D0592428

DE WITT PUBLIC LIBRARY
13101 SCHAVEY RD.
DE WITT, MICH 48820

APR 19 2002

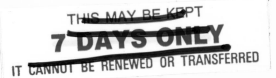

THIS MAY BE KEPT
7 DAYS ONLY
IT CANNOT BE RENEWED OR TRANSFERRED

THE
YOUNGEST
HERO

Novels by Jerry B. Jenkins

The Left Behind series

Hometown Legend

Though None Go with Me

'Twas the Night Before

The Operative

The Margo Mysteries

JERRY B. JENKINS

THE YOUNGEST HERO

WARNER BOOKS

An AOL Time Warner Company

Copyright © 2002 by Jerry B. Jenkins

All rights reserved. No part of this book may be reproduced in any form or by any
electronic or mechanical means, including information storage and retrieval systems,
without permission in writing from the publisher, except by a reviewer who may quote brief
passages in a review.

The Youngest Hero was originally published in a completely different version as *Rookie*
© 1991 by Jerry B. Jenkins.

Warner Books, Inc., 1271 Avenue of the Americas, New York, NY 10020

Visit our Web site at www.twbookmark.com.

 An AOL Time Warner Company

Printed in the United States of America

First Warner Books Printing: April 2002
10 9 8 7 6 5 4 3 2 1

ISBN: 0-446-52903-6

LCCN: 2001098327

Book design by Giorgetta Bell McRee

To Robert W. and Mike H.
With thanks for your confidence

THE
YOUNGEST
HERO

1

Don't be giving me the credit. I'm just the mother. Seems like yesterday it was just Elgin and me on the Trailways from Hattiesburg. That was four years ago. He was ten.

"You're not gonna go barefoot in Chicago," I told him. "And you're not gonna say 'not gonna' up there neither."

" 'Either,' Momma," he said, turning from the window to face me. "You mean 'either.' "

I pursed my lips. "Thank you, Mr. Know-It-All."

My hair hung heavy from sweat. I shook my head, but I wasn't really upset. I was the one who taught him to read when he was four. I'd watched him devour baseball books and schoolbooks ever since.

Elgin climbed over me and into the aisle where he stood on tippytoes and dug an aluminum bat out of his bag. I saw the driver watching him in the mirror. "There's no room, El," I whispered.

He climbed over me again—this time with the bat—to sit by the window. "I just want to hold it," he said. "Daddy told me—"

"If you're gonna play with that thing, you can go sit by yourself."

Elgin let the bat slide between his knees. "You shouldn't have said that, Momma. You know I'd rather sit with you than even feel a bat."

It was the highest compliment I could hear from him. I wasn't much bigger than Elgin, but when I hugged him I felt strong. Ownership and responsibility, I guess.

"Elgin, just don't—"

"I know," he said, closing his eyes. His arms were moist and cool against mine. "Don't talk about Daddy."

Elgin and I lugged four suitcases from the bus station to a Chicago street littered with trash. A transient hotel was all I could afford. In my purse I carried nine hundred and ten dollars in cash. I had squirreled it away over seven months on a salary that would have made a panhandler blush. I only broke even when I sold our house trailer. That cash was my net worth.

By the end of the day, we had settled into a two-bedroom flat on the sixth floor of a building that smelled like the rescue mission in Hattiesburg. Like I told Elgin, at least it was better than living where people knew your business.

I know Momma was worried cause I was sitting there so quiet while she cooked red beans and rice. There was stuff I missed already. Like screen doors. Room to move. Buddies.

Momma said, "If I never see another IRS form as long as I live, it'll be too soon."

"But you were good at it, weren't you?"

She snorted and nodded, setting a full plate in front of me. "I don't believe I saw more'n two, three adjusted gross incomes lower'n mine."

She had her wish. She was out of it, away from it, away from Hattiesburg. If only she could explain it. I didn't understand why we had to move. She'd tried to tell me enough times. I learned to quit pestering her.

*   *   *

The next day Momma found a job in the accounting department of a distributing company four and a half miles away.

"You could act a little more excited," she told me. "This is food and rent."

But I had my own news. I had discovered a game close enough to baseball to hold me until Momma could find a real league she could afford. "They call it fastpitch," I said. "You stand on one side of the street with a building behind you and the strike zone chalked on the bricks. The pitcher stands in the street with a tennis ball that has the fuzz off it. He tries to strike you out before you get a hit. You make singles, doubles, triples, and homers by how high your hit goes on the front of the building across the street."

"How did you do?"

She would ask that. "Haven't hit a foul yet. But I will. A couple of Puerto Ricans can really fire."

Three days later, Elgin came home crying.

"A kid stole my bat," he told me. "And we can't get it back cause he's not from around here."

"Can't you use someone else's?"

"All they have are broom handles with black tape. And I was just starting to hit with my bat. I'll never hit anything with a broomstick! Anyway—"

"I know, Elgin," I said. "Your daddy gave you that bat." I gathered him in. "A broomstick is about all I can afford right now. Everything costs so much more up here."

"Daddy says I should hit with a wood bat anyway. Get a better feel of the ball."

I sighed. "Money never meant much to your daddy. If he had his way, you'd have had a breakable bat whenever you needed one."

Elgin shook his head and pulled away.

"I don't want to hear about it all the time, Momma. I know. Okay?"

It burst from me before I could think. "You would've had a sister by now if it hadn't been for that man."

"I hate when you call him 'that man.' He has a name."

"Yeah, and he's also got a number."

He brightened. "Daddy's playing ball again?"

Just like Elgin to assume the best.

"That's not what I meant." I reached into a cupboard and handed him an index card.

> Neal Lofert Woodell
> Lockbox 092349
> Alabama State Penitentiary
> Birmingham, Alabama

The pain in Elgin's eyes pierced me. "What for this time?" he said.

I stalled and sat next to him. "Reckless homicide."

"What's that?"

"You know. Figure it out."

"Why do you have to make everything like school? Homicide is like murder, right?"

"Um-hm. Drivin with no papers, drivin while drunk, hit an old man on a bike."

Elgin stared at the card. "Then he's not going to come see me? He said he would."

"When did he say that?"

"My birthday, and also the last time I talked to him on the phone. Just after Christmas."

"He was already in jail by then."

"He didn't tell me."

"Probably embarrassed."

Elgin nodded, his eyes wet. "Can I go see him?"

I shook my head. "What do you want to see him for when he's only seen you once in more than a year?"

Elgin shrugged. "That's why."

*   *   *

On my way to the bus the next morning, I mailed a letter from Elgin to his father. It had taken him most of the evening to write it. I told him I wouldn't read it unless he said I could.

"You can."

How are you? I am fine. I didn't know you were in prison. I'll bet you're as sorry as I am. Momma says it could be lots of years. I hope not. I miss you and especially talking and playing baseball. Is there anyone there that can strike you out? I'd like to see them try!

I'm switch-hitting like you taught me. My metal bat got stolen, so I'm going to get a wood one when I get enough money. I lost my batting helmet too. Sorry.

Chicago is different, but we like it. At least I do. I can't go barefoot. I'm not looking forward to school, but Momma is. She doesn't like leaving me all day. I have to call her from the pay phone in the hall at the same time every day. Once I forgot, and once I got my money stolen. I got whipped the first time and haven't forgotten since.

I didn't get whipped for getting my money stolen, but Momma told me how to tell the manager so he could call her. She worries too much, but I'm not scared. I just play fastpitch all day. I'll tell you about it when I see you. How much would it cost for me to come see you?

I love you and miss you, Daddy. I wish you would have told me what happened. It's bad, and I know you're sorry, so don't worry about me not loving you anymore or anything like that.

You still love me, don't you? Mom doesn't love you anymore because of that night, you know. I was mad at you too, but I knew you meant it when you cried. I'm never ever never going to drink beer or anything like that, Dad. It makes you do stuff you don't want to do, and it makes people quit loving you, but not me.

Love, Elgin

2

It was September before I started to get the broomstick on the tennis ball. I was in school most of the day, and they didn't allow fastpitch during recess. Too many broken windows last year, I guess.

Every day at 3:40 I had to call my mother from the hotel pay phone in the hall. Usually, I was still catching my breath from the run home.

"No letter from Dad," I'd tell her, wishing she would care. She'd just tell me what to put on for supper so it would be almost ready by the time she got home. She let me play fastpitch as long as I was home when the streetlights came on.

Work kept my mind off being lonely, but getting supper on the table wasn't enough to keep me from missing Elgin. He played only a few blocks away, but five minutes after I expected him, I would think about heading out to find him. I fought darker thoughts, thoughts of something happening to him. I couldn't risk embarrassing him again. I had wandered over to watch him once, but the game stopped until the others found out who the woman was. They teased him unmercifully. No adults allowed. Not even to watch.

Elgin always made it home just before dark. Every day he told me that the next day he would get the letter he wanted so bad.

"You think Dad still loves me? Could he forget about me?"

"I never knew anybody who could forget about you," I said. "I'm sure he loves you the best he knows how. He was never much good at lovin anybody but himself."

I knew I shouldn't bad-mouth Elgin's daddy, but I was tired of covering for him. For a year before we moved to Chicago, we lived in a trailer park in Hattiesburg with bad memories. Before Neal had moved away and then been sent to prison for what was probably the last time, he had raced stock cars on a dirt oval and hit something like .550 in a local semipro league.

I never thought I asked for too much. Just a husband who kept a job and came home after work and didn't get drunk. When Neal got drunk, he got crazy. He had never attacked Elgin, but I know Neal terrified him when he was drunk. Even when I was pregnant with our second child, I felt like I was Elgin's protector, keeping Neal's attention. I swore I'd leave and take Elgin with me if Neal dared hurt him. I wouldn't even let Neal spank him. "I don't trust you," I'd tell him. "You could kill that boy and call it an accident."

One night, drunk and sobbing, Neal fell on his knees in front of me when I said something like that. "You can't hurt me more'n sayin I could ever hurt my own child, Miriam!"

"You can hurt *me* and I shouldn't think you'd hurt *him*?"

"He's my own flesh and blood! You're not!"

"I'm your wife!"

"That was my mistake," Neal said. "We're only related by law."

"You can say that after all we've been through?" I said. "The nights I've bailed you out, put you to bed, made excuses for you, forgiven you?"

Neal was still on his knees, but I saw his muscles tighten. "I had a momma," he said, rising. "I don't need another."

I told him I didn't want to mother him, that I didn't want to have to. Neal cursed me and called me ugly names. That I could take. I'd done it many times. But when he punched me in the stomach, the pain shot through me and made me dizzy. As I lurched forward he drove his knee into my abdomen and I slammed to the floor, desperate to protect my baby. Lying there I saw Elgin, standing frozen in the doorway of his tiny bedroom.

Neal immediately started in with his apologies. "Oh, honey, sweetie, I'm sorry! I'm sorry! I'm sorry! Forgive me! I'll kill myself if I've hurt you! Oh, God! Oh, please! Jesus, don't let anything be wrong with the baby!"

I fought for breath as I struggled to my knees, keeping an eye on Neal. He reached for me, but I wrenched away. "Don't touch me," I said. "You will never touch me again."

While he cried, I dialed the phone. "Yes, sir," I told the cop, "I'm willin to press charges this time."

Neal sat at the kitchen table with his head in his hands, sobbing. He said, "Forgive me, Mir, I swear I'm sorry. I'll never—"

"If anything happens to this child, Neal," I said, "I hope you die in prison."

Neal spent sixteen months in the county jail that time. And I lost the baby, a girl. The prosecutors couldn't prove the beating caused the miscarriage.

It seemed to me Elgin was as sad and almost as mad as I was, but he believed his dad was sorry. "That's what matters, right, Momma?" he'd say. "If he's truly sorry, we have to forgive him, don't we?"

"I don't," I said, though I knew I shouldn't be countering what he learned in Sunday school. "Someday you'll learn to never believe a drunk, no matter what he says."

During more than a year in jail, Neal went to the hospital twice with delirium tremens. I never visited, wrote, or called. A sheriff served papers on me, requiring me to let Neal see his son. I let him go with his great-grandmother Lofert.

Elgin told me Neal spent each visit holding him, crying, and pleading with him to try to convince me he was truly sorry.

"Tell him it's too late," I said. "Better yet, don't tell him anything. Don't even promise him you'll give me his messages. He has no right to ask you."

When Neal was finally set free, I got a court order to keep him from coming to the trailer. We'd bought it used, eight years before, in my name because I was the one with a job.

I let Elgin visit Neal at a park close to town, while I watched from a distance. I didn't change my feelings about Neal, but at least something good was happening. Elgin was learning to play ball. Not only that, but I had to admit he was learning the game from one of the best players I had ever seen.

Against everything I ever knew as a Christian, I had grown to hate Neal, but I could never deny he was a marvelous baseball player, born to the diamond, a man everybody loved to watch play. *Play* was the perfect word for what Neal Woodell did on a ball field. He was a center fielder, but he could play any position. He knew what to do, when to do it, and how to do it. He was fast, graceful, powerful, and smart. Most of all, he seemed to truly love the game. If only he had loved me as much.

Even when it was just Elgin and his dad, playing catch, hitting fly balls, pitching, and batting, I watched in awe. I did not, could not, would not ever again love or accept or even want to talk to Neal. But as he taught Elgin rules, strategy, technique, even style, I had to watch. Whenever he noticed, he hollered something to me, often something about Elgin's progress. I just stared, acknowledging nothing. He finally quit trying to connect with me and concentrated on Elgin.

"Aggressive, boy!" he would say. "Always look for the extra base, the advantage."

Elgin threw right-handed and batted left. Neal taught him to switch-hit. "See how you can see the ball better, El?"

When Dad and I would take a break and sit under a tree, he would tell me his favorite stories—of childhood games, of incredible plays, of his four home runs in a rookie-league doubleheader.

"If I'da stayed off the bottle, El," he told me more than once, "I'd be a big leaguer today."

I wanted to believe it, of course. "Is that true?" I'd ask Momma later.

"No doubt," she'd say.

I was impressed that a born liar could speak the truth at all. Watching Neal field and throw and hit with effortless fluidity, I was carried back to seeing him in a Pirate uniform, posing for his spring training pictures. He started in the rookie league and moved all the way up to triple-A ball, but his scrapbook was full of pictures of him in the big-league uniform even the minor leaguers wear during spring training.

I didn't need the Pirates to tell me Neal Lofert Woodell had been a bona fide major-league prospect. But now he was a sandlot player, a race driver who made twenty-five dollars a night Fridays and Saturdays and barely enough more to live on by bagging groceries.

In Elgin's eyes, of course, his dad was a giant.

"I'm praying you'll forgive him, Momma," he'd say.

"I'm bitter," I told him. "And it tears me up. But I don't believe the man, and I don't think I can ever forgive him. I know I can't trust him. I don't even like you bein with him. You ever smell liquor on his breath, you get away, you hear?"

"I asked him if he still drank," Elgin said.

I looked at him. "You did? Good for you!"

"I told him he didn't have to tell me if he didn't want to."

"Oh, I'm sure he told you. But did he tell you the truth?"

"Yeah, he did."

"How do you know?"

"He said he was a lot of things, but that he doesn't lie when he's sober. He has a six-pack every night after ball games to help him sleep, and he says he knows enough to stay off the road. On Fridays and Saturdays he has only a couple of beers because they're testing drivers at the track now, and any more than that shows up."

"He can't afford to lose that ride."

"That's what he said, Mom. He needs the money."

"What about weekends? He drinkin on weekends?"

Elgin nodded.

"Saturday night after the races and all day Sunday he drinks a good bit. He says he's pretty wiped out till he goes to work on Monday mornings."

I'd seen Neal in the grocery on Mondays, his eyes red and puffy, tiny slits against the sun that streamed through the plate glass.

On muggy summer evenings in Hattiesburg, I had taken Elgin to the library where I taught myself the tax return filing business. For a year I couldn't get him to read anything but baseball books: how-to's, biographies, histories, you name it. If it had to do with baseball, Elgin read it, including every baseball novel for children.

When he ran out of stuff at his reading level, I moved him up to adult baseball books. He expanded his vocabulary by checking with me on words he didn't recognize. I'd been an honor roll student and had dreamed of college. When I didn't know a word, I made Elgin look it up. Whenever I felt impatient or frustrated with him, I hid it. I had to do the loving for two parents, and I wanted Elgin to feel deeply loved.

"Momma," he would tell me, "there's no game like baseball. It has so many things happening at the same time. It's a team sport but every play is also individual. You know what I mean?"

All that talk of baseball made me think of Neal, but I worked at never shutting Elgin off.

"No," I'd say. "What do you mean?"

"Tennis and golf are sports you play alone. I mean you're against everybody else, but it's just you and the ball and there's no team to help or hurt you. Baseball is a team sport, but when the ball is hit to you, it's an individual sport until you catch it. Then it's a team sport because you have to throw it to someone else. And when you're batting, it's all up to you. You have to get the sign, do what you're told, and get on base. But then it's a team sport because the next hitter has to do something or you die on base."

I understood what he was saying, but I couldn't see the beauty, the importance of it. That was all right. Someday I would see him play, and that would be even better than watching Neal play. My love for him was long gone. Elgin often asked if I liked watching his dad play.

"Everybody likes watchin your father play, Elgin. He's gifted. But I suppose I resent that he's that good at anything. Sometimes I wish he was as bad a ballplayer as he is a race driver."

Even Elgin had to laugh.

Neal hardly ever won a race, but I guess his sponsors kept him in because he was so daring. He was always on the brink of disaster, scraping guardrails or tapping other cars into the infield. Fans loved him. He seemed to love to drive fast without having mastered the sport. Two guys he drove against graduated to the NASCAR circuit, but Neal drove for beer money and for fun.

Elgin badgered me into taking him to Neal's baseball games, but he was an obnoxious fan. He combined play-by-play with desperate coaching from the stands, trying to urge on his dad's awful Zephyrs. They won about half their games.

"Full count and two outs," Elgin would holler. "Runners will be going! Runners should be going! Runners aren't going! There's the hit! C'mon, Shaw! Move with the pitch and you score on that play!"

After each game, Elgin would debrief with Neal.

"Outfield was too deep for their shortstop in the sixth, weren't they?"

Neal nodded.

"Would you have taken Crawford out so soon in the seventh, Dad? Why not let him walk the hitter to load the bases and give Mehlis a little more time in the bull pen? Mehlis wasn't ready. He got behind on the first guy and then had to come in with that candy pitch."

I could see Neal was impressed. "You saw that too, huh?" he

said. "You also see that I've lost a step to first and that my arm has no pop anymore?"

"You've lost two steps, Dad. But your arm is as good as ever. Ask Ernie."

Ernie was the Zephyr catcher who had taken a throw from Neal to cut down a runner. Ernie had made the tag and come up shaking his hand.

At the park in town, Neal hit Elgin harder and harder grounders and line drives. He pitched faster and faster until we were forced to save our money and get Elgin a batting helmet.

The helmet gave me a feeling I can't describe. Dad told me to open my stance and make sure I was getting both eyes on the pitch. Now I could do that without worrying about getting beaned. It made Dad laugh, though, the way I stuck my face right into the pitch before trying to drive it somewhere.

I loved to hit!

3

My family and my church taught me God hated divorce. Well, I didn't believe in divorce either, but I knew something about hate. It was what I felt for Neal. As for biblical grounds, I happened to know I had those too, but that was nobody's business but mine.

I lived with the pain and the embarrassment as long as I could. Neal quit trying to get me back. I guess I convinced him I was through with him, and I hoped he was grateful he still had some contact with Elgin.

A bad marriage was good gossip in Hattiesburg. I saw scorn on faces, heard it in tones of voice. I was a failure, pitiable, wife of that violent drunk who washed out as a professional baseball player and was now just a good ol' boy, racing cars, bagging groceries, and playing a little ball on the side.

I guess there was irony in my choice of a lawyer, but I didn't know anybody else. Billy Ray Thatcher was an old friend of Neal's family and had been his agent. He had worked on Neal's contract with the Pirates, a five-figure deal that let Neal live like a king until he drank his talent away and the money ran out.

Billy Ray's claim to fame was that he had represented Bernie Pincham, a poor rural basketball player who became a six-time NBA all-star and was now worth millions. The newspaper said the agent's commission on Pincham's salary and endorsement deals alone more than doubled Thatcher's firm's gross receipts for several years. Billy Ray had also advised Bernie on investments. Pincham was worth many times in retirement what he had made playing basketball. The Woodells had assumed the same would be true for Neal.

Mr. Thatcher had done his best, but unlike Bernie Pincham, Neal had not listened. He had not heard Billy Ray when he insisted that "everything, all of this—the bonus, the salary, the deals—hinges on what kind of a steward you are of your talent. If it doesn't happen on the field, it doesn't happen in the bank.

"The bonus is yours. You can pay your bills and put the rest away. You know as well as I do that the odds are one hundred to one against a rookie-league player making a living as a big leaguer."

"I'll make it," Neal had told Billy Ray and me as we sat in his office so many years before.

"I believe you very well could," Mr. Thatcher said. "But you want to be smart with this little nest egg. It looks like a lot to you now, and if we're careful with it, it can be a cushion for you if anything happens to your career."

"Do I get it in cash or like, what?"

I saw Billy Ray Thatcher's eyes roll.

"It comes to me in the form of a check, Neal. I recommend that you allow me to subtract my commission, pay your debts, put a quarter of it in a savings account, put a few thousand in your checking account, and invest the rest in some safe, conservative stocks."

Not only did Neal refuse, but it was like he was insulted.

"No way, Jose! Huh-uh! We agreed on your percentage. You take that and you give me the rest. And you can tell me one more thing: how to get a check that size cashed. I tried to cash a big check at the bank one time, and they said they needed a couple of days' notice."

"They would require a week's notice on a check this size, Neal, but surely you don't intend to—"

"You're gettin your cut, so just let me know when I get the cash."

"I'd be doing you a disservice if I allowed you to—"

"You'll be fired if you don't. Now stick with me, Billy, because we gonna make lots more money together."

Neal was up and out of Mr. Thatcher's office that day without even waiting for me. Billy Ray stood when I did and touched my elbow as he held the door for me. "Miriam, if he squanders that money, he'll ruin his career."

I just nodded. If I'd tried to say anything I would have burst into tears. It seemed like Mr. Thatcher was putting the responsibility on me to keep Neal from messing up. No one else knew yet that Neal beat me when he was drunk and that he was drinking during the week for the first time. Nobody could tell him anything. I had quit bringing up even minor things. We lived in the same house. That was it.

I watched Neal slide from the frittering away of his signing bonus to borrowing ahead on his small, minor-league paycheck, and finally to where he began asking the ball club for his daily meal money in advance.

The day after the Pirates first warned him his career was in jeopardy, he hit four home runs in a rookie-league doubleheader. That had to be why they stuck with him as long as they did, that and what they had invested in him. Neal rose to triple-A but soon dropped back to double-A and then A, and finally the Pirates told him they weren't going to make room for him again with the eighteen- to twenty-year-olds in the rookie league.

I was amazed he could come back to Hattiesburg with his head high, admitting, *admitting* that drinking had done him in. I finally figured out that the last thing Neal wanted anyone to think was that he hadn't had the talent to make the majors. The saddest thing was that he was right. Someone less gifted became that one in a hundred from the rookie league to make the big leagues.

After years of beatings, drinking, lost jobs, and bankruptcy, I could hardly recognize the person I had been so attracted to in the first place. He had been the best-looking boy in high school, a star in three sports, homecoming king. He was my dream from the day I first tutored him in algebra. I didn't help him as much as I distracted him. He said he couldn't take his eyes off my red hair, my freckles, and my figure. His algebra grade went from an F to a D. I felt like a failure.

He was charming and funny, and he claimed he believed in Jesus, but he was not bright. In the end, Neal Woodell was only physical. And when alcohol had left him just a better than average local jock, and me a struggling young mother with no more sympathy or patience, I got an appointment with Billy Ray Thatcher.

"How long since you threw him out, Miriam?"

"More'n two years, plus his jail time."

"He sendin you any money?"

I snorted.

"Can I talk you out of this?" Mr. Thatcher said. "Tell you he's worth the effort, that you don't wanna be a divorced, single parent in this town?"

"I'm not going to be in this town much longer, Mr. Thatcher. Soon as I can get some money saved, I'm sellin that trailer, and Elgin and I are going to Chicago."

"Why there?"

"I had an aunt who moved to Chicago with her husband when I was little. She wrote the most beautiful letters about it. The culture and all." I sat with my hands folded, eyes focused on the floor where my tears puddled. "I just want to get as far away from here as I can," I managed. "My family knows what I'm doin, and they don't like me for it. Well, they can just hate me long-distance."

Mr. Thatcher sat with his legs crossed, fingers entwined. "Can he accuse you of adultery?"

"No, sir," I said. "He accused me of a lot of stuff when he was drunk, but he knows better."

"Could *you* use adultery as grounds?"

"I wouldn't, but I probably could. You know that girl at the grocery with the blonde hair and—" I caught myself. "Mr. Thatcher, I don't want any more mess."

"But he beat you, didn't he? Isn't that what he did time for?"

"I don't want charges and countercharges. I don't want anything but to be out of this for as little money as possible."

"Miriam, I could never charge you."

"I didn't come to you for any deal."

"I know, but please, let me do this for you. I would be hurt if you insisted on trying to pay. Don't give it another thought. I'll throw a little stationery at Neal and follow through with the paperwork. It shouldn't take long."

"Stationery?"

"I send him a letter on my office letterhead and use lots of legal jargon designed to convince him he has nothing to gain and everything to lose by contesting this. Now what do you want from him? At least child support."

I shook my head. "He has nothing."

"You're too generous."

"But he really doesn't. If he gave up drinkin he'd have a little extra, but I really want to be done with him."

"Just the same, I'm going to get a list of his assets. You can decide then if there's anything you want."

I couldn't imagine anything of Neal's I would want. Everything would remind me of the horror years. I didn't even want his money to help raise Elgin. I thought of Elgin as mine alone.

The letter from Mr. Thatcher sent Neal into a spin. He said he was offended that his former agent would take my side. He pleaded for the chance to make our marriage work, hired a local public defender, and threatened to sue for custody of Elgin.

"I've talked to his representative," Mr. Thatcher told me. "You're right that he has little to offer, but I can tell from his lawyer's language that at least he knows they have no hope. Here's a list of assets and debts."

I hated even looking at the sad list of junk and obligations. I had no interest in his eight-year-old car. I wouldn't need that in Chicago, and I had already promised my beater to my little sister. Neither was I interested in his Harley, which he had bought off a junk dealer and never had the money to get into running condition.

"So, he's still got that old pitchin machine," I said, studying the sheet. "Wonder where he keeps that."

Mr. Thatcher studied his own copy. "At a community college in Mobile. Friend of his coaches there and borrowed it. It's in storage, not being used, but probably still worth a thousand dollars, so it's listed."

"You got him that thing," I said, "didn't you?"

Thatcher leaned back in his chair and smiled. "I was rather proud of that," he said. "Got it thrown in with his signing bonus. Helped Neal a lot, at least for a while. He'd forgotten about it, though. I had to tell his lawyer I knew Neal had it somewhere. It's of no worth except to the team that borrowed it."

"I want it," I said.

Mr. Thatcher shot me a double take. "Whatever for?"

"For Elgin."

"Oh, Miriam," he said, "Elgin's a lot of years from being able to use that. This isn't one of those toys they use in batting cages. It's a monster. Where would you put it?"

"Wonder if that coach would store it for me."

"Maybe, but do you really want me to go after it? It's gonna look a little silly in the divorce action. And won't it remind you of Neal anyway?"

"I don't want money, not even child support. I just want Neal to admit the trailer is mine, give me that pitchin thing, and let me have this divorce."

"I could get you more."

"I don't want anything more."

When the divorce was final, Neal left town without a word. I was insulted. When his career blew apart because of his drinking, he had come back home without a second thought. When I had kicked him out of the trailer, he found a cheap room and stayed in town, working at a grocery where everyone knew him. Most knew he had beat me. Some even knew I believed he had killed my unborn girl. But now, after his year-plus in jail and a couple more years living apart, I finally divorce him, and he gives one hour's notice at the grocery and leaves town.

I began planning my own escape to Chicago. I slowly paid my debts and started salting a little away each month.

Neal visited one more time and played catch with Elgin, not even telling his son he had moved away. I heard nothing more of him until Mr. Thatcher drove out one night with the news. The rest of Neal Lofert Woodell's sorry life would be spent in the Alabama State Penitentiary. That news would get around soon enough. It was time to move on before time passed us by.

I didn't know whether to ask Momma if she knew more than she was telling me about Daddy. All I knew was that I missed him. He always clapped me on the back, looked me in the eye, and told me I was "gonna be a great one someday."

Every night in bed I prayed my dad would come back. I wanted him to keep teaching me baseball, to touch me, to live in the trailer, to be Momma's husband again, to make us a family. Other kids had dads. I wanted mine.

4

When Elgin first started asking when he would see his dad again, I said, "I'm not sure exactly where he is." It was true. I didn't know which wing, which cell block.

"Well, am I supposed to meet him at the park this week?"

"We won't know till he calls," I said. Now that was a lie. Neal wasn't ever going to see that park again.

It didn't take long for Elgin to figure out that his father was no longer bagging groceries, racing cars, or even playing local baseball.

"Has he moved, Momma?"

"I expect he has," I said. "You know I don't care."

"Well, *I* care! What am I supposed to do? I'm just starting to get good at baseball!"

"You can keep playing."

"Yeah, but not with anybody who knows what he's doing! You know our gym teacher was trying to get everybody to throw off their right foot the other day? Right-handers! He was having right-handers step with their right foot and throw!"

"Is that wrong?"

"Is that wrong! Mom, look!"

He went through the motion. I smiled. "You look like me when I try to throw," I said.

"I flat out wouldn't do it. I told him if this was some sort of a drill, then maybe, but if he thought that's really the way you're supposed to throw, he was wrong. You know I usually don't talk back, and I called him sir and everything, but there was no way I was gonna throw a ball stepping with my right foot."

"What did he say?"

"He said you get more power that way, and I asked him how come then that big leaguers don't do that. He said he was sure they did. I asked him to show me how a pitcher would do it, if it would give him more power. He tried to do it and then he said, 'Well, I think outfielders do it on the big throws.' It was crazy. That's the kind of coaching I'm getting without Daddy."

I couldn't believe the prices of aluminum bats. The salesman told me I would be ahead "in the long run, because it will never break."

I told him how tall Elgin was and asked for a bat he wouldn't grow out of too quickly. The man went on about length and weight and thickness and made me wish I'd brought Elgin with me and forgotten about surprising him for his birthday that April. How different could bats be? I only hoped Elgin would like it.

He did and he didn't. He'd never had his own bat before, but he had always talked about having a wood one. This one was a little too long, a little too heavy, but I could see in his eyes he didn't want to say anything bad about it.

I was desperate. Elgin was my life. I lied again. "El, your dad sent me the money for that bat and had me pick it out for you. He probably could have done better himself, or maybe I could have with you there, but we wanted it to be a surprise."

Elgin's eyes shone. "Dad hates aluminum bats, but he probably knew I'd break a wood one."

I nodded, hating myself. I was going to feel bad in church again Sunday. That night I wrote Neal: "I told Elgin his birthday gift, a metal bat, was from you. If you talk to him, cover me. Neal, I would rather a man like you have no influence on my son, but I don't think he could handle never hearing from you again. Don't do that to him. Sincerely, Miriam."

A little more than a week later a card came for Elgin with a lockbox number as the return address. I had no idea whether Elgin would be able to figure out anything from it, but to be safe I gave him only the card, not the envelope.

Crafty as ever, even though he had clearly forgotten Elgin's birthday until he heard from me, Neal had dated the card the day before Elgin's birthday. It was a silly card with a cartoon ballplayer on it. It read, "Today is special in every way, swing for the fences and Happy Birthday!"

On the back, Neal had written, "Hope this reaches you in time. Hope you liked the bat. Had to follow work to Alabama. I'll come see you when I can. Love, Dad (#16)."

"He put his old uniform number on here, Mom."

"Did he?" I said, trying to hide that I wasn't impressed.

"I was starting to feel real bad about not hearing from him," Elgin said.

"I don't blame you."

"I mean, it was my birthday! He never forgot my birthday. The card must have got lost in the mail."

"Must have."

For Christmas I made Elgin a sweater but couldn't afford anything more besides two rubber-coated baseballs. I figured they would stand up to the weather better than regular baseballs. I told him they were from his father, but I forgot to inform Neal. He called the day after Christmas.

"Oh, I'm so glad you picked up, Mir," he said. "I was afraid Elgin would answer and thank me for some gift and I wouldn't know what I got him. What did I get him?"

"He's right here, Neal. He wants to thank you for the two rubber-coated baseballs."

"Rubber-coated? Miriam!"

"Here he is."

"Dad? . . . Yeah! . . . Great! How are you? . . . Yeah, they were nice. I've already played catch, but it's been cold out. Hurt my arm a little. . . . No, it's okay. When are you coming to see me? . . . Well, let me know when you get a vacation or something. . . . Yeah, here's Mom."

I took the phone.

"Good-bye, Neal."

"Wait a minute, Miriam. Just tell me why you went and bought—"

"Good-bye, Neal."

"Miriam!"

I covered the mouthpiece. "El, could you give me a minute?" He hurried to his little room at the back of the trailer, and I feared I saw hope in his eyes. I didn't want him to think there was some hope of our getting back together just because I wanted to talk to Neal alone. But I didn't want Elgin knowing yet that his dad was in prison, and especially why.

"I'm back, Neal."

"I wanna know—"

"Listen to me, Neal. I don't have to tell you anything. If you want to get Elgin somethin for his birthday or Christmas, then you better remember and save your money and buy him something right. How do you think I feel trying to buy him the right stuff and not knowing and not having enough money? Who do you think you are, scolding me for doing the best I can? I'm not giving you the credit for any gifts anymore, so you better plan ahead next time."

"I don't have any money, Mir! How'm I s'posed to do that?"

"Well, you should've thought of that a long time ago."

"Well, lemme just tell you this, Mir: If you think about gettin him a glove, and you don't hafta say it's from me, make sure it's a Wilson A-2000. Got it?"

"Neal! Where do you think I'm going to get the money for a ball glove? You have any idea what those run these days? Cheap ones are over fifty dollars!"

Neal laughed. "Fifty dollars! It'd be just like you to get him a vinyl glove. You're lookin at three times that for a good one."

"Well, you can forget that. He's using your old glove."

"That's old, all right. And dry. And too big for him."

"Neal, I am through talking."

"My time's up anyway, Miriam. I'll call you sometime soon."

"Don't bother."

"Well, I can call the boy, can't I?"

"I wish you wouldn't. I haven't told him where you are."

"I'm getting out soon."

"Oh, Neal, don't start playing games with me, and quit promising Elgin that you're coming to see him."

"I was framed, Miriam. I'm gonna get outa here soon, and I *will* come see him. I wanna talk to you, too."

"No."

"I'm telling you I was framed, well, not framed, but railroaded."

Mr. Thatcher had given me the details. "You weren't driving with a suspended license?"

"Well, yeah, but I was going to work and—"

"You weren't drunk?"

"I was officially under the influence, but only a hundredth of a—"

"And so, what, someone pushed that man out in front of you?"

"It was dusk, Miriam, and I should have sued his family for letting their dad ride that three-wheeler that late in the evening."

"He was on a three-wheeler?"

"And just pokin along! I couldn't stop. I honked and he panicked and stopped."

"He didn't swerve out in front of you?"

"No, but if he'd swerved the other way, I wouldn't have hit him when I slid onto the shoulder."

"Oh, Neal! You're never gonna get off from a charge like that!"

"You just watch!"

"I'd rather not."

I wanted to come up with a great closing line that would put Neal in his place. But words weren't my game. I would not be calling or writing him again, I decided. The last thing he needed was encouragement from me. I hung up.

The next day I asked Billy Ray Thatcher to see if Neal had filed an appeal on his sentence. He called back that evening.

"He doesn't even have a lawyer, Miriam. And the case was so open and shut that there would be no hope. He was driving while his license was suspended. Witnesses saw him get thrown out of a bar for being too rowdy. They say he was laughing and crying as he staggered to his car. A friend offered to drive him home and Neal took a swing at him. He laid rubber screeching out of the parking lot, then flew through radar at over sixty in a thirty zone. The officer saw Neal's car weaving as he pulled out to pursue him, and just as he was turning on his flashing lights, he saw the accident. Neal appeared to have not even seen the old gentleman on the bike. It was lucky no one else was on the sidewalk."

"The sidewalk?"

"Neal drove off the road, between two trees, and up on the sidewalk where he hit the man. The old guy was hardly moving."

"Neal said something about the man being in his way."

Mr. Thatcher sighed. "Neal was a born liar." He paused. "Open and shut, Miriam. He's in there forever."

When Momma told me we would be moving to Chicago that summer, I worried about Dad. "Won't it be harder for him to find me and get there?"

"Might be," Momma said. "That's *his* problem."

"It's my problem too," I said. "You gonna let me play in a league up there?"

"The summer after we get there."

"A league with uniforms and all?"

"I don't know what they have."

"I want to play in a league with real uniforms. I can't stand this playing with just a team T-shirt. I'm ready."

"I know you are. But we'll be getting there too late to try to join one right away."

I played in just five games before we took off for Chicago. If I'd have known how I would do in those five games, I'd have fought harder against leaving.

5

The children's baseball program in Hattiesburg had one league for nine- and ten-year-olds, one for eleven- and twelve-year-olds, and another for thirteen- and fourteen-year-olds. I was hoping Momma would handle signing me up, but she seemed as shy as I was when we walked in. I finally went up to one of the tables and a woman shoved a sign-up sheet toward me. A man leaned over and looked me up and down.

"Before you tell me your age," he said, "I guess. I'm within a year ninety percent of the time."

A man and woman at the cash box smiled and nodded. "He's been especially accurate today."

I was taller than most older boys, so when the man guessed thirteen—"Am I right, huh, am I right?"—I wasn't surprised.

"I'm ten," I said.

The man roared. "Well, we'll see what your momma puts down for date of birth, and if it comes out to ten, we're gonna hafta see what Matt wants to do about it."

"Who?" I said.

"League rep. He can ask you for a birth certificate."

That got Momma's attention. "The boy is ten," she said. "And I didn't bring any papers. I'm sorry."

Somebody went and got Matt, a huge fat man with an unlit cigar at the corner of his mouth.

"Trouble?" he said.

"No," Guesser said. "Just that this boy and his momma say he's ten."

Matt seemed to study Momma more than me. "Pretty little lady says her son is ten, he's got to be ten. But ma'am, you understand we're gonna get challenged on this every time we turn around. You have papers somewhere, right?"

"Of course."

"Just bring a copy of his birth certificate to tryouts."

"My dad is tall," I said. "That's why I'm tall."

He said, "If you're as good as you are tall, you're gonna need that birth certificate. If you're not, nobody will care."

"My dad is a good player."

"Someone I should know?"

"Neal Woodell."

"No kiddin? He was some kinda player before, ah—he was some kinda player."

The man at the cash box said, "Maybe he would like to coach a team for us. We're still looking for help for the—"

"Uh, no, Clarence," big Matt said. "He's, uh, not a local man. Now let's get this boy signed up and tell him where to report for tryouts."

I was nervous at tryouts, but I tried to hide it. The other kids all seemed to be dressed in new shoes, sweats, hats, and gloves. I wore raggy sweats, one of my dad's old, too-big caps, and that floppy glove. I wore year-old sneakers that were already smooth on the bottom.

I quit telling other kids about my dad after the first three didn't know his name. But I couldn't wait to run and hit and throw and catch. I was glad Momma was there to watch. Matt explained to the parents how the tryout would go.

"We'll run them for time, hit em a coupla grounders and flies, and give em three swings apiece. We grade em from zero to five or A for automatic. Each coach gets a certain number of nine-

year-olds and a certain number of ten-year-olds on his team, and
they bid on players of different levels. We don't claim to be perfect, and we don't tell anyone what the ratings are. Don't call us;
we'll call you."

They lined us up near home plate and told us to stand in the
batter's box, one at a time. We were to swing and drop the bat
and run all the way around the bases, touching each one. We
were timed from the plate to the plate.

Most of the kids swung, set the bat down, and then ran. They
ran in a huge circle, touching first base and running almost into
right field on their way to second and into left on their way to
third. A lot of kids slid into home, even though that slowed
them down. Some stopped and jumped on the plate with both
feet.

When my turn came I stepped quickly into the box. I
crouched with the bat ready, pretending I was in a game. Daddy
had drilled into me that every play in practice came with a man
on second and two outs, or bases loaded and no outs, or whatever. My dad would tell me the inning, the standings, the score.
"Practice doesn't make perfect!" he would shout. "Perfect practice makes perfect!"

I had to run out every ground ball or pop-up and step and
throw on every practice toss. Now I imagined running out an inside-the-park home run where scoring would tie the game and
being out would mean a loss. I stood in left-handed to give me
an edge toward first.

"You a lefty?" a man asked.

"Switch-hitter, sir."

"Sure you are. Which hand do you throw with?"

"Right."

"Bat righty for this."

That made me mad. I moved to the other side of the plate,
stepped and swung hard. I was moving before I dropped the bat,
and within three steps I was at top speed.

I heard other kids gasping and saying, "Whoa, watch this!
Look at that kid."

I raced toward first, sixty feet away, and I must have looked like I would never be able to slow enough to make the turn. A few feet from the bag I darted to the right and leaned hard to the left. My left foot slid into the bag and straightened me up and put me on a line toward second, where I did the same thing.

I was hardly two feet out of the base path all the way around. I got ahead of myself on the way to home and almost stumbled, then righted myself and sped across the plate.

"Man!"

"Wow!"

"Unbelievable!"

I peeked at Momma in the bleachers. She raised her fist and smiled.

The timers looked at their stopwatches and then at each other.

"Can't be right," one said.

"The watch doesn't lie. He looked pretty quick."

"He didn't look this quick. I don't think a fourteen-year-old has run this fast. Maybe I was late punching in at the start."

"Me too. We were both off?"

"Could have been. He got out of the box fast."

Another man came up to them with a clipboard.

"Time?"

"We're not sure."

Both showed him their watches.

"You want me to write that down? Or should I just note that you both think you're funny? C'mon, what's the time? I expected him to have the fastest time, but faster even than the big kids by more than a second? Are we sure this kid's only ten?"

"He's ten."

"Sure he is."

"Woodell!"

"Sir?"

"When you catch your breath, get back in line. We need to be sure of your time."

When I catch my breath? I was hardly panting. I went to the back of the line.

Twenty minutes later, when I was up again, kids and coaches from all three tryout areas watched. That just made me faster.

I swung harder, started earlier, flipped the bat a little higher, and dug straight for first. I hit every base with my left foot, and this time I didn't stumble coming around third. My time was faster on both clocks. I had been 1.6 seconds ahead of the best-ever time for nine- and ten-year-olds and a tenth of a second slower than the best fourteen-year-old that day.

Very few kids my age could catch a grounder or a pop-up without luck, and the coaches gave up trying to teach them after the fifth or sixth kid. They had been shouting, "Head down, glove down, butt down!" for ground balls, but most kids wouldn't even stay in front of the ball.

I had done this with Daddy so many times that when my turn came the ground ball right at me looked too easy.

"Take two more," the coach yelled, "and you guys watch!"

The next was hit sharply to my left and would have skipped past if I hadn't angled back and cut it off. I went down for the ball and came up throwing, right to the catcher. The next went to my right. I'm quicker that direction, and I hustled so I wouldn't have to turn my glove over, and I kept my hands in front of me. I fielded the ball low and fired it home.

My curiosity got the best of me. I knew parents weren't supposed to ask, and I'd never have the nerve to call. But with everything going on at a noisy tryout, I knew I could walk right behind the coaches without being noticed. I heard, "Woodell."

"Birth certificate."

"Automatic."

"Best I've seen."

During the hitting tryouts I learned what Neal and Elgin meant by candy pitches. Easy, simple, slow, arching tosses were the only things these kids had a chance of hitting. Elgin came to the plate eleventh and, batting right-handed, ignored the first two pitches, one high, the other outside. No one else had let a pitch go without swinging.

"Swing at this no matter where it is!" the adult pitcher yelled. He lofted a high outside pitch with a three- or four-foot arc on it. Elgin drove the ball over everyone's heads, almost two hundred feet into right field.

The boys whistled and gasped. The pitcher looked insulted.

"I'm going to throw harder," he said.

Elgin nodded as if he appreciated that.

The next pitch was a fastball, low and inside. Elgin stepped a little farther than usual and drove the ball right back up the middle, making the man dive out of the way. He lost his balance and fell. Most of the kids laughed, but Elgin didn't.

"Nice hit," the man said. "Get ready."

"Can I bat lefty?" Elgin asked.

"It's up to you, hotshot. But I'm throwin just as hard."

6

I hardly ever hit righty. Daddy was a right-hand thrower, so when he pitched to me, I usually hit lefty. I could hardly wait.

A couple of dozen boys had ringed the infield, hardly any even on the outfield grass until I had hit the long one to right. Now everyone had backed up ten feet or so, but when I switched to hitting lefty, they moseyed back in.

That was unlucky for a chubby kid with glasses low on his nose and his hat pulled down almost over his eyes.

The first pitch was waist-high and harder than the ones before. I stepped and swung and the ball rocketed off the bat, rising and spinning left over to where the second baseman would normally play.

It sounded loud even to me, pinging off that aluminum, and I noticed everybody turned to watch as the ball barreled into the outfield and kids scattered. Chubby ducked and turned his back, but the ball seemed locked on him like a missile and hit him in the right arm just below his shoulder as he spun.

The ball bounced all the way to the fence while the boy went down squealing, his hat and glasses flying. I didn't know what to do but run out there. Coaches came running too and surrounded him, telling the rest of us to back off. I couldn't move.

I was afraid I was going to cry myself. The kid was moaning now, and a bruise was already showing.

"Can I apologize?" I said as they helped him up.

"You don't need to," the boy said. "I never seen any kid hit a ball like that. I just couldn't get outa the way."

"I'm real sorry."

"You ought to be!" a man shouted, rushing to the boy.

"Now, Earl," one of the coaches said.

"Don't 'Now, Earl' me! You're as much at fault, lettin this big kid try out with these young ones."

"He's ten, Earl."

"Ten, my rear end! If he plays in this league, my kid doesn't! Somebody's gonna get killed out here; then what—"

"Dad," the boy whined, "at least find out if we're on the same team. I don't mind if I'm on his team."

Everyone laughed, but the father said he wanted to see a birth certificate and that "something should be done."

I felt bad for Elgin and was glad the other boy wasn't hurt worse. As we were getting into the car, a man with a clipboard came up.

"Ah, ma'am, would you have a few more minutes? I'd like to see the boy throw a few."

"They didn't say anything about pitchin," I said.

"I know, and usually we don't worry about that until the teams are picked, but I know I'm going to get your son, so—"

"How do you know that?"

"Well, we've already flipped for first pick, and I've got it, and there's certainly no one else out here who could compete with Elvin for first pick."

"Elgin."

"I have down here 'Elvin Worrell.' "

"It's Elgin Woodell."

"Really? Is he related to—"

"Neal is Elgin's father."

"Well, that sure explains a lot."

Does it ever.

I turned to ask Elgin if he wanted to try out for pitcher, but he was already out of the car.

"You're going to be on the Braves, buddy," the man said, shaking Elgin's hand. "Just call me Coach Kevin. Want to throw a few?"

"Sure!"

"My son John here is our catcher."

They walked off the distance from an imaginary rubber to an imaginary plate near the parking lot, out of the way, but still several dozen kids and parents crowded around.

Elgin looked nervous, but I could tell he was excited. He reminded me of Neal, throwing easily and quickly, pitch after pitch right to the glove.

"Just let John know when you're ready to throw harder," Coach Kevin said.

"Isn't he going to wear a mask?"

"Not without a hitter in there. Just let er fly."

"My dad always wore a mask when he caught me, in case of a short hop or something."

"Just cut loose, Elgin," the coach said.

The pitch was a strike, but it wasn't down the middle like the slower stuff had been. It came in like a laser, a pitch that would have probably crossed the corner of the plate. John moved late and the ball tipped the edge of his glove and whizzed past. He looked as if he knew he should have caught it, so he sprinted after it as he would have in a game. It bounced twice and rolled more than a hundred feet.

John ran back with it, and Elgin wound and fired again, this time a pitch at John's ankles that sneaked under his glove and rolled as far as the last one. John scowled at Elgin and swore, then jogged after the ball. When he got back he threw the ball hard to Elgin.

"Sorry," Elgin said. "I thought it was an okay pitch."

"It was low," John said.

"You don't have to apologize for pitching a ball," Kevin said.

"That pitch was catchable, even if it wasn't in the strike zone. Right, John?"

John said nothing.

"Right, John?" his father demanded. The catcher shrugged.

"You got a curveball, son?" the coach said.

"My dad said I shouldn't throw a curve till I'm thirteen. But I've got another fastball that I hold a little different and that moves some."

"Moves how?"

"It'll look to rise as it comes across the plate. Daddy says it doesn't really. It just looks that way cause I throw it harder."

"Harder than the first two?"

"I try, yes, sir."

"Be ready, John!"

Elgin wound up slowly. Though he looked older than most ten-year-olds, he still had to kick high and follow through to create his tremendous arm speed. It was a good thing John had been warned. The ball smacked into the web and drove his catcher's glove into his chest. He wound up on his seat, and some people laughed.

"I'm not catchin this guy," John said, his eyes filling. "He's too wild."

"Wild?" his father said. "You just got knocked on your can by a strike. Give me that glove."

John skulked away.

"Now, big boy," Kevin said, "put me on my butt."

I couldn't. In fact, Kevin caught everything I threw. I could tell he had done some catching.

"How does 1.2 million over two years sound?" Kevin said when we were finished.

I didn't know what he meant at first. "What?"

"Just kiddin. Show up Monday at six for practice."

*   *   *

Even though most of the kids wanted to be on the Braves, probably because Atlanta was the closest big-league team, Coach Kevin's team was pretty bad. He wound up with a bunch of kids who couldn't catch lobs from the coaches, let alone hard throws from me.

John and I were the only kids who could throw the ball over the plate, and even though I could catch John, John didn't want to catch me. We both wanted to pitch and play shortstop. The kid I had hit with the line drive was on the Braves, I guess to keep his dad quiet.

Elgin came home with his uniform T-shirt and cap, and displayed it for me. I thought it looked great, but he said he still wished it was a "real uniform."

He was also upset that whenever he came up to the plate, no one would play the infield. They would laugh and run for cover or play deep in the outfield.

"Coach Kevin can't even make them stay in the infield."

"You can hardly blame them if you're hitting the ball that hard," I said.

"Momma, this is like a league for babies. Nobody knows what a force-out is. I said something to one of the kids about John and me being like Ruth and Gehrig, batting third and fourth, and the kid didn't even know who I was talking about. How can somebody play ball and not know who Ruth is?"

"Who is she?" I said, even though I knew, and he knew I knew.

"Oh, Mom!"

Kevin had told him he was going to hit him fourth in the lineup.

"He said, 'How do you like that?' as if I was supposed to be thrilled."

"Weren't you?"

"No! Nobody puts their best hitter fourth. That's the place for your power hitter. Your best hitter hits third. And if your best hitter is also your power hitter, you hit him third and let your next best power hitter hit fourth."

"Why?"

"To make sure your best hitter gets up in the first inning. It also gives him a better chance to come to the plate one more time during the game."

"Did you tell Kevin that?"

"Yeah. He said, 'You play and I'll coach, okay?'"

The Braves were the visitors in their first game. Elgin was on deck with two outs when John hit a one-hopper to left field and was thrown out at second trying to stretch it to a double. As Elgin was tossing his helmet in the dugout and getting his glove, he looked up at me in the stands.

"See?" he mouthed. "If I'd been on base, that hit would have scored me."

Kevin motioned him over with a waggle of his finger and spoke loud enough for the adults to hear.

"We'd better get something straight, superstar. You may know more baseball than me, but I don't want to hear it, all right? And I don't want you talkin to anyone during the games."

Elgin shrugged. I could see he was near tears.

He threw about three-quarter speed so John could catch most of his pitches. The other team was out three up and three down on strikeouts. Batters ducked and stepped out as each pitch came.

I sensed a rumble in the crowd.

"Unfair."

"Too big."

"Gonna hurt somebody."

"Like to see his birth certificate."

"This isn't right."

"How are beginners s'posed to hit this kid?"

I couldn't help but put myself in their position. I wouldn't want Elgin facing a pitcher so much bigger and better and faster than he was. I mean, I was proud of him, but I didn't want people thinking bad about him just because he was big and a good ballplayer.

The pitcher on the other team was a right-hander who threw huge rainbow pitches, most over the catcher's head. His first three to Elgin were balls, and I could tell by his pleading look to Kevin that he was hoping he wouldn't get the take sign.

He must have got the signal to hit away, because when the pitcher finally let one fly that came in close enough to reach, Elgin drove it between the first and second basemen. Each dove away from the ball as it whistled past, and the other parents gasped. It skipped past the right fielder and bounced, breaking a piece off the top of the snow fence and rolling all the way to another diamond.

Elgin stood on second with a ground-rule double. I clapped, thrilled with his first ever official hit in a real game. But he looked disappointed. He couldn't have been thrilled with hitting a double off a pitcher who could hardly get the ball to the plate. But what if he had pulled the ball a little more or less and hit an infielder in the face?

One of the parents said something about his being "an older kid using his little brother's birth certificate." Others started in again about how dangerous it was to have a player like him on the field.

It was hard to disagree with that.

7

No one on our team except John and me could really hit the ball, and we lost 12-2. With the ten-run slaughter rule, the game was called after four innings.

I didn't say anything to Momma all the way home, and when I got out of the car, I threw my glove on the ground and kicked it. I flung my bat so hard I had to crawl under the trailer to get it.

"Stinkin, lousy, stupid stinkin team!"

I let Elgin vent and waited to talk to him until he had flopped onto his bed.

"Your temper reminds me too much of your daddy," I said. "I pray you don't inherit all his traits."

"Daddy woulda been disgusted today," Elgin said. "Do you believe that team? We can't throw, hit, run the bases, nothin."

"The other team wasn't much better."

"They wouldn't have been able to hit me if I'd had a catcher who could catch me."

Hardly any opposing hitters got the bat on the ball, but Elgin kept throwing slower and slower, hoping for some kind of an out. He allowed one hit and several grounders that should have been outs but weren't.

I could tell he was getting madder and madder as the score got worse, and in the third inning with two outs and the bases loaded, he lobbed a two-strike pitch to a decent hitter and saw him hit a sharp grounder to third. All the third baseman had to do was catch the ball and step on the bag for the force-out, but he bobbled it. Elgin charged over to him, yanked the ball from him, and fired it to first.

The first baseman was startled and stuck his glove up in self-defense, and the throw pushed him back over the bag where he and the runner tumbled to the ground. Out.

In the next inning, with a runner at first, Elgin got the next batter to hit a grounder toward the second baseman. But rather than let him try to catch it, Elgin darted back and snagged the ball, tagged the runner, then beat the hitter to first himself, even though the first baseman was standing on the bag.

"Use your defense!" Kevin shouted.

Neither the shortstop nor the third baseman could throw the ball all the way to first, so Kevin told them to shovel it to Elgin. He would then relay it across the infield.

Because he had pitched only four innings in the first game, he started the second as well. The defense was no better, and the Braves were massacred again. The trouble came with Elgin's hitting. As I feared, he hit a ground ball so hard at the second baseman that the boy closed his eyes and turned away. The ball hit his foot, glanced off his glove, brushed his forehead, and rolled to a stop between the infield and outfield.

As the boy went down, looking more scared than hurt, Elgin never slowed, rounding first as the center fielder checked out the injured second baseman and the right fielder picked up the ball and froze. Elgin didn't even turn to look.

"Third! Third! Throw it!"

The right fielder finally threw the ball, which bounced and rolled to third just as Elgin steamed in. But he didn't slide, didn't stop, didn't look. He made his turn and barreled for home. The third baseman bobbled the ball, then threw wild, and Elgin scored easily.

"This isn't even fair," someone said. "He's going to hurt somebody."

The second baseman stayed in the game, rubbing his foot. But when Elgin came up again, the first baseman backed fifteen feet down the right field line and the second baseman ran over and stood at second.

I knew enough about baseball to know that Elgin could have pushed a bunt up the first baseline past the pitcher and probably run all the way around the bases again. Instead he launched a line drive through the hole at second that seemed to never get more than eight or nine feet off the ground. It didn't drop until it had landed about two hundred and twenty feet from the plate.

Elgin received polite applause even from the opposing fans, but a couple and another man left the bleachers, heading for the concession stand where the league officials hung out.

By the time Elgin was up again, leading off an inning, several men from the league board were watching. With nobody on and nobody out, the opposing pitcher began walking Elgin intentionally.

"Ho! Wait! Time out!" the league president hollered.

The umpire, a young man in his late teens, whirled around and looked mad until he realized who was talking.

"Time is out!" the ump yelled.

The president went to the opposing coach and Kevin followed. "Clarence, what do you mean by an intentional walk with nobody on? We came down here to see this boy hit, not to see bad sportsmanship."

"Bad sportsmanship? If we don't walk this kid, he's gonna take somebody's head off."

Some of the fans hollered that they agreed.

"Pitch to him," Kevin said, "and I may have him bunt."

"Don't be doin that either," the president said. He turned to the other coach. "Play your kids deep and let him hit. We'll decide if he's too big for this league."

Elgin hammered a foul down the first baseline, and half a

dozen fans dived for cover. Everyone looked at the president. He seemed to be pretending not to have seen.

Elgin drove the next pitch as far as he had hit his first home run, but foul. The other team was giggling, dancing around on the field as if looking for a safe spot.

A few wild pitches later, Elgin reached for an outside pitch but got too far under the ball and sent it into left field, the highest pop-up I could imagine. He looked disgusted and sprinted to first, making the turn and almost reaching second before the ball finally came down between the left fielder, center fielder, shortstop, and third baseman. The pitcher and catcher stood watching. No one was covering third. Elgin kept running and, though he was the only one near the bag, the center fielder threw the ball anyway. Of course, Elgin scored.

The league president slapped his palms to his thighs, rose, and, said, "That ball wasn't gonna hurt nobody."

He left amid a wave of boos and complaints.

"You should stay and watch!"

The Braves lost big again, but at least in the next game Elgin got to play shortstop. Unfortunately he couldn't find the arm speed slow enough so his first baseman could handle his throws, yet fast enough to get the runners out.

"Mom," he said later, "there's nothing more fun than baseball, and nothing worse than playing it the way we are."

By the end of the fifth game the Braves were one-and-four, but Elgin was ten-for-eleven, all extra base hits, including four homers, plus a bunch of walks. While we packed for our move, I asked him if he had had any fun.

"Not really. It was too easy. And our team was too weak."

The phone rang. It was the league president.

"Mrs. Woodell, it would be very helpful to me if I could come visit with you this evening."

"This is not the best time. In fact, we're—"

"I would be only a few minutes. I have good news for Elgin."

I didn't know how to turn the man down, but I knew it would have to come out that we were leaving.

"Ma'am," he said a few minutes later, a sweaty glass of tea in his hand, "we're going to promote your son to the next level."

"Sir?"

"He's clearly too good for where we have him at now, so we're making room for him on the Pirates of the eleven- and twelve-year-old league."

"Yes!" Elgin said. "The Pirates! Just like Dad! And they have full uniforms, don't they?"

"Indeed they do, son. I've got one in the car."

I said, "Sir, I'm afraid I have some bad—"

"Just let me get that uniform, ma'am, and see how it looks on the boy."

"Yeah, Momma, let me at least try it on."

It was against my better judgment, and when Elgin came out of his bedroom looking like a miniature version of Neal at his first spring training, I could hardly breathe.

"The fact is," I said, my voice shaky, "we are leaving, moving to Chicago this weekend."

"Can't the boy stay with friends or family so he can finish out the year? It's hardly fair to—"

"The only person it's not fair to is Elgin," I said. "It won't make a bit of difference to the Braves, and the Pirates don't even know they have him yet, do they?"

"Well, their coach does, and he's going to be plenty upset."

"I'm sorry."

"I can't stay with Grandma, Momma?"

I gave Elgin a look that shut him up. Later, I scolded him for crossing me in front of somebody. "It was hard enough for me as it was," I said, finally breaking down.

"I'm sorry, Momma," he said, and I looked up at the emotion in his voice.

"This is harder on me than it is on you, isn't it, El?"

He nodded. "I won't miss the Braves, but I didn't know about the Pirates. Playing with the bigger kids would have been fun."

"But I can't leave you here, Elgin."

"I wouldn't want you to, Momma. I wouldn't want to be here

without you, and I sure wouldn't want you in Chicago without me."

"You wouldn't?"

"Are you kidding? You'd get to watch two big-league teams play whenever you wanted, and I'd be down here hitting home runs and pitching no-hitters you'd never see."

Three days later we headed north.

8

One thing that could be said for fastpitch was that I could play it until late fall when the sun set too early after school. Even then I played most of the day on Saturday and after church on Sunday.

"I kept track," I told Momma after a nonstop, six-hour game with just two players on each team. "I had sixty-two hits today and thirteen homers."

"Not a bad day," she said. "Can't do that in Little League, can you?"

We had been to see several games in organized leagues, including the one I would play in the next spring, when Momma could afford it. The league played all its weeknight games under the lights, and they had beautiful uniforms. The equipment and the field were not kept up the best, but the competition was way better than in Hattiesburg.

Elgin pestered me to take him whenever I could, and though I was exhausted from working all day, I often did. Tell you the truth, I was fascinated with Elgin's baseball mind. He sat fidgeting, hollering, and pointing, and he commented on every play. Nearly everything reminded him of something he had seen on television or read somewhere. He gushed stories of baseball from the past and the present, and I wondered what else might be in that head of his.

"With guys on first and second," he said one night, "they're not even watching the guy at first. But unless they're afraid the pitcher or catcher will throw the ball away, the first baseman ought to duck in behind him either just before the pitch or just after so they can pick him off. They'd still have time to get the guy going to third. They're just handing him a huge lead this way. He's got as much chance to score on a single as the guy on second does."

I grew up with brothers. I knew how boys could be about sports they loved. But I had never seen anything like this. Not even Neal had loved the game the way Elgin did. It was too early to tell whether he had Neal's ability, but if I could keep him off booze and anything else that might destroy him, his desire alone could take him far. If only Neal had loved baseball more than the buzz of a six-pack.

Maybe it was my loneliness that kept me from being bored by Elgin's constant baseball chatter. The only thing I grew weary of was tossing a sock ball to him all the time. If I hadn't protested, he would have kept me throwing it for hours. Whenever there was a commercial or a break in the action on television, he would toss me the sock and run and dive on the couch. I had learned to lead him so he could catch it in the air and then flop onto the couch, as if saving a dramatic home run.

In the late evenings, when I was watching an old movie on television and he was supposed to be asleep, he would call out to me.

"Momma, can I come tell you just one thing?"

"Just one."

He would pad out with some bit of trivia I could hardly believe anyone could remember.

"Cool Papa Bell, from the Negro Leagues, could run around the bases only a second slower than Maurice Green can run the same distance in a straight line. That's how fast I want to be."

When he was finally asleep I would pace and long for someone to hold me. I knew men noticed me. Here in the North they were bold enough to comment on my looks. They often complimented my clear, pale skin and my red hair. Three different men at my office had asked me out. Two of them were married.

It was nice to be noticed and thought pretty, but I didn't feel available, didn't feel free. I would have loved to have an adult to talk with about something other than business or kids—something I hadn't had since the early days with Neal. We had halfway intelligent conversations at one time. But when the alcohol took the place of his career and he saw everything falling apart, he took it out on me. There was no adult conversation after that.

My family had been little help. My mother and grandmother reminded me that there had never been a divorce in our family, and that a real woman could hold a man, regardless. I could have "held" Neal. There would have been nothing to that. He wanted a punching bag and a bed partner who would pay his way, pick up after him, and let him do what he wanted. I might have done all that except put up with the beatings. The rest was not a fair trade, but it was a trade.

But who knew when the anger would be directed at Elgin? And what good would I be to him or any future children if I were injured? Sadly, I left one fight too late. And on those nights when I dreamed of a mature, soft-spoken, loving man merely holding me, hearing me, I could just as easily shift to a wrenching need to cuddle my baby girl in my arms.

Tears dripped in my lap as I sat curled up on the couch, watching TV but not really watching. I would fold my arms across my chest and imagine cradling a newborn, a helpless, feathery girl with wisps of hair and a pink bow, huge blue eyes and a rose petal mouth. In my mind I enveloped the child without hurting her, protected her, made her feel warm and secure and loved.

When I imagined that sweet, unnamed child at my breast, the pain became too intense, and my hands curled into fists and my nails dug into my palms. I wanted to scream, to wail, to yes, cry like a baby. Sobs caught in my throat as I forced myself to remain silent. Elgin would never understand.

I buried my face in my hands and wept, renewing my resolve. I would pour my grief, my loneliness, my passion, my motherly and wifely instincts into my surviving child. This was the reason I had fled Hattiesburg. I had hated the shame, but even more, I didn't want Elgin to live with it. To have a daddy in prison, to have the whole town know of your legacy of failure—no, I would not subject him to that.

I knew Elgin had wanted to stay, to play ball, to be around friends and family. He had come because I did. I had tried to take the blame for leaving, making it sound as if it were my problem and that I hated to make him the victim. But if I had my way, he would not be a victim. I had already succeeded in getting him away from Hattiesburg, away from his daddy, away from bad influences and dead-end possibilities.

I didn't know what Chicago held for him, but I had been able to find work and a place to live. We were getting by, not falling into debt as had always been predicted for me. I knew Elgin wanted nothing more than to play baseball, and if he was anything like my brothers and his father, he wanted to make a career of it.

But I also knew the incredible odds against that. I didn't hope for a big-league career for him, even if that's what he and every ballplaying kid his age wanted. What I wanted for him was an unlimited horizon. I based his privileges on his success at school.

"I don't expect you to do better than you can do; I just expect you to do as well as you can do. Then you can play and have lots of time for fun."

Elgin had risen to the challenge as I knew he would. He was such a good reader, so inquisitive. And competitive. Within the first two weeks of school, he'd told me he knew who the girl was he had to beat for best grades.

"She's got me in arithmetic now," he said, "but not for long."

He had been right. By early spring he had the highest grades in the class, including arithmetic. I allowed myself to entertain broadcasting as a potential career for him in spite of his shyness. With my first raise, which came six months after I arrived, I began putting aside money for college.

I had asked my boss what he recommended for financing college for a kid who was almost ten now.

"How do you feel about crime?" he said, smiling. I laughed.

Maybe Elgin could earn a scholarship. Did colleges offer baseball scholarships? If I were trying to get him into the big leagues, I would have stayed in a climate where he could play year-round. Chicago held other opportunities. Reading did not depend upon the weather. With his brain, his memory, his scholastic ability, the future was his.

We rarely talked about it, but I could see him anchoring a sports roundup show, maybe doing play-by-play or even color work for major events on a network. I knew there were many levels of broadcasting before that and lots of competition— everyone in the business looking for the same plum assignments—but that didn't have to deter Elgin any more than it had deterred me. Leaving Hattiesburg for Chicago in the face of uncertainty and criticism had been like taking off for Mars. But I had a feeling. I had to do what I had to do, and no problems were too great.

I wanted a nicer place to live, would have loved to be able to afford the suburbs, but there was no way. Any extra money would go for sports equipment, sign-up fees, and the college fund. Everything would point toward Elgin's success. That was the greatest investment I could think of.

Could he be even more than I dreamed? Could he do something for people far beyond what would bring him success and money in a profession he loved? Was it possible he could be a doctor, a lawyer, or a college professor? Who knew? It was delicious to think about all the options. Everything about Elgin spoke of the future, not of the past.

The past was gone, a painful, bitter memory that sneaked up on me late at night when I needed a baby in my arms or to be a baby in someone else's arms. In my mind, I would take Elgin's face in my hands and turn him toward the future, toward the rising, not the setting, sun. I wouldn't push; I would merely enable. I would steer, guide, help, provide. He had the tools, and so far he seemed to have the drive.

I would give him what I had never had: freedom. I didn't want him to be perfect. I knew he was not. For all the skills and talents and the wonderful mind, he could still be selfish, sometimes obnoxious, sometimes angry. Sensitivity and maturity would come with age. I desperately wanted to stay close enough to be assured of that. But I also knew the day was not far off when I would have to let him become what he wanted to be, not what I had mapped out for him.

I was amused one evening when he did a play-by-play of our sock-tossing game.

"Woodell goes back, back. He may never get to this one!" He motioned to me to throw the sock ball. "He leaps!" I tossed it higher than ever, just missing the ceiling and heading for the faded drape above the couch. Elgin got a finger on the sock, causing it to tumble end-over-end. As he settled onto the couch, he reached up with both hands and gathered in the sock.

"He's got it!" he cried. "Elgin Woodell, youngest player in the history of baseball, saves the game for the Cubs! The ten-year-old center fielder climbed the vines for that one, tipped it, and came down with it!"

That line of Elgin's was one I had never heard from my brothers. They had always imagined themselves as Braves, making the game-saving catch or the game-winning hit when they grew up.

This was something else that set Elgin apart from others in my life. They all waited and hoped to get the big promotion, to win the lottery, to get a break. But Elgin didn't dream about being a big leaguer when he grew up. He dreamed about being a big leaguer now.

9

I tried to get Elgin interested in football and basketball throughout the fall and winter, but though he enjoyed following the Bulls and Bears, baseball remained his true love. How could a boy his age care so much about box scores and statistics? We were learning a lot from each other. He had inherited my knack for math, and he used fractions and percentages to teach me how to figure earned run and batting averages. I pretended to care.

"It isn't just the numbers," Elgin told me. "Every game starts with an empty box score, and no two are alike. There's always the chance for a perfect game, or a no-hitter, or a shutout, or a blowout. Games have patterns. Sometimes you'll go along with nothing happening for five or six innings, then one team will explode. Sometimes both do."

One night he made me wonder if he was gifted. Was there some dormant gene from a distant ancestor?

"Baseball is, like, sort of balanced," he said. "You're supposed to suffer when you walk too many people, and usually you do. But sometimes you get out of jams when you shouldn't, and then you see things fall apart with no one on and two outs. The best play of a game might not work. It's just like how we live."

Could he have been thinking of the choices I had made, the

divorce, the move, my leaving him alone every day until I got home from work? I wanted to ask him, but he quickly moved back to baseball.

He went on and on about how sometimes a great play doesn't work while a mistake can work out for good.

"Uh-huh," I said.

"Don't you see it, Momma? On a bad play, out of position, lucky, a guy makes a double play that gets his team out of trouble and keeps them in the game. Then, on the best play he makes all year, the runner is safe anyway and the game starts to turn. In the scorebook, his best play looks like his worst and his worst is scored a double play."

"So what's the moral of your story, El?"

He smiled. "The moral is, you talk to your mother about baseball stuff and you get to stay up later."

I chased him to bed.

"There really is a moral to that story, though, isn't there?" I said as I tucked him in.

He shrugged.

I said, "I think that if you do the right thing because it's the right thing, sometimes you win and sometimes you lose, but it evens out. You can do the right thing and fail, or you can do the wrong thing and get lucky. But you can never do the wrong thing on purpose and get lucky often. Isn't that just like life?"

He shrugged again.

"That works in life as well as in baseball, El. Don't you think?"

I didn't know what Momma wanted me to say, so I just scowled and concentrated on getting better situated under the covers. She was talking about adult stuff now, and though she seemed to think I understood, it made me uncomfortable. I just didn't want her to make such a big deal of it.

"I tried to do the right thing with your dad and nothing worked out," she said. "I tried to do the right thing by moving to Chicago. We won't know till spring if that was the right thing, at least for you."

"You mean if I get to play in a good enough league, we'll find out how good of a player I really can be?"

"El, I didn't come here just to find out what kind of a baseball player you would become."

"I know."

"If I only wanted to see how good you were, I would have kept you down there where you could play most of the year and where they would have moved you into a higher league."

"They better do that here, cause I'm better than the kids my age here too."

"Are you sure?"

I nodded.

"I wouldn't mind playing with the men in the softball league."

Momma threw her head back and laughed. "Let's not get carried away," she said.

I was glad the conversation found its way back to baseball, as our talks usually did. I felt guilty trying to steer such a young boy into adult talk. I longed for the day when he would be old enough to understand.

The Chicago winter had been depressing for both of us. No snowdrifts or traffic jams like the locals predicted, but it was bitter cold. Hot water was sometimes scarce. A hot meal charity mistook our address for someone else's and tried to deliver dinner one night. I explained that we were not needy, and that our dinner was on the stove.

Elgin was curious to know whether what they had to offer— hot turkey—was better than the ravioli in the kitchen. It was, he decided, but I dragged him from the door and explained the situation to him. We had a good laugh over it, then I went to my bed and cried.

I didn't understand my own emotions. The sun setting so soon after Elgin's school let out depressed me. The sweetness of people delivering hot meals to shut-ins or the elderly touched me. But being mistaken for a charity case, probably because of the building we lived in, reached my soul.

Yes, we were needy. But I couldn't bring myself to accept handouts. We were not eligible and did not need the hot meal, but when a church group came by with warm winter coats, it took all my reserve to send them away with a thank-you.

Sub-zero temperatures were new to me, the windchill piercing as I waited for the bus and made the frigid walks from the bus to the transient hotel. I had taken to wearing several layers of clothing, but there was something about my porous cotton overcoat that made me long for something down-filled.

I had bought Elgin a warm parka. I would not have been able to live with myself if he'd had to get to and from school and play outside without it. For me, earmuffs, a hat, a scarf, and decent gloves helped make up for my flimsy coat. By spring, if it ever came, I would have not only my savings, Elgin's college fund, and my bills up to date, but I would also have enough to register Elgin in a real baseball league.

As the days grew longer, but hardly warmer, Elgin began playing fastpitch with his friends a few blocks away on weekends and for a little less than an hour on school days. He devoured the sports pages, which Mr. Bravura saved for him from the lobby.

Ricardo Bravura was a man in his late fifties, short with spindly legs and arms but a waistline that belonged to a much larger man. His remaining wisps of hair were greasy and unkempt, and he only occasionally kept his teeth in all day. He was not intimidating, but he ran the place for some absentee owner, which pretty much meant no breaks for anyone. He threw out the drunks who wandered in to doze in the warmth of the lobby. And he evicted tenants who didn't keep their rent paid in advance.

He made clear he was not there as a referee for the residents. It was up to us to keep out of one another's way. He might threaten to keep people quiet, but once a renter got past Bravura's desk, he was on his own. Two maids changed the linens once every three days or with each new client, unless you rented by the month—which we did. Then you did your own housework.

I could tell Mr. Bravura was enamored with me. For all I knew he might have been a devout lecher in his day. But now he was old and tired and seemed content to just notice and compliment women when the mood struck him. He was overly friendly to me, but he had never been inappropriate. I tried to carry myself in a way that made that impossible.

I appreciated that Mr. Bravura was nice to Elgin. He let him use the office phone in emergencies, though Elgin was to use the pay phone whenever he had change. Best of all, Mr. Bravura finally caught on that Elgin was willing to tidy up the dingy, smelly lobby in exchange for the day's newspaper—specifically the sports section.

So, every morning after the early risers had cleared out, Ricardo would find the most unwrinkled sports section from those that had been left, and save it for his young lobby attendant. Elgin breezed through the dusting of dark, greasy wood and cracking leather in just a few minutes, clearing and tossing the trash. Then he would move past the cluttered, glassed-in cubicle with "Manager" stenciled on it. He would take the *Tribune* or *Sun-Times,* promise to greet his "lovely mother," and head to our apartment.

There, with just enough time between breakfast and school, while I dressed for work, Elgin memorized the numbers that defined his world. All through the dark, cold days there had been little mention of trades, deals, and winter meetings. But with February had come spring training.

"The scores mean nothing, Momma," he tried to explain. "The managers are experimenting, trying everyone, working on plays, pitches, situations. But the batting averages mean a lot. The veterans don't care if they're facing the Cy Young award winner or some guy who will never play in the big leagues. They're there to prove they still have it. They don't want a rookie proving it's his turn."

I half listened as I steeled myself for the day. With every layer of clothes I reminded myself that this was worth it. This was why

I had come to Chicago. Today it would be spring training box scores. Tomorrow it would be Little League. But someday, it would be broadcasting. Or something. Anything. Elgin would be more than his daddy, more than anyone who had ever bore that name. I would make it possible, give him all the opportunities, and he would not squander it.

10

"How are you doing with your fastpitch hitting, El?" I called, pulling on a boot.

"I'm the best hitter every day, and I'm still the youngest."

I stopped and looked out the door at him. "Are you serious?"

"Yes, ma'am. Hardly anybody can get me out twice in a row."

"You caught on to that pretty fast."

"Seemed like forever to me. Using a broom handle to hit a tennis ball, pitched from up close like that, seems like the hardest thing to do. But once you catch on, it's fun. You should come and watch sometime."

"Last time I got shooed away."

"I don't care anymore. You can come."

"Maybe when it starts getting lighter. By the time I get off work now, it's already pitch black."

The day I decided to make good on my promise to Elgin was also the day Charlie from marketing decided to make his latest move on me.

"At least let me walk you to the bus."

I thought I had somehow kept from my coworkers the fact that I rode a bus to and from the office.

"I'm watching my son play ball on the Near West Side."

"Bad neighborhood," Charlie said. "Pretty little redhead like you ought not to—"

"I'll be fine," I said, not looking at him. "Thanks anyway."

"Any time," he said, as if he meant it.

The white mark on his ring finger told of his fresh second divorce. The reasons for that failure sat at desks and phones within a floor of mine.

I knew the neighborhood was bad where Elgin played fast-pitch. We lived close enough. When I got off the bus I thought about dropping my stuff off at the hotel, but the sun was setting fast and I didn't have the time or the energy to endure Mr. Bravura's fawning. He would offer to look after my things or even deliver them to my apartment, but that would cost precious minutes of polite small talk.

So despite that the total walk from the bus to the fastpitch game was a half block more than a mile, and that I would have another quarter-mile walk back home after that, I kept trudging. The walk home with Elgin would be no ordeal. He was my existence.

Spring was around the corner, but no one had told Chicago. I was dressed almost as I had been for the dead of winter, though I wore walking shoes rather than boots, and my scarf hung inside my coat, not wrapped around my neck and face. I wondered how pretty I looked now, in bulky outerwear and a floppy knit hat pulled over my hair.

I sat on a stoop across the street from where the kids batted. There were three kids to a team today, and Elgin was waiting his turn to hit. He gave a small, shy wave, as if not wanting to draw attention to me. I smiled at him and remained in the shadows, though it was even colder there.

A black kid of about fourteen was pitching. He was wild, but he threw the bald tennis ball so hard I wondered how anyone could see it, let alone get a stick on it. The bat was exactly what Elgin had said it was: a broomstick with electrical tape wrapped around one end for a handle. No wonder his palms were black every day.

The hitter stood in front of a wall, and if the pitch got past him and slammed into the chalk-drawn strike zone (which was the same for everyone, regardless of height), the pitcher called it a strike. That led to countless arguments, of course, but everyone wanted to keep playing so they were kept short.

"Oh-and-two," the pitcher hollered as he began his windup. I thought I recognized that windup. Who was it? A Cub? Sure! The tall black pitcher for the Cubs, Joe Davis, would be this kid's idol. He lifted his hands together, just missing the brim of his cap, kept his body straight, drew his leg back and swept forward, his arm beginning slowly and finishing in a whip action that sent the ball whooshing toward the hitter.

I squinted, trying to pick up the flight of the ball. The hitter, a big white kid with long, dark curls, spun to get out of the way, but the ball hit him in the temple. It skied high above the pitcher and drifted back toward the buildings on my side of the street.

"He hit that?" one of the two fielders said as he settled under it.

"No!" the pitcher squealed, doubling over. "It hit him!"

Everyone was laughing, even the hitter. It had to have stung, but I guess unless you get hit in the eye or some other sensitive spot, a tennis ball can't seriously hurt you. And apparently there was no hit-by-pitch in fastpitch because the hitter stayed in and the pitcher hollered out, "One-and-two," as he wound to fire again. This time he threw a lazy change-up that started toward the hitter and broke way to the outside. Curls started to bail out, then realized the pitch was slow and tried to stay in and swing. The ball curved away from him so far that he missed it with a weak swing and looked silly. The boys all laughed again, including the hitter.

"I burned you, man!" the pitcher said. "You shoulda seen yourself, man! Two down! Okay, El-El, get in there. Big stick, heat against heat. Let's see what you got."

That was the first time I had ever heard anyone call my son El-El. Were they teasing him, as if he were a baby?

"You already know what he's got, man," Elgin's Puerto Rican

teammate sang out. "He seven for nine against you already and three homers."

The Joe Davis imitator threw a pitch so hard that it bounced off the wall and back to him on one hop.

"Strike one!" he said.

Elgin had stepped into the pitch and opened his hips, but he had held his swing at the last instant. I wondered how anyone could react that quickly, and I figured his teammate must have been kidding about his already getting several hits off this kid today.

The pitch had been at about Elgin's eye level, but the strike zone had been chalked for the older kids. Elgin's shoulders slumped, and he cocked his head and pursed his lips at the pitcher.

"It was in the zone," Davis explained in a high, squeaky voice.

"It was in the zone," Elgin mimicked, and I was stunned. To make fun of a black person, especially the way he talked, constituted the fixings for a fight where we came from. I watched in amazement as everyone laughed, including the pitcher. "Come on, Darnell," Elgin said, "I'm not a seven-footer here!"

"That pitch was in the zone, wasn't it, boys?" Darnell said, turning to look at his fielders. They both nodded.

"Oh-and-one," Elgin sighed. "Now I dare you to bring that pitch down six inches."

Darnell went into his exaggerated windup again, and the fastball hurtled toward the wall. This pitch was slightly lower, but just when I expected it to bounce off the wall and back to the pitcher, I saw my son, as if in slow motion. Could I lay the credit for his incredible swing at the feet of Neal Lofert Woodell? Someone deserved the praise.

Elgin had stood there, bat cocked. He followed the pitch with his eyes, keeping his chin down and his head steady as he stepped and pivoted and swung as the ball came in at about chest level, and blasted it straight back at Darnell. The pitcher flinched and tried to move, but I was sure he hadn't moved a muscle until the ball was well past him, though it had come within inches of his ear. One of his fielders across the street instinctively shot out his glove and the ball slammed into it and ricocheted out and back to Darnell, where it hit him just below the knee and bounced away.

I had not entirely caught on to the game yet, but plainly this was an out. The team in the field whooped and high-fived each other and ran in to hit. Elgin and his teammates shook their heads and grabbed their gloves. The ball had not reached the building across the street, so it wasn't a hit; it was as simple as that. Though Elgin had hit it as hard as I had seen a tennis ball hit, he was out. Those were the rules, and they were having fun, so who was I to consider it unjust? In spite of it, he was the youngest, the smallest, and the best hitter. And from what I could tell, this was wonderful training for the real thing. If he could hit that little, speeding ball, thrown from so close by kids so big, and with that sorry excuse for a bat, real baseball was going to seem easy.

Elgin hit three more times before dark. Once he lofted a high pop-up that was uncatchable but fell as an out in the street. The other two times he rifled doubles off the wall across the street. As we walked home he explained his new nickname.

"I don't really like it, so don't start calling me that. But they took the first syllable of my first name and the last syllable of my last name."

"Clever."

"But I don't like it."

"I heard you, El. I can still call you El, can't I? Aren't you cold?"

"I'm still sweating," he said, his parka slung over his shoulder.

"That's a good time to stay bundled up," I said. "That wind will chill you."

"C'mon, Momma. I'm no baby anymore."

I looked at him, and to my horror realized he was right. He was smaller than the kids he played with, but for his age he was tall, lankier than ever.

"So, how'd I do?" he asked at home as we ate.

"How'd you do? You did fantastic! I don't understand how you can hit that ball."

"I don't either. I remember when I couldn't hit that thing to save my life. It would come in there and bang off the wall before I had time to think."

"So how do you do it?"

"I don't think."

"What do you mean?"

"I mean I really don't think about it. Daddy used to tell me to use my instincts rather than my mind. I didn't know what he meant until I had to try to hit a small ball, pitched from close in, by kids this big. I mean, Daddy pitched as hard as he could to me, but from—"

"Did he really?"

"I think so. He said he did, and I know I couldn't hit him."

"You hit him a lot, El."

"But not when he was pitching his fastest. Nobody could. At the end of each practice he would throw me a dozen or so of his hardest pitches. I don't think I fouled off more than one or two ever."

"Did he throw faster than this Darnell?"

Elgin nodded. "Yeah, but I'd have to say this is a little tougher, because a tennis ball is lighter and can move a lot more, and it does come in from so much closer."

"How do you do it?"

"I started to hit fastpitch when I finally realized that I didn't have time to think. I could guess, that's all."

"That doesn't make sense."

"Sure it does. Big leaguers guess. They try to guess what pitch a guy will throw and about where he will throw it. It gives them a little edge."

"Only if they're right."

"Exactly. But there's not enough time to think about where the pitcher's arm is and the spin of the ball. Daddy says that all goes into the hitter's computer."

"His brain."

"Right. But you just see that and react and hope for the best."

I shook my head. "Do you realize that baseball tryouts are next Saturday?" I said.

"Momma," Elgin said, "I know how many days and hours there are to go."

11

I found myself one of hundreds of parents who showed up with their kids for the baseball tryouts the following Saturday. Elgin had not slept well. I had heard him up in the night several times.

We sat in bleachers, huddled in our coats, as kids continued to sign up and pay.

"This league goes from age eight to twelve, El. Lots of competition. It's okay to be nervous, to wonder how you'll do."

"I don't wonder that at all."

"You don't?"

"No. Now what's the deal with the ages?"

"The man told me that they have a minor league and a major league. He said it's just as likely to see a twelve-year-old in the minors as it is to see an eight- or nine-year-old in the majors. It's all based on ability. Don't worry. I'm sure you'll be one of the younger ones in the majors."

Elgin leaned forward, elbows on his knees, and looked into my eyes. "You don't get it, do you, Momma? What I'm excited about."

"What's there to get, El?"

"I'm not nervous, that's what. I'm not worried. I'm excited because I can hardly wait to get out there and play. You know there's nothing I'd rather do."

"But don't pretend that you're not just a little worried—"

"I'm not."

"A little nervous?"

"I'm not."

"Then why are you sittin here fidgeting?"

"You're gonna think I'm bragging."

"Well, I probably will. You've been getting a little showy here lately."

"Then I'd better not tell you why I'm so excited."

"Go ahead."

"I don't want you thinking I'm too big for my britches, like you always say."

"Go ahead and tell me."

"Momma, what I'm starting to really like about baseball is that I'm so good at it. I love for people to see me play. Nothing makes me feel better than for you to tell me I did good. And I love it when everybody stops and watches."

"That would make me so nervous I would just fall apart," I said.

"Not me," Elgin said. "I pretend not to notice, but I do. It was great when people in tryouts or at practices talked about me. But when we got into games and I did something that made people clap and cheer, well—"

I looked at him. He seemed unable to find the words.

"A little humility would do you some good, Elgin."

"Now, see, Momma, I told you you would think that. But I'm not bragging. I'm just trying to be honest. I don't know how I got so good, except Daddy was good and he taught me everything. I'm fast and I'm tall and I've got a good arm. But I don't think that's that important."

"What is?"

"I just love the game so much. You know I love the game."

"Do I ever! You love it more than anybody ought to. I mean, you see things in this game your daddy never saw, and that's the truth."

"It's a beautiful game, Momma."

"I know. I didn't always know. But you're teaching me, and more than your dad did."

"Really?"

"Honest. I can't get into all those statistics you love and everything, but the little things you notice, the strategy you come up with, well—maybe you oughta be a coach someday."

"You mean after I've played twenty years in the big leagues?"

I smacked him on the shoulder. "Mr. Humble," I said. And I hugged him. He stiffened and pulled away and I realized he was getting past the age where he would let me do that in public.

The eight- and nine-year-olds were cavorting on the field, baseballs flying everywhere. When the ten- through twelve-year-olds were called to a nearby football field, Elgin jumped up and began to run. He skidded to a stop, raced back, shed his coat, and took off again, this time forgetting his glove. He whirled to get it and I tossed it to him. I surprised him and he missed it.

"Hope you get an ovation for that!" I said. "If you can't catch a big old floppy glove thrown by an old woman—"

"You don't look that old to me," a man said from behind me.

I hated myself for turning to look, but it had been instinct.

"Good morning," the man said.

He looked younger than I, no wedding band.

"Good morning," I said lifelessly, turning back as if to watch the tryout.

"My son is just starting," he said. "Your boy?"

"Second year," I said, turning only enough so he could hear. "He's almost eleven."

"Go on! I'm talking about the one who was just here."

"So am I," I said, my hands in my pockets, one fingering a copy of Elgin's birth certificate. Would it always be this way?

"That boy's eleven?"

"Almost," I said, unable to mask the sarcasm. "Almost eleven is ten."

"Well, it sure is, isn't it?" he said, scooting down to my row. I looked the other way, frustrated and disappointed. I wasn't that lonely. And I wanted to watch Elgin play. The field where he was trying out was to my left, and when the man noticed I was looking that way, he moved to that side of me. Now I was angry and would not look at him. I answered him in the least cordial ways I could think of, short of rudeness.

The man kept trying to get me to watch his Robin. Robin! Who would name a boy Robin?

"What's your boy's name?"

"Elgin."

"Elgin! Now there's a name for you! I don't think I've ever heard of a person named Elgin before! I mean, there's Elgin Watches, and the city of Elgin. Oh, course there was the basketball player, Elgin Baylor, but I think that's the only other one I've heard of."

"Really?" I said, as if I didn't care.

"Yeah! How bout you?"

"Me?" I didn't want to tell him my name.

"Yeah! Have you heard of any other Elgins, or is he named after somebody?"

"He's named after one of my husband's great-uncles."

I hadn't meant to refer to Neal as my husband; I really hadn't. I was glad for the slip, though, because I heard the life die in the voice of this new "friend."

"Do you have an unusual name too?"

"No, sir. I'm Mrs. Neal Woodell."

That time it was intentional.

"What does your husband do?"

Oh, please! Would he really like to know? Should I tell him that he serves time? That he beats women, kills babies, runs over old men on three-wheeled bikes?

"He's a professional racecar driver."

"Have I heard of him?"

"How would I know that?"

"What did you say his name was?"

"I didn't."

"Yes, you did. You said you were Mrs.—"

"That's my name."

"Well, then, without the 'Mrs.' that's his name too, isn't it? Now what was it?"

"Jeff Gordon."

"You're putting me on!"

"Yes, I am. Now, do you mind? I just want to watch my son."

"Well, sor-*ry*! I just wanted to make sure you didn't really see yourself as an old woman, like you said to the boy there. Elgin. I mean, someone as lovely as you—"

I stood and moved five rows down where I stared straight at Elgin. I was relieved to hear the man behind me get up and move back to where he had come from.

The other kids and I had been told to find a partner and warm up. I hooked up with a kid who couldn't throw or catch. I had to toss the ball easily so the boy could grab it. And I had to chase just about every one of his throws.

A coach noticed and paired me with a better player. But even he stepped out of the way and took my throws out to the side, away from his body.

They had us run a lap around the goalposts. I beat everybody by a long way.

"You get to hit first," a coach called to me. "Pick out a bat."

I stood waiting while a teenager strapped on the catcher's gear and an adult warmed up from the pitcher's rubber.

"All right," the man said. "Step in there and take six cuts. Hey! You're only eleven now, right?"

"Ten," I said. "Well, officially eleven. Almost eleven."

The pitcher looked at another coach and shook his head. Then he stepped and threw. The ball was a foot over my head. The next one was outside. The next low.

"I'm still getting loose," the man said. "But let's not be too picky in there."

What was I supposed to do? The next pitch was inside and high, but hittable. I ripped it to right field on a line, about two hundred feet.

"That woulda been a homer in this league," the pitcher said, grunting as he released another.

It was a fat pitch, a little faster than the last. I hit it in the same spot, maybe twenty feet farther. The pitcher spun to watch it go. "I must not be as loose as I thought," he said.

He went into an exaggerated windup and I knew his best, fastest pitch was coming. I crushed it, driving it high and deep to center, at least two hundred and fifty feet.

The pitcher turned his back on me to watch the flight of the ball. He stayed facing that direction until all the balls had been tossed back. He cradled six in his big glove and turned back around. "All right, son, listen up. I want you to take six more swings. I'm gonna throw you my best stuff, sliders, curves, changes, fastballs. As soon as you've swung, I'm comin with the next one, so be prepared. Ready?"

I dug in and stole a glance at my mother in the stands. I had to search for an extra second, because she had moved. She raised a fist to me, and I turned back to face the first of six quick pitches.

I fouled the first pitch straight back, then hit the next five solid, every one a line drive to the outfield. People had stopped to watch. I was embarrassed because the other kids were waiting to hit and the coach asked me to stay in there. I had already taken more swings than they had planned for, and now they were bringing in another pitcher, an older teenager, a friend of the catcher.

"Can you hit breaking balls?" the coach asked as the new pitcher warmed up.

"You said you were going to throw me some," I said. "Did you?"

"You trying to be smart?"

"No, sir. I just never had anybody throw me anything but straight pitches except my daddy, and I don't remember what breaking balls looked like."

"Well, the last three I threw you were half-decent sliders for one of my vintage. I pitched at Purdue and was in the White Sox organization for a couple of years."

"Did you know my dad? He was with the Pirates in the minors. Neal Woodell?"

The man shook his head. "Don't think I ever ran across him. He probably came along later." He turned to the pitcher. "You ready, James?"

"Yeah!"

"Now, son, this guy's a lefty, so be careful not to bail out."

"I never bail out," I said. "I switch."

"You switch! Now ain't that somethin! Go ahead, then. Hit righty for a half dozen pitches. If you can hit this guy like you hit me, we're gonna hafta have a look at that birth certificate."

"My mother has it."

"And is she here?"

"Yes, sir."

"Where you from, boy?"

"Hattiesburg, Mississippi."

"You play ball down there?"

"Not much. A few games before we moved last year."

"I sure coulda used you then."

"Can't you use me now?"

"Oh, I believe we'll find a spot for you, son. Yes, sir, I believe we will. Right now we're just trying to figure out where."

I moved to the other side of the plate and stood about ten feet away, watching the rangy Jim, a tall, powerfully built left-hander, throw his last two warm-up pitches. I finally felt afraid. This guy threw hard enough to hurt somebody. Maybe I *would* be bailing out.

I don't think my dad had ever thrown that hard to me. The coach certainly hadn't. This kid could fire. I wondered who he was.

"Get in there, Woodell," the coach hollered.

The first pitch popped the glove before I could react, except that my lead foot had stepped toward third base, seemingly on its own. "Strike one!" the coach yelled. "Right down the pipe! Where you goin?"

The next pitch was inside, and though I was determined not to step in the bucket, I almost fell down trying to get out of the way. But the pitch was not really close to me. It caught the inside corner.

"Strike two! You were a flash in the pan, son. You were hitting off a broken-down old pitcher. C'mon, show me what you got!"

The young pitcher came straight over the top and the ball appeared to be spinning vertically. It dropped through the strike zone and I swung and missed. The coach laughed. The pitcher smiled. The catcher said, "Would you like to see that one again?"

"Yes, sir."

"I'm callin for the same pitch. Trust me."

Sure enough, the motion was the same. I reacted without thinking and shot the ball right back at the pitcher. He caught it but it spun him around. I stepped out of the box, shaking my top hand.

"That's a heavy ball," the coach said. "The harder it's thrown, the heavier it feels on the bat. Did you feel the resistance when you hit it? Did it feel like it was drivin your bat back at you?"

I nodded.

"Okay, listen, Elgin. Jim here is the ace of the local American Legion team. He's already been scouted by the pros. Has a promising future. I've seen him pitch three games where nobody got that much bat on one of his pitches. Was that luck, a fluke?"

"I don't know. I don't think so."

"Try three more."

"What's he throwing this time?" I asked the catcher.

"Huh-uh. I'm already gonna hafta answer for tipping you off on that one. You're on your own now, buddy."

The next pitch was a sinking fastball, down and in. I got around late and hit it to where a second baseman would have been. The bat was solid on the ball.

Jim pumped another fastball, this one with more on it, and I couldn't catch up with it. Swing and a miss.

I stepped out and pretended to be getting a better grip. "Do me a favor," I said quietly to the catcher. "Call for the same pitch."

The catcher did, and I drove the ball deep to the opposite field. Jim stood on the rubber, eyebrows raised. The catcher grabbed me and pulled me close.

"That was nice," he said. "Even I don't hit him like that. But remember, your two best shots came when you knew what was coming. Nobody ever knows what's coming."

I nodded. The coach asked someone else to take over the try-out while he asked me to bring my mother to the registration table in the hallway of the school.

When we got there he introduced himself as Mr. Morrison. "This is your mother?" he said. "Maybe you *are* as young as you say. Ma'am, do you have proof of the boy's age?"

She showed him.

"Uh-huh. Ma'am, we have a little problem, which could be an opportunity for your boy if you approve of it."

"A problem?"

"Well, yes. One of my jobs as league commissioner, in fact my most important job, is to ensure the safety of everybody on the field. We spare no expense for the best helmets, and we hire the best umpires—who also look out for the boys. I have to make difficult decisions about individual players, and I've made one about your son as it relates to the safety of other kids in this program. I confess this is the first time I have outlawed a boy under twelve, and I'm still finding it hard to believe this boy is only nearly eleven, but—"

"What more proof do you need?"

"Oh, I'm taking your word for it, ma'am. But I need to tell you from the perspective of a parent, a commissioner, and as one who pitched to this boy, he does not belong at this level of baseball."

"But he's only—"

"I know. And we go up to twelve, and we have some twelve-year-olds who might give him a run for his money. You know we have a boy in our program, well, he'll be in the thirteen- to fifteen-year-old league this year, but he got his picture in *Sports Illustrated* last year when he hit five straight homers."

"In one game?" I said.

"Well, no, in two games, but it was five straight. And son, not one of those homers was hit as hard as three of them I saw you hit today. Don't get me wrong. His were impressive. They all cleared the fence, four of them by a good margin. But when he hits a ball, it's not of any danger to anyone on the field. The infielders back up and a couple have taken his hard grounders off their chests. But I don't think I'd ask anybody to stand in there when you're hitting. Mrs. Woodell, I'm going to have to ask you to let me try him out for the next level. He'll be eleven by the time the season starts. I know that doesn't seem to make much difference, but—"

Momma glanced at me. I think she could tell I was so excited I could hardly stand it.

"I don't know," she said. "If those kids are as big as the ones who pitched and caught today—"

Mr. Morrison laughed. "Oh, no, ma'am. Those were both eighteen-year-old American Legion players. He won't be facing anything like that."

"Well, I don't want him pitching or catching or playing the infield with kids too much older and bigger than he is, for the same reason you don't want kids in the infield while Elgin is hitting."

"Well, I can certainly understand that," Mr. Morrison said. "I just need your written permission to try him out at that level and see where he lands."

"You mean I might not make a team?" I said.

"That's the bad news," Mr. Morrison said. "And I want to be straight up with you. I've already made the decision to keep you out of the younger league. I'm not gonna change my mind about that. I mean, I might have let you in if you agreed to hit only lefty, or only righty, but you're equally strong from each side. I'm not the commish of the higher league, and I can't make them take you. They might be afraid to, or you just might not be good enough. Personally, I think you're better than average for a kid starting out in that league, so you shouldn't have any trouble. But you need to know that you just might find yourself in no-man's-land."

"Sir?"

"You might find that you're too big and strong and accomplished for our league, but not ready for theirs."

"Then what happens?"

"Then you sit out a year and we look at you again."

Momma looked at me and squeezed my knee. "That might be for the best, El," she whispered.

"Are you kidding, Momma? I'd die! You know how long I've been looking forward to this! I need better competition."

"But thirteen- through fifteen-year-olds. Elgin, I don't know."

"At least let me try out, Momma. Please!"

"I don't guess there'd be any harm in taking a look at you on the field with those kids. When do they try out?"

"This afternoon, ma'am. But let me put you in touch with that league commissioner first. There's no sense makin any promises before I get a chance to talk to him."

The four of us met in a classroom away from the registration table. Mr. Richter, the older league's top man, was tall and bald. He held a red cap in his hand as he greeted Momma and me.

"You have another son who wants to try out for our league?" he asked.

"No, Carl," Mr. Morrison said, "this here is the boy."

"Fine. What's the problem?"

"Well, he won't be eleven till the season starts."

"Eleven? Have you seen the—"

"Yes, I've seen the birth certificate."

"What happens if he gets hurt in the tryouts?"

"If you saw him hit, you wouldn't worry about it. His mother won't let him pitch, catch, or play the infield anyway."

"Well, neither would I. But can he run like the older boys and catch up with fly balls? What's the sense of having a younger kid on a team if he's going to ride the bench? How about we have a look at him, and if he doesn't make it, you take him back."

"I've already explained to them, Carl, that this boy will not be playing at our level."

"You afraid of him? Afraid you won't get him on your team and he'll show you up?"

Mr. Morrison smiled at Mr. Richter. "Carl, if I'm afraid of anything, it's that I'll get him, and he'll kill somebody with a line drive in the first inning of the first game."

12

By the first practice of the Tigers, the thirteen- to fifteen-year-old team I was assigned to, I had turned eleven. The kids new to this league because they had turned thirteen looked young and inexperienced, except maybe Barry Krass, the one who had made *Sports Illustrated* by hitting five consecutive homers.

Momma said I was the talk of the team and of the league. I guess I was the reason so many other kids and coaches showed up to watch us practice. But I couldn't think about that, unless it made me play better.

The pitcher stood fifty-four feet from the plate, nine feet farther than I was used to. I thought that was great. More time to see the ball. I would have to get used to the new distance between the bases, seventy-five feet rather than sixty. For once I would not be the fastest runner on my team. I was about fourth, and the only thirteen-year-old faster was Krass.

The Krass boy especially intrigued me, because Elgin was mostly quiet about him. It was a new experience for Elgin to be outrun by someone only a few years older, and I watched for signs of jealousy. Elgin was clearly going to be a star, but it did not appear he would lead this team in anything. He had found a level where he could compete equally.

"There's a lot of pressure on the boy," his new coach, Maury Rollins, told me. "I don't believe he has the arm to pitch at this level, which means he can't catch either because you need a strong gun to second base. The infield is too big for his arm, and he's too small to play first base. I put him in the outfield like you asked, which he admitted he's not too excited about, but he didn't argue because he knows the game."

"You noticed that?"

"Yes, ma'am. He might drive me crazy, but I could almost make him an assistant coach. I'm seriously thinking about having him coach one of the bases, but I'd probably get in hot water. I have to be careful not to favor him."

"Um-hm."

"He told me that if he was the manager and this was the American League, he'd make himself the designated hitter. I told him he'll have to wait a few years to make the American League! Anyway, I think he might have himself underrated as an outfielder. He has much better than average speed for a thirteen-year-old, and we both know how old he is. He gets to the ball well, senses it off the bat, hits the right cutoff man—not with a huge throw, but he gets it there—and I think will make a fine left fielder. I'll probably hit him in the lower third of the batting order."

I raised my eyebrows. "I don't guess he'll like that."

"Oh, probably not, but there are five or six hitters on this club who deserve to hit ahead of him. Krass is one. He'll be the only player under fourteen hitting ahead of Elgin in the lineup. Have you seen that boy hit?"

"No. Is he fixin to hit today?"

"He's in the hole," Maury Rollins said. "Stick around."

I watched from the stands. One of the assistant coaches was throwing three-quarter-speed batting practice, and the kids sent a lot of fly balls and line drives into left where Elgin seemed to be having great fun chasing them down.

From what I could tell, and from what I had heard, Krass

would be difficult to dislike, even if he was better than Elgin. He was polite and good-natured, and though he may not be as obsessed with the game as Elgin, he clearly enjoyed it. Everybody knew when it was his turn to hit.

The home run fence was two hundred fifty feet down the lines and two-eighty to center. Krass was a right-hander, and Elgin played him closer to the left field line than he had the other hitters. Of the fifteen balls he hit, I counted six that would have been homers on the smaller field. He hit none over this fence, but one chased Elgin to the warning track. He lost the ball in the sun and saw it bounce over the fence. I could tell he was angry. He kept looking behind him and resetting himself, as if he'd love to have the chance to have that play over.

Krass hit nearly as well as the older boys, but they had a little more strength, most putting one or two over the fence, the big first baseman sending one over the center field wall. Krass went out to play second after he hit, and when it was Elgin's turn, he stepped in left-handed against the right-hand coach.

I sensed everyone watching carefully, and I could see Elgin was nervous. I wanted to tell him to just relax and loosen up. The coach had not been throwing hard, so Elgin should just work on his swing, not trying to impress anyone.

That must've been his plan, because on the first pitch, he swung easily but was way late. He looked embarrassed, but I knew what had gone wrong. Elgin had been studying the coach's pitching for half an hour and had his speed down, but the coach threw harder to Elgin. He was ready for the next pitch and lashed a screamer so hard at Barry Krass's feet that all he could do was skip out of the way. I heard low whistles of approval from the crowd and wanted to see Elgin hit one over the fence. Just one. One more than Krass.

Listen to yourself! I thought. *Now who's jealous and competitive?*

Elgin was fooled on a couple more pitches, missing one and fouling one off. But then on ten straight he drove line drives into center and right. On the second to last pitch he bounced one over the left field fence. I wondered if he had done it on purpose, to show that he could hit as far as Krass but to the opposite field.

"Exactly," he told me later.

"Are you serious?"

He nodded. "I'm glad you noticed."

I smiled. "You little scoundrel."

"Tell me you didn't love it, Momma."

"I did. That Krass boy sure seems nice, though."

"Oh, he's a great kid. We have a good team even without me. We've got trouble, though. Last year's left fielder. His dad's not happy. He hit ninth all last year anyway, but this year he won't play much."

"Because of you."

"Right."

"Uh-oh."

"Momma, it doesn't have to be that big of a deal, does it?"

"You don't need that kind of pressure."

"It's no pressure. I run faster, throw harder and farther, and I hit better from either side of the plate."

"So what's his problem?"

"His dad said something to Mr. Rollins about a little kid pushing a fifteen-year-old out of the lineup. Coach told him no decision had been made yet, and that he was sure both of us would see a lot of playing time."

"That didn't satisfy him?"

"He said he was going to take it to the board."

"Oh, great."

"I'm not going to worry about it, Momma. What can they do? They won't let me play with kids my age, so I tried out and made this team. If I'm the best left fielder, that's where I should play, right?"

I shrugged.

"Am I wrong, Momma?"

"Course not. But we're lookin at it from our own point of view. How would you feel if you were that boy?"

"Like I got my butt whipped by a kid."

"Elgin!"

"Well—"

"Don't talk like that."

"That's how I would feel, and I'd start working on my game till I won my job back, or some job anyway."

"Don't be getting conceited on me."

"I'm not! You asked me and I told you."

"I don't mind tellin you, young man, that if the shoe was on the other foot, I wouldn't like it one bit."

In his first game of the season, Elgin batted seventh behind Barry Krass. The Tigers won 7-1. Krass was oh-for-two with a walk, a strikeout, and a groundout. Elgin was two-for-three with a double to right center, a single to left, and a deep fly to left. He stole a base, was caught stealing once, and caught everything that came his way. After the game, I saw the father of last year's left fielder standing toe to toe with Coach Rollins.

"Say what you want, Maury, but you're gonna find a place for my kid, or—"

"Ralph, he pinch-hit in the last inning and struck out!"

"His timing is off cause he's not gettin enough action!"

"Where am I supposed to put him? You still think he's better than my new left fielder?"

"I didn't say that. I'm just sayin he's a veteran with a lot of experience and he ought to be starting."

"When he beats somebody out or somebody gets hurt, I'll put him in, but until then, I'll coach and you watch, okay?"

"You haven't heard the end of this, Maury."

Elgin was still excited as we walked to the bus. When I took a left instead of a right, he stopped and looked at me.

"What're you doing?"

"I thought you deserved a cheeseburger for each of your hits today."

"Really? We can afford it?"

"I put a little aside for this."

"Yeah!"

Kids in various uniforms sat with their friends and families in the fast-food place.

"I can't do this every game," I whispered.

"I know, Momma. I can hardly believe we're doing it now."

"I know it's been hard on you, El. We've never had much."

"It's all right."

"No, it isn't. I wish you could have a bat bag and your own bat again, a newer glove, wristbands, all that."

"I wish I could go to a movie once in a while."

"That we *really* can't afford. Honestly, Elgin, I don't know how suburban people do it. Those kids are always at movies, buy the latest CDs, wear expensive gym shoes, and dress in style."

Elgin sat staring out the window after he had finished eating. There were long lines at the cash register and people looking for places to sit, but it was as if he didn't want to leave.

"Those kids don't work, though, Ma, and they aren't very good ballplayers. Even the ones who are in shape, and there aren't many, don't know not to throw behind the runner. They never take the extra base, they throw too many times on a rundown, or they run a man to the next base instead of back to his old one."

"You don't mind not havin all that stuff then?"

"Sometimes. I don't like people knowing where we live, and my baseball shoes are too small. My clothes never look like much, so I'm glad I've got a uniform. On game days I look like everyone else."

"But how about when kids play their music or talk about the movies they've seen?"

He nodded. "Sometimes I wish I could see what everybody else is seeing, but I know we can't afford it."

That hurt. How I wished I could afford whatever this child needed and wanted!

Elgin slid to the end of the booth but stopped before he stood to leave. "There's something I want more than any of that stuff, though."

"What's that?"

"A letter from Daddy."

13

By the end of the regular season, when it came time to choose the all-star team, I had had a great year. I wasn't the best player or even the best hitter on my team. But my average was almost five hundred, fourth among all players and second on the Tigers only to the leading hitter in the league.

I had played every inning of every game and had made just two errors, one on a fly ball and one on an overthrow of home from in front of the foul pole. Though it was an error, it was the play of the game; nobody believed a kid my age could throw a ball that far.

Elgin had moved up in the batting order to second and finally to lead off, where he had a great on-base percentage. He hardly ever struck out, and it seemed to me that every time I turned around, Elgin was spraying a single or double into the gap. He faced only a few left-handed pitchers, but when he did he was nine-for-twelve from the right side of the plate.

Barry Krass had shown well for his age. He wound up hitting in the eighth spot in the lineup, starting at second base, and hitting just over .250. He did not make the all-star team.

Best of all, especially to me, there had been little trouble. Ralph had taken his son out of the program because the league refused to force Coach Rollins to start him, and they wouldn't put him on another team either. And no one was saying that Elgin hit the ball so hard that their sons were in danger. He wasn't hitting home runs left and right the way he would have in the younger league. And he wasn't pitching, so no one was making any noise about that.

After my great throw to the plate, even though it was an error, Coach took me behind the stands and watched me pitch.

"Your dad didn't teach you much in the way of mechanics, did he?" he said.

"No, sir. He wasn't a pitcher."

"Well, you're not either, but you could be next year. There's a pitching instructional book at the library."

I named it.

"Get it."

The next time Coach Rollins watched me pitch, he said, "Difference between night and day, kid. You're gonna pitch for me some next year."

"And play short some, I hope."

"No question. For now, do your best in the all-star tournament. You should have a lot of fun and get some good experience."

Experience was an understatement.

"What I love most about this team is the uniform," Elgin told me.

He savored everything from stirrups to sanitary hose to colored-sleeve undershirt. He padded out in stocking feet to show me. He looked like a major leaguer, all red and gray and white from head to toe.

"I only wish I could afford to get you new shoes," I said.

"That's all right. Hardly anybody else has new ones either."

Elgin's teammates were all city kids, most barely able to afford the registration fees. When they traveled to the suburbs, they faced teams that had the latest equipment, bat bags, gloves, wristbands, batting gloves, glove pads, even weighted rings for swinging a heavy bat in the on-deck circle. Even more impressive, they had warm-up jackets made of brightly colored nylon that made them look professional. To me, Elgin and his teammates looked intimidated when the other teams ran in a line onto the field, circling the home run fence, displaying all their fancy stuff, doing exercises, singing, and chanting. One team chanted, echoing their leader:

"Everywhere we go . . . (echo) People want to know . . . (echo) Who we are . . . (echo) Where we come from . . . (echo) So we tell them . . . (echo) Who we are . . . (echo)!" Then, in unison, "We are Granger! Mighty, mighty Granger!"

They also practiced a chant for when they got runners on base. They would say of the hitter, "Billy is a friend of mine, he can stroke it down the line. Stroke-it-down-the-line, stroke-it-down-the-line!"

In the event of a rally, they'd practice, "Rip, a-rip-city, rip-a-rip-a-rip-city, come on now, rip!"

I felt self-conscious, and not in a good way. Our team didn't look like more than a bunch of guys with pretty uniforms and old gloves and shoes. A couple of them even had high-top black tennies, which made the Granger guys laugh. We didn't have any chants or routines.

Coach called us around him before infield practice.

"Listen up. Some of you guys are finished already. I can see it in your eyes. Are these kids older than you?"

"No!"

"Yes!" I called out, and everyone laughed.

"Okay," Rollins said, "but they're not older than the rest of us!

And you know what? All that stuff, the chants, the equipment, none of it wins ball games, does it?"

No one responded.

"Well, does it?"

The players shook their heads.

"I don't know if you guys are scared or just jealous. You want cool stuff or you want to win?"

"We want to win!"

"Then let's show em how a real team plays ball! Take the field!"

But we were tight, and we didn't show much during infield practice. Granger didn't just laugh at our shoes and gloves, they cackled when we goofed up.

"Fortunately," Coach said when we came back in, "we're batting first. There's no science to this. They throw their best kid; we swing the bats. The team that scores the most runs still wins. There are no runs added or taken away because of how you look."

When I dug in left-handed against the Granger right-hander, the other coach moved his outfielders back.

"This is him!" he shouted. "This is Woodell!"

That quieted the crowd. There was a low buzz as everyone stared. I had stepped in and stared at the pitcher as he took the sign, so I stepped out.

"Atta boy! Atta boy, El!" Coach hollered. "Good thinking! A heads-up kid!"

I wasn't sure why Coach Rollins thought I showed such wisdom and maturity by stepping out. He said later I had put the pressure on the pitcher and took some control.

I almost always took the first pitch of a game, because I wanted to see what the live game-situation fastball looked like. This one was straight and hard at the waist, and it split the plate. That would be good news for my teammates. If this guy grooved it, no matter how fast, they would do some hitting.

Because I hadn't even hinted at a bunt, the first and third basemen backed up even with their bases. I had a spot picked out in left center where I wanted to hit an outside pitch, and another in right center where I wanted to hit an inside pitch. Another plate-slicing fastball I would try to send back up the middle.

The big right-hander seemed to hang on to the ball a fraction of a second too long, and the next heavy fastball came right at my middle. I spun and dropped, and it just missed me. The whooping and laughing from the Granger bench told me it had been thrown on purpose.

I stood and brushed myself off, looking for the signal from Coach. I was on my own. I was to get on any way I could. I dug a deep hole for my left foot, trying to show the pitcher he hadn't scared me. There was no hitting a pitcher like this if you bailed out.

This time he tried to catch the outside corner with an off-speed pitch. The speed fooled me, but the location didn't. I figured the pitcher thought I would be shy about diving across the plate, but I expected a fastball. That's why I was a little early about squaring around for the bunt, and here came the fielders from the corners.

The first baseman was almost on top of me when I let the ball hit the bat and directed it between the pitcher and the second baseman, who had darted toward first. It was perfectly placed. No one would get to it in time to even attempt a throw. But as I raced to first, I noticed the shortstop had come over to field the ball on the first-base side of second.

He swiped at it and tossed it to the pitcher, then turned his back to me to trudge back to position. No one was covering second, so I never slowed. I was halfway to second before the shouting started.

"Second! Second! He's going!" The shortstop whirled and tried to get to second in time for the throw, but the pitcher tossed it wildly. It had been only a flip, so there wasn't enough on it to get it far into center field. There it sat, with the center fielder coming in and the shortstop racing out as I slid in head-first, squinting toward the outfield. As soon as my fingers touched the bag I pulled my feet up and headed for third. It was a long shot, probably foolish, but it would take a perfect throw to get me.

Coach wildly pointed down, so I went into another headfirst slide. The throw was a couple of feet high, and I was safe. I saw a look in the pitcher's eyes like the one that was in ours when we first saw the Granger team. With nobody out, we had a fast man at third, leading off, faking, distracting, looking for a passed ball to score on. It never came, but with one out, a grounder to second was deep enough, and we scored first.

It wasn't much of a game after that. We broke it open with a five-run second inning that included a home run, a double, and two errors. Granger had stopped chanting. The fancy equipment looked silly. We were just shabby-looking kids from the city, but suddenly we were the team to beat in the tournament.

Three days later, we finished second, losing 2-1 in the championship game to the defending state titlists. I made the all-tournament team and had two homers in four games, the last one our only run in the final game. All the way home we pestered Coach Rollins about getting into another tournament.

"If I can get some money from the league," Coach said, "I'd love to see what you guys could do."

The league told Coach that we would have to pitch in several dollars apiece to get into another tournament, but not enough of us could afford it. I could hardly believe the season was over already.

I still played fastpitch every day, and that made baseball look easy. It was sad, though, that fastpitch was all that was left for another year, but I forgot about that when I noticed the return address on a letter addressed to my mother. It was marked "Personal and Confidential," and it was from the Alabama State Penitentiary.

14

I wasn't as eager as Elgin was to read the letter from Alabama.

"You should have waited to start the rice," I said. "Now it's gonna be sticky."

"Sorry, Momma."

"Please quit callin me 'Momma'! You sound like a baby!"

He squinted and turned on me. "That's what I always call you. And I'm not a baby."

I hated when we squabbled, but we both had to vent sometimes. I busied myself with details so I could ignore the letter.

I couldn't stand it when Momma was mad, especially when I couldn't figure out why she was. I sat at the table, drumming my fingers.

"Ain't the Cub game on or somethin?" she asked.

"Ain't!? Momma, you haven't said ain't in months! You're excited about this letter from Daddy too, ain't you?"

I was just trying to be funny. She stopped and stared at me, hands on her hips. "First off, I can talk any way I want, and I don't need some child prodg—some child progeny, or whatever, tellin me—"

"Prodigy."

"Whatever. The letter is not even from your dad. It's from some official at the prison, and if they thought you should see it, they wouldn't have marked it personal."

"You think it's bad news," I said, "like Daddy's sick again, or hurt, or dead?"

"I thought you said bad news."

"Momma!"

"Stop callin me that!"

"But that was mean. I sure don't want anything happening to Daddy before he comes to see me."

Momma dried her hands and sat down with me. "There's something you got to get straight, son," she said. "Your daddy's never getting outa that prison."

I started to say something, but she cut me off.

"I know more about it than he even remembers, and what he did is the kind of thing they throw away the key for."

"But he said—"

"I know, but I had Mr. Thatcher look into it. It was bad, El. Your dad did something that can never be fixed. He can be as sorry as he wants and he can come up with all his typical excuses. But he was driving without a license, ran full off the road, and killed an old man poking along. I hate to have to make it so plain to you, but do you see why your daddy got life in prison and was lucky he didn't get worse?"

I couldn't speak. Daddy had made it look to me like the whole thing could have been the old man's fault.

"Will he get out like when he's old?"

"He was given sixty-five years, Elgin. And he was in his thirties when he went in."

"He'll be almost a hundred!"

"He'll never live that long, El. Not in prison."

I couldn't keep from crying.

"Momma, could you read the letter and tell me what you can?"

I took it to the living room. It was on Prison Chaplain Alton Wallace's stationery.

I had been under the impression that you and Neal Lofert Woodell were divorced. He assures me this is not the case. If he is being other than truthful with me, I would appreciate your advising me so that I not trouble you with his requests that I contact you.

If a document would clarify your marital situation, that would suffice.

Meanwhile, Neal is hospitalized yet again, but this time not for delirium tremens. He has largely recovered from the effects of alcohol, due to time and medication and his inability to procure the same.

This time, sad to say, he attempted to take his own life. He used a sharpened spoon to tear a gash on the inside of his elbow and lost considerable blood. He left a note, addressed to me but concerned with you. It is enclosed.

I have talked and prayed with Neal and find him still despondent and, in my psychiatrically lay opinion, also still suicidal.

He wants your love and attention, but this suicide attempt was more than a cry for attention. He almost succeeded. Any worse and he would have been shipped to an intensive care unit. As it is, he is rarely lucid.

Mrs. Woodell, I know from Neal of some of the very difficult times you endured with him. I would not be surprised to find you still bitter and even hateful toward him. But as you will see from the enclosed, this is a man with a life-or-death need to hear from you, regardless of whether he is still your husband.

If you would reply directly to me, I will honor your wishes. My prayer is that you will thoughtfully respond to Neal, but I will understand if you wish to wash your hands of him.

I am sorry to trouble you, and I hope you understand that I am only trying to do what I think is right.

I remain cordially yours,

Rev. Alton Wallace, Chaplain
Alabama State Penitentiary

P.S. I have honored the request in his note.

"Well?" Elgin called from the kitchen.

"Nothing to speak of," I said. "Just a letter from an official."

"About Daddy?"

"Um-hm."

"Anything from Daddy?"

"I'll let you know, El. Now stop bugging. Beans done yet?"

"I'll let you know," he said. "Now stop bugging."

Any other time I would have found that funny. I ignored him and opened the dingy, twice-folded note.

By time you find this, Ill be dead, I hope. I appricate everthing youve tried to do for me. Like I told you, I know Jesus died for my sins when I was a littel boy, but Ive done so many bad things sence then, I jist dont know. Thanks for praying with me anyhow.

I cant go on. You tell me God forgives me if I'm truly sorry. I don't know how sorrier I can git. What I want is for my wife and boy to forgive me, but I cant tell my boy what I done. He knows a littel but not all and I dont want him to.

My wife knows everything I gess, and she dont want to forgive me. She hates me. I jist wish she could see that I dont want nothing from her that would make her life worse. Her forgiving me for what I done to her would just make my life a little easier. I aint going nowhere anyway. I wont be any more truble to her.

Reverned, I got something like over a hunderd dollers in my account here. Could you use that to git my frend in Mobile to send my old pitching machene to my wife. She wants it real bad for some reeson.

Thanks again for everything, and Im sorry to let you down. Tell my wife and my boy I love them and that Im sorry. Tell my boy I wouldve wrote to him sooner if I hadnt been sick. Good by, and I hope to see you in Heaven.

Neal L. Woodell

I slid the letters back into the envelope. I stood and reached for the wall, shutting my eyes.

"Momma, what is it?"

"Not now. I need to take a little walk."

"Can I read the—"

I gave him a look and pulled a sweater from the closet.

"Anything from Daddy?" he tried.

I didn't look at him. "If I'm not back soon, go ahead and eat your supper. Put mine in the oven."

"But, Momma—"

The elevator was slower than the stairs, and as I turned at each landing the aroma of food overpowered the usual stench. I smelled the dinners of tenants of all different nationalities, heard babies screaming, couples bickering, kids fighting.

"Good evening, Miz Woodell," Mr. Bravura said, standing quickly as I passed. "Everything all right?" His teeth were on the desk, and he looked as if he wished he'd known whose footsteps he'd heard on the stairs.

"Good evening," I said, not looking at him.

"Anything I can get for you, ma'am?"

"No, thank you. Just out for a stroll."

"A little warm for that, ma'am. And not the best neighborhood."

"I'll be careful," I said as I breezed out the door into the darkness. As soon as I was clear of the entrance, I felt the humidity. The sky was not black yet, and I feared no danger if I walked as if I knew where I was going. The problem was, I had no idea. Where do you go and what do you do, what do you think or say when the problem you thought was behind you raises his head and reaches for you from inside prison bars?

I walked a couple of blocks to where Elgin played fastpitch every day, and I sat on the stoop from where I had watched him in the early spring. That had been one cold day. From across the street I could just make out the fading chalk strike zone.

How neat and tidy that there was a drawn box. If the pitch hits within the borders, it's a strike. If it doesn't, it's not. Why couldn't life be like that? I had not sent Neal to prison. I had not forced him to kick me and kill our unborn daughter. I had not been responsible for his killing an old man out of drunken stupidity.

I admit I was glad he had been sentenced for life. That was tidy. Not pleasant, but final. If I could have gotten him to write to Elgin once in a while, maybe with some baseball advice or something, it would be perfect.

Did I feel bad for Neal? No. He got what he deserved. In fact, he had deserved it long ago, and if he had been sentenced for what he did to my baby, he never would have been free to kill the old man.

Was it up to me to try to keep Neal from killing himself? Was that being laid at my feet too? For sure, that's what Neal had in mind. He was a manipulator to the end, even using the prison chaplain!

And what should I do about forgiving Neal? I could not forget, which was another way of saying I could not forgive. But would there be any value, any harm, in telling him I wasn't holding it against him? That wasn't true, but what could he do from behind bars? He might get the idea that there was some hope, some chance for us as a couple. I wanted no part of that.

I put my elbows on my knees and my head in my hands.

Neal, how could I have ever fallen for you in the first place?

15

Neal had been great-looking and a gifted athlete, and he was charming in his own good-ol'-boy way. He was always polite around girls, nodding, pretending to tip an imaginary hat whenever one walked by, which was often in our big county high school. He gave off enough self-conscious shyness to take the edge off his swagger. We girls swooned.

Everybody knew he was no student, but teachers and coaches liked Neal. He was all aw-shucks in front of a microphone, but he knew how to draw a laugh.

"I ain't much fer talkin here, as y'all know, but I jist believe we're gonna whip some, ah, Spartan tail tonight and I hope y'all'll be there to cheer us on. Thank you." Then he would look to his buddies and give them a thumbs-up as he shuffled off the stage.

Neal wasn't a rich kid, but he set trends with how he wore a plain shirt and jeans. Some said he was a behind-the-barn smoker and an in-the-barn drinker and romancer. But by the time we were going steady as seniors, I doubted that reputation, as least as a lover. It wasn't that he didn't want to. I set limits and stuck to them.

As for the smoking and drinking, well, most everyone except athletes smoked openly. I hardly knew any boys who didn't drink. The problem with Neal wasn't his vices, though there were many. His problem was his outlook, what some people call worldview.

I didn't have trouble making Neal behave before we were married. I gave him the silent treatment when I smelled tobacco on his breath and lectured him on his responsibility as a star athlete. He never drank in front of me, but I knew when he'd been drinking.

For a while I was dreamy about landing the school's heartthrob, but Neal Woodell was simple and plain, and I could see right through him. He seemed surprised at what his body and physical abilities brought him. They became his security, his identity. But what shaped the man he became was something else. It was his family outlook.

I visited his home for the first time about six weeks after we started dating. The Woodell place was a lot like my own family's. Low marshland in the Gulf coastal plain made for a rich, deep green, sweet-smelling grass that covered the back of the property. The front was bare dirt. There was a shed, parts of old cars, and a stone drive that led back to a chicken coop and what was left of a red and gray barn. Inside the small house, eight children—Neal was the oldest—shared two tiny bedrooms. Their mother had one to herself, except on weekends when her husband returned from shrimping near Biloxi, half a day's drive in a rattly pickup.

I felt at home at the Woodells' right away. My family was not quite as large, just six children (I was fourth). Neal seemed to be treated the same way my brothers and sisters and I treated my oldest sister. There was a pecking order, and here it started with Neal.

His mother seemed a hard woman, small with black eyes and thin lips. She never attended Neal's games, but a few of his brothers and sisters showed up. Mrs. Woodell was pleasant enough. She rarely had time to sit and talk, except at mealtimes, and even then she seemed to do all the work.

What struck me about her and her husband (when I happened to catch him on a weekend) was their view of the future.

To them, everything was temporary. It all pointed to a day, someday, when their number would turn up, their ship would come in, they would get that break, that job, that phone call, that inheritance.

I knew from TV and magazines that out there somewhere was a life far beyond my own, and I was desperate to find it. But I was also realistic. I wanted to marry Neal Woodell and stay in Mississippi, not necessarily Hattiesburg, but maybe down on the coast or up closer to Jackson. A university town might be nice. That was the extent of my dream. My aunt had prattled on about Chicago, but to marry somebody who would move to an international city like that—well, to even dream such a thing would make me like Mr. and Mrs. Woodell.

There was no extra money in that home, not even enough to move closer to Mr. Woodell's work. Yet they always seemed to be playing the local numbers racket, an illegal lottery that made someone in the county richer by twenty to five hundred dollars every week and by three thousand dollars every two months. By the time someone had spent five hundred dollars with no return, they had been hooked on the chance at the three grand. Lots of people, including the Woodells, borrowed to play.

Four years before I had even heard of Neal Woodell, his family had won a hundred and twenty-five dollars in the county game. Neal told me they had been just as dirt poor then, but rather than use the money to fix their car or put tires on the pickup, they celebrated. His family was still talking about it after Neal and I had married. What a weekend they had had in Biloxi.

Mrs. Woodell had played the winning number. She had chosen it from the birthday of a dead uncle, a no-account drifter named Clovis Woodell. The story went that Uncle Clovis had looked his new niece-in-law-to-be in the eye at the church just before her wedding and told her she was about to become his prettiest relation. He shook her hand and welcomed her warmly into the family.

"I wish you the very best," he said.

She still told the story with a sparkle in her eye. "He din't even try to kiss me like all them others done. He was just real nice, and he always treated me with respect, right up till the day he died."

"How did he die?" I asked her the first time I heard the story.

"Somehow tripped and fell down the basement stairs over to the church. Hit his head somethin ugly awful, was in a coma for a coupla days, and never woked up. Nice funeral, real nice. He never married, so there wasn't no wife or kids or nuthin to worry bout. He left us his estate, such as it was."

I hadn't felt bold enough to ask, but Neal's mother told me anyway. "Mostly just stuff from his shack. He only ever worked on the railroad, so there was some lanterns and some kitchen stuff. Nuthin else worth anything. Somebody told me once that there was some antique-buyin couple makin a swing through here what woulda give me a few dollars for the lanterns, but it wouldn'ta seemed right to me anyway, know what I mean?"

I nodded, but it was beyond me how Mrs. Woodell could have been so sentimental about a dead uncle's junk and yet see nothing wrong with using his date of birth as a numbers racket entry.

Anyway, that one victory, out of the thousands of dollars the family had spent trying for the big one, was known—by the time I had become an item with Neal—as the "Clovis Payoff." All that small bit of luck did was to forever marry them to the game. In fact, I thought, some quick-thinking numbers racketeer may have simply decided it was time for the Woodell number to come up. Years later, having never won again, they were still playing.

That hundred and twenty-five dollars had revealed some bedrock generosity—or recklessness—on the part of the Woodells. They didn't hoard it, weren't selfish with it. They piled all the kids into the truck and spent two days and one night in Biloxi, at a modest hotel that left them enough money to play and eat.

The Clovis Payoff was anything but an end. It was living, breathing evidence that they were destined for fortune. Their ship, from wherever, had set sail. Who could know when it might appear on the horizon?

It was only after I was married and working that I heard a

name for that kind of thinking. My boss at my first accounting job referred to someone with a "blue-collar mentality."

I resented the remark for weeks, though it had not been directed at me. My people and my husband's people, and most of the decent people I knew, were blue-collar. As far as I knew, there was no general blue-collar mentality. Most were hard-working lovers of the land, and we scratched out a living the best we could.

But then I started listening more to Neal. I saw him counting on talent alone to carry him in professional baseball. His conditioning was not what it should have been. He smoked and drank openly, and now that he had won my heart and my hand, I had no more to say about it. I learned that quickly, violently, and completely.

He was going to get the big break, the great contract, the right agent, the right coach, meet the right executive. His four homers in a doubleheader while he was on the brink of destruction were—to me—like another Clovis Payoff. It proved to Neal in the saddest, sorriest, worst way that if he could just do that again, show some incredible talent, he could make it in spite of everything.

His whole life and legacy were wrapped in unrealistic hopes and dreams that had Clovis Payoffs built in. Some power, some force, some evil allowed these brief glimpses of success during his darkest hours. It reminded me of the only time I had ever tried a slot machine, at Las Vegas Night in the local VFW hall. I fed two dollars' worth of quarters into the machine.

With my second to last quarter, I won a dollar. I should have realized I was not going to do better than spend a dollar seventy-five to "win" a dollar. Rather than lose the whole two dollars and get one in return, I considered the four quarters I had won as gravy, not really mine, just something to keep playing with. How can you do better than to play with the machine's money? I wouldn't realize until later that this *was* my money, that I could have reduced my losses.

Before I had finished, I had spent my own two dollars and two of the four quarters I felt I had won. Five quarters dropped into the pan, and I was hooked. One of these was going to pay off big. The bell would sound, the light would flash, and people would gather to see me trying to contain all the quarters.

But of course that didn't happen. Those four- and five- and even another four-quarter payoff were just Clovis tricks. Every time I seemed to be close to cashing out, I got a reprieve to keep me in the game. Finally, I had spent my two dollars and about another three I had won in small increments. I didn't like that. I got another five dollars' worth of quarters and went through that in about twenty minutes.

When it was over, I felt stupid. I hated myself, and I saw my husband and his family in a new light.

The more Neal drank and the more he counted on dumb luck to not just pull him through but to also make him a success, the more miserable he became. He evolved into something totally other than what I had fallen in love with. I didn't know this man, yet I knew him all too well.

And now, on the stoop across the street from where the new, true, real love of my life played fastpitch, I knew what I would do and what I would not do. I would not tell Elgin everything; I would do that much for Neal. I would cover for him. Yet neither would I write him a letter that relieved him of guilt for what he had done to me, to my unborn daughter, and to my son. I would not provide him another Clovis Payoff at the most critical hour of his life.

I wouldn't be looking for any payoffs either. I would, as I had done since I left that trailer, fighting tears, make my own good fortune. I didn't want riches. I didn't want comfort. I didn't want luck.

I wanted my son to know how to work and how to think and how to set his priorities. I had the feeling that everything I could see and feel and touch would blow away one day, while only the truly valuable stuff—the love, the people, the values, the honor, the honesty—would remain.

I looked up and sighed a thank-you, assuming God had allowed me a bit of His wisdom. And I started home.

16

The sweater had proved needless. The sky was now black, but it was still hot out. I hadn't realized how tired I was until I heard my sandals scuff the pavement. How old must I look, walking that way in the prime of my life?

As I rounded the corner toward the hotel, I passed a young couple in front of their brownstone. In the light from the street lamp they sat, not moving, not even talking. They weren't looking at each other or at anything in particular. I guessed them in their late teens, maybe early twenties.

As the young man stared vacantly across the street, the woman caressed his back with long, light strokes. It seemed an almost unthinking, idle gesture, and yet it stabbed me with pain. Did they know, could they know what they had? I wanted to run to them, to tell them. Capture this! Keep this! This is love, casual and easy and comfortable, but not to be taken for granted! One of you will change, your true colors will emerge, and the caresses will stop, the relationship will change. It will fade like the light on a summer's night, here all day, bright, in your eyes, then gradually disappearing as the darkness sneaks up on you.

I lowered my eyes and hurried, pain deep in my soul, the agony of loneliness and need. I wanted to sit on the steps somewhere and touch someone or be touched.

I got off the ancient elevator and sat on the creaky steps within earshot of our rooms. I heard the television, Elgin switching between a late Cub game and a show I had forbidden him to watch. He was so deprived. No movies. No good clothes or sports equipment. What was wrong with the program? I couldn't remember. Too adult, I guessed. A lot like Elgin. I felt generous, a mother full of mercy, making noise opening the door so he had time to switch back to channel nine.

I could see from Elgin's face that he had decided not to say anything about the letter. He just stared at me, clearly wondering if I was okay.

"How're the Cubs doin?" I asked.

"Down by two in the sixth," he said. "What else is new?"

"It's hot out," I said.

"It's hot in," he said.

I smiled. "You're a sweet boy, El. A good boy." A flicker of guilt passed his eyes, probably about the TV.

He changed the subject. "Second and third and no outs in the top of the fifth, and they don't score."

"Strikeouts?" I said.

He shook his head. "Groundout to third. Looked the runner back. Then a liner to short, doubled off Hobson at second."

"Was he too far off?"

"Nah. Elliott and Sanders both should have been trying to hit to the right side and at least get one of those guys in. Doesn't anybody play the percentages anymore?"

I shook my head and shrugged. "Turn it off a minute, son."

Elgin all but ran to the TV. Then he sat on the couch, looking expectant.

"Your dad's been hospitalized again."

"With those tremors or whatever they are?"

"No," I said, and moved a kitchen chair to sit facing him. "He cut his arm and—"

"How bad?"

"Pretty bad, I guess. I don't know all the details, so don't ask."

"But—"

"It looks like he's gonna be okay. He sends his love to you and—"

"And to you, Momma?"

"To you, Elgin, now stop interrupting. He wants my forgiveness."

"He's always wanted that."

"Elgin!"

"Sorry."

"You may not be old enough to understand, but I'm gonna tell you a story to explain why I'm gonna do what I'm gonna do."

I tried to tell him all about the Clovis Payoff, but he wasn't buying.

"Momma, forgiveness is just forgiveness. He's not gonna go getting his hopes up about anything just because you do what you were supposed to do a long time ago."

"So I've been wrong all these years?"

"Seems like it. I mean, Daddy's been saying he was sorry and begging you to forgive him ever since I can remember."

"And ever since I can remember, I've seen no change, no repentance. Nothin's changed except how bad he feels. Well, maybe I shouldn't have told you all this. You're too young to understand."

"I understand all right," Elgin said. "I'm not saying Daddy deserves it. It just seems like forgiveness has to be without any, um, any—"

"Strings attached?"

"Yeah, isn't that what you always say?"

"That's when you and I are squabblin about something and we ask each other to forgive. That's unconditional. That means there's no ifs. You know."

"So what's the difference with you and Daddy?"

I had heard enough. I didn't know if it was because Elgin was so young and naive and stubborn, or because I knew he was right. Neal needed grace and mercy and unconditional forgiveness. That wouldn't mean I was saying he was right or innocent or worthy. It certainly wouldn't mean I still loved him or wanted him back. The question was whether Neal would understand it. For his own good, for his own protection, for the sake of everybody—especially Elgin—I couldn't take the risk. Unconditionally forgiving Neal would cost me nothing but pride in trying to get the words out.

The boy I had fallen in love with in high school and the man I had grown to hate were as different as angels and demons. Here he was, sober and unable to get booze in prison, and what kind of a man was he? Like before he had turned to alcohol? No. Still a child, whimpering, selfish, a dolt. I was not about to let myself be used by him again. I may have held some cards in his game of life, but now was not the time to play them.

I dragged my chair back to the kitchen.

"So, we're done talking?" Elgin said.

I nodded. "I am. I wasn't asking your advice, you know. I was tellin you something."

He said something under his breath.

"What did you say, young man?"

"I said, 'Truth hurts.'"

"Because I don't do what you say, I don't like hearing the truth?"

He turned on the TV again. "Well, it *is* the truth."

"Maybe when you grow up and go through a few of life's valleys, you can start tellin me how to live."

"I wouldn't even try."

"Don't get smart, Elgin."

"I'm not trying to be smart, Momma. I just—"

"There is a lot you don't know, and I wish you'd just trust me. If I can't tell you stuff without this happening, then I just won't tell you stuff anymore."

He had turned his back to me and was watching the Cubs fall farther behind.

I was suddenly ravenous. I retrieved what was left in the oven and remembered that this was the same fare we had eaten the day we moved in.

I ate quickly and more than I should have. I had always been trim and never worried about my weight, but when I overate I felt uncomfortable. Plus I had argued with Elgin, which I hated more than anything. I couldn't begin to tell him what he meant to me. How do you tell someone his age how committed you are to making him into the opposite of his father? If Elgin had an inkling of his importance to me, it would be too much for him.

How I hated to have anything between us!

I cleaned up the kitchenette and went to sit with him. He was clearly not angry. I doubted he had backed down from his position, but he wasn't the type to make me suffer, even when we disagreed. I put my arm around him and he let me cuddle him. I couldn't get interested in the game. I was thinking of that stupid pitching machine.

I had wanted it at one time, thinking of Elgin's future and knowing it was one of the few things of value Neal owned. But we had no place to set it up. Elgin obviously didn't need it. Apparently, it was on its way anyway. That would be fun to see: Ricardo Bravura taking delivery of a several-hundred-pound contraption he wouldn't even recognize.

I decided to write the chaplain and inform him that Neal Woodell was indeed not my husband, but that he was the father of our son. I would say that I was—what would be the right word?—upset, troubled, saddened, something, to hear of Neal's latest troubles. I would not be mean, not say he was getting what he deserved and I was sorry he hadn't succeeded in killing himself. I would be careful to be cool without being nasty, and yet I wanted Mr. Wallace to tell that no-good—to tell Neal to write to his son.

"That's all the boy lives and dies for," I would write later. "Every day he looks for that letter from his daddy. And then we get this. Mr. Wallace, if you have any influence on Neal, get him to write something, anything to his son. And please look it over if you have to. I will read it before I show it to my son, and I don't want any of this mess in it.

"As for forgiving Neal, you can tell him I didn't speak to that. I'm still thinking and praying about it. Maybe someday I can talk to you about it. It's not as simple as it seems, that's all I can say."

As I sat on the couch with Elgin, framing the letter in my mind, Elgin suddenly turned and stared at me.

"Just one question, Momma," he said, unsmiling. "When was the last time the Cubs had a pitcher who could get a bunt down?"

I swatted him and went to write my letter. "I'm serious," he called from the couch. "Did you see this? The runners were going! He pops it to the pitcher and we were lucky they didn't turn a triple play on us!"

The game wound down as I finished writing. Elgin wandered out and sat as I folded the letter.

"Can I see?"

"Private," I said. "Sorry."

"If it was lovey-dovey I could understand," he said. "But you're probably just telling him how much you still hate him."

"I'm not even writing directly to him."

"I'm not either," he said.

"What do you mean?"

"I'm not writing him again until he writes to me. I'm sorry he got hurt, but why couldn't he even write and tell me?"

I shrugged and looked away.

"Momma, I want to go see him."

"Elgin! It's been months since you heard from him. If he's not worth a letter, how can he be worth a visit?"

"I just think he's forgotten me, and if I go see him, he'll remember me."

I embraced him. "No one could forget you."

"How much would it cost to go?" he said.

"More than we've got."

"I'd hitchhike."

"Sure you would. And I'd sit here in Chicago and work and eat alone and pray you were okay. And then the people in the white coats would come and ask me if I was the mother who let her eleven-year-old son hitchhike alone to prison."

17

Five weeks later I received a polite reply from the prison chaplain, informing me that he had relayed my messages to Neal.

"I can't guarantee he will accede to your wishes," the Reverend Wallace wrote. "Your son will be pleased to know that his father is recovering. I urge you to continue praying about your own response to him, though I would not presume to advise you."

It didn't take a brain surgeon to read between the lines. The response had taken so long, I guessed, because the Reverend Wallace was not happy with my letter. He had apparently hoped for more. It was clear that he assumed I had told Elgin everything. I would keep praying about my own response, but I was at peace with my decision not to tell Elgin about Neal's attempted suicide.

When Elgin's letter from his father finally arrived, I could tell the chaplain had written it and had Neal copy it. It read: "Dear Son, I'm sorry I haven't written you in such a long time. I have been ill. I miss you and love you and wish I could see you. Maybe someday soon we can get together. Keep up the good work with your baseball. Love, Dad."

It didn't sound like him, and not one misspelling. Elgin didn't notice.

"Mom! Do you think he's gonna get out after all?"

I shook my head. "I think he's hopin you'll come and see him someday, Elgin."

"Can I?"

"Maybe someday. You're growing up and he's gonna be there a long time."

Elgin scowled at me.

I loved the fall in Chicago, but when the temperature began to bite, I wondered if I could squeeze a few dollars out of my budget for a warmer coat. For six weeks I put a ten-dollar bill in a small envelope in the cabinet above the refrigerator. A couple more weeks and I would be able to afford a coat I might actually look forward to wearing.

The day before my four-day Thanksgiving weekend, I trudged home exhausted. Pre-Christmas orders had taxed everyone in the office. Tempers were short, and bosses whose passes I had ignored seemed to take their frustrations out on me. I was working an hour extra each day and still getting criticized and corrected. I worried about my raise, which had been promised and then delayed and then promised again before the end of the year.

A drunk on the bus circulated among the women passengers, asking for money. I could not understand why these men thought women had more money or were more sympathetic than men. I shook my head and looked away, but the drunk stood staring at me with a hateful look. He scared me. The door of the dingy hotel actually looked inviting. It would be warm inside. Mr. Bravura would say something nice, though I would be only cordial. And the slow, rickety elevator would connect me with the reason I endured all this.

Mr. Bravura was occupied with another tenant as I walked past, but he sang out, "Oh, Mrs. Woodell, a word please, if it's convenient."

"I need to get to my son," I said, slowing.

"Just a word. Anyway, your son only just arrived."

I looked at my watch. It was an hour and a half after dark. "Is he all right?"

"He's fine, ma'am, and if you could just give me a second . . ."

He finished with the other tenant.

"Now, Mrs. Woodell. Please, sit down."

"I really don't have a lot of time."

"If you knew what I did for you today, you would give me all the time I need."

Why did he have to play games? Had he rescued Elgin from some danger? Caught him hanging with gang members? I sat. Ricardo leaned forward far enough that I could smell him. Tobacco. Alcohol. Sweat. Breath. I fought to keep from wrinkling my nose.

"I did something for you today that I have never done for another tenant. When C.O.D.s come, I usually turn them away. Oh, I have paid a few extra pennies, but never have I done what I did for you today."

He looked as if he expected a thanks before I had even learned the nature of the favor. I pressed my lips together, determined not to beg.

"Well, it wasn't C.O.D., thank God. I would not have been able to advance you that much. But look at this." He produced a carbon sheet from a stack on his desk. "The total cost of shipping this, this contraption, is hidden under these squiggly lines, but you can see clearly the difference between that figure, which was paid in advance, and the amount that had to be paid before they would make the delivery. I told them there was some mistake, that you were not here and that I couldn't imagine your ordering such a—a monstrosity. It must weigh over two hundred pounds. I had to help get it to the base of the stairs, but they would not take it down for me. Maybe I should have refused it, but then if you were expecting it, what is a person to do?

"I knew for sure you would be good for the, let me see, sixty-three dollars and seventy-seven cents."

It had to be the pitching machine. *There goes my coat.* "Elgin doesn't know about this, does he?"

Ricardo shook his head.

"Good. And thank you for doing that for me. I'll have Elgin run the money down in a few minutes, if you promise not to tell him about it. May I see it?"

He led me down a dark hallway to a steel door that led to the cellar. I hadn't realized the building even had a basement. "Does anyone ever go down there?"

"Not often," Ricardo said. He flipped on a bare bulb that hung from the ceiling and gestured toward the shipment.

I had seen the thing before, but never quite like this. Every protruding piece had been twisted or pivoted or folded down and wired to keep it as compact as it was, which was not very.

"May I ask what it is?" Ricardo said.

"A pitching machine."

"Like a robot that throws the ball?"

"You could say that. Only it doesn't look like a robot. It's just a box that shoots baseballs at you."

"I can probably store it for you downstairs."

"I appreciate it."

"It will probably take your son and you to help me move it. We can't leave it here, and you don't have room for it."

"Can we do it tomorrow morning?"

"Of course. Tell me, is this normally an outside toy?"

"I've seen them in field houses," I said, "but yes, it is intended for outside."

"May I ask one more thing? Do you intend to leave us, maybe move somewhere with more space? I would hate to see you go."

I shook my head. "If you can find a spot to store this, we'll be here quite a while."

Ricardo looked relieved and busied himself in his cubicle while I waited for the elevator.

"Why were you late?" I asked Elgin a few minutes later.

"Who said I was late? Big-nose Bravura?"

"He's a nice man."

"He should mind his own business."

"I want him to look out for you, El! Don't blame him. Where were you?"

"At a secondhand store."

"A couple of blocks over?"

He nodded. "Chico was looking for something. I had never been in there before. They have everything! It's like a pawn-shop. I got to looking at everything and lost track of time."

"You should have been able to tell it was getting dark."

"I know. It won't happen again."

I sat in the kitchenette with my coat on and the envelope of ten-dollar bills in my hand. I took sixty dollars from the envelope and the rest from my purse in exact change.

"Run this down to Mr. Bravura, will you, El? Then we'll have supper, and tomorrow I have a little Thanksgiving surprise for you."

"Turkey?"

"Better."

18

Being able to sleep past six-thirty on a brisk Chicago morning was heaven. Problem was, Elgin was up and around. I hoped he hadn't noticed the small turkey in the back of the refrigerator. Neither of us could hide anything in that tiny two-and-a-half rooms and a bathroom.

Elgin spent as much time at the stove as I did. Still I was amazed to hear the cabinets opening and closing, the match being struck, the rattle and tap of pots and pans. He sounded as much like a born housewife as an eleven-year-old boy.

When I smelled breakfast I lay on my back with my hands behind my head, wondering what Elgin was up to. I finally padded to the kitchen where Elgin greeted me with a grin and a set table. Coffee was brewing, bacon was sizzling, French toast frying, and scrambled eggs ready. To be able at his age to get those dishes ready within seconds of each other astounded me.

"Happy Thanksgiving," he said.

"Ain't you somethin?" was all I could think to say.

"Yeah, I'm somethin," he said, for once not correcting my English. "I figure if you have a surprise for me, I can have a surprise for you."

After we ate, Elgin started clearing. "You just get dressed so we can get to my surprise." I shot him a double take and he smiled. "Don't trust Mr. Bravura."

"Don't worry," I said as I went to get into jeans and a sweater. "He'd be the last person I'd tell anything."

We raced down six flights, laughing and bumping each other. Just before we turned into the lobby, we heard Mr. Bravura.

"What's that racket?" he hissed, but he softened when he saw us. "Good morning, madam! Are we ready for our little chore?" He said he had found a length of chain and a rubber bungi cord that might assist us in lowering the contraption down the stairs.

Elgin looked stunned by the device. With its metal tubes and protrusions, it made a mass of parts about six feet tall and four feet wide. It was on wheels, but not all of them rolled. Elgin put his hands on the sides and shook it to feel the weight. The thing hardly budged.

"I hope the three of us will be enough," Mr. Bravura said as he fed the chain in and around a couple of metal bars. He did the same with the bungi cord.

"I'll hold by the chain," I told Elgin, "and you can guide it down the stairs by the side. Whatever you do, don't get in front of it."

We maneuvered into position, centering the machine in the square landing at the top of the concrete stairs. It took all three of us scraping and grunting to get it facing the right direction.

"We should just let it fall down the stairs," Elgin said. "I'm gonna have to put it all back together anyway."

No one laughed.

Elgin moved down two steps while Mr. Bravura and I got behind and bent to push. When the front wheels slipped over the top step, just before the weight of the machine made it tilt forward, we stopped and repositioned ourselves, carefully wrapping chain and bungi cord around our hands.

I lowered my shoulder into the machine. Mr. Bravura did the same. Elgin held the side, hoping to keep the thing straight as we planned to go step by step to the cellar. But as soon as the weight of the machine shifted, the whole thing pitched forward and began to walk itself down the stairs, faster and faster.

"Whoa! Whoa!" Mr. Bravura cried, following as if taking a gigantic robot on a walk and finding himself dragged behind.

"Don't let go!" I squealed. "Elgin, get out of the way! Get up here and help us if you can!"

Elgin flattened himself against the wall as machine, landlord, and I lurched by, picking up speed. He reached around Mr. Bravura and got both hands on the chain, but that only made my side move more quickly. The whole thing was turning to the right. Elgin let go and it straightened itself, but when he grabbed the bungi cord on my side, the thing jerked that way. Now it was humping and jumping and banging down the stairs with the three of us trying to hang on. I had the cord intertwined in my fingers, something Mr. Bravura could not do with the chain.

"I'm losing my grip!" he shouted.

"Hang on!" I said.

Elgin was crushed between Mr. Bravura and me now, trying to grab the chain again so one side wouldn't rip free. Just as Mr. Bravura's hands slipped off the chain, Elgin grabbed it. The landlord's weight shifted to his rear and he sat on the stairs, unable to hang on or help.

Elgin may have been as strong as I was, but he didn't weigh quite as much, and now our dead weight, trailing the lumbering appliance, was all that kept it from tumbling end-over-end.

When Elgin screamed that he too was losing it, I knew I was in danger. If he fell back too, it would be just me and heavy metal rolling down those ungiving stairs, my fingers and hands stuck in a contracting rubber cord. My weight moved forward, and I tried to plant my feet to keep from rolling over the top of the machine. Now I knew what a rodeo rider feels like when he's thrown off an animal but his hand is still locked into the rope.

As the machine began to hurtle and crash down the stairs, Elgin pushed off with one foot and got his knee atop it. As he was going over backward with it, he somehow unhooked my bungi cord from the metal. I sat back and he jumped off, landing hard on the stairs as the three of us watched the thing reach the basement floor with a terrible crash and roar.

Elgin sat rubbing his thigh, where he had hit the edge of a step.

"Everyone all right?" I asked.

When they nodded, I began to laugh, and soon the three of us were howling. Dust rose from the basement, along with the smell of oil and grease. We went down to survey the damage.

"I wonder if you can hurt one of these things," I said.

"Two wheels are bent in," Elgin said.

"I hope we can still drag or push it somewhere," Mr. Bravura said.

We scouted the musty, dark basement. Every imaginable piece of junk was stored in that cellar, from surplus furniture to tools, rags, gadgets, and moldy junk decades old. As my eyes adjusted to the light, I got an idea. I could tell from the look on Elgin's face that he had the same.

Just around the corner from where the pitching machine lay in a heap were two walled-off areas. Both were windowless, and each had one bare lightbulb that looked like it was on its last tungsten. One was a square room piled three or four feet high with junk. I had my eye on the other room, which ran almost half the length of the building and was about twelve feet wide.

"What would you guess was the size of this area, Ricardo?" I said idly, trying to keep him from suspicion.

He straightened and looked to all four corners. "Oh, twelve or fourteen by thirty or forty."

"I would have said twelve by forty myself," I said. "There'd be more than enough room to store it in here."

"Mr. Bravura," Elgin began slowly, "is there an outlet in this room?"

Ricardo squinted. "Why?"

"Maybe someday when I get the thing figured out and put together a little, I could plug it in and see if it works."

"Oh, I don't think so. This is not an inside thing. And you might break something."

"I'd move everything into the other room."

I was afraid Elgin would offend Mr. Bravura. "Maybe, Ricardo," I said, "the boy has a good idea. I'll bet a thinker like you could come up with an idea of how we could make this work. Maybe I could give you a few dollars a month for your trouble and for the electricity."

The light returned to Ricardo's eyes. "I will consider it, of course. I was an engineer in the past, you know."

"I didn't know that," I said, feeling sleazy. "But it doesn't surprise me."

"Maybe if the boy moved everything into the other room."

"Yes," I said. "Then you wouldn't have to worry about what he does in here with the machine."

"Precisely," Ricardo said. "I would entrust you, ma'am, with a key to the basement. You would be responsible for whatever happened down here."

"That's great!" Elgin said. "I'll—"

"But," Ricardo said, holding up a hand. "No one must ever be in this basement who does not live in this building. No boys from your team, no stickball players."

"Stickball?" Elgin said.

"Whatever they call it these days."

"Fastpitch," Elgin said.

"Are we agreed?"

"If I got the thing working, I'd want to show my friends and have them try to—"

Mr. Bravura raised both hands. "No! No! See, ma'am? He does not understand liability and expense and a person's job. Just store the machine wherever you can find room! No setting it up, fixing it, getting it to run, anything. And no key to the basement."

"Ricardo," I said. "Depend on me to carry out your wishes. I understand completely, and I'll make sure your rules are followed exactly down here. You can trust me, and we both appreciate it."

"You'll explain it to the boy?"

"For sure."

19

Mr. Bravura made a point of giving the key to me and not to Elgin. "Whenever you or whoever you designate is in the basement," he said, "I want the door locked behind you."

"Yes, sir," I said. "Elgin?"

"Yes, ma'am."

"You can always get out," Ricardo continued, "but it's a big steel door, so no outsider can get in without a terrible racket. I'll run them off. I will not allow anyone to threaten my tenants."

I told Elgin to wait for me upstairs. He looked puzzled and didn't respond, but he slowly went to the elevator.

"Take the stairs," I called after him. "Keep you in shape."

"Oh, Momma," he said. But he obeyed.

I could tell Mr. Bravura was already regretting his decision. "Ricardo," I said. "Let me just say again how much I appreciate this. Next time you look in that basement, it'll be straightened up, and we'll be sure your rule is followed. You made me very happy today. Can I send you and your wife down a plate of Thanksgiving dinner later?"

"Why, Mrs. Woodell," he said, beaming. "I'd be more than honored."

Back upstairs, Elgin was sulking.

"What's your problem, buddy?" I said, pulling him to me.

"That is the best thing you've ever given me, and I can't wait to start working on it. Where'd you get it anyway?"

"You can see it's not new."

He nodded.

"It's from your daddy."

Elgin sat in a kitchen chair and shook his head. "Momma, you gotta let me get at it. Let's skip lunch, and then let's have the big meal later."

"Big meal?"

"I saw the turkey, Momma."

"Not much to speak of, is it?"

He shrugged. "I love turkey. Now can I have the key?"

I shivered when I finally got to the basement, but it wasn't long before I had to take off my sweatshirt. I kept thinking that in ten minutes or so the machine would be ready, but so far I hadn't touched it in forty minutes. I made trip after trip from the big room to the smaller one, trying to find places to put half-used cans of paint and heavy containers of who-knew-what. There were suitcases, trunks, oil drums. It was all I could do to push them, slide them, roll them into the other room. I would be tired and sore after this.

By noon I was hungry, but I put off running upstairs for a snack. I knew I couldn't last till the turkey dinner that afternoon, but I didn't want to quit working either. I had never been so industrious. Everything I was doing, every step I made, pushed me closer to checking out the rickety pitching machine. Trouble was, even if I could get it to fire up, I had only one bald tennis ball. Would that even work?

It was another hour and a half before I had cleared the big room. I leaned against the wall and surveyed it. There were pipes overhead, a utility box in one corner, and the single bulb hanging in the middle of the room. That left the ends of the room nearly dark. The machine could be set up at either end, and since one was just ten feet from where the thing sat now, that would be the best bet. I heard a knock at the door.

I jogged up the stairs to find Momma with a couple of apples. "I'm glad you're here," I told her.

"Need some help?"

"Wait till you see." I grabbed the apples, thanked her, and chomped a huge bite as I led her down the stairs.

"Elgin! You're ready to move the machine already!"

"I've been working forever."

"I can't believe how much you've done."

"I need help dragging the machine. I'm gonna set it up at this end and have it pitch toward the other wall."

"How hard will this thing throw, Elgin, and what will it throw?"

"No idea how hard. I've seen em at batting cages where they throw slow and medium and fast, but I don't know how you set that. I'll have to look at it. I don't even know how to aim it."

"Aren't we gonna need Ricardo?"

"I don't think so, Momma. We're on flat ground now, and the chain is still attached. We can put the bungi cord back on, and I can try to get the thing up on its wheels."

We laughed, remembering what happened on the stairs.

"We can try," she said as I put the uneaten apple in my pocket and tossed the core of the first one into an empty can in the other room.

I hooked the bungi cord to a strategic spot on the machine, and we leaned and braced and pushed and pulled until it stood upright. Two wheels were still bent, but at least it was pushable now.

Every time we got it going a few inches it seemed to turn on its own and head the opposite direction. I couldn't help but laugh when Momma did. As the machine started through the door, I ran to the side and leaned into it, bumping and pushing so it wouldn't drag against the doorframe. Momma had got up some speed behind it, and as it cleared the doorway it swung into the open room and spun almost in a circle.

"I've got to get back to the turkey," she said, "unless there's anything else I can do."

I shook my head. "You think Ricardo would mind if I used the tools down here?"

"Looks like nobody's used em for years. Be careful with the electricity now, hear?"

I nodded. "Only socket I can find is in the light fixture."

She looked up. "Funny place for it. At least you know it works, cause the light's working." She looked at her watch. "I'll come get you at dinnertime, around four. I promised Ricardo and his wife some turkey dinner."

"Oh, no, Momma! They gonna eat with us?"

"I'm just bringing them a plate; now don't be so selfish. Having them join us would have been a nice idea. Wish I'd thought of it."

I found a hammer, pliers, a huge monkey wrench, and a couple of screwdrivers. I removed the chain and the bungi cord, then loosened every bolt connected to something that should stick out rather than fold in. Soon I had the machine looking more like those I had seen at the batting cages. The difference was that the ball was delivered not by a mechanical arm on a spring that picked up one ball at a time and whipped it toward the plate, but rather by two horizontally spinning wheels. The balls apparently rolled between the wheels and were spit out by spinning friction on each side.

I couldn't wait to get the machine plugged in and on to see which direction those wheels turned. It seemed they had to be able to be adjusted to put all different kinds of speeds and spins on the ball so you could order up fastballs, sinkers, curves, sliders, whatever.

What looked like it might take days was finally finished. The machine stood there, awkward and clumsy-looking, awaiting my decision. I felt around in the metal housing and found a long, coiled cord. As I pulled it out I noticed the plug was hanging from the rest of the three-pronged cord by a thread. Could I fix it, or would I wind up electrocuting myself?

20

I fed the cord from the machine across the floor until I was sitting directly under the lightbulb in the center of the huge room. I felt under the machine to where the cord began, snaking its way from some sort of special box. That seemed intact, and the connection from the box to the cord was firm. I ran my fingers along the cord and found that the only frayed spot in more than twenty feet was right at the plug.

I used a screwdriver to separate plug from cord. I was careful to remember which color wire attached to each copper connection. There was no sign of burning or wear, just loosening.

Like a woman from the electric company showed us at career day at school, I used pliers to cut away loose bits of wire and the rubber coating until I had shortened the cord by about a half inch and was left with clean, connectable wires. I wound them around their various posts and tightened the screws. Then I replaced the plastic covering with the three prongs sticking through and tightened that down.

I was pretty proud of what I'd done. Momma thought I was something because I could cook a simple meal. Wait till she saw this!

Before I plugged it in, I found the on-off switch on the pitching machine and checked the other moving parts. The container looked like it could hold six or seven dozen balls. It turned in a circle like the mixer on a cement truck and delivered the balls to a short trough that fed the two spinning rubber wheels.

The shape of the container made the balls stack and come out one at a time to the trough, which balanced on a fulcrum and dipped to receive each ball and roll it slowly on its way. The spinning wheels thrust the ball toward the hitter. Adjustable screws and knobs determined the speed, distance, and direction.

I wanted to be sure of everything before I turned it on. My friends would have to see this to believe it. I couldn't believe my luck. This was worth the months of hearing nothing from my father. I couldn't imagine a better gift.

I stood at the hitting end of the room. The machine leaned to the right. I tried adjusting the wheels by banging on them with the big monkey wrench and the hammer. The machine looked straighter. It still looked old, but I figured it should work.

I stood on a chair in the middle of the room and carefully inserted the plug in the light socket, half expecting to be blown across the room. As soon as I let go the plug fell out and bounced on the floor. I widened the copper protrusions to make them tighter and decided electrical tape would keep it in for sure. It was trickier than I thought to hold the plug in and wrap the whole thing with tape. My shoulders were sore.

Rooting around in the junk I found an old bicycle basket, perfect protection for the lightbulb. I jury-rigged the basket upside down on the ceiling with screws and bent nails and tape.

I found sheets of drywall with crumbled corners and used the insides for chalk to outline a strike zone on the far wall and sketch in a plate and batters' boxes. I went upstairs to borrow Momma's tape measure.

"I was just about to come get you," she said as I burst in the door. "Get cleaned up for dinner."

"Oh, Momma, can I have about twenty minutes?"

"I guess. You wanna run a plate of food to the Bravuras on your way back down?"

"How soon?" I said, rummaging in the junk drawer. When I pulled out the tape, I dragged a bunch of other odds and ends with it and they scattered on the floor.

"Why didn't you just let me get that for you?" she said, helping me gather up the stuff.

"Momma, I'm eleven years old. I don't need you doing stuff for me all the time."

"Apparently you do."

She took a fork and a carving knife to the oven where she removed the tin foil from the little bird and sliced some turkey for Ricardo and his wife. She added stuffing, a couple of rolls, a scoop of corn, and a slice of canned cranberry mold. She added gravy and wrapped the plate in foil.

"Oh, man, is this making me hungry!" I said. I stuffed the tape measure in my pocket so I could carry the plate. I had to spread my fingers under the plate to keep from burning myself.

Mr. Bravura was ushering a drunk out of an easy chair in the lobby.

"This isn't a mission! Now get out of here! Find a place that's giving out meals today!"

The old man shuffled out, swearing and trying to make an obscene gesture, which he had not quite accomplished by the time the door slammed in his face.

Mr. Bravura hurried back to his desk where a tiny black-and-white TV played one of his soap operas.

"Oh, young Mr. Woodell! How good to see you! And what is this? What a treat! Tell your sweet mother how grateful my wife and I are, would you?"

Before I could turn away I saw him remove the foil, find the silverware, and shovel a huge mouthful of dressing and gravy in as if he hadn't eaten for days. I hurried toward the basement.

"Enjoy your feast!" he called after me.

"You too!"

The batters' boxes and plate turned out even better than I'd hoped. I got rid of the scraps and leftover materials, then came back to survey my work. It looked great.

The moment had arrived. I knew enough to be wearing rubber soles and not touch anything metal when I flipped the switch on the machine. There was a low hum, then a rattle, then a slow acceleration until the whole thing vibrated. The motor wasn't loud, but the machine creaked and squeaked, and gradually the ball container began to rotate. I moved around to the front and watched, my eyes darting over the entire surface of the thing.

When the container was in a position where the first ball would have dropped out, the trough automatically dipped toward it. It stayed that way, the container turning and the trough leaning toward it, as if waiting to accept a ball. I wondered what made the trough tilt the other way and the pitching wheels spin. It could be only the weight of the ball.

I reached for the trough and tipped it toward the wheels. When it reached a certain spot of tension, the wheels kicked in and spun. When I let go, the trough tilted the other way and the wheels stopped. I could tell from the noise that the moving parts needed oil. I turned off the machine and found some in one of the cabinets in the other room. I applied it to anything that looked like it could use it.

The machine hummed and whirred as if new, until I heard the rumble and clatter. Had a gear slipped? Had something fallen off? It sounded like a tennis shoe tumbling in a clothes dryer. I moved to the front where I could peer into the container with a sliver of light at my back.

The noise changed. It was no longer a bump and tumble but a roll, as if a ball was in the machine. I leaned over as far as I could and saw a dark, almost black, baseball-size sphere rolling neatly around the container, edging up toward the trough. Could it be? Had an old ball been stuck in there and been dislodged by all my tinkering? How could it have stayed in there during the shipping? It must have been pinned in a crevice somewhere.

When it reached the trough I could tell it was a regulation baseball, but badly weathered and probably waterlogged. It rolled slowly until it reached the midway point, then its weight made the trough tilt forward with a clang and the pitching wheels began to spin, faster and quieter now because of the oil.

I suddenly realized I was standing in front of a pitching machine that was about to fire an old, heavy, rock-hard baseball right at me. My knees buckled and my eyes were just sinking out of range when the rubber pitching wheels gobbled up the ball and hurled it toward the far wall.

The ball rocketed from the machine with a rubbery *thwack!* and from the floor I watched it slam off the wall near the ceiling almost forty feet away. It made a crunching sound, rebounded and hit the side wall, and rolled unevenly on a split side almost all the way back to me. Shaking, I picked it up and examined it. The seams had split and the stuffing stuck out.

As I stood there I thought I heard another rumbling in the container and dropped again, my heart racing. It had been only in my mind, but to be safe I crawled to the back of the machine and turned it off. I felt around in the container to make sure there weren't any other surprises. Finally I headed up to the lobby and the elevator.

I knew I should take the stairs, but my legs were still like jelly. That ball would have killed me for sure. I tried to calculate how to adjust the machine to bring it down into my strike zone. Here was a machine designed to throw fastballs from sixty feet six inches, the major-league distance from rubber to plate. What in the world would it do with a bald tennis ball?

"You look like you've seen a ghost!" Momma said.

I told her the story over dinner. By the time I had eaten too much and thought about how thankful I was to God for a mother who cared about me so much and a father who would send me such a gift, I had regained my courage. It would be a long afternoon, having to feed the tennis ball back into the machine by hand, but it was better than nothing.

21

My friends and I had agreed to play fastpitch at five-thirty, though there wouldn't be much daylight left. Now it was the last thing I wanted to do. I asked Momma to tell the guys, if they came by, that I wasn't going to play today. I also asked if I could have five of the twenty-one dollars she was holding for me.

"What're you lookin to buy with five bucks?" she said.

"A baseball or two."

"Can you get two for five dollars?"

"Maybe at the secondhand store. You never know."

"I'd be surprised if you could get two new ones for five," she said. "I was lookin for one for Christmas last year and I didn't see any that cheap except those rubber-coated ones."

I stared at her. "*You* bought those rubber-coated baseballs?"

She hesitated. "Well, your dad told me what to—"

"He did not. You bought those, didn't you? And you told me they were from him. I knew he wouldn't buy me those."

"I'm sorry, Elgin. It's never right to lie. I was tryin to protect your image of your daddy, and I just thought—"

"It's all right, Momma. I should have known anyway. I guess I knew, but I did believe you."

"Will you forgive me, El? It was wrong, just wrong."

"Yes'm. How about the other gifts?"

"I'm sorry."

I plopped down on the couch and shook my head.

"What is it, honey?"

"Now you're gonna tell me that pitching machine isn't from Daddy either."

"That was his, El. I wouldn't lie to you about that."

I sighed. "So you're telling me it was his idea to up and send it to me."

"He had somebody at the prison tell the guy to send it."

"Who?"

"The chaplain, Mr. Wallace."

"And Daddy had him tell the coach to send it to me?"

"Right."

"To me?"

"Of course it's for you. What'm I gonna do with it?"

She smiled at me.

"The name on the tag was yours, Momma, not mine. How come it was sent to you?"

"I don't know. Maybe they thought I might have to pay for delivery."

"All I want to know is, was this your idea or Daddy's?"

She looked away. "What's the difference? He had it sent and now you have it."

"How'd you get him to send it?"

"What makes you think I—"

"Momma! You already lied to me about the other gifts, and you said you were sorry. You know as well as I do that Daddy didn't up and decide to send me a pitching machine after not writing me or calling me for so long. How did you get this out of him?"

"I won it as part of the divorce settlement, if you must know."

I wished I hadn't asked. I got my glove and broomstick bat and bald tennis ball. If I got tired of using the same ball over and over, I would go play fastpitch. I trudged down to the basement, still excited when I saw the machine, but not as thrilled as when I thought Daddy was still interested in my baseball career.

I stashed my other equipment and dropped the tennis ball

into the container. The thing whirred to life, but the tennis ball never rolled to the top toward the trough; too light, it just bounced around inside the cylinder. I fished it out and set it in the trough. It was even too light to tip the trough and start the pitching wheels moving, so I held it in and tipped the trough myself. The wheels spun, but the ball was too thin for the space between the wheels and it dribbled through, skipping to the floor.

I studied the machine until I discovered what to loosen to push the wheels closer together, then tightened it again. I still had to feed the ball into the trough and tip it toward the wheels, but this time the wheels were too close together and they caught and mashed the ball almost flat before spitting it out about ten feet to the right. It bounced off the wall and rolled into my newly chalked batters' boxes.

This machine was just not designed for soft balls. I played with the adjustments again and got it so the tennis ball fit just right, but when I sent it through, the ball floated from the machine and looked like anything but a pitch. I finally decided that because the pitching wheels were made of rubber, they would work only with hardballs. I shut the machine off and went to look for my friends.

"Where you been, man?" Chico asked as I rounded the corner. "It's gettin dark and we need another guy."

I took over pitching and tried to keep the ball away from the strengths of the other team of two. But I was still thinking about the machine and didn't pitch well. I didn't hit well either, averaging about three hundred for an hour or so.

"Man, you're losin it," Chico said.

"Yeah?" I said. "You want to trade me?"

"No way, man. Still you and me all the way!"

We sat on the sidewalk.

"Hey, Chico, you think that store you showed me yesterday would have baseballs for sale?"

He shrugged. "Closed today anyway. We can look tomorrow, eh?"

I didn't understand Elgin's mood when he got home. The life, the excitement, the enthusiasm seemed to have gone out of him. I tried to get him to talk, but he was quieter, more sullen than he'd been in a long time. I felt terrible that I had lied to him, worse now that I had been caught than when I had misled him in the first place.

I tried apologizing again, more for my sake than his, but he waved me off as if I shouldn't worry about it. "You'll be able to find something that will work in your machine," I said. "I'll be back in a while. Goin for a walk." I told him he could watch the football game.

I didn't take a sweater, and if Elgin had been thinking, he'd have realized I wasn't going outside. I took my key and slipped downstairs, unfortunately running into Mr. Bravura. I had hoped I could just duck down to see Elgin's handiwork. Maybe I could encourage him somehow.

"Oh, Mrs. Woodell!" Ricardo said. "A feast fit for a king and queen! Wonderful! Wonderful!"

"Did you want some more?"

"Oh, we couldn't eat another thing! You were most kind. I tried to wipe the plate clean, but I didn't do too well."

He gathered plate and silver, and though I wasn't really ready to take them back, I accepted them and told him he was welcome. I'm sure I was nicer to him than anyone else in the building was, but I just wanted to do the right thing because it was the right thing. He was one greasy, tacky man, but he had needs and had suffered the way most of us in that building had.

I smiled at Elgin's chalk work and his ceiling basket to protect the light. I ran a hand along the edge of the pitching machine as I walked around it. If anybody could get this contraption to work, it was Elgin. I wondered if the cord in the middle of the room distracted him and whether he could get the machine to pitch around it.

I found the switch and wondered if there would be any harm

in starting it up. I jumped when I pushed the button and the machine hummed. The container rolled and I quickly figured out how it would work. *What fun.* I wished I had the money to buy Elgin a dozen new baseballs. How would he see old ones in this dingy place?

"I'm proud of you," I told him upstairs.

"For what?"

"Your own personal batting cage."

"It's kind of good, isn't it? It's going to take me a long time to adjust it and all that. It wasn't meant to pitch from that close up."

"You'll figure it out, El. You've got one fantastic opportunity. Once you get that thing workin, you'll be able to take batting practice anytime you want, year-round."

He looked up at me and smiled. "I will, won't I?"

"It might get a little lonely, but anybody who ever did anything worth a nickel had to go through a time of training, don't you think? Like me with my accounting work. All that library time."

"When I get to the big leagues," he said, "and make millions of dollars, you won't have to be a bookkeeper anymore. You can live anywhere you want. You can be my bookkeeper."

I laughed and hugged him. I didn't know whether I wanted him trying for a big-league career or not. But now that he was thinking about it, as he did so often, he couldn't quit talking about it.

"You know, Momma, I will have lived again as long as I have now when that happens. I mean, I should know whether I'll make it by the time I'm twenty-two, but I might not be making millions yet."

"Oh, not right away, no," I said, teasing him. "And eleven years may be another lifetime to you, but the last eleven have flown by pretty fast for your momma. It won't be long before we know what life has for you. Just keep track of the basics and—"

"I know," he said. "And do the right things because they're the right things."

22

Lucky's Secondhand Shop between the transient hotel and our fastpitch diamond was a new world. Chico took it in stride. "I got no money, man, and less I get some money, all I can do is look or steal, know what I mean?"

"Just like a base runner, Chico."

"Say what?"

"A base runner can only look or steal."

"You crazy, man."

"Yeah, but you're not gonna be stealing anything when you're with me. I don't steal and I don't need trouble."

The store had a red-bearded biker type behind the counter. On his belt he wore one of the many hunting knives for sale in the store. Chico's eyes grew wide when he saw it, and I knew he wouldn't be trying to pull anything that day.

"Take yer time, boys," Biker said. "Touch what you want, take what you want, pay for what you take."

"Yes, sir," I said, saluting, and we laughed. So did Biker. *Fortunately*, I thought.

Chico moved back into the military hardware area, checking out knives and canteens, belts, shoes, and boots. I was fascinated with the uniforms and fatigues too, until I remembered what I was there for. I looked at old ball gloves, none of them any good.

I was stopped by a cardboard box full of old, brown softballs, all twelve-inchers. I tried to remember if I had been able to separate the pitching wheels far enough for such a large ball.

I went to the counter.

"Do you have any more baseball equipment?"

"I got some stuff in day before yesterday that's in the back. I can't go back there while I have customers in the store. But you could check it out yourself. You can't get out that way anyway, so I don't hafta worry about you stealing nuthin."

"I wouldn't anyway."

"It's just through there. You'll see a big green canvas bag with bats and catcher's equipment. Looks like it's from a Little League team. If you wanna know the truth, I think it's hot."

"Any baseballs in there?"

"You know, I don't think there is. You can look, but I went through the stuff real quick to give the guy a price, and that was one thing that was missin. Guess he had use for those. Probably took the best bats too, but take a look. You can dump out the whole bag, but put anything back you don't wanna buy. I haven't put prices on anything yet, but I know what I paid for the lot, so we can figure something out."

Chico started to follow me but Biker held up a hand. "Just one back there at a time, boys."

I had never seen such an assortment of junk. Everything from lawn furniture to old clocks and golfing equipment was stashed in that place, ready to be priced, I guessed. I wrestled the green bag to the floor, opened the top and lifted the bottom. Half a dozen aluminum bats, including a long, skinny, weighted fungo bat, clattered to the floor. There was a catcher's mitt, a chest protector, and shin guards, along with several navy blue batting helmets. One fit perfectly.

The bats were of different lengths and widths, and though all of them felt okay, I was most interested in the fungo. I had seen wood fungo bats before, the kind big-league coaches used to hit fly balls to their outfielders. I had never seen an aluminum fungo. I wondered what a bat like that would do to a fastpitch tennis ball. Probably rip it in two.

Biker was right. There were no baseballs. I left the helmet on
and carried the metal fungo as I looked at the other stuff in the
room. In one corner it looked as if someone had ripped off a
golf course. There were several golf bags and even a wire basket
full of golf balls, each ringed with red stripes and reading
"Range." Nearly half of them had deep cuts.

I had money in my pocket, but I didn't need a batting helmet
for fastpitch. I couldn't use a metal fungo for fastpitch. I had my
own broomstick handle bat, which would probably not work
with my pitching machine, but I didn't have baseballs for that
yet anyway. I took off the helmet and put it back in the bag. I
hung on to the bat, moving into the center of the small room
where I had room to swing. What a great weight and feel.

"Findin anything back there?" Biker called out.

"Not much!" I hollered. "I'll be right out!"

I talked myself into the fungo bat. It was about an inch and a
half in diameter, perfectly straight from the handle to the other
end, with no fattening or tapering. When I found some baseballs for my machine, this would be the perfect bat.

Biker grunted when he saw it. "Never seen one of them before. What the devil is it for?"

I told him.

"But what do you want it for?"

"Just to play with."

"What's it worth to ya?"

"What do you mean?"

"What would you pay for it?"

"I don't know. I've only got—" I reached in my pocket for the
five but Biker cut me off.

"Whoa, whoa, whoops, don't tell the seller what you've got to
spend. You tell me how much you've got, and I'll tell you that's
how much it is. Understand?"

I shook my head.

"This is a secondhand store, son. I know what I paid for that
bag of junk and roughly how much I wanna get for it, but there
are no hard-and-fast prices. If I can get you to pay twice as much
as I really need, good for me. If you can find out how really low

I'll go, then you'll get a better deal. I'm not gonna go below a certain point, but your job is to get as close to that as you can."

"How?"

"Make me an offer and see how I react."

"You're not gonna react with that knife, are you?"

Biker found that hilarious. "You're a good kid! I like you! Now come on, let's deal on that fine bat. It's unique. I don't know where you'd find another one like it. It's in perfect condition. Lot of people come in here looking for those. I could sell that this afternoon for three, four times what I paid for it."

"You could?"

"Course not, but come on, kid. You gotta play the game. This is how I make my livin. You gotta tell me what's wrong with that thing and why it's practically worthless. You gotta try to convince me you'd be doin me a favor by takin it off my hands without chargin me to do it."

I enjoyed the twinkle in his eye. Chico thought we were both crazy and said so, then went out and sat on the sidewalk, his back up against the metal grating that would be pulled across the front window when the shop closed.

I ran my hands up and down the bat. "I don't know what I'd do with this piece of junk," I said.

"Yeah," Biker said. "Like that! Good!"

"Thing looks like a mistake. S'posed to be a bat, but it's just a straight metal rod. You'll never find anybody who wants this. I'll give you a dollar for it."

Biker roared. I could see he loved the game, especially teaching it.

"Why, I paid three times that for it, and I have to make a profit."

"Two dollars, tops," I said.

"I gotta lose a dollar on the deal? I'll tell ya what, buy somethin else and I'll consider takin a loss on that, that whatever it is."

I thought a minute before it hit me. If I could get this bat for two dollars, I could get the basket of golf balls for three. I was sure I could make them work in the machine. Swinging at a smaller ball with a smaller bat would be great for my hitting eye. I left the bat on the counter and headed into the back room, trying to decide what to say to lower the value on the basket of golf balls.

When I returned with it, a woman was at the counter, dickering over the price of a fancy Swiss army knife.

"That's a forty-dollar piece of merchandise I'm gonna let you have for just thirty-five," Biker said, winking at me when the woman looked down in disgust.

"It's not worth five," the woman said, "but I can go ten."

"Ten? Lady, I paid a lot more than that for it. I can come down to thirty-two-fifty."

"Fifteen is my limit."

"Well, then we got a problem. I got a limit too, and it's twice where you are now."

"Sorry," the woman said, and she turned to leave.

Biker raised his eyebrows at me, as if to say he was impressed by her tactic. "Ah, ma'am," he said, "I can meet you halfway. Twenty-two-fifty and we got a deal."

"No." The woman was heading out the door.

"Twenty's as low as I can go," Biker called.

The woman returned. "Twenty is what I was hoping to pay."

"Pleasure doing business with you, ma'am."

I shook my head as the woman left with her knife in a small paper sack.

"You like that?" Biker asked.

"It was fun."

"Yeah, for me too. You know what I paid for that knife and what I wanted to get for it?"

I shrugged.

"I paid six. I was hoping to sell it for twelve. Always try to get twice what I paid for something."

"You told her it was a forty-dollar knife!"

"It is if she'll pay that."

"Does anybody ever pay the first price you tell them?"

"It happens. Not often."

"How much for this basket of useless golf balls that nobody

else in Chicago would want because there's no place to use them?"

"Good! Good! Well, let me see, there must be sixty, seventy balls in that basket."

"Less than sixty," Elgin said. "I counted them."

"Oh, that was good that you didn't tell me exactly how many. Okay, if there's, say, fifty-five at a quarter apiece—" He wrote on a piece of scrap paper. "That would be thirteen dollars and seventy-five cents. Let's make it an even ten."

Uh-oh. "Would you sell me just ten of them or so?"

Biker looked at me with a smile. "I want you to have the balls and the bat. We're down to two bucks on the bat if I can make a little profit on the balls. What've you got?"

"You mean honestly, not dealing anymore?"

"Yeah."

"Five dollars, and I'm not gonna have any more for a long time."

"Five will do it, buddy. I hope you learned a little today. I paid ten dollars for that bag of equipment, so I want to sell it for a couple, three dollars a bat or the whole lot for twenty or more. The catcher's equipment, if I had time to clean it up a little, could get me fifteen. So, the skinny bat for two is okay."

"And the basket of balls?"

"Those are obviously hot. I bought a couple of golf bags, including clubs, one a complete set, and the guy threw in the balls for another buck."

"And I have to give you three dollars for them?"

"You sure do! Part of that profit goes for today's lesson. We got a deal?"

"We do," I said as the man pulled out a large paper bag. Actually, I couldn't believe my luck. And I couldn't wait to get back to the basement.

"Where you goin in such a rush, man?" Chico called after me. "Ain't we gonna play today?"

"Later!" I said. "Just like yesterday."

"You ain't hittin my fastpitch ball with that thing you just bought!"

"I know!" I said, running for home. I doubted my new bat would ever see the light of day again. It was for batting practice in my own cage, a secret weapon no one would ever have to know about.

23

Elgin had promised to be back as soon as he found, or didn't find, what he was looking for. Of course, he might not come to the apartment first, now that he had his private hitting place. If I didn't see him by ten, I planned to mosey down there and see what he was up to. The last thing he told me was that he needed baseballs to do a final adjustment on the machine so it wouldn't pitch over his head.

As I sat at the breakfast table with my toast and coffee, I had the niggling feeling that I had never turned off the batting machine the night before.

I let the heavy basement door shut and lock behind me and felt for the switch on the wall. Just before I turned it on I stood stock-still on the steps and listened. My heart raced. What was that noise? The machine was on! Who would be down there in the dark with the machine running?

It could only be Mr. Bravura. No one else had a key. I carefully set the paper bag in the corner. Carrying the fungo bat I crept down the stairs in total darkness. I raised the bat as I flipped the light switch in the big room. No one was there.

I trotted back up for the basket of golf balls. I wondered if I had left the machine on myself. I hoped Mr. Bravura hadn't been down there and decided he didn't like my setup. I felt the machine and found the casing warm around the electric motor, but I figured it always felt that way when it was running. I wouldn't worry about it unless it became too hot to touch.

I turned the machine off and got a wrench so I could loosen the pitching wheels and set them closer together for the golf balls. For the first time I became aware that the rubber on those wheels was old, dried, and cracked, especially in the indented middles of the wheels where the ball was gripped. I wondered what effect that might have on the spin of the balls when they were thrust out and hurled toward the plate.

The pitching wheels were set flat like a pair of record turntables and spun close to each other. I squatted and closed one eye, peeking between the wheels as I drew them as close together as possible. Their outer edges almost touched, and there appeared to be just barely enough room for a golf ball to squeeze through with friction from each wheel. I forced a ball through by hand, and found I could hardly make it budge. I thought about trying it with the machine on and the wheels spinning, but I didn't want to risk getting a finger caught between ball and wheels.

With the ball stuck between the two wheels, I turned on the machine. When it warmed up, I tilted the trough, which started the wheels. They stuck and grabbed, then they squirted the golf ball out, spinning it wildly. It landed about ten feet in front of the machine and bounced back and forth before rolling to the side.

I wondered if I should spread the wheels a bit, finally deciding that I wanted to see what would happen if the wheels were at full speed before the ball was fed through. If it still stalled, then I would allow more room for the ball. I tilted the trough until the wheels began spinning at top speed. With my other hand I held a ball over the far end of the trough and let it go.

The ball rolled quickly to the wheels where there was a loud *phfft!*

I had a fraction of a second to wonder if the ball had been

launched. In fact, it had happened so fast I didn't see it. I only heard it. It slammed off the wall nearly forty feet away and came hurtling back past the machine and right at my face. I jerked my head left without thinking, but the missile caught me on the right side at the top of my forehead and my head snapped back as my legs buckled.

The ball hit the ceiling and dropped on my ribs as I lay on my side, dazed, not moving, groaning. What had happened? All I was aware of was the cold cement floor on my cheek and on the back of the hand that was tucked under me. My other hand cradled the quickly rising bump on my forehead.

I struggled to my knees but felt dizzy and sat on the floor Indian style. The machine was still humming, but the trough had fallen back to its original position and I heard the wheels stop spinning. I blinked, feeling pressure on my right eye from the wound above it. How was I going to explain this to my mother?

Within seconds the bump on my forehead was hot and tender and felt an inch high and scared me. I knew I should get some ice on it, but how could I do that without scaring Momma and losing my privileges with the machine? I decided that though the bump was probably ugly and awful-looking, I was not really hurt. My name is Elgin Woodell and I live in Chicago, I told myself. I wouldn't know that if I was hurt bad, would I?

I stood and staggered and wondered how close I had come to losing an eye or even getting myself killed. How fast must that ball have come off the wall? It had traveled more than thirty feet each way and had still knocked me off my feet. I chuckled at the thought of trying to hit or even catch a pitch like that. I had only heard it hit the far wall, so I didn't know about the trajectory. The way it came back, though, made me guess it had hit high off the wall, the way the old baseball had.

I turned off the machine and looked for a way to adjust the trajectory. I finally found that the two front wheels could be raised and lowered. When I raised them, the front of the machine sat closer to the ground, and when I got behind the machine and lined it up, it was clearly pointing at a lower spot on the far wall.

I was tempted to try another pitch, but first I wanted to find a place to hide. How could I watch the pitch and still protect myself? I decided that if I let the machine deliver the balls automatically, the way it was designed, I wouldn't have to be standing and could peek out from behind the machine.

I was still woozy when I dumped the bucket of fifty-six golf balls into the container and picked up the fifty-seventh and tossed it in too. Before turning on the machine, I walked around it, looking for the best place to stay out of the way and still be able to see where the balls hit off the wall. I was sure that once I could control where they hit and how fast they were going, I could stand in there with my new bat and take some hitting practice.

I decided to crouch directly behind the machine and peek out around the right side. If the first ball came back that way, I would just duck back in and stay there until the balls ran out. What I had not thought about, however, was the back wall, just six or seven feet behind the machine. That first pitch had not hit the back wall only because it had ricocheted off my head.

Something else I had not thought of was the difference in weight between golf balls and baseballs. When I turned on the machine, the container rolled and rolled, and I could hear the balls inside aligning themselves to be delivered one at a time to and from the trough.

However, because they were so much lighter and smaller than baseballs, rather than cooperating with the intent of the machine, they rolled in a steady stream from the container to the trough, which picked them up, tilted, started the pitching wheels spinning, and drew all fifty-seven balls through the apparatus in a straight line.

The wheels never slowed, and the trough never tilted back until all the balls had been sucked through and fired at the far wall, sometimes as fast as two a second. It was as if the pitching machine had been transformed into a submachine gun with golf balls as its ammunition and the far wall as its target. The bigger problem was that the walls were all concrete, and with nothing to get in the way of the balls except the basket on the ceiling, the cord hanging down, and the machine itself, most of the balls kept bouncing off the front and back walls until they had lost their momentum.

I couldn't believe what I was seeing and hearing. It was deafening. I was sure I saw one ball bounce off the wall and then hit head-on the next one just a few inches behind. Two of the first five balls skipped off the cord hanging down in the center of the room and made it swing and sway, creating a weird shadow. Two balls banged on the wire grate around the light, and it came loose and began rocking.

But then the machine seemed to settle into a cadence and began firing the balls every half second or so, right to the same spot, low on the far wall. The balls smashed off the wall and rose quickly over the machine on the rebound. I kept watching until I heard a ball strike the wall behind me and in the next instant I felt the thud between my shoulder blades. I couldn't believe it. The blinding power of the one that had hit my head was worse, because it had not hit a second wall, but this one stung. And here came another, and another.

I scooted away, but the balls that hit both walls also hit the sides and seemed to hunt me down.

I knew I should get in front of the machine because the balls were coming back over the top of it, but I couldn't risk that. My best hope was to make a break for it and try to dive out through the doorway to the landing at the bottom of the stairs. But if I got hit with a line drive off the wall on the way, I would be hurting.

Six balls hit me hard in the seat and back and I covered my head and curled up into a ball behind the machine. I wasn't going to just sit there and take that. I rolled to my left, getting hit a couple more times. Finally, I gave up caution and scrambled to the door, peeking at the far wall as I went. I had made the mistake of pushing off against the machine as I made my break, and I had redirected it to shoot into the far corner. Three balls struck me as I reached the doorway and three more bounced low off the far wall and came back high, two hitting what was left of the cage and the third knocking it loose and banging it into the light fixture.

Just as the last few balls were being fed into the wheels, two balls hit the fixture and the cord, bringing the whole assemblage crashing to the floor, cutting out the light, and shutting down the power to the machine.

I lay there, dazed and hurting all over as I heard the machine slowly wind down to a hum and a whine and then stop.

That was unbelievable! I thought. *When I get this thing figured out and adjusted, it's going to be great!*

24

I knocked on the basement door but didn't hear anything at first. Then I heard footsteps coming up, and finally the door opened.

Elgin looked so terrible, I shrieked, "What happened to you?"

He shushed me and I was certain someone in the basement had attacked him. "Tell me!" I said.

"Upstairs," he said, leading me to the elevator. As the doors shut, I examined his head under the light. "What in the world?"

"It's just not working yet, Momma. It's my own fault. I'll get it right. Just don't worry about me. My basket didn't work either, and I broke the light."

"Oh, no!"

"I'm sure it just needs a new bulb. I hope."

"I hope so too, Elgin, because we've got no more extra money for this thing."

"This thing was your idea, Momma."

"Don't get smart with me or you won't see it again."

"I wasn't being smart! I just don't want you acting like this is some crazy idea of mine that you have to pay for."

"Did the ball hit you?" I said. "Were you trying to bat before you knew where the thing would throw the ball?"

"Not exactly."

"Not exactly, what? Did the ball hit you or what?"

"A ball hit me."

A minute after we were in our apartment and before Elgin could even explain, I heard a knock at the door. It was a tiny black girl with pigtails.

" 'Scuse me, ma'am, but Mistuh Brava say he wanna see you right now. Say you know where to meet im."

"Thank you, honey," I said. I shut the door and turned to Elgin. "What would he have found in the basement?"

"You don't want to know."

"Yes, I do. I want no surprises."

"I haven't got time to explain."

"You comin with me?"

"I'd better not, Momma. You'll do better cooling him off without me there."

"True enough," I said, and I ran down all six flights to the basement door. I had forgotten to get the key from Elgin, so I had to knock. It seemed strange, as if I were asking to be bawled out.

Mr. Bravura was huffing and puffing when he reached the door. "I gave you a key," he said. "Why do you knock?"

"I forgot it, I'm sorry," I said. "It sounded like an emergency."

"An emergency is right! This will not do! Look at this mess!"

"I know about the light," I said, following him down the stairs. "Elgin told me."

He shone a flashlight into the big room. "And what did he tell you about the golf balls?"

"Golf balls?"

"I am telling you something, Mrs. Woodell. You know I think the world of you and the boy, I really do. I have tried to treat you with more than courtesy."

"I know."

"In fact, I think you are most charming and beautiful, and you have been wonderful to me."

"I know. Forgive us."

"Forgiveness is not what this is about, ma'am."

"Mr. Bravura—"

"Call me Ricardo, but for now, don't call me anything and let me finish. I want this place repaired, the light replaced, and the cord plugged in somewhere else. There is a socket in the smaller room, but you will need a heavy-duty extension cord, which I don't have. I want the glass swept up, and I don't ever want balls left on the floor when the boy leaves the basement."

"That's certainly fair, but he injured himself or I'm sure he would have cleaned up the—"

"If that is too much to ask, then I must ask for the key back."

"It's not too much to ask."

"Good, because we're talking about my job here. You know that my wife is ill and in bed all day. I get my room free plus my small salary, which puts food on our table and gives us medicine for her. I cannot be without this job. We would be homeless and she would die."

"I understand."

"I don't think you do. You have a good job and can pay your rent and buy fancy equipment for your boy."

I nearly laughed but thought better of countering Mr. Bravura, who had by now worked himself into an unattractive lather in the faint light from the basement stairs.

"I wonder if you know what it means to be desperate, to have a life-and-death need to keep a job. I know for certain that if the owner of this building saw this, I would be out. Out! No severance pay. No warning. No notice. Out, gone, finished, over and done with."

I thought of what a dive the rest of the building was. It stank. It was moldy, greasy, filthy. What owner in his right mind would even come in there? And then to the basement? And would he really expect the basement to be spotless when the rest of the place was such a rat hole?

"Ricardo," I said, "accept our apology. We'll get this cleaned up right away and you'll never have to worry about it again. I'll talk to the boy about what you've said, and I know he'll be careful to follow your orders, because he thinks so highly of you."

That quieted him for a moment.

"Well, I like him too," he said. "But this, this will just not do."

I had figured out a few things. First, ice hurts before it helps. My forehead throbbed. I took off my pants and shirt and looked at my back and legs in the mirror. Several red spots would become bruises, I knew. I looked like the victim of a stoning. I was standing before the mirror with a washcloth full of ice on my forehead when my mother returned.

"Guess I should have told you about the golf balls, huh?"

"That would've been nice. You can imagine what he said."

"He throwing us out?"

"No, he's not, no thanks to you."

She told me everything Mr. Bravura said.

"I'm sorry, Momma," I said, and I told her how it had all happened.

"How is your head?" she said finally.

"It's all right, and why are you smiling?"

"I'm not," she said, but then burst into laughter. "I'm sorry, El, but that musta been a sight! I wish I could've seen that!"

"I'm sure glad you care about me so much," I said, but I couldn't help laughing too.

Over the weekend, I worked on the light fixture, which needed only a new bulb, and the machine. I added a few pieces to help balance the trough to make up for the weight of the golf balls, but I wasn't ready to try the machine yet. I was able to pick up a used extension cord for fifty cents (after hard bargaining at the secondhand store), so there would be nothing hanging down in the middle of the room except the lightbulb. I made a smaller cover for it that would be harder to hit, and I knew I could adjust the machine so it wouldn't pitch the ball at the light or even bounce off the wall and hit the light. The only way to hit the light after that would be if I hit it with a batted ball. At this point, I couldn't imagine getting the bat around fast enough to do anything more than just bunt a ball.

Most important, I was doing odd jobs for my mother and for Mr. Bravura, saving a little each day so I could afford some large sheets of canvas. I would hang those from the ceiling on the back wall behind the pitching machine. If a pitch got past me— as I knew most would—and banged off the far wall, that was fine. But I wanted it to hit something flexible at the other end so it wouldn't keep bouncing around and hit me. That way, if I hit a ball, it would hit the canvas and drop near the machine. If I missed a ball, it would bounce off the wall behind me and fly to the other end where it also would hit the canvas and drop.

My only problem was that the canvas sheets I found at the secondhand store, cheap as they were, were white. I was making this the most difficult batting practice area I could.

I was not going to slow down the machine. I had no idea how fast it could throw the golf balls, but I knew from having watched it when I got nailed so many times that it was faster than anything I had ever seen. No pitcher and no pitching machine threw the ball so fast that it looked like a white streak.

If I could get it to throw strikes, with a white canvas background, while I was swinging a skinny but heavy aluminum bat, well, that would be some kind of training. I hoped it would make live pitching with a bigger ball, and hitting with a bigger bat, look slower and easier. I didn't know if anything like that had ever been tried before, but it seemed to make sense.

I washed the golf balls until they gleamed white. I was grateful for their colored stripes; without them I would never have been able to see the balls against that background.

My last purchase was the batting helmet that had fit me so perfectly in the secondhand store. My new friend, the man behind the counter, showed me how to cut down the foam rubber around the ears as I got older and bigger. "That should fit you for three or four more years, if you do it right. If you have any questions or problems with it, just bring it in here when it needs cuttin, and I'll do it with my bowie." He patted the blade at his hip, and I decided that was something I would want to see: a man who knew what he was doing, adjusting sports equipment with a hunting knife.

By the time I had rearranged the room, hung the canvas, and made all the repairs, I was back in the swing of things at school and had only a few hours after homework every night to make final adjustments. I kept making excuses to my friends who played fastpitch, but the fact was, I was not getting good enough competition there. I didn't want to tell them that, but it was true. The game was still fun and challenging, but I was hitting about seven hundred. And after a lot of dry swinging with the heavy fungo, the broom handle seemed like a toy. I could smash that fastpitch ball.

Every afternoon I played an hour of fastpitch, went home for supper, did my homework, and tinkered with the machine in the basement. I finally got it to where it would fire the golf balls, one every few seconds, right into my strike zone. By adjusting the wheels, I could make it curve in or out or up or down, but of course I had to have it throw all the balls one way before adjusting it to throw them another way.

I had not yet stepped into the box against the steel monster. I was waiting for final adjustments and lots of time. That would come at Christmas break when I would have almost three weeks to take my cuts or, I hoped not, my lumps.

25

The Chicago snow came as what the local TV newspeople called a lake-effect dump during the first week of December. They predicted minor flurries followed by Indian summer days that would clear the white stuff, but the city was frozen nearly to a halt till March.

One day the sun would melt the drifts to slush, making people on the side streets hope for plows to clear them with the same enthusiasm that streets in the Loop and the expressways were cleared. But as evening fell, so would more snow, and everything reverted to the way it was. Soon even those sunny days became rare. Little flags on long metal rods were attached to fire hydrants so they could be found in the snow. People took to attaching the same to their car antennae so other motorists could see them at corners over the five- and six-foot piles and drifts.

I found it depressing. Walking was treacherous. The wait for the buses seemed interminable. The shipping charge for Elgin's pitching machine had eaten most of my coat money, so I chose a pair of cheap boots and a shawl to wear between my sweater and my old coat.

I kind of liked the snow. I had never seen it before, and I liked running and jumping in it, climbing the piles, making snowmen with my friends. There was no fastpitch in this weather. Our "field" had to be flat from the pitcher and outfielders on one side of the street to the hitter on the other. But snowdrifts and parked cars blocked ours. I had found one of my rubber-coated baseballs and adjusted the pitching machine to see what it would do with the ball. I changed only the distance between the two pitching wheels. I didn't want to mess with the trajectory, because it had taken me too long to adjust it for the golf balls. Though I was interested in the baseball, I wasn't about to adjust the whole machine for one ball I would have to retrieve and toss back into the container every time.

Mostly I was curious to know if the machine only seemed superfast because it had been throwing golf balls, or if it was malfunctioning. I wasn't sure I would know, except to compare it to what I remembered seeing at batting ranges.

One night after dinner I fired up the machine and fed the ball into the pitching wheels. Even though the ball hit the floor about three feet in front of the wall, instead of right in the strike zone as the golf balls had been doing, the machine put the same spin on it. The baseball flashed toward the wall, spinning and sweeping to the right. When it hit the floor and then the wall, it bounced high toward the light and blasted into the canvas at the far end, dropping to the floor.

There had to be something wrong with the machine. It was throwing the ball faster than I had ever seen and faster than I could have imagined. As I reset the wheels to accept the golf balls, I thought of all the reasons I should not be able to hit them:

They would come in faster than it was possible to react.

The machine itself was a third closer to the hitter than it was designed for, even if it had been throwing at normal speed.

There was no clue as to the rhythm of the deliveries, as there was when you could watch a pitcher wind up. I would have to learn to anticipate each pitch by watching the tilting of the trough.

The room was dark at both ends. I would see the pitch better when it passed under the light than I would when it left the machine or reached the plate.

The balls were small. They were white, except for their rings of color.

The backdrop I had installed to keep the balls from attacking me from every angle was white.

The bat was skinny, like a fastpitch bat, but heavy, almost like a weighted on-deck bat.

Why did I think I even had a chance of getting the bat on the ball?

Still, I couldn't think of any reasons not to try it.

I dumped the entire basket of golf balls into the container. With all of them in there, I could turn on the machine and run to the batter's box in time to set myself and take a practice swing before the first pitch came.

Before turning it on, I untied my shoes and pulled up my socks, then tied my shoes again, firm and tight. I loosened my belt and tucked my shirt in till I felt comfortable. I put on my batting helmet and shoved it all the way down, banging the top with my fists until it was snug.

I swung the bat above my head and stretched it across my shoulders. I was as nervous as if I was facing the toughest pitcher ever. Daddy always told me to think only about looking for my pitch, having a plan, and attacking the ball. I was to work for bat speed and confidence, not just trying to get the bat on the ball. That seemed impossible now.

As I put my fingers on the switch, I tried to talk myself out of this. Was I sure the machine had not shifted? Would it start throwing several balls every few seconds, despite my adjustments? Would I be hit, drop to the floor, and be unable to get out of the way of the rest of the balls? I told myself this was no time for more excuses. I had forced myself to become a better-than-average player for my age by doing the tough things, working on the fundamentals, running longer, working harder. Anybody could get along on his talent, but I was Elgin Woodell, son of a man who had almost made the Pittsburgh Pirates.

I flipped the switch and ran to the other end of the room, desperate to get in the box and stay there. The machine whirred as I went, and I stepped in right-handed. I could almost feel the ball smacking me in the rear end as I hurried past the plate and got set. I tingled from my seat to the back of my head.

"You'll learn to hit the off-speed stuff," Daddy always told me. "The curves, the changes, the sliders—they say that's what separates the big leaguer from the amateur, but don't you believe it. The day comes when you hope a guy throws you junk because it's the only thing you can catch up with. What really separates the men from the boys is that drop-dead, freight-train fastball that's in on you and dancin before you can move. That's the pitch you dream about. That's the career-ender, right there. Show me a man who can stand in there against a big-league fastball and I'll show you a man who can hit a curve in his sleep."

The balls were tumbling, then rolling smooth but loud in the container. I had reached the box quicker than I expected. I took a couple of practice swings while trying to position myself where I could reach the ball with the bat but where I wouldn't get drilled.

I was as close to the back wall as I could be without hitting it with my bat, and I was as far from the plate as I could be without being out of the box. If I couldn't reach the first few pitches, I decided, I would just creep in until I could. I had fifty-seven pitches' worth of adjusting available.

The trough tilted back, picked up a few balls, and tilted forward. I saw and heard the cream-colored pitching wheels whine into action. The first pitch would be at top speed, I decided. The mechanism was working. The wheels had reached their maximum rpms before the ball was fed through.

I heard the *phfft!* and the *whoosh!* but hardly saw the pitch before *crack!* it slammed the wall behind me, *whoosh!* it flashed to the other end of the room, *thwack!* it smacked into the canvas and then bounce, bounce, bounce, bounce, roll.

I had not even flinched. There was no swing, no half swing, no step, no thought except, *Don't let that thing hit you.* I could tell from the sound that the ball had come through the strike zone but that I probably would not have been able to reach it if I had swung at the perfect time. I was tensed and ready because the next pitch would follow the first by just a second or so, enough time for me to pull my bat back and get set after each hit—if I ever hit one.

I squinted and told myself to at least watch the flight of the ball this time. I heard the first two sounds almost simultaneously, cocked my head and bat, almost stepped, and peeled my eyes. I saw the blur, heard the bang off the wall, and watched the ball fly to the other end. I had just about enough time to appreciate my own handiwork with the canvas and wonder if I would hit any of the balls, before the sounds came again and another blur hit the wall.

I had hardly stepped, still hadn't swung, and was almost as amused as I was scared. For the briefest instant, every few seconds, the brute seemed connected to the wall by a flash of white. The ring of color on each ball disappeared in flight, and I wondered if my mind and my eyes would ever adjust. If they did not or could not, I would be forced to modify the machine and find some baseballs.

But as the flashes kept banging and I noticed that the streak was whiter near the machine and a dirty gray as it left the light and flew past me, I realized that I might be hundreds or even thousands of pitches away from actually making contact. Yet somewhere deep inside me was the feeling that if I could somehow catch on to this, master it, practice it, it could make me as a ballplayer.

What I did not know then and could not have realized was that I was facing an inanimate, brainless, muscle-less, tireless thing that threw a ball tinier and harder than a baseball from less than two-thirds the major-league distance at a speed of more than one hundred and thirteen miles an hour.

After about the tenth pitch, I made up my mind to start swinging, even if I was a half second behind. Which I was. I stepped and swung at waist level, regardless where the pitch was, and tried to pick up the cadence so I would at least be stepping and swinging in rhythm with the machine, even if I wasn't making contact.

I stepped and swung, stepped and swung, stepped and swung. Not hard, not overpowering, not much bat speed. I quickly came to the place where all I wanted was to get lucky, to hit a foul tip, to dribble one away.

Step and swing.

Step and swing.

Step and swing.

Step and swing.

Miss.

Miss.

Miss.

Miss.

Step and swing.

Miss.

Thirty, forty pitches into it, I felt anger and frustration rise in me. I started swinging harder and faster, telling myself that I could and I would catch up with a pitch. I seemed to be swinging through a couple of them, convinced it was only a matter of time now. But then my timing would leave me and I felt as if I was swinging after the ball had already hit the wall.

The room was filling with golf balls, some rolling lazily almost back to the batter's box. I would have to do something about that, maybe drape a blanket or extend a rope across the floor to stop those so I didn't have to worry about stepping on them.

I was determined to keep my head down, my swing level, my step the right distance.

"Perfect practice makes perfect," my dad's advice rang in my ears. "No matter what the drill—running, hitting, fielding, throwing—you do it right every time. Even if you swing and miss, make sure your mechanics are right, that you're puttin in your mind's computer a perfect picture of how it oughta be done."

I imagined that I was hitting line drives with every swing, but I couldn't beat back the truth. I was missing, missing, missing, not even coming close. I guessed there were about ten balls left when I squared around.

I am going to make the ball hit this bat at least once, I told myself. *At least once.*

Strangely, squaring around allowed me to pick up the flight of the ball better. Man! That thing was moving! I carefully stuck my bat out and kept it level. The pitch was high. I followed it, keeping the skinny, aluminum bat steady.

No dice.

I tried it again, and again. Just a few pitches left now. I just had to touch one, foul one off, get something on it, anything.

26

But I didn't. I was just enough afraid of the slamming golf balls to keep me a few inches from touching them with my outstretched bat, even to bunt.

My anger and frustration exploded. I was madder than I had ever been. All the work, all the adjusting, all the waiting and anticipation, and I hadn't even been able to bunt or foul off or even tip one of the fifty-seven pitches.

I drew the bat back into my normal swinging position and whipped it through the strike zone, letting go of it with both hands when I normally would have pulled the top hand off. The metal bat clanged off the side wall and whirled toward the machine. I hoped it would bang it, but it didn't. I couldn't hit anything I wanted to that day, except the wall.

I wanted to kick something, but everything I looked at was cement or metal or round. I clenched my teeth so tight I gave myself a headache, and as I cooled down, I got the wire basket and gathered up the balls. This time, I decided, I would hit lefty. The balls were moving from left to right across the plate, so I told myself that I needn't be afraid, even if the pitches seemed to be coming at me.

As if I can see them at all.

But from the left side, I could. On the first several I bailed out without swinging. It was one thing, I decided, to tell yourself you didn't have to be afraid, but it was another to stand in there with only a helmet on. I was grateful to find that the machine was consistent within inches, firing every ball to almost the same spot on the wall. A couple of times I looked back as it hit. Eventually I became aware that the machine jarred itself slightly out of position with each pitch and that I would have to re-adjust it with every two or three buckets of balls.

After more than twenty pitches, with no better luck than I'd had from the other side, I began wondering why I had made it so difficult for myself. I wondered if I could adjust it to throw the old, torn-up baseball, my bald tennis ball, that box of softballs I'd seen at the secondhand store. Mostly I wondered how my mind could mull over all those things while streaks of light, as if from a laser, blasted off the wall behind me. *Concentrate,* I told myself. *Concentrate.*

I was mad, frustrated, and sweating a half hour later when I had stood in from both sides twice and never touched a pitch with the bat. I wondered if the pitches were catchable, let alone hittable. I got my glove, stood in the left-hand batter's box, and kept reaching farther and farther, getting closer and closer to each pitch.

Finally, one touched the web of my glove and the thing almost flew off my hand. The ball seemed harder and heavier than when I hefted it with my hand. What was this? What did speed and movement do to a ball?

Five more pitches flew past before I touched another with the thumb and got the same sensation, that my glove could come flying off at any second. How my father would ridicule me if he saw me like this!

"Only sissies step out of the way and catch the ball to the side," Daddy had always said. "They're afraid it's going to hit them or bounce off their gloves and catch them in the nose. You watch me and you watch your pros; we catch the ball right out in front of us. Does it ever skip off and get us in the ribs or the face? Sure. But have you ever seen a guy go to the hospital because he missed a ball in a game of catch? Nah! Maybe hit by a pitch or a

big throw by accident, but not from playin catch. Only guy I ever
heard of gettin hurt from a ground ball was Tony Kubek when
he took one in the neck for the Yankees in the World Series
years ago. A Cub got hurt playin catch in front of the dugout,
but that was only because he was talkin to somebody and the guy
throwin to him didn't know he had looked away. He turned
back just in time to take it in the mouth. Cost him a few teeth,
but then he played eight more years. Catch it in front of you,
El."

But here I was, standing gingerly in the batter's box, reaching
out on tiptoes, hoping to feel what those nasty pitches even felt
like. By the end of that basket of balls, I had caught two, but the
first had made me overconfident. I reached a little farther for
the second, but the machine was just inconsistent enough to
bring it a half inch closer to me. I got a bruise just above the
palm of my hand and just below my index finger.

I yanked my hand out of the glove and shook it, waved it,
stuck it between my legs, jumped, and hollered.

"Nice pitch, you—"

Meanwhile, the machine just kept firing. I decided to try one
last basket of balls to see if I could just hold the bat out with one
hand, moving it and adjusting it slightly with each pitch, trying
to guess where it would be coming. I flexed my left hand all the
while I was picking up balls. I knew, as my father said, that I
wouldn't be going to the hospital, but this was painful, almost
like a bone bruise, and it would be a long time healing.

I took a different approach with the machine this time. I
dumped the balls in and turned it on, staying behind the machine for the first few pitches to study the trajectory. By now I
knew exactly where the ball would fly off the wall and where to
walk to stay away from it.

When I was ready, I walked to the other end while the machine delivered pitches. They came within three feet of me. I
wondered if I was being foolish. I knew guys who had been hit
in batting cages because the machine threw a wild pitch right at
them. I prayed this one would never do that.

I stepped into the box and took my normal swing for the second dozen or so pitches. As I expected, I didn't come close. Now I crouched low and held the bat in my left hand from the lefty side of the plate, stretching it out horizontally in the direction of the pitches, which swept away from me over the outside corner. I could tell I was within a half inch of touching a few.

Finally, I reached far enough and held the bat level enough so that a pitch ticked the end of it on the top side and skipped back to the left off the wall. It cracked into my helmet, hit the wall and helmet again before I went down, and I found myself in the righty batter's box with the machine seeming to take aim.

I was not hurt, just stunned by a buzz in my head, but I knew I had to get out of there. When I tried to step, I slipped, so I lay flat on the ground and felt a pitch miss me by a foot. I tried to get up and move to the other side again, but I was too panicky and didn't get traction and had to spread-eagle myself again. Eventually I was able to roll out of the way.

There were still a dozen or so balls left in the machine, so I got back into position. If I could tip one, maybe I could get more of the bat on another. I missed several, but the second to last pitch hit the top side of the bat about six inches off the end, hit the wall, and slammed into my side, just under the shoulder and above the rib cage in a fleshy area that seared with pain.

I hit the deck again, this time in the lefty box. I knew I was out of danger of being struck with a pitch, but I wondered how stupid a guy could be.

How many times was I gonna do this before I learned that fouling off a pitch like that made it bounce off the wall and try to kill me?

The last pitch sailed past me, hit the wall, and flew to the other end. Maybe because of where I was on the floor, maybe due to having been hit in the hand, the head, and the side, I was able to see this one. I finally decided that it was because I was on the floor, looking up into the dim light in the center of the room, and the ball was silhouetted before it.

Whatever the reason, I was fascinated by it. The pitch, as were all the others, was a screamer. It wasn't as if I could see it in slow motion, I decided, but because I had been watching hundreds of pitches already, I was able to break this one down as it came. I was aware of it snaking its way from the container to the trough, the tilt of the trough toward the wheels, the wheels grabbing and shaping themselves around it, seeming to mash it between them before slinging it out. It spun wildly and darted more than a foot and a half from left to right as it traveled less than forty feet to the wall. It swept past where a left-hand hitter would stand, breaking over the outside corner.

I had seen it all the way. I longed for the day when I had developed my eye-hand coordination, bat speed, and strength to where I could not only swing at that pitch at the right instant but also be able to hit it. I wasn't thinking about just getting my bat on it. I wanted, as I always planned, to attack the pitch, hit it with authority, drive it somewhere.

I had seen Chipper Jones turning with that ferocious power stroke on Randy Johnson and actually pulling a fastball in the high nineties into the upper deck in left field. That was the way I wanted to hit. Not just spraying the ball, but turning on it, driving it, sending it to the gaps or to the seats, no matter what it had on it when it left the mound. I slowly gathered up the balls, occasionally reaching to rub the sore spot on my side. That would be another bruise. I was sure glad I had invested in the batting helmet. The question now was, did I need a piece of canvas on the batting wall too, so when I did start fouling off pitches I wouldn't hurt myself?

I decided against it. I imagined foul balls and missed balls hitting a tarp and dropping at my feet. I couldn't imagine rigging up some sophisticated device to keep the balls from rolling forward and tripping me. That would be all I needed: to be sent to the floor while swinging at a demon pitch. I'd be killed for sure.

Something nagged at me as I retrieved the balls. Had this been a perfect practice? I had swung hundreds of times, and always tried to do it right. I had stood in against unbelievable pitching, and though I was frustrated at not hitting, it was certainly understandable that I hadn't.

But had it been profitable? I decided not. When the balls were in the basket, I dumped them in the container in the machine and left the machine off. I dug out my rubber-coated baseball and stood by the machine. For the next half hour I threw against the far wall, aiming at tiny spots in the strike zone and fielding the ball as it came back to me.

When I threw the ball high, it came back in two or three bounces. When I threw it waist-high off the wall, it came back as a skipping grounder. When I threw it low, it skittered along the floor, hardly bouncing. I worked up a gigantic sweat and concentrated ferociously. When I wanted a liner, soft or hard depending on how I threw it, I made the ball bounce on the floor just before hitting the wall. The harder I threw, the harder it came back.

There was little challenge in catching balls you threw yourself, but I was a perfectionist. I wanted to cleanly field a hundred in a row, every time with my left leg forward, head down, glove down, butt down. The glove was like a vacuum cleaner, my dad had said. There was only one right way to do it.

"Lots of guys can bend at the waist and spear a ball one-handed," my dad had said. "They might even have a big gun of an arm and be able to throw the guy out at first. But that's the wrong way to do it. Do it right, same way every time. Head down, glove down, butt down, left foot forward. Move to the ball, keep the hands and arms relaxed and out front. Play the ball; don't let it play you. Gather it in, pulling both hands across your body to the right as you take one step and make a crisp, hard throw all in one motion."

I repeated the motions over and over and over. My breathing became shallow. I huffed and puffed and sweat some more. Off the wall, to the glove, you can always come up on a hopper; you can hardly ever get the glove down if you start in the wrong position. Do it right, every time. Be in a position to whirl and start the double play. Don't be lazy. Perfect practice makes perfect.

Perfect practice. Perfect practice.

27

I had sweet-talked Ricardo Bravura into a second key for the basement. That way, I assured him, I could check on Elgin and make sure everything was tidy. It also, of course, allowed me to go and find the boy when he had been in the basement too long. Like now. It was bedtime. When I opened the door and peered down the stairs, I saw him turn from where he was sitting, on the bottom step with his back to me, and smile. He looked beat.

"What're you doin with that helmet still on?" I said.

"Just forgot," he said, pulling it off.

"Have a good workout?"

"In a way."

"Do any hitting?"

He laughed. "I tried."

"No luck?"

"That's for sure. Look at this." A purple spot had already risen on his palm.

"Did you try to block a pitch? You know what your daddy always said about that: only block it with your hand if it's comin at your head or face. Protect those hands."

"I know, Momma. I was trying to catch a pitch."

"Bare-handed? A golf ball?"

"Not bare-handed."

He explained his entire evening.

"So, you got in some good fieldin practice anyway, huh?" I said.

He nodded wearily.

"You need a shower, buddy."

He nodded again.

"It's fun to work out alone, Momma. But I don't know how long I'm gonna be able to stand not hitting the ball."

"What kinda attitude is that, El? This thing got you beat?"

"Momma, you should see it. I feel like I'm a year away from really hitting the ball."

I sat next to my son and put my arm around him. He was wet all the way through his sweatshirt.

"Boy, you're hot."

"Um-hm. Be careful."

"Of what now?"

"My side. Look at this." He lifted his shirt.

"Elgin! I can see the imprint of the dimples from the ball! You got that one battin righty, didn't you?"

"No. I was hitting lefty and reached out and tipped it. It bounced off the wall and got me."

"If anybody at school sees your bruises, they're gonna send the authorities after me for child abuse."

He laughed. "I'd love to see that!"

"I'll bet you would. Now get upstairs."

"I gotta turn that light out."

"I'll get it. I promised Ricardo I'd check up on you, anyway."

He turned and started up the steps and I moved into the batting room. *Tidy,* I thought. I idly flipped the switch on the machine and heard the container begin to turn and the balls begin to roll.

"Momma!" I heard from the stairs. "Take cover! Get out of there now! The machine is loaded!"

I froze, not knowing what to do or where to go. Was I to hit the floor? Hide behind the machine, what? Elgin appeared just as the first ball was being fed to the spinning wheels. He raced to me, yelling, "Get down!" and I ducked behind the machine. For the first time, I heard the unusual, violent sounds of the grab, the pitch, the flight, the wall, the second flight, and the canvas behind me.

"Whew!" was all I could say.

" 'Whew' is right," Elgin said. "Lucky for you, they're all flying that way."

He reached around and turned off the machine.

"They do go fast, don't they?" I said, my voice weak.

He laughed. I didn't know if I could laugh until I saw him. He sat there, smiling, sweating, bruised, tired. I knew he was frustrated at not having been able to hit the pitches, yet he still seemed excited at having tried. Had anyone ever loved baseball as much as this boy? I couldn't imagine.

He was like a newborn calf that wanted to run, a new bud reaching for the sun, a tender shoot eager to sprout and blossom. For the briefest moment, in the middle of a miserable Chicago winter, I was glad we had moved there.

My bruises turned ugly and were hot and hard to the touch. They stung whenever I brushed against anything. My limbs ached from the harder and longer than usual workouts, but after a few weeks, I was in shape and could handle them. In fact, I looked forward to them.

I forced myself to stand in the batter's box for three buckets of golf balls from each side of the plate before I did my fielding and throwing work. Though I tipped only one pitch, batting lefty, in several days, I kept swinging and felt I was getting my timing down. There were times, of course, that I wondered if swinging over or under or ahead or behind thousands of pitches was doing anything for me. But my chest and back and arms grew stronger.

When I had gone several weeks with just a few tips of the ball from each side, I added something. I began taking one hundred swings from each side as hard and fast as I could with no pitches coming. I wore myself out, tore down my muscles and built them up again doing that, hoping to increase my bat speed. That had to be it, I decided. The only reason I was missing those pitches was because they were so fast and the ball and bat were so small. I had to learn, to force myself, to catch up with the pitches.

Chico came by one day to complain about the snow and the sad state of the fastpitch area.

"Man, I could use a good game of catch, you know?"

"I hear you, Chico. It gets lonely working out alone."

"You're workin out?"

"A little."

"Where?"

"The hotel."

I was afraid Chico was going to keep asking questions or suggest that he join me, so I changed the subject.

"Our sidewalk is cleared. Let's play a little catch."

"With what?" Chico wanted to know.

"I've got a rubber-coated baseball."

"It's cold out here, man."

"We'll take it easy. I need to throw just like you do."

Chico ran home for his glove. He returned with a big grin. "My mother and my brother think we're crazy," he said.

"We are!" I said, following him out.

We began about twenty feet apart, throwing easily. I knew it wouldn't show yet, but I felt good and strong. I had wanted to get into some kind of game or at least throw with someone just to see if my workouts were paying off. The first thing I noticed, of course, was that the ball looked huge to me, much the way it did when I threw it off the wall after watching more than three hundred golf balls whiz past me.

But outside, playing catch with someone to whom I had been used to throwing a bald tennis ball, I really got the perspective. Chico seemed tight, almost awkward. I threw like I meant business.

"Hey, man," Chico whined, "back up if you're gonna throw like that."

I smiled. "You loose, Chico?"

"Yeah, but put an arch on it or somethin. Just don't make me stand there and catch fastballs."

I had not been aware that I had been throwing that hard. I felt I had some snap on my delivery, but Chico had always been able to catch me. Of course, we had always played with a rubber ball. This one, despite its coating, was hard, especially in this weather.

As we backed up from each other, I still felt strong. I whipped throws right to Chico's glove, hardly making him move more than an inch. Chico shook his head with every throw.

"Man, you're hot!"

Hot was exactly what I felt. I loved this, but I was also sweating. I took off my coat and put it next to the building. The frigid air felt good on my face and neck, and it breezed through the thin material of my long-sleeved shirt.

I threw long and straight, popping Chico's glove. Chico smiled, shook his head, and lofted the ball back. Every time I caught it I imagined a different game situation. A runner was tagging or leading off too far or in a rundown or represented the second half of a double play. Catch and fire, catch and fire. How I loved the game, the sheer joy of it, the great fun of throwing a baseball!

But I lived to regret my foolishness. I had not known I was being careless, of course. I felt a dull ache in my arm, near the shoulder, at bedtime. I had just been telling my mother how great it had been, how strong I had felt. I said nothing to her about the pain.

In the middle of the night I awoke with a burning sensation in my shoulder and biceps. My elbow hurt too. What had I done? It wasn't worth waking my mother, but I ran the sink full of cold water, got on one knee, and dunked my arm to the shoulder. By morning, I could hardly bend it. The muscle was swollen and tender. Dressing and eating were a chore. I felt like an old man with, what was it my mother called it? Bursitis?

Throwing in cold weather was not something I'd had to worry about in Mississippi. And the winter before had been mild enough that the guys got used to the weather because we played in it the whole time. It had been nearly two months since I had played fastpitch, and we all had worn warm jackets.

What had I been thinking? I should have known better.

My teacher grew tired of my excuses for having to write with my left hand. I may have been able to switch-hit, but writing lefty was not one of my strengths. I felt like an idiot and knew I had brought all this on myself. I hated the idea of not being able to practice my fielding. There would certainly be no stopping my hitting practice, if you could call it that. It hurt to hold the bat in my usual manner, so I had to swing with one hand. I swept through with my top-hand power stroke from the left and pulled through with a smooth, level cut from the right.

Who knew? Maybe I would start hitting these crazy pitches when I could come at them with just one hand.

The first night I tried working out with my bad arm dangling. I couldn't even stand the pain that came with swinging with the other hand. Eventually my mother rigged me a sling. I felt more comfortable with the arm bent and close to my body, but I felt more like a cripple too.

It took longer to set myself and practice-swing with one hand, and I was able to swing at only every other pitch. When I first began fouling off one of every ten or so, I knew I was making progress. I had only done that well with both hands.

It took me longer to retrieve the balls and to get them into the machine, but then it had taken me even longer to get out the apartment door and down to the basement too. I found as I walked through the motions of my batting workout that I merely looked forward to the day when my arm would be back in shape and I could see if I had made real progress at the plate.

I missed my throwing and fielding workouts, and I vowed to

never again risk injury because of enthusiasm. Nothing was more frustrating to a perfectionist than not being able to train.

I guessed my arm was a month away from being back to normal, and then I would have to build up the muscle again. That seemed like an eternity away.

28

I had never had reason to doubt Elgin before, but neither had I ever experienced a cold-weather arm injury. Elgin had gone through the typical childhood stage of duplicity, but it had been two full years since I had caught him in an outright lie. Still, I had to ask.

"El, are you sure all you were doin to hurt that arm was throwin without your coat on? I mean, you weren't wrestling or roughhousing or something, were you?"

He insisted he was not. He told me how he had felt so good and how his throws were crisp and right on the money.

"I got warmed up, the cold air felt great, and I guess I just got carried away."

I had insurance at work, but the deductible alone would have threatened my various weekly savings programs. I was willing, of course, to take Elgin to a doctor, but he told me he was sure the arm was just strained.

"I don't think anything's broke or pulled," he said. "I just got to wait it out."

Waiting it out was as tough a thing as I had ever done. It was two weeks before I could use my right arm to help pick up the golf balls at the end of each hitting session, and two more before I could start throwing easily. The muscles had atrophied and I couldn't fully straighten the arm for a few more days. It wasn't long, however, before I could bat with both hands.

That was what I had been waiting for. The Christmas vacation had been lost to what I considered profitable workouts, though even standing in against the pitching machine with one hand and fouling off a few did more for my eye and my timing than I imagined.

For a few days after resuming my normal right and left batting stances, I had as much trouble catching up with the pitches as I always had. But then the day came when I was batting righty and was also relaxed. After weeks of being rigid and tense in the box, I had learned the rhythm and cadence of the machine and knew what the pitches would and would not do. It didn't bother me—as it once had—to just wait on a few pitches, not swinging or even looking at them, but rather getting myself set for a future pitch, say the fourth or fifth one coming up.

The pitches still hummed in, moving from left to right, coming on the inside corner to a righty. I took a few practice swings, ignored a few pitches without moving, then set myself and drew the bat back. I was ready for the next pitch, having memorized the timing from when I first heard the *phfft!* from the spinning wheels until the ball whizzed past me.

I stayed in my crouch with knees bent, eyes on the ball, stepping slowly about six inches as the sound was emitted. I turned on the ball, driving my bat through the strike zone and keeping my chin down, eyes level. I smacked the ball on a direct line past the machine and into the hanging canvas. I dropped to one knee just to think about it and appreciate it. It had not been luck. I had nearly gotten to the place where I thought it might be possible. Pitch after pitch came banging off the wall as I knelt there, smiling. Man, that felt good! It wasn't a foul tip; it wasn't even a pop-up or a grounder. That had been a solid line drive, maybe a homer. So, it was possible to time these pitches, follow them in, and get the bat around!

I couldn't wait to do it again, and I didn't mind that the machine emptied itself of golf balls while I sat reveling in my success. This was something to be savored, to ponder, to enjoy. It had been almost worth the wait. Almost, but not quite. If I could now get a shot like that during each set of fifty-seven pitches, then I might think the lengthy ordeal had been worth it.

Batting lefty a few minutes later, I found that I could reach the outside corner by forcing myself to step into the pitch. I would rarely try to hit a pitch like this into left field because I simply couldn't get enough on it, but until I was ready to adjust the machine to either start spinning the ball the opposite way, redirecting it so the ball cut across the inside or the heart of the plate, I would try this.

I hit four foul tips and what would have been a weak pop-up, probably to the third baseman. In a way I felt better about that performance than even the solid shot I had gotten from the right side. I had come a long way, getting my bat on five pitches. It was less than ten percent, but it was so much more than I had ever done before. My goal was to be able to somehow drive the ball from both sides the way I had—one time—from the left.

I refilled the machine and used my rubber-coated baseball for a little infield practice. My arm was still delicate and I felt feeble, not being able to snap the ball on the throw. Still, I knew it was good for the arm to just loosely arch the ball to the wall and then play the easy hops. I would take it slow, not try to hurry my comeback. I wanted to be ready by spring to become the best player on my team and maybe in the league.

I was glad Elgin had found some success in the basement. I loved to hear him tell of his progress. Occasionally I would stand in the doorway and watch him, ready to duck behind the wall if necessary. The difference between the first time I had done that—just after Christmas when he was able to foul off maybe ten pitches out of a whole set and hit grounders on one or two more—and the second week in March was amazing. By then he was at least tipping every other pitch, and he hit a half dozen solid every time. Only once in every two rounds of pitches would he hit a hard liner, but I was still astonished by his progress.

As the weather cleared and Elgin's fastpitch buddies began making noises about starting up the games again, I cautioned him about throwing too hard too soon outside.

"Oh, don't worry," he told me. "I don't ever want to go through that again. If I play, I won't pitch, at least till next month."

The only problem I had with Elgin's obsession was that it made me lonelier. He was doing homework or reading when I got home, for which I was thankful. We talked during dinner, and he helped me with the dishes. Then he finished his homework and headed for the basement, usually not returning until bedtime. We talked a little more when I was getting him settled in, but still I felt I had less and less time with him and for him. He didn't seem any the worse for it, but I felt deprived.

He was becoming a charming, quick-witted kid. He was sensitive, though a loner. I worried that all that time alone would affect how he got along with other people, but his teachers said he was an outspoken leader in class and everyone seemed to like him. He had a reputation as a local baseball star, but he assured me he had said nothing to anyone about his private training room and regimen.

I used the time in the evenings to read and sew, and I watched more television than I felt I should. I worried when I began to pretend there was a man there, one I could talk to about important things, trivial things, anything at all. More than once I caught myself thinking aloud, imagining that someone who loved me cared about what I had to say. I spoke of Elgin, waited for a reasoned response, then talked some more. I knew it was silly, wondered if I was crazy, and eventually went to sleep trying to picture the man who would come into my life.

My bed was lonely and cold until I curled into a ball and embraced the extra pillow, often waking in the morning in the same position, feeling as if I had hung on all night for my very life. But when I saw my son, my precious son, the one who was worth any sacrifice, I decided every morning to postpone my own needs for his. He didn't know this, I recognized. He seemed to take life as it came, believed that baseball was all there was and, I hoped, realized that I loved him. That was all I wanted for now, for him to know that he was loved—to know something I had never really known or felt.

There had been too many children in my family, too many sons, too many daughters. I felt as if I had slipped through the cracks, as if I were just one of the kids and not special to my parents. Being one of the youngest, I was convinced my parents had run out of time and energy for me. I was not a rebel, not a troublemaker, but I was a troubled soul. I desperately needed and wanted attention, and not being a socialite or a rich kid, I settled for dating the campus heartthrob. That was almost enough, but it had evolved into a nightmare.

I had read and seen and experienced enough to know what it meant to be a caring parent. I didn't want to overdo it, but I compared myself to TV moms, movie moms, even moms of my friends. Few had experiences any different from mine, but I had one friend whose mother was fun and funny, who listened and seemed to care. This woman didn't embarrass her kids by trying to be like them or by trying to impress their friends. She just was who she was, and seemed comfortable with it. Who she was, was a mother who didn't spoil her kids or let them run her, but who cared deeply for them—and it showed.

That was the kind of a mother I wanted to be. I had friends and acquaintances in the work world, as I grew older and got married and divorced, who liked to blame their troubles, and mine, on the way we were raised. We commiserated about neglectful parents, too harsh parents, too permissive parents, too busy parents. I grew sick of it. I believed in my soul that what happens to you does not have to be the result of the way you were raised, but rather can be a result of how you responded to the way you were raised. For a while, especially when I doubted myself and believed I had brought many of these marital troubles on myself, I believed that my upbringing had a lot to do with it. Had I become an enabler? Was I making it convenient for Neal to be alcoholic, abusive, self-destructive?

Eventually I separated myself from that kind of thinking. I convinced myself that I would be a good mother and could have been a good wife, not because of the way I was raised but in spite of it. I told myself that though, yes, perhaps my family was dysfunctional and never learned to interact properly, I had known all along it was wrong. I never got swept into believing that this was simply the way things were and the way they should be. I had a brain, I had eyes and ears, I had experience and years, and it was time to grow up, to take responsibility for my own actions.

I still felt my divorce was not right in the eyes of God. I hadn't felt good about giving up on the marriage, or giving up on Neal. But he had bled from me every vestige of energy and dignity. When my reserves were gone I decided that God would certainly not expect one of His children to live in fear for her life and that of her children, born or unborn. I wasn't sure I was right, but I knew I had to take control.

In just seven or eight years I would see my son off to college, and maybe he could help me financially after that. Maybe I could be open to another relationship. For now, though, I was content to let my guiding principle be to devote myself quietly and almost secretly—for eleven-year-olds rarely sensed such things—to giving my son a life I would have died for as a child. I didn't want to be blind and spoil him; I didn't want to center my life on him to where I would have nothing to live for when he was gone. But in my small ways, with my humble financial means, I intended to deny myself—and him in many ways—so that in the long run he would have the opportunities I never had.

Then, regardless what he did with those opportunities, he would know what I had tried to do. He could have obscenely expensive athletic shoes and other equipment now, and then have to work and not go to college one day. But I would not do that to him. I knew the day would come—in fact, I was amazed it hadn't already—when his values might not be my values and he might start badgering me to give him what everyone else seemed to have. Then I would just try to explain things to him. I would tell him about my budget and why we lived beneath our means on a salary that would be poverty-level for most. Unless I missed my guess, Elgin was one kid who would understand. He may not like it or agree with it at first, but he would be grateful for me and for my philosophy one day, the day that it counted. He would not be looking for any ship to come in. He would know the value of love and family and work and diligence, and he would know that you make your own way in this world. He would become a man of responsibility and discipline. That I prayed for above all.

Chico came by looking for Elgin one afternoon after I had returned from work. Elgin was in the basement, but I didn't want to tell Chico that and make him feel bad that he couldn't join him.

"I'll tell him you came by."

"Tell him we gonna play fastpitch till dark today. First game of the season."

After Chico left, I hurried to the basement to give Elgin the news. He was picking up golf balls and sweating.

"I think I'm ready for a little fastpitch," he said. "I'm not ready to pitch, though. Chico always wants to pitch. I'll get on his team."

An hour later, just after dark, I heard Elgin on the stairs from a couple of floors below. He was the only person in the building who could run up that many flights. He rarely did it at the end of the day, though. Usually, especially after playing hard and long, he took the elevator. He must, I decided, have news.

Did he ever.

29

I was sure it was Elgin banging on the door, but the rapping was so insistent that I peeked through the peephole just to be safe.

"C'mon, Momma! Open up!"

I removed the chain and twisted both dead bolts. Elgin had already turned the knob and the door swept in at me. I stepped back just in time to miss being slammed in the nose.

"Elgin! What's wrong?"

Nothing was wrong. I could see that from his face, but I wanted to send him a message. Nothing but an emergency should require that kind of enthusiasm at this time of the day.

"Momma, you've got to come with me right now. Chico is waiting."

"Why? What?"

"Please, Momma, get your coat."

"Dinner's on the stove, El."

"Turn it down, turn it off, put it in the oven. Just come on."

"No, you gotta tell me first."

"You just have to see this, Momma, what I can do in fastpitch. You will not believe it. Chico promised to throw his hardest and to do whatever he could to get me out, but you gotta watch."

"It's after dark! You can hardly see the ball now!"

"It didn't make any difference when the sun went down. I could still see. I mean I see it leave his hand and—"

"I thought Chico was pitching on your team."

"He was, but we won so big because of my hitting that the other guys finally left. Chico said he thought the other pitcher must have been throwing me candy pitches, because he sure couldn't hit the guy. Momma, I must've made only three outs in an hour, and there were only two guys on our team, just Chico and me."

"Just three outs?"

I could see there would be no bargaining on this. I put the pans in the oven and turned it on low, then grabbed my coat. We hurried a couple of blocks, and sure enough, there sat Chico.

"I try to get him out, ma'am, I really do. I pitch after dark, my best, my fastest. I can't even see the ball after the pitch, but he hits it and then I see it, very high."

"I'm watching," I said. It was unlike anything I had ever seen. If I hadn't been there myself, I would not have believed it. It wasn't that Elgin was one to stretch the truth, but this would have been hard to swallow. He stood up to the chalked-in plate.

"Tell her what happened first, man," Chico said, grinning.

"Oh, yeah, that," Elgin said, laughing. "Well, when we first got here, nobody else was here, so we pitched to each other."

"You weren't going to throw in this weather," I scolded.

"Oh, I was just lobbing it."

"Yeah, he was, ma'am. In fact, I was hitting him pretty good!"

"But then when I tried to get some practice hitting against Chico, I couldn't hit a thing. The bat seemed so light I couldn't control it, and I was way out ahead of everything. He started throwing harder and harder, and just before the other guys showed up, I got used to it."

"Yeah," Chico said, "and then—well, watch this!"

Chico wound and fired, a high fastball, outside. Elgin turned and smacked the ball high off the eighth or ninth floor of the twenty-story building across the street. Chico chased the ball by listening for the bounce, then both boys looked to me.

"What's a home run again?" I asked.

"Anything over the fifth story, ma'am," Chico said, grinning and pointing.

I raised my eyebrows and nodded.

"That's nothing," Elgin said. "I can't miss!"

Chico fired again, hard and low. Elgin golfed the shot from his ankles, another fastpitch homer. Chico changed speeds. Elgin was way ahead of it.

"Strike one, man!" the pitcher yelled.

The next pitch nearly hit Elgin in the knee before he hit it for a homer.

"Watch this!" Chico said.

He bounced the ball to Elgin as hard as he could. Elgin hit it for a homer.

Chico threw sidearm, then submarine, then an overhand pitch that dropped through the strike zone. Elgin hit them all out.

"If he don't quit this, ain't nobody gonna want him to play fastpitch anymore!"

"Okay, Chico," Elgin said, "let's show her the biggie."

I couldn't believe there could be more.

Chico said, "Are you sure?"

"Yeah. Come here."

Chico cut the pitching distance almost in half. He was now throwing from about twenty feet away. His first couple of pitches were over Elgin's head. I could not imagine how the boy could see them. They bounced off the wall behind him and almost all the way back to Chico. I heard the slap against the wall and then several echoes. From the sound of it, Elgin's friend was throwing as hard as he could.

"Be careful of your arm," I cautioned.

"No problem."

He finally found the range at the new distance. Of the next ten pitches, nine were hittable. Three were lined right past Chico for doubles low on the wall. One was slightly higher for a triple. The rest were homers.

"Momma, usually I at least have a strike or two before I get a hit. This is unbelievable!"

"It sure is," I said. "It most surely is."

Elgin was still wound up on the brisk walk home. I tried to slow him down, trudging along with my hands deep in my pockets.

"How do you account for this, El?" I said.

"I don't know! I just think it's fantastic!"

"Now, hold on. Wait a minute. You can't tell me, baseball mind that you are, that you haven't tried to figure this out."

"I don't want to think about it. I just want to do it."

"Think about it, El. Tell me. What's happening?"

I stopped under a street lamp. Elgin leaned back against a building.

"Well," he began, "I've been doing a lot more swinging with a heavier bat since the last time I played fastpitch. So I'm getting the broomstick bat around a lot faster."

"But you're hittin fastballs pitched close up in the dark."

"I know. I guess that's from hitting in the basement with the low light and the golf balls coming so much faster than the tennis ball. You know, the pitching machine must be throwing two or three times faster than Chico and the other guys."

"But you could see it almost in the dark! How?"

"I wasn't really seeing it all the way, Momma. It was strange. You know I've always had good eyes. That school doctor told you that."

"Yeah, better than twenty-twenty, he said, which I didn't even know was possible."

"I know I can see things far away that other people can't see."

"But how were you picking up that tennis ball in the light of a street lamp a half block away?"

"I saw just enough of it as it came out of his hand that I could judge the speed and where it was going to be. I don't know how I do it, I just do. I guess trying so hard to watch the golf balls makes this easy."

"It looked easy," I said. "You made it look like you were tossin those balls up and hitting them yourself."

He nodded. "I felt like I could hit anything I could reach, and I could smack it anywhere I wanted. The ball looked huge and slow to me."

I signaled with a nod that it was time to keep moving.

"Do you think this is gonna affect how the golf balls look to you tomorrow?"

"I hope not. I'm gonna do both every day and see if I can get used to that."

"What if nobody can get you out in fastpitch? You won't like that, will you?"

"I'll probably get tired of it. But I love it. When I first tried to play this game I couldn't even hit a foul ball. Now it seems like in one day I'm hitting better than even the best kids. I've never seen anybody hit like this. After about ten homers in a row, the guys were laughing because I seemed so lucky. They'd change pitchers and move closer, which isn't even fair—but nobody cared, not even me—and I just kept hitting them. It got scary after a while. The other guys finally went home shaking their heads. Even if I never do this again, they'll be talking about it for years."

It was all I could do to get Elgin settled down enough for bed that night. All he wanted to do was talk about his feats. I could hardly blame him. I lectured him on humility and steered the conversation to something else. As usual, it came back to baseball.

"They say Willie Mays learned to hit playing stickball. They used a ball made out of rolled-up tape, so it was small and moved a lot, but he got to where he could hit it hard no matter where it was pitched or how hard or what it was doing."

Three days later Elgin came home early from fastpitch, looking glum.

"Have you lost it?" I asked.

He shook his head. "Maybe I should. Couple of the guys told me it really wasn't fair anymore, that my home runs could count but they would also be outs. Otherwise, whatever team I'm on stays up too long."

"What did Chico say?"

"Same thing. When a guy on your own team thinks you make the game too long, you start seeing what they're saying."

"What are you gonna do?"

"Quit, I guess."

"Do they really want that?"

"I think they do."

"You still have friends at school, right?"

He nodded.

"I think the fastpitch has been hurting my basement practice," he said.

"Really? You're having a tough time adjustin?"

"Yeah. But you know what, Momma? I have a new goal, and it's real important to me. I want to start hitting the golf balls off the pitching machine the same way I can hit fastpitch."

I shook my head. "Lofty goal."

"I mean it," he said. "I'm gonna work like crazy till I can do that. Think what that's going to make baseball pitching seem like to me."

30

As a returning player, I didn't have to try out for my baseball team that spring. I watched, though, and was surprised by how big and slow the ball looked. I still hadn't been able to test whether hitting a baseball would be easier because of my pitching machine.

I wasn't really playing fastpitch anymore. Once in a while Chico would show me off, but nobody wanted me unless I could be on their team. I quit showing up for the games and they quit asking me. It was a game I had finally mastered.

From then until the first day of practice with the Tigers, I spent every spare moment in the basement, either working on my fielding or standing in against the machine. I experimented by changing the speed of the wheels and getting the thing to throw pitches that broke in and out, up and down. I even rigged it to throw all the pitches in the dirt to see which were hittable and which I should take.

The best I had ever done in a one-hundred-and-fourteen-pitch stretch, fifty-seven from each side of the plate, was to hit three pitches solidly from each side and foul off more than a dozen. The greatest part of that was about midway through the left-hand batting segment when I smashed two solid line drives and what would have been a clear pop-up on three straight pitches.

I had stepped and driven the ball, quickly moved back into position and done it again, and recoiled in time to get a good part of the fungo bat on the tiny ball. The rush was almost like what I had felt when I realized I could hit fastpitch. I wanted to drive and drive and drive the ball off the machine some day.

Next I stood in the middle of the room and threw as hard as I could in all four directions, diving and jumping to catch the balls off the walls. Sometimes I did this for more than an hour at a time. I sweat through my clothes. After a few weeks, I was used to it and didn't ache the next day. I got to where I looked forward to the workout. I never missed a day.

My twelfth birthday passed with no word from my father. Momma gave me a few dollars and took me out for a fast-food meal.

"Sometimes I wonder, El," she said, "if you're not in better shape than most of these kids just because you don't eat this junk all the time."

"Oh, Momma," I said, "it's only because I work out. Who do you know who plays ball as much as I do?"

She shook her head. "Who'd have ever thought you'd have your own place to play in this city?"

The Tigers' first practice was set for a Saturday late in April. It was still blustery and wet, but I couldn't wait. I badgered my mother into taking me to the library just before closing the night before. I checked out a book on hitting like a big leaguer.

"Can I read till I fall asleep?" I asked her.

"You may never fall asleep. Lights out at eleven, no matter what."

The next morning I was so eager I could hardly stand it. I was starved for competition, for the real thing. I hung around in the infield, filling in for whoever was hitting. I wondered why Mr. Rollins's assistants were throwing so slowly.

"Is that all the faster you'll be pitching?" I asked.

Fred, an assistant coach, turned. "This is the first day back for us too, Elgin. We don't want to wake up with no arms tomorrow.

I can crank it up a little for you, but your eye and timing will be off too. We're just loosening up, seeing where everyone is."

When it was my turn to hit, Fred was still throwing easy. The first pitch down the middle. Batting left-handed, I swung viciously and dribbled it off the tip of the bat foul down the third-base line.

"See?" Fred said, "Your timing is off. Just swing easily and make contact."

The next pitch was over the outside corner. I hammered it so hard foul down the first-base line that players waiting to hit had to scatter.

"See? You're way out front. You been playing fastpitch?"

"Not for a long time, Coach."

I pulled another outside pitch even farther foul, banging it off the bench and sending it skipping back to the mound. Fred fielded it and put his hands on his hips.

"You're way out front! You know to go with the pitch! C'mon!"

I wanted to tell him the pitching was too slow, that the baseball looked like a basketball. Probably just to cross me up, Fred came inside next, and if I hadn't swung, the pitch would have hit me. It wasn't unusual to see a self-defense foul, but no one had ever seen one hit more than two hundred feet. The pitch was a little faster than the one before, so I didn't have time to duck.

Players and coaches watched the ball land on a soccer field where spring players stopped and glared at us.

Fred said, "All right, Elgin, I'm ready to throw some heat."

He wound and fired his best fastball, just below the knees, maybe two inches off the outside corner. I kept my chin down and eyes steady, and I knew the swing was perfect. The ball cleared the fence in center, easily three hundred feet away.

I stood watching till it stopped rolling. No one said anything. I waited until the ball was found and thrown to him. He held it up for me to see and threw it again. I hit an opposite-field home run, and Fred went through the same routine. "It's flying off your bat like a golf ball."

My face burned. No way Fred could know what he was saying.

"I'm not that bad a pitcher," he said. "Hit this out again, and I'll switch balls on you."

I did, and Fred did. But still I rocketed line drives, making infielders back onto the grass. I cracked a couple off the fence and hit two more homers.

"Not a bad first batting practice," Fred said. "Not bad at all."

After that I played the infield, fielding grounders and liners and pop-ups and firing so hard to first that the first baseman complained. Some of the guys reminded me how much younger I was than the first baseman.

"Just keep throwing," the big kid said.

I knew I shouldn't have, but on the next one-hopper, I placed my fingers across the seams and threw sidearm. The ball swept across the diamond, looking like it was headed up the line toward second. But to catch it, the first baseman had to cross his legs and fall into foul territory. I could tell he wanted to cuss me out, but he probably didn't want to take any more heat for not being able to catch a throw from a twelve-year-old.

When we ran the bases and took a lap around the football field, I finished way ahead. Mr. Rollins came up when practice was over.

"It doesn't surprise me to see you keep improving," he said. "It's a little scary to think about how good you could become. We'll try you pitching next week and see if we can get any mound work out of you this year."

To keep from the arm trouble I'd had in the winter, I would have to practice my pitching in the basement. I looked forward to that season like no other. And I could hardly wait to tell Momma about the first practice.

31

I never got a chance to pitch in that league. That first practice was the last time I had any trouble adjusting my timing from my own BP in the basement to hitting my coaches and teammates. The way I hit astounded everybody.

I was shocked myself. I was still not hitting more than three or four golf balls at a time against the machine, so I didn't expect that much improvement in baseball. But during the fourth practice, I bombed a liner back at Coach Fred, just below his left cheekbone. The crack was heard all over the field. Fred reached for his face with his gloved hand as he went down, but by the time he hit the ground, he was out. His eyes were open and an ugly raspberry was already showing.

"If that had hit him any higher," Barry Krass said, "it would have broken his cheekbone."

"Bet it's broke anyway," someone said.

"Out of the way!" Maury Rollins said. He knelt by Fred and rolled him to his back. Rollins pushed Fred's eyes closed and someone gasped.

"Gee, he ain't dead, is he?"

"Shut up!" Rollins said.

I couldn't drag myself away.

"C'mon, talk to me," Rollins said, holding Fred's head in his hands. He poured water on Fred's face, making him flinch. Fred coughed and tried to sit up.

He swore. "What happened? I'm all right."

"No, you're not," Rollins said. "Just sit there."

"I'm okay, really."

"I'm taking you to the emergency room myself," Rollins said.

"For what? I'm all right." He tried to stand and fell back to his seat.

Rollins told him what had happened.

"Never saw it," Fred said. "Nice goin, Woodell."

I could tell Fred meant it, but I felt terrible. Maybe this golf ball thing was making a hitting monster of me. I didn't want to hurt anyone.

When Fred was finally standing, he moved his lips and jaw and winced. "Wow. Was I out or something?"

"You didn't know you were out?" Rollins said. "Let me get you to the hospital. That looks nasty."

"Can I come?" I said.

"Okay, but I can only bring you back to the el, all right?"

I nodded. I could call my mother from the hospital. But somehow getting to ride along didn't make me feel any better. I tried to apologize.

"Hey, Champ, it happens," Fred said. "If I thought you did it on purpose I'd ask you to teach the other guys to hit back up the middle, right?"

I nodded, wanting to sob. I had seen that ball crash into Coach Fred's face as if in slow motion. I wondered if I would ever be able to erase that from my mind.

After Fred was treated, we rode most of the way to the el without talking.

"I have to ask you something," Coach Rollins said finally, turning to me. "How is it you have so much strength? You're big for your age, but you're not big for this team. You've got the tools and I don't guess I've seen as good coordination in a kid, but what's giving you this power?"

"I don't know," I said.

"Where'd you learn to hit like that?"

"My dad."

"He must have been some coach. You hit like you know what you're doing, and it's working."

"I sure hate hitting people."

"That's part of the game, part of the risk," Fred said.

I didn't hit in the basement that night. I was glad my mother didn't try to make less of it than I did.

Two nights later everyone watched as usual when it was my turn to hit. I picked the only wood bat in the bag. Mr. Rollins pitched while Fred joked about hiding behind the backstop. I smiled, but I didn't think it was funny. I was scared to death of hitting someone else, especially Rollins.

I swung at about half my usual power. I was lofting easy flares into the outfield, going with the pitches. After a dozen such hits, Rollins slapped his glove at a throw from the outfield and whirled to face me.

"I can pitch just as slow as you can swing, kid, and then what'll you have? One wasted batting practice! C'mon, hit the ball!" The next pitch was outside, but I pulled it to left. Rollins said, "What're you doing?" I shrugged, fighting tears, and stood in. By now, everyone was quiet, watching. "I'm going to throw you a fastball, Elgin. I'm going to throw it as close to seventy miles an hour as an old man can, and I'm gonna split the plate. Normally, you'd drive a pitch like that all the way to tomorrow. Now, are you gonna hit, or are you gonna be a pansy because you gave somebody an owie? Quit bein a baby!"

I swallowed and dug in, but I couldn't make myself swing. Rollins shook his head. "Another!" he said, and threw the same pitch. I checked my swing. "Unbelievable," he said. "One more and then you can go play on the swings."

I was more embarrassed than mad, but I knew I'd better swing. If I could just relax, not think about anything, make it automatic—

I felt light, as if I were floating. The pitch was coming and my front foot was off the ground. The bat was back, my hands feathery on the handle. My weight was back, now moving forward. My front foot touched the ground, my back foot pivoted.

The sound of the bat on the ball brought me back to reality. The sound of the ball on Coach Rollins's left knee made me burst into tears. I slammed the bat on the ground as the coach screamed and everyone came running.

Now it was Fred's turn to help Coach Rollins. I raged. I picked up the bat and ran across a parking lot. Had I heard a bone break? Had I ruined his knee? I didn't want to know. I hurried to the corner of the brick school building and swung the bat as hard as I could, driving the trademark into the bricks. The bat split and the handle snapped back into my chest.

It hurt but I was glad. As I beat the bat to pieces, I imagined I was the target. I would have loved to smash my own head for hurting people. Why had the coach made me do it? I could hit five hundred in this league without hitting hard line drives. How could I ever hit again? If I hit a kid in the face or in the head, I could kill someone.

I couldn't force myself back to the field. No one was trying to move the coach. I ran all the way home, nearly three miles. I bounded up the steps, carrying only my glove.

My mother waited in the open doorway, her face grave.

32

I was sewing Elgin's tournament shoulder patch onto his new uniform when a message came from Mr. Bravura that I had a phone call from one of the boys on Elgin's team.

"Coach asked me to call you. He just wanted you to let him know when Elgin got home. Wants to make sure he got home, I mean."

"Why wouldn't he?"

"He left before practice was over, and Coach wants to talk to him."

"What happened?"

"Coach Rollins got hurt, and he wants to come over and talk to Elgin."

"How'd he get hurt?"

"Line drive."

When Elgin reached the top of the stairs, it was obvious he was exhausted.

"You run all the way?" I said, taking him in my arms.

He nodded. He was boiling, his soaked sweatshirt steamy.

"Mr. Rollins is on his way over."

"Here? Please, Momma, anything but that."

"You ashamed of where you live?"

"Momma, I need to quit baseball."

I knew when to keep quiet.

"I wasn't even thinking. Just like with Coach Fred, I just swung hard and nailed him."

"Why'd you run, El?"

"I can't stand it! It smashed him right in the knee!"

"Elgin, you can't quit," I said, and we heard a knock at the door.

It was Mr. Rollins, Coach Fred, and Tim, an outfielder from a couple of miles farther south.

Rollins limped in, a heavy bandage bulging from beneath his jeans. Fred was strangely quiet, and Tim nosed around the flat, looking at everything I had on the walls.

"Elgin," Mr. Rollins said, "I wanted you to know I was okay and that it wasn't your fault."

"Wasn't my fault?" Elgin said. "Who hit the ball?"

"Who dished up the candy pitch?" Rollins said.

"That was no candy; that was heat."

"Well, sure, but a straight fastball is no challenge for a hitter like you."

"I don't want to hurt anybody else ever," I said.

"You won't. We're going to get one of those little fences that protect the pitcher, like they have for big-league batting practice."

"That's going to make me feel like a freak."

"Let me tell you something, Elgin: you *are* a freak. You hit like an adult, son. But we'll leave that barrier up for everybody; it won't be just you."

"Everybody will know why it's there."

"Boy, you've got something nobody should be ashamed of. You've got talent that should make you proud."

Proud? I didn't feel proud.

"You've got that quitting look," Coach Fred said. Tim yawned. "You're not thinking about quitting this team, are you?"

"Thinking about it, yeah."

"We don't want you to," Rollins said. "We're the two you hit, and we're saying stay, you're good, we need you, we want you. Got it?"

I nodded, but I still wasn't sure I wouldn't quit. I wanted to be a good ballplayer, even a powerful hitter, but I didn't want to be a monster.

My coaches seemed nervous. They talked a lot and were still talking on their way out. "So, don't give it another thought, Elgin. You won't have to worry about hitting anybody else."

"What about during games?"

"That's a different story," Rollins said.

I reached to tap fists with Tim as he followed the coaches out. "You sure live in a hole," he whispered. That bothered me worse than what I'd done.

When they were gone, my mother sat next to me on the couch. "You're hittin uncatchable liners up the middle. Even I know enough to know that's what hitters want to do."

"If it means hurting people, it's not what I want to do."

"You hardly ever hear of big leaguers being hurt by line drives, do you?"

I shook my head. "And those guys hit a lot harder than I do. I guess it's just the difference in the distance between the mound and the plate."

My mother sighed. "Is it possible you're already too good for this league?"

"Could be. But who's gonna let me play in an older league?"

"Whoever sees what you can do."

"You know what I feel like doing?"

She shook her head.

"Like hitting where no one can get hurt but me."

"Go ahead. You didn't hit last night, did you?"

"Nope."

"Do it, El. Your chance will come to play where people can compete with you. And you want to be ready."

Either because I had taken one night off or because my mother had encouraged me much more than my coaches, something was different in the basement. I felt more relaxed, more comfortable. In the batter's box I let pitches come within an inch of me, even though I could hardly see them. I didn't try to hit every pitch. I waited for ones that broke just so, spun just right, came into not just the strike zone but *my* strike zone.

That night I hit six solid shots in one session and five in the next. If just standing in against the machine had made me a dangerous hitter, what would happen if I mastered it? Was it possible? I went upstairs to bed in a better mood.

Several parents showed up at the next practice. They looked grim. From shortstop I studied the protective screen. The first eight batters seemed to be trying to hit the thing, despite Coach Rollins's advice—from a chair behind the backstop where his leg was elevated—that they ignore it and hit as usual. Coach Fred was on the mound. It took him a while to get used to the screen. His first dozen pitches were high.

I was embarrassed that the man on the mound had a purple blotch from just above his mouth to his eyebrow. The white of his eye was filled with blood. I had also, of course, been responsible for Coach Rollins's injury. No wonder there was a crowd.

I made a couple of good plays, but I knew people were there to see me hit. By the time it was my turn, I'd made a decision. I was not going to hold back. I found my favorite aluminum bat and felt everyone's eyes on me. I hurried to the plate. People came to see a show; they would see a show.

Fred started by whistling a fastball to the plate. It was better than the stuff he had been throwing the night he'd been hit. *Interesting,* I thought. *Fred's thinking about the audience too.*

I wanted to explode on that first pitch. Start with a homer. Set the pace.

33

I unleashed just as I realized that the coach had let the ball roll out of his palm and off his fingers. It floated before my eyes as my swing carried me in a circle and spun me to my seat. As I sat in the dirt I heard the laughter—first from Fred, then the catcher, then Rollins, then everybody.

So that was how it was going to be? I would be fooled, even in batting practice? Well, maybe I had it coming. Either I was a good hitter or I wasn't. Hitting against a thinking pitcher was even tougher than facing the machine, no matter how hard it threw the tiny balls.

I was wondering now, thinking. Had Fred's smile faded? As he rocked back, he actually waved his glove at the catcher—back of his hand first, the way pitchers signal a breaking ball during warm-ups. So this was it? He was going from busting me with a change-up to telling me what he was going to throw?

If I was wrong, I'd be on the ground again. I wanted to catch up to this stuff and show Coach Fred who was better. So many things raced through my mind as that spinning, high-and-outside pitch came in: if it was just a spinner, I would never reach it. Fred couldn't break off a curve of more than a few inches. At best this pitch would barely touch the corner of the plate. It might drop into the strike zone at the letters, but no one would criticize me if I let it go.

But I didn't want to. It was not as slow as the change-up but way slower than the golf balls. I watched for that tiny movement, that rotation that signaled me that the ball would move within reach.

My eyes were locked on the ball, chin tucked almost to my chest. As I uncoiled, Fred was safe behind the new pitcher's screen. I realized as I hit the ball that it had not dropped as far as I hoped. But I got all of it and drove it two hundred feet to left center, and before the fielders could react, it bounced all the way over the fence.

I had no time to admire it. Fred was into his windup again, signaling curve again. This one broke on the inner half at the belt. I ripped it over the right center field fence. I hit a slider to the fence down the right field line. I smacked a fastball back up the middle, just over the protective barrier.

"Trying for the other eye?" Fred said. Everyone laughed.

Fred came back with a fastball inside, and I smashed a one-hopper to the first baseman in shallow right. Raleigh Lincoln Jr., a skinny black kid, stabbed it but was completely turned around by the force. He lobbed the ball in to Fred, then held his hand over his heart as everyone laughed.

A gigantic black man came out from behind the backstop. "Can I pitch to this kid?" he rumbled.

"Be my guest, Raleigh!" Fred said, tossing him his glove and pointing to the bucket of balls.

"Know who that is?" Geoff, the catcher, said.

"Must be Raleigh's dad," I said, staring.

"Raleigh Lincoln Sr. threw the only no-hitter in an Olympic game. Almost made the big leagues with the Red Sox."

The catcher was taking off his gear.

"Where you going?" I said.

"Deep," Geoff said. "I can't catch him, and I'm not gonna try to stop your shots."

"Ho, hey, whoa, stay there," Mr. Lincoln called. "At least warm me up. It'll take me a while to get loose. If nobody can catch me, we'll move the hitter back and I'll pitch to the backstop."

Mr. Lincoln looked at least six-three and well over two hundred pounds. He was a friendly looking man with big eyes and high cheekbones, but he looked mean on the mound. He yanked down the pitching screen and set it aside. "One thing I don't need is this!" He put Fred's glove on his right hand and began throwing easily lefty. From the first pitch, I knew he was the type of pitcher I had seen only on television. His mechanics were perfect. He wore deck shoes and dressy clothes, but he looked at home on the mound.

Mr. Rollins motioned me over. "This guy still pitches, you know."

"Looks like it. Where?"

"City League. They say he can still throw in the eighties."

"Uh-oh."

"Well, hey, Elgin, I never saw anybody you couldn't hit. Give it a try."

I couldn't wait. I didn't care if Mr. Lincoln made me look like a fool. At least I would know that I fell somewhere between the league I was in and a man who had been an almost–major leaguer.

As he got loose his fastball began to pop into Geoff's glove. Everyone seemed mesmerized. The man began to sweat, dark circles appearing under his arms and in a line down his back. It looked like Mr. Lincoln was going to enjoy this as much as I was.

Finally, Geoff had had enough, so Mr. Lincoln moved several feet in front of the mound and began throwing at the middle post of the backstop. He came close with every pitch, banging at least six out of ten off the post.

"I'm ready!" he hollered. "Get in there and take your cuts."

Fred's fastball was better than any of the kids', but Raleigh Lincoln threw harder warming up. And I wasn't going to be seeing any of those warm-up pitches once I stepped in. If there was anything readable in the man's face, it was that he was not about to signal any pitches or make things easy on me.

It was written all over him that he wanted to show there was one man in the crowd who wasn't intimidated by some kid. There was little ceremony, no pretending to take a sign, no waiting between pitches. Mr. Lincoln held four balls in his glove and just kept throwing. It was like facing the machine. But this machine had a brain and a heart and pride and experience.

This machine was one mean pitcher.

34

That evening I moseyed to Elgin and Chico's old fastpitch street and watched others playing. I recognized a couple as old acquaintances of Elgin's.

A crazily spinning foul ball dropped to my right and skipped into my lap. I surprised myself and the boys by catching it and tossing it back. Several would whisper and one would look, then others would whisper and another would look. A big black kid looked defiantly at me, but I stared right back.

Then I noticed it. An aluminum bat against the wall near where the kids hit. One said, "Ricky, c'mon, man, let me use the bat, huh?"

"No way!"

"Yeah!" someone else said. "You stole that a long time ago. That boy's gonna come bust you for that."

"Uh-huh," big Ricky said. "He send his momma already."

I felt a chill. So this was the boy who had stolen Elgin's bat. He had stayed away until he heard that Elgin never came around anymore. I wanted that bat back. It was only right.

Ricky looked about sixteen, hard and wiry as a grown man. When it was his turn to hit, he grabbed the bat, glared at me, and stepped in. He took the first pitch, then skied the next one for a home run near the top of the building across the street. As the ball caromed about the street, Ricky let the bat clang to the pavement and went into his home run trot. Coming around first brought him as close to me as he would get. He stopped dead when I whispered something.

"What'd you say?"

"I said you ought to bring me that bat. It belongs to my son."

He squinted. "*My* bat belongs to your son?"

"His name is scratched in the end of it."

"What's his name?"

"Elgin."

"I'll tell you what, lady. You want that bat, you can come and get it."

"I can?" I said.

He laughed and continued his home run trot. "You can try."

My heart slammed off my ribs. I stood, but Ricky had his back to me as he headed toward third base. When he reached the plate, he saw me coming slowly. I looked right at him and headed toward the bat. He walked briskly to meet me. Was I risking my life for a hunk of metal?

From a block and a half away I heard a slamming door and the rattle of a steel grate across a storefront. I wouldn't hear the jangle of keys on a belt until it drew closer, but something deep inside me hoped an adult would walk my way.

Ricky beat me to the bat.

"That's my son's," I said.

"Yeah?"

"His name is scratched into the end there."

Ricky turned the bat on its end and read aloud, "E-L-G-I-N. Hm."

"Hm, what? May I have it, please?"

"What's it worth to you?"

Now I heard the keys, louder as they came closer.

"It's worth what I paid for it originally."

"Which was what?"

"I don't recall."

Ricky's eyes grew dark as the other boys giggled.

"Ten bucks'll buy it, honey."

"I don't have ten dollars, and I wouldn't pay for a bat twice anyway."

The keys stopped. "What's the trouble here?" a bearded man asked.

"Nothin that's none of your business," Ricky said.

"Just give her the bat," one of the boys said. "You know it's hers."

"Maybe I'll give her a beatin with it."

"You'd better be kidding," the man said. "Because to hurt her you're going to have to hurt me."

Ricky turned on the man. "What is your problem, dude? You'd best mind your business."

"Stealing in my neighborhood *is* my business. And threatening people is my business. Let me tell you something, son, you don't want to tangle with me. Give the woman the bat, and we'll be on our way."

"You're together?"

"We are now."

Ricky swore and handed me the bat. "C'mon, guys," he said. "The air stinks here." He started off, but no one followed. "Well, come on!" Still no one. He waved at them and swore again, disappearing around the corner.

Embarrassed, the boys resumed their game. I turned to the stranger. "I can't thank you enough."

"Glad I came by," he said. "Walk you home?"

"I'd appreciate it. I just live—"

"I know where you live."

I shuddered and tried to keep my voice steady. "You do?"

"Course. The hotel over here, right?"

I nodded.

"I know your son. Sold him some baseball equipment."

"Oh! You're the one he calls—" I stopped, not wanting to offend.

"What? What does he call me?"

"Biker," I admitted.

He threw back his head and laughed. "Know what he told me once? That I had the same hair color as his mother. I saw you come over to watch him play once, and I thought, *Hey, the kid's right! Almost the same length too.*"

I stopped at my corner. "I'm grateful," I said, taking a good look at him in the fading sun. His face was ruddy and freckled. He appeared in good shape, mid- to late thirties, a generous smile. I offered my hand. "Miriam Woodell."

"Lucas Harkness," he said. "Friends call me Lucky or Luke. You can call me Mr. Harkness."

He was laughing, but I thought that was a good idea. "I will," I said.

"Do me a favor," he said.

Uh-oh, I thought. *Already he wants to see me again. I'm so tired of this.*

"Tell Elgin I have more stuff he might want to see."

"Sure. What've you got?"

"A wood bat for one thing."

"Really?"

"They're hard to come by. I couldn't give him much of a deal on it, but you know wood bats are used only in the pros, so it's the real thing. A light thirty-three-incher. Probably too big for Elgin, but he said he was looking for one."

"Sounds like a great surprise," I said. "Maybe I could come see it and he wouldn't have to know."

"I'll look forward to seeing you. You should be safe now, especially with that bat." Mr. Harkness smiled and walked away.

I watched to see if he would sneak a glance back, but he didn't.

At home I looked in my cash stash to see if I could afford a no-occasion gift. I had less than twenty dollars. What could a big-league wood bat cost?

I was watching television when Elgin came in. "Got something for you," I said.

"Good. Listen, Mom, I've got to tell you about practice."

"Let me show you what I got you first. Something you thought you'd never see again."

"Daddy?"

I scowled. "You'll see him again someday."

"So hurry, Momma. I've got a lot to tell you."

I reached behind the couch and brought out his aluminum bat.

"I don't believe it," he said. "Where in the world—? Did Chico bring it? He knew who stole it."

I shook my head. "I got it myself."

Elgin turned it on its end to be sure it was really his. "This I've got to hear."

35

"Lucky, huh?" Elgin said. He sat shaking his head. "I can hardly believe it. I mean, I know you're tough, but what if that Ricky guy had started beating you with the bat?"

I shrugged. "I could see he was scared. He just wanted to play big."

Elgin told me about facing Raleigh Lincoln Sr. "He didn't even use the pitching screen. He waves me into the batter's box and tells me, 'I'm gonna say only two things, kid. You don't have to worry about me knockin you down or even brushin you back. I'm not lyin, so you can just stand in there. I've got better control than anybody you ever saw.' And then he says, 'Don't feel bad if you can't hit me. Nobody can, really.' "

"So did you?"

"At first I didn't know whether to believe him. His kid is a good guy, but you never know. So he throws the first three right past me, and all three of em bang right off that center post of the backstop about waist-high."

I smiled. "Bet you wished you'd been swingin."

Elgin nodded. "He says to me, 'Trust me, boy. Swing the bat. Show me what you can do.' So I ground the next one right back to him."

"Hard?"

"Not really. He caught it behind his back. Both Fred and Mr. Rollins holler at him, telling him not to try that once I get my timing. Rollins points to his knee and Fred points to his eye and everybody laughs. 'He ain't gonna get no timing!' Mr. Lincoln says, and he blows another one past me. He was throwing smoke. I say, 'Give me another of those.' He says, 'Just like that one, same speed, same location?' and I say, 'You wouldn't dare.' Well, he thinks that's the funniest thing he's ever heard. He's laughing and jumping, and he keeps repeating it.

"I say, 'Yes sir, I dare you.' He laughs and says, 'Okay, white bread, here it comes, and I mean you're gonna get all of it.' I could see in his eyes he was gonna do it."

"Did you or didn't you?"

"I did. I drove it right back at him. It was a hard shot too. I just about died. Before he snagged it in that wrong-handed glove, I was sure I'd hurt my third pitcher in a row. I swear I would have quit."

"What did he do?"

"He did like this," Elgin said, mimicking Lincoln's double take. "You knew he had to have caught it on instinct because there wasn't time to think. Then he went and got the pitching screen while all the parents laughed. While he was kicking it into place, he said, 'You're gonna see nothin but heat now.'

"Momma, I just loved it. Zing, zing, zing, they came barreling in. Some were tight, some outside, some up, some down. He set me up, made me reach, jammed me, everything big leaguers do."

"How'd you do?" I asked him.

Elgin sat back on the couch, grinning. "I hit him, Momma. I hit him pretty good. I swung and missed maybe six times, fouled off a bunch, took a few. I only popped up a couple. I hit at least five off that pitching screen, one that would have killed him. Two over the fence, both to right center. Lots of grounders."

"What'd he say?"

"He said, 'Folks, I'm not kiddin you. I'm throwing my best hard stuff. This is as fine a hitter as I've faced in a long time, and I mean of any age.'

"Mr. Lincoln wiped his face and said, 'One more pitch, boy. Hit this and we'll make room for you on the city team.' I knew he was kidding, but I sure wanted to hit that pitch."

"And—?"

Elgin shook his head. "I don't know what he put on it, but it was faster and had more movement. He busted it in on my hands and I just couldn't get the bat on it. A few people clapped and cheered him. He came off the mound pointing at me. 'Be clappin for him,' he said. 'We all will be one day.' Later he told me he was going to tell Mr. Rollins not to let me play this year."

"What?"

Elgin nodded. "He said the whole thing was a setup. They wanted Mr. Lincoln to pitch to me. He didn't bring his glove on purpose because he wanted it to look like he'd just thought of it."

I sat shaking my head. "What are you supposed to do if they don't let you play?"

"Mr. Lincoln said there's a high school summer team for sixteen- to eighteen-year-olds."

"Oh, Elgin, I don't know!"

"Momma, I need this!"

"What did Mr. Rollins say?"

"He said he'd be surprised if the league lets him keep me. But he also said, 'Son, you'd better not get your hopes up about that high school team. It's carrying fourteen all-stars right now, and there's not one who would be willing to give up his spot.' I asked him what am I supposed to do if I can't play for him or the high school summer team. He said he didn't know. He said lots of people would be happy to coach a kid like me, but he also said he couldn't promise I'd be playing ball at all this summer."

36

When word finally came that I could not play for Maury Rollins's team anymore, I went to a last practice, threw a little, ran a little, said my good-byes, and heard my good-lucks. I would miss these guys. They didn't know my secret, and I wasn't going to tell them. Worse, they didn't love or care about the game the way I did.

Coach Rollins told me the way had been paved for me to try out for the summer high school traveling team. "Raleigh Lincoln Sr. put in a good word for you, and Hector Villagrande is looking forward to giving you a look."

"I'll make it," I said.

I had been running, throwing, doing sit-ups and push-ups, practicing my fielding, and of course, hitting. I figured out how to adjust the machine to throw high, low, inside and outside, breaking balls from two directions. With each new setting I went through hours of not being able to even foul off a pitch, but slowly I caught on. Now I could hit nine or ten decent shots off the thing at its original setting, and two or three from each of the new ones for every basket of golf balls.

Mr. Rollins told me, "They're practicing at the old Lane Tech field Saturday morning at ten. Hector will give you a look at noon. It's a long shot no matter what. Understand?"

I just smiled.

During the few days before my tryout, I worked out more, read more, saturated myself even more with baseball.

I had never seen Elgin like this. Living with him had been like living with baseball history, but now his constant chatter and confidence were even getting to me. But I could hardly blame him. This was the break of a lifetime. Making this team would get his name in the papers, maybe even in *Sports Illustrated.*

"I'd have to be the only kid on a high school team who's not even in junior high yet, wouldn't I, Momma?"

"I guess."

"You know I would."

"I s'pose you would."

He was so hyper I wondered how he could sleep. But I didn't hear him tossing or turning or getting up in the night. It must have been those grueling workouts. Sweat dripped off him, even in that cold, damp cellar, and I imagined his muscles maturing, growing, tightening. I just knew he would shine for Mr. Villagrande, and I was thrilled the tryout was on a Saturday.

"I want to go with you," I said. "I won't say anything. I won't even let on who I am."

"Momma, you'll probably be the only woman there. They'll figure it out."

"You don't want me to come?"

"It's all right. The more people, the better I do."

"Elgin, what size is your bat?"

"Thirty-two inches, twenty-three ounces. Why?"

"Just wonderin."

"Is there any way I could get some metal spikes by Saturday?"

I shook my head and closed my eyes. "I'll tell you what, El:

You make this team, and we'll figure out a way to get you some metal spikes."

"Momma, how could I not make this team? I'm hoping to lead the team in hitting!"

"I hope you do, but let's not get ahead of ourselves."

Friday was payday, and I was home a little early. Elgin was watching the end of the Cubs game.

"Did you work out today?" I said.

"Everything but hitting."

"Don't wear yourself out before tomorrow."

"Momma, I'm in the best shape of my life."

"Still planning on doing some hitting?"

"When the Cubs are over. Maybe for an hour before dinner."

When the Cubs won on a clutch hit, Elgin seemed to take it as a sign. "Everything's gonna go right this weekend," he said, grabbing his aluminum bat.

As soon as he was gone to the basement I hurried out. Lucky's Secondhand Shop was a little farther than I had remembered. As I had hoped, Lucky himself was there.

"Mrs. Woodell!"

"Mr. Harkness! I came to look at that bat."

"It may be a bigger bat than your son's ever used," Mr. Harkness said, "but it is very, very light for its length. You can see it bears the stamped name of a former Kansas City Royal who liked light bats. Elgin chokes up on this baby and he'll be able to get it around. I've seen him play fastpitch, and he tells me about his exploits with the ball team."

"I'm sure he does," I said. "You wouldn't believe he used to be humble."

"He's got nothing to be humble about, ma'am. Kid that age makes a team for older kids, well—"

I told Mr. Harkness about the next day's tryout. He whistled through his teeth. "Makes me wish I could give this bat to you at my cost."

"Which was?"

"I could have paid thirty dollars for it."

"I heard on TV that bats like this, even for big leaguers, go for a little more than half what you're saying."

"You're offering me twenty?"

I smiled. "No, sir, but I just found out you were lying about the thirty, didn't I?"

Lucas Harkness looked stricken. "I never said I paid thirty! I said I *could* have. But for a genuine big leaguer's bat—"

"I have twelve dollars," I said. "And I'll bet that would double your investment."

"Well, it'd be more like breaking even."

"Oh, come on," I said, still smiling. "You telling me I couldn't go to Kmart and find this same bat?"

"No, and I'm telling you that honestly."

"But everything else you've said is dishonest?"

The pained expression returned. "Now why do you want to say that?"

"You're the one who said you were telling me something honestly, as if the rest was just—"

"I know, okay. You drive a hard bargain. Let me show you my original receipt." He rummaged in a cardboard box behind the counter.

"You have to prove to me that twelve dollars would make you only break even," I said.

"I said twelve would be more *like* breaking even. Closer to breaking even than doubling my investment. Here, see, I paid eight dollars for this bat."

The twinkle was still in his eye, but my financial mind was whirring. "I've finally caught you in a lie," I said.

"No, please. You didn't. I don't lie. I bend and twist and imply to get the best price I can, but don't accuse me of that."

"My offer of twelve is four dollars more than what it would take for you to break even, right?"

"Right," he said carefully.

"So I made you an offer that is just as close to your breaking even as it is to doubling your investment."

He thought for a moment. "You figured all that out just standing here?"

I smiled at him.

"I want to give you the bat."

"No way, Mr. Harkness. Twelve is a fair offer. Take it or leave it."

37

I stood in against the pitching machine, hoping to break my record of ten solid hits for fifty-seven balls. I grabbed my old aluminum bat, the one that had been too heavy for me when I lived in Hattiesburg. I hit only five good drives then grabbed the lighter, fatter bat.

I started by fouling off a half dozen pitches, then hit four line drives in a row. By the end of the first basket of balls with the aluminum bat, I had hit fourteen solid shots. I felt guilty, as if I had cheated. I would never completely give up using the fungo bat, but this was fun.

When I finally trudged back upstairs, my mother seemed to have something on her mind. I told her how I had been able to adjust the machine to throw a variety of pitches. I said, "I wonder what would happen if I took that old piece of plastic railroad track, from the train that kid traded me, and stuck it between the wheels."

"What would that do?"

"Seems like it would fit real tight between those wheels. It would jam them when the little ties came through, then release before the next tie. Some balls would just drop through, but other ones would have all different speeds and directions."

"You think of that yourself?"

I nodded.

"I have something else for you," she said, smiling.

"What, another bat?" I was teasing.

Momma's smile disappeared. "How'd you know?"

"Oh, right! I'm sure you got me another bat."

"I did!"

"C'mon, Mom!"

"I did!"

"Let's see it."

She pulled it from behind the couch. For once, I was speechless. I could only shake my head as I hefted the new wood bat.

"Where?" I managed finally.

"Lucky's," she said.

"He rip you off?"

"Nope. He paid eight dollars for it. I paid him twelve."

"No way. He lied to you. If he paid eight, he would have sold it for sixteen."

"Hey, I'm a good bargainer."

"Not as good as he is. Did he show you what he paid for it?" She nodded.

"He's got a lot of phony receipts he can pull out from under the counter," I said.

"That scoundrel!"

"Ah, he wouldn't lie to you, Momma. He asks about you all the time."

I rummaged under my bed for the piece of plastic railroad track, then headed for the basement. I had to choke up about an inch to make the wood bat feel as light as my aluminum one, but what a wonderful feel! My dad had always told me I should switch to wood bats as soon as I could afford it, even if everyone else in my league was using aluminum.

"It'll cost you in your batting average," my dad had told me, "because you can get hits off the handle of a metal bat that would break a wood bat. And you can figure a metal bat is gonna push the ball about twenty percent harder. But the sooner you get used to wood bats, the better."

I had been so young when my dad said that, I didn't even

know what a career was. I hadn't even played in an organized league by then. Now, the advice sounded good. I would use the wood bat in my tryout the next day.

It was late, but I wanted to try my experiment. I poured a basket of balls into the machine and started it up. I fed one end of the plastic track through the underside of the spinning wheels. The machine whined and groaned and nearly stopped. Then it seemed to heat up and struggle as the plastic was drawn through in a slow, herky-jerky motion. The contraption smelled of electricity. I counted sixteen pitches affected by the plastic. What those pitches did amazed me.

Some hit the ceiling, some hit the floor, some shot out either side. But about five seemed to break three or four feet before banging into the wall for what would have been strikes.

The machine slowed and strained, and then began to smoke. I tried to pull the strip out, but it was already halfway through and would go only in one direction. The machine nearly came to a stop, yet the motor kept grinding, emitting gray smoke.

I yanked at the plastic from both ends, and now it wouldn't go either way. By the time I turned off the switch, the smell sickened me. The switch clicked but the machine was still running. The cord! I yanked it and the machine slowly wound down.

I found my tools and loosened a wheel so I could dig out the mangled strip of plastic. I quickly reassembled the machine, but when I plugged it in and flipped the switch there was only a low hum, heat, and that tiny column of smoke. I was sick. What did I know about fixing an electric motor?

The last thing I wanted was worry about my pitching machine when I was supposed to be getting a good night's sleep before the tryout. With a huge screwdriver I removed the whole motor, amazed at how heavy, and still hot, it was.

Upstairs I told my mother the story. "I'm hoping Biker can fix this for me."

"What makes you think he knows anything about motors?"

I shrugged. "He knows everything about everything."

*   *   *

"How bad do you need this?" Luke Harkness asked me the next day. He plugged in the motor and flipped the switch.

"Did I ruin it?" I said.

"Smells like somethin's melted in there. It's froze up good. I got a friend who works on these things, but I could probably get you a rebuilt one for the same price, maybe better."

"How much?"

"Thirty, forty bucks."

I scowled.

"I could carry you for a while," he said. "You could even work it off. Do odd jobs for me."

"I'd love that! Only thing is, I'm trying out for the high school summer league all-star traveling team this afternoon, and I don't know when they practice and play and all that."

"We'll work around it. See if you can give me a couple of hours a day."

"All right!"

"Listen, just because you're a good kid and you have a nice mom and I'm not payin you real money doesn't mean I won't expect you to be here on time every day and work hard."

"You just wait and see."

"One more thing, buddy. You didn't say anything about that bat."

"I love the bat! Thanks!"

"I gave your mother a good deal on that. Didn't do more than four bucks over breakin even."

I laughed. "Which worked out to a fifty percent profit."

Harkness smiled sheepishly. "You would be the kid of a numbers woman."

38

My mother was under the weather Saturday morning, which was okay with me. I had wanted to go alone anyway and didn't know how to tell her.

I felt conspicuous at the dusty practice field across the street from Lane Tech. A dozen of the fourteen all-stars showed up, and they all had metal cleats, of course.

The distances were major-league—the mound sixty feet, six inches from the plate, the bases ninety feet apart. A strange-shaped outfield fence was three hundred feet all the way around, about as far as I had ever hit a ball.

I introduced myself to the coach, a stocky Mexican who wore a straw fedora with a black band, nice loafers, and a pullover shirt and shorts. He had a neatly trimmed mustache. He asked me to sit in the stands and watch until noon, when I would get my tryout. His accent was thick.

"Could I sit in the dugout?" I said.

He seemed to study me. "In the stands, *por favor.*"

"Will I be facing you or one of your best pitchers?" I said.

Again, Mr. Villagrande hesitated. "I will decide when I decide. In the stands, please."

"I brought a wood bat. I hope that's okay."

Villagrande looked at me and then back to the field.

"I mean, I can hit with either, but I'd like to get used to wood. My dad told me that. He was a ballplayer. Almost made the majors with the Pirates."

The coach turned his back on me.

"Um, do you think someone could warm me up a little before noon, so I don't have to start cold?"

Mr. Villagrande hollered an instruction to the batting practice pitcher, a real tall guy in his late twenties who threw hard and straight. The coach turned back and looked at me with dark eyes.

"This is not the stands, is it, *Señor* Woodell?"

My face burned. "No, sir."

"Let us see how well we can follow instructions and respect a man's time and responsibilities; then we will see what kind of a ballplayer we are. Okay?"

I felt terrible. I still wondered about starting cold, but I sure wasn't about to ask again.

"At about ten to noon, take a slow jog around the field. Don't wear yourself out in this heat."

"Where should I leave my stuff?"

I knew as soon as it was out of my mouth that my just-one-more-question had angered the man. Villagrande's eyes narrowed. He tilted his head and sighed. "Anyone who qualifies for this team takes care of certain things himself."

I wanted to apologize, but I didn't want to open my mouth again. I trudged high in the stands, where I sweat in the sun until almost noon. Even from up there, the players looked huge. Throws were crisp. No one was criticized for an error, but they were if they got out of position or threw to the wrong base. Hector Villagrande's rage was hottest for anyone who didn't hustle.

"We have ballplayers," he said, "standing in line for your jobs!"

When the time came, I hurried down and dropped my bat and glove next to the first-base dugout. As I jogged slowly around the field, outside the fence, I watched the last few hitters take batting practice.

They crashed hard liners and long fly balls all over the field against the big right-hander, who was throwing harder now. I hoped to face him. There was not a pitcher I feared, and I day-dreamed about standing in against a major leaguer.

Shortstop and second base were played by twins who looked as smooth and strong as any double-play combination I had ever seen, even on television. I wondered where I might play. Maybe in the outfield.

Hector called his boys in to the third-base dugout. I got my equipment and walked across the diamond to hear. When he noticed me he stopped and spoke quietly. "*Señor* Woodell, if you would excuse us a moment, please."

When will I learn? I wondered, humiliated as I stepped out of earshot. I might enjoy this team if I could quit irritating Mr. Villagrande.

The boys filed out and took a hard lap around the field. As they headed toward their cars, a couple of them approached me, which drew a small crowd.

"You're the rookie we're supposed to worry about?" one said.

"I guess," I said, smiling.

"What position?"

"I can play any position."

"Oh, really?"

"Yup."

"What's your batting average?"

I shrugged. "Haven't found anybody who can get me out yet."

"You're batting a thousand?"

"No! But nobody can get me out regularly. Not even adults."

"Whoa! Excuse us!"

I knew they were being sarcastic.

"Well, we'd stay and watch you take our jobs, but—"

"Yeah, all our jobs! He can play every position!"

"—we were told we couldn't. Guess you'd make us feel bad, or we'd make you nervous."

"You wouldn't. I do better with more people watching."

"Oh, he does better with more people! Let's stay!"

"Coach said no. We gotta go. How old are you, kid?"

"Twelve."

"I'm sure."

"I am!"

"Yeah, okay. Well, good luck."

I said thank you, but the players laughed as they left.

"Mr. Woodell," Hector said, "what time is it?"

"I don't have a watch, sir."

"It remains your responsibility to be on time. You are four minutes late."

"Sorry."

"Coach Michaels will time you around the bases. One chance and one chance only."

I took off with the command from the assistant coach. I slid in the dust around each base, but I felt fast. Coach Michaels raised his eyebrows and showed the watch to Hector, who pursed his lips.

"Do you own metal cleats?"

"If I did, I would've brought them."

Hector Villagrande glared at me. "Was that supposed to be an answer, or are you a smart aleck?"

"No, sir. I was just saying that if—"

"Do you own metal cleats, yes or no?"

"No, sir."

"Thank you. I am curious to know how fast you would be with real baseball shoes."

"Where would I rank on your team?"

"Fourth or fifth," he admitted.

"And I'm not even thirteen yet," I said, beaming.

"Run two more times, but this time—"

"You said just one chance."

The coach squinted. "Listen to me. Here is what I want to say to you. If something sounds not like something I already said to you, you do the last thing I say, okay? You don't argue, you don't ask, you don't explain, okay? You just do."

"Okay," I muttered, looking at the ground.

"And with a good attitude," Hector added. "Now I want you to run around the bases two more times, as hard as you can, without stopping, and not for time. I will watch you for speed, endurance, and technique. Go!"

I sped twice around the bases as fast as I could, hitting each sack with my inside foot. It did not surprise me to see that Coach Michaels had a watch running.

"Very impressive," Hector announced. "Are you not winded?"

I shrugged. "A little. But I could run it again if you wanted."

"I will let you know."

Coach Michaels swore, just above a whisper. "Man, any one of our kids would be on the ground suckin air right now! He got faster as he went and he could go again!"

I smiled.

"Want to do some hitting?" Hector said.

I ran for my bat.

"You are a switch-hitter, right?"

I nodded.

"Bat righty against the righty, anyway."

The tall pitcher hurried to the mound with a huge plastic bucket of balls.

"Uh, sir, do you have a screen to protect the pitcher?"

Hector stepped close to me. "You worry about getting your wood bat around on Neil's fast ball, and I'll worry about his safety, okay?"

"Okay, but I've hit two adult pitchers, and I—"

"Were they throwing from this distance?"

"No, sir."

"Then their pitches didn't have time to do what Neil's pitches have time to do."

I shrugged. Coach Michaels pulled on the catching gear. Hector moved to the third-base coaching box, but rather than giving signs, he merely hollered out what he wanted me to do.

Lucky for me, even though Neil was accurate, he was not nearly as strong or powerful or fast or intimidating as Raleigh Lincoln Sr. And he certainly was no match for the pitching machine. The pitches looked fat and inviting, and the feel of the wood bat made me as comfortable at the plate as I'd ever been.

39

I'm not one for hunches, but somehow I knew the way I felt that morning had as much to do with dread as any illness. I padded around the flat in my robe and slippers, not eating and feeling faint by noon. I finally talked myself into a shower, a sandwich, and a cup of coffee, then sat reading an old magazine Mr. Bravura had saved me from the lobby.

I admired Elgin's devotion, his brain, and his abilities, but they were also taking him from me. I was excited at his progress and intrigued by his confidence, but I didn't like his new cocksureness. It didn't wear any better on him than it does on anyone, yet Elgin's certainty was based on his talent. How could I fault him when he was so obsessed, so unwilling to compromise? I wasn't questioning his confidence or his methods. It was his expression of it.

Kids his age love to talk about themselves, to boast, to see where they fit in. He could not brag much on his daddy, except to say what he used to be and might have been. So what could make Elgin half as proud as what he had done with his skill? He had done this himself. Reading, studying, watching, trying, doing, he had turned himself into a hitter and fielder and thrower far beyond his years.

I couldn't shake my depression. I went down to get my mail.

"Ah, lovely Mrs. Woodell," the greasy Mr. Bravura said as I approached. "You have something we rarely get here." He pulled a few pieces of mail from my pigeonhole, including a Federal Express envelope. "And from an unpleasant place."

"What time did you sign for this?" I asked coldly, noticing the return address: the Alabama Department of Corrections.

"This morning," he said. "I would have run it up to you myself, had I not been swamped."

"I would have appreciated that," I said, turning.

"No need for a tip," Ricardo said softly.

I spun to face him.

"Just kidding," he sang out. "Next time I will personally deliver it."

The first two pitches were high and outside, and the third was tight at the letters. I stepped but didn't move my bat on any of them.

"Reachable?" Hector Villagrande asked Coach Michaels from the third-base coaching area. The catcher shrugged and nodded.

Hector moved up the line toward me. "You have a good eye, but this is batting practice. I—"

"Oh, I thought it was a tryout. If you want me to hit like I have two strikes, I will."

Hector nodded, not smiling. "That is what I want you to do."

I took a low, inside pitch right down the line at Hector, who skipped out of the way. I grinned. "Sorry."

"Did you do that on purpose?"

"Not really. I was trying to hit it fair."

"You can come that close to where you want to hit it?"

"Even on an outside pitch."

Hector thrust out his chin, as if thinking. "Neil, move the ball around. Elgin, I will tell you where to try to hit each pitch. No matter where it is pitched, hit this to center field!"

The ball split the plate. I barely swung, lofting a soft liner over second.

A very hard, low pitch off the outside corner. "Same spot!" Hector shouted.

I stepped farther, bent my left knee, and got around quicker. I pulled the ball over Neil's head. I could read nothing on Hector's face. Neil looked impressed, maybe a little embarrassed. He threw the same pitch, a bit harder.

"Left field," Hector said as it left Neil's hand.

It had been a chore to hit a low outside pitch to center, but to pull one to left, one with more on it—

I did it. I was pumped. I loved this game.

Throw me anything, tell me to hit it anywhere! I thought, and only the winding motion from the mound kept me from saying it out loud.

"Right field!"

The pitch was outside, just what I was waiting for: the chance to hit a pitch where it was thrown. I drove it on one hop to the fence.

"Left field line!"

I took a waist-high strike down the line, my hardest shot so far.

"Now," Hector said to Neil, then shouted to me, "hit this one out of here, wherever you can."

I revved up, but as Neil went into his motion, Hector's saying "now" made me wonder. Was he calling for a certain pitch? I decided to take a chance. I would guess breaking ball. I still wanted to try to hit the ball out, but I wouldn't allow myself to tense and set for a fastball.

I could barely keep from grinning as Neil's arm swept toward me and I saw the turn of the curve. The ball had good rotation, and though it appeared to be coming at my left shoulder, the pitch would get into the strike zone. Had I been thinking fastball all the way, I would have spun myself into the dirt trying to get at it.

Was it possible Hector had had Neil throwing fastballs all during the previous batting practice and then on the first several pitches to me, just to set me up for this?

I got out in front of the ball and under it too much. I sent a 275-foot towering fly ball to left, then stole a glance at Hector. The coach's face had softened. Hector pointed at Neil, who nodded. The next pitch was a fastball, to the left of my rear end. Hector had not called out a field, and I fought the urge to back away, just like any hitter would. But if you do that, you wind up backing into those pitches and getting fanny bruises. I had done it more than once against the machine.

The next pitch was at the back of my head. I didn't like that. Follow your instinct to back away from that, and you can only hope the helmet does its job.

I ducked and glared, first at Neil, then at Hector. Neither was smiling. The next pitch was at my feet. I danced to avoid it. I had hit pitches like that from the machine. How I hoped Neil would throw that same pitch again. How could I make him do it? I laughed aloud, as if to say that anyone could get out of the way of a pitch like that.

Neil wound fast and quick-pitched me, a fastball in the same location and, if anything, lower. I took a chance, stepped and swung as if golfing. I ripped a shot at Hector, who had to dive to evade it. He came up dusting off his shirt and shorts.

Neil came in under my chin with the next pitch, and I blasted it back up the middle on one hop. Neil somehow got a glove on it and, without winding up, fired it right back at me. I fought it off, fouling it back. And here came another pitch, right at me. I stepped back and lined it to Neil's glove.

Now I was scared. What if these guys didn't let up? Could I outrun them? Would they both start throwing baseballs at me? Were they really trying to hurt me?

Rules were out the window. I jumped around to the left-hand hitting side of the box and drilled the next pitch into the outfield. I fouled off a few more, swung and missed a few, and felt tears rising. I willed myself not to cry, and Hector began calling out fields again. I tried, not as successfully as before, to hit the balls where Hector said. But Neil's control had left him. I swung at everything, in the dirt, over my head, behind me. I huffed and puffed and sweat, and I was mad. I wanted to fling my bat at the hulk on the mound. Oh, for a few good pitches!

And with the thought came the pitches. I hit four towering fly balls into the outfield.

"Routine fly outs," Hector said.

I tried hitting harder. I wanted to hit one out. That was a mistake. I was not a power hitter except against kids my age. I knew my long hits would come naturally with my normal swing. I hit a few shots, a few liners, and a lot of hard grounders. I fouled off a half dozen pitches and missed three more.

"One more," Hector said. "Give him a home run pitch, Neil."

For some reason, I didn't suspect any deceit. They owed me a home run pitch. And here it came.

I set the colorful, cardboard envelope on the kitchen table and avoided it like an intruder. It had to be from the chaplain, and it had to be bad news. I picked through my bills, a form from the personnel office, and a silly, no-occasion card from Lucas Harkness. What a nice friend he had become to Elgin.

40

My power did not reach three hundred feet. Otherwise, I might have hit the fat pitch over the center field fence. My choice now was to take off someone's head. But whose? Neil seemed like a nice enough guy. He had only done what Hector told him to do. Hector was the target. And Hector had been warned. He said he was in charge of safety, and I figured that meant his own too.

I did not want to hurt him and would have felt terrible if I had. I lashed Neil's letter-high, inside fastball down the third baseline, and Hector's eyes grew wide as he ducked.

I didn't smile. I didn't even look at him. I could tell Hector was glaring at me, but I wanted to hit some more.

"Are there any more balls in the bucket?" I said.

Neil looked to Hector, who shrugged.

"A half dozen or so," Neil said.

"Bring em on!" I said.

Hector nodded to Neil again. All seven pitches were fastballs on the inner half. I swung easily, driving each on a line into right field, almost into the same area. When the bucket was empty, I ran for my glove and waited for instructions. I had left Hector and Neil speechless.

Coach Villagrande motioned to the balls in the outfield.

"Fetch them and loosen up your arm by tossing them easily to Neil, please."

When I finished, I was hot and dripping, but I felt good. Surely, this strange coach had to be impressed. Could any of his regulars have done what I did?

Neil stood at first base. Hector hit grounders to me at short. The first few were easy and right at me. I charged slow rollers, angled back on ones away from me. My throws to first were fast and true, though each took tremendous effort. I had never played on a field this big.

Soon Hector was smashing liners and grounders at me harder than anyone had ever hit them in practice or a game. I enjoyed diving for them. A couple skipped off my glove. One bounced off my chest, causing me to grunt. On about fifty ground balls, I had three bad throws, two over Neil's head and one that pulled him off the bag. Otherwise, I was flawless. I was exhausted, but I would have done it all day.

Hector waved me in, and as Neil and Coach Michaels loaded the equipment into his car, I sat with the coach on the first row of the bleachers.

"You are very young," Hector began quietly.

"Yes, sir, I know, but—"

"You are very young and gifted and impressive, and—"

"How did you like it when—"

"*Señor* Woodell, I would like you to not speak until I am finished. Do you understand?"

"Yes, but—"

"Yes or no is all I need. Do you understand?"

"Yes."

"I want to talk about what I saw today and a little about my team. First of all, I saw a young boy, big for his age, but not big for a high school team. You are a better-than-average fielder with a better-than-average arm, but I think your arm is at its limit from shortstop on a regulation field. In fact, were you to play for me, I would probably not risk putting you anywhere in the infield other than at second base."

Better than average? What was I supposed to do, catch everything?

"Your range and mechanics are good. You show tremendous potential as a fielder. I like the way you use your feet and your glove. You have been well trained and coached."

By myself, mostly.

"You are a fine hitter, very strong for your size and age. Power will come with growth. You have a little boy's immaturity, and I would wonder about team spirit and attitude."

I wanted to tell Mr. Villagrande that I had always been a team player, but the coach kept talking.

"You are full of yourself, that is clear. I say this not because you nearly hit me with batted balls. It is seen in your face, your walk, everything. You know how good you are, and I fear you will be satisfied to remain at the level you are now. That would be a tragedy, for you have unlimited potential."

I wanted to argue, but I had learned not to interrupt. I wanted to tell the coach that too.

"I do not have a place for you on my team," Hector said.

I felt paralyzed. My head buzzed; my breath came in short gasps.

"I know this is a disappointment to you, and I know also that you may not be able to play ball at all this summer. That is not good but not all bad either."

I was barely listening. How could this be? How could this fool have watched me and not realize what I could do for this team? Surely I was better than half the players I had seen that day.

"Continue working out. Look for a league that will accept you. I know Mr. Lincoln was impressed enough that he would be willing to pitch to you. I would work on humility. You are not the best ballplayer who ever lived."

Not yet, maybe.

"You did not see anyone congratulate himself on this field today, no matter what he did. My players encourage each other, but there is no self-aggrandizement. Do you know what that means?"

I nodded.

"Many a player has come to me the best on his high school team. Each has his sights set on American Legion and the pros. One player every five years gets a contract. But each comes to me thinking he is the best. Those who learn quickly what it means to be a humble team player are the ones I keep. The others go elsewhere, and I have never seen one succeed. You have a great advantage because of your youth, but let me warn you. You may plateau while everyone else catches up to you. If you keep improving, you will be something special."

I'm something special now. It was like he could read my mind.

"If you are convinced you are already something special, you will probably be a good high school player someday. Then, because you are not better, you will be more interested in cars and girls and money, and you will drift from the game."

"Never," I said. "No way, ever. I may have a lot to learn, but I will never drift from the game."

"Well, good for you," Villagrande said, slapping my knee and rising. "I wish you the best, and I invite you to try out for me again next year."

"But what if I—?"

"That's all I can offer, *muchacho.* I am sorry."

Sobs were dammed up in my throat. I wanted to scream, to threaten, to accuse. Who was this man who thought he knew so much? I moved stiff-legged to the field where I picked up my glove and found my bat in the third-base dugout. I was suddenly weak and tired. I pressed my back against the end of the dugout and slid to the ground. Without meaning to, I had hidden myself from Hector and Neil as they chatted by their car.

As I sat there, letting the tears come, the coaches' low tones grew louder.

"Where would Michaels have left the mask?" Neil said.

"I thought I saw it near the dugout."

They approached.

"There it is."

They stood on the other side of the dugout wall, apparently unaware that I was right there.

Hector sighed. "Was that kid something today, or what?"

"Good, huh?"

"Good? Neil, that was the most unbelievable hitting exhibition I've ever seen, especially for a kid that age."

"Who you tellin? Almost cost me my head."

I took my time opening the FedEx package, which bore Chaplain Wallace's return address.

Re: Neal Lofert Woodell (092349)
Dear Mrs. Woodell:

I thought for the sake of your son that you would want to be informed of your former husband's condition. He has suffered acutely from a new attack of delirium tremens, apparently brought about by yet another difficult withdrawal from alcohol. I know this comes as a shock to you, because he was not assumed by anyone, myself included, to have access to alcohol here.

As you can imagine, such substances can be smuggled in, unfortunately only by prison employees. He was supplied with vodka, which could not be detected on his breath, though it was detected in blood and urine samples. He denied knowing how his system could evidence signs of the same.

Apparently he ran out of whatever mode of payment he had been making, and his supply was cut off. An investigation continues here to determine who was bringing in the liquor. Meanwhile, his condition is not good. For several days he suffered the typical hallucinations. He now tells me they were more vivid and terrifying even than last time, which was the worst I had seen anyone endure. He may wish to inform you of the details, but I will spare you that for now.

More important, according to the physician here, Neal suffered from profound perspiration leading to dehydration, a dangerously elevated heart rate during convulsions, and a blood pressure reading in the critical danger zone. He has suffered two heart attacks, one severe and the other not so severe except for a man in his condition, and also kidney failure.

He is on heavy medication to sedate the central nervous system, is on IVs for constant hydration, along with whatever fluids they can get him to take orally, electrolytes for salt, multivitamins, and a strict diet. Of course, his strict avoidance of alcohol is key, but I fear he has no self-control in that area and would eagerly take a drink if he could get one.

The doctor is most concerned with the kidney and heart failures and, I must tell you, is pessimistic about Neal's survival regardless. Were you to elect that your son see his father again, the doctor urges that you consider a trip within the next thirty days.

Very truly yours,
Rev. Alton Wallace, Chaplain
Alabama State Penitentiary

41

A week from the following Monday, Momma and I sat on a train in Chicago that would take us all the way to Birmingham, Alabama.

"Bet you don't like wasting your vacation like this," I said.

My mother shrugged. "It's for you. It's okay."

"Am I still going to be able to go to college?"

Momma smiled. "I didn't take all your college money, El. I just borrowed it and will be paying it back, okay?"

"I'll put money in that fund someday," I said. "Soon as I get my motor paid off, maybe Mr. Harkness will start paying me."

I had walked all the way home from Lane Tech, hiding my tears from passersby. With every step I determined to work harder than ever to show Hector Villagrande and anyone else that I could play with anybody.

"I hate to say it," Momma had told me, "but I have seen the same things in you lately. You used to be the sweetest, most self-less child, but you've become impressed with yourself."

"I'm impressive," I said.

"But only until people know you're aware of it, El. Then it's obnoxious, and it's only going to get you what you got today. Let people discover you."

From now on I would let my play do my talking. It had taken

that shot between the eyes from Hector Villagrande to make me
see the light. Maybe I would still like to play for Hector some
day.

At the secondhand shop a few days before my mother and I
left for Alabama, Lucky's electrician friend showed up. We sat in
the back room, just me and the tall, skinny man with a bobbing
Adam's apple. "This here is a good motor," he said. "It's not new.
Fact, they hardly make 'em this good anymore for less than several hundred dollars. My question is, what's it from and how did
you burn it up?"

"I can't tell you what it's from," I began.

"Because you don't know, or because it's somethin illegal?"

"Neither. I just don't wanna tell."

"Well, were you jammin the thing somehow?"

"Yeah."

"With what?"

"Plastic."

"Why?"

"I can't say."

"Give me a general idea what you were trying to get it to do."

"Start and stop at different speeds without turning it off."

"That's all I needed to know. You probably put your resistance
out here, am I right?" He pointed to the end of the spinning
shaft.

"Actually, I put it out at the axle that's driven by a belt."

"Even worse. Puts too much torque on the—well, you don't
need to know all that. So what you want is a heavy-duty motor,
this size, that you can turn on, get warmed up and running, and
then have it change speeds, what, sort of at random?"

I nodded.

"You want a different animal," the man said. "It's got a clutch
in it, and a cooling system, and I can build right into it your random, spring-loaded, metal resistor. It shouldn't ever jam or over-
heat or break down, as long as you let it warm up before you
start askin it to change speeds."

"Sounds fantastic."

"Well, it is. Industry has some uses for motors like that, mostly for mixing food and such, needing those unpredictable changes of speed, but I can't for the life of me figure out what a kid would need one for. I'd sure like to see your contraption."

"Maybe someday," I said. "How long before I can have this one?"

"I'd say two weeks and a hundred dollars. It'll be rebuilt, but almost indestructible."

Now, on the train, I said, "Wouldn't it be something if that thing was ready when we got back home?"

"Don't get your hopes up," my mother said, looking out the window.

I may never get my hopes up again. I couldn't wait to get back to the pitching machine and see what the new gizmo would add to my workouts. But the rest of the way, all I could think about was seeing Daddy again and all we would talk about.

I phoned Chaplain Wallace from the train depot near the taxi stand.

"Get yourself a room nearby," he said, "and I'll come get you. You may see Neal at four this afternoon. You'll be happy to know he is ambulatory and will be able to walk into the visitors' picnic area to greet you."

I was grateful Elgin wouldn't have to see his daddy in a hospital bed with needles and tubes running in and out of him, but the chaplain didn't say the prognosis was any better.

Elgin and I showered. He dressed up. I dressed down. There would be no encouraging Neal on this visit, though it felt strange to think I might be seeing the last of him.

Reverend Wallace was a kind-looking man, perhaps softer and plumper than I expected. He had fleshy hands and wore thick glasses. When he picked us up, he spoke to me in code. "The incarcerated individual," he began, looking at me over the top of his glasses to see whether I was following, "remains in a negative prognosive state. He must be very careful, however, to avoid anything that would exacerbate his hypertension or threaten his cardiovascular system."

"Uh-huh."

"It's so good of you to come, ma'am," he said. "Have you thought more about that of which we corresponded?"

"Yes," I said. "I'm not prepared to reconcile, if that's what you mean. I don't plan to be nasty, but I'm here for the boy. I don't mind seeing Neal again, but I will not be encouraging him."

"Ma'am, I think he knows what's happening here, and I doubt he's looking for any romantic encouragement."

"I know what he's looking for, sir," I said. "He's not going to get absolution from me."

The chaplain showed his card to the guard and began the process of getting himself and his guests inside the maximum-security facility.

"A little mercy or grace to a terminal patient is an inexpensive but precious commodity."

I took that as a rebuke and fell silent. Wallace turned his attention to Elgin. "I'll bet you'll be glad to see your dad after all this time."

"Momma says he's sick."

"He might not look like what you remembered, but you'll recognize him."

The chaplain led Elgin and me to a picnic table beneath a huge tree. "I am happy to stay," he said, "but will be just as happy to make myself scarce."

"Thank you," I said. "We prefer to see him alone. But would you mind staying within sight in case I let Elgin and Neal spend some time together? I don't know what to do with myself here."

"After I have pointed you out to him, I will be over there." He gestured to an area where several tables had been pushed together.

I found myself nervous and curious. It wasn't that I wanted to see Neal, but I had long wondered what age and illness and prison had done to him. Surely he wouldn't be the vision of athletic prowess he had once been.

Elgin said something I didn't hear. I had watched the chaplain until he disappeared. Now I watched wives and children embracing men and laughing and crying. I planned to do neither, and I certainly would not touch the man.

"What?" I asked Elgin.

"There's Mr. Wallace," he said. "Where's Daddy?"

The chaplain now stood where he said he would wait. He waved at me with a small flick of his hand and smiled politely. Several prisoners milled about, looking for people. I did not see Neal.

I raised my palms at the chaplain in a question. He pointed past me to the corner of a building. I saw no one I recognized. It would be too much for Elgin if Neal could not join us. It wouldn't be fair to make him wait another day.

I scanned the grounds again and told Elgin to wait as I hurried to the chaplain. "Where is he?" I said.

Reverend Wallace pointed back toward Elgin. "Right over there," he said. I looked. "Right there."

Past a group of families and about twenty feet from Elgin, slowly, carefully making his way toward his son, was Neal Lofert Woodell, number 092349. Over his prison blue dungarees he had wrapped a drab green woolen blanket around his shoulders.

My knees buckled and the chaplain caught me as I sank to the bench.

42

There had never been one clue that I could ever lose my resolve to hold against Neal the loss of my unborn daughter. The man had cost me a child, my dignity, my security, a normal family life, my childhood dreams. He had lied as a matter of course, even when lying benefited him nothing. He was evil and worthless.

But now as I saw the broken husk of the boy I had fallen in love with in high school, I was overcome with pity. Perhaps he deserved this. Perhaps I should be glad he finally got his due. But what a sad and sorry price! I had not even recognized him, had looked right through him.

Barely into his thirties, he was wan and frail. His gait was deliberate, his step unsure. He clutched the blanket around his shoulders as a wisp of a ninety-year-old would. I felt the warm, soft hand of the chaplain on my shoulder and fought to control myself. I needed to make sure Elgin didn't bolt from his father. It would be no good for either of them.

I dabbed at my eyes and forced myself to watch. Elgin stiffened and stared as his father approached, prison-issue hat mocking the baseball caps that had looked so smart on him in his youth.

Elgin stood, and I felt myself rising too. I pulled away from

Chaplain Wallace, insisting I was all right, and moved a few feet behind my son. Neal glanced at me.

"Dad?" Elgin said, his voice thick.

"El," Neal said, and the boy rushed to him, embracing him. Neal put one arm around his son and held the blanket up with his other hand. "How ya doin, boy?"

His voice was weak, his face dark and shadowy. He looked as if he had lost more than thirty pounds. His eyes were sunken and dark, his teeth bad, and thin strands of hair poked out under the cap. I was impressed when Elgin helped his father get one leg under the table so he could straddle the bench. The boy hurried around to the other side and leaned forward.

"Did we surprise you, Dad?"

Neal hesitated, thinking. "I believe the chaplain told me you might come." A flicker of amusement came to his eyes. "I never was much for bench sittin."

"Me either," Elgin said, and went into a long explanation of why he was not playing on a team yet this summer.

"That's a crime," Neal managed. "I oughta write somebody and tell em I'm gonna sue em if they don't let you play."

"It's all right, Daddy," Elgin said. "If I don't get to play till next summer, I'm gonna be something because of that pitching machine," and he proceeded rapid-fire to bring him up to date on that. Neal, whose attention seemed to flag, merely smiled and nodded occasionally.

What I felt for the man was compassion and sympathy, not love. Still I wanted to embrace him. What would be the harm? There would be no false encouragement in it. The man was clearly dying. Anything and everything he had ever done had caught up with him, and now he was in an irreversible spiral, years before his time.

"El," he whispered, "there's things I got to tell you, and then I want to talk to your momma. Listen to me. Remember me for the good things, you hear? For what I could do on the ball field when I was healthy, for teachin you all that stuff. Know what I mean?"

Elgin nodded. "I inherited my baseball from you, Daddy."

"Sounds like you're already better than me at your age. But let me tell you somethin, boy. I been a liar all my life. I two-timed your momma from the day we started dating. You know what that means?"

"You had another girlfriend?"

Neal nodded miserably. "She wasn't someone you'd marry, just have fun with. Bad news. Bad thing to do. I even had other girlfriends after we was married."

Elgin winced, and I wished Neal could spare him this. It was little surprise to me, though I had tried to believe otherwise.

"I been an alcoholic since high school. Not just drinkin, but needing it, doing anything to get it, lettin it run my life. There were times I controlled it a little, sometimes in the minors, just after your mom and I got married. But I never got a handle on it. My job was drinkin and everything else was just to finance it, right up till the time I killed that old man."

"You said that was an accident."

"Elgin, I'm tellin you I was a liar. Believe what I told you about baseball. But everything else I ever told you, you can take to the dump. You know your mom believes I killed our baby."

"Yeah, but I know you—"

"Well, I did. I didn't mean to, but I was drunk and not thinkin and raging mad. Just because they never busted me for it don't mean I didn't do it. I live with it every day. That baby girl comes to me in the middle of the night sometimes and—"

Elgin recoiled, and I stepped from behind him to put my hand over Neal's. His lean, cold fingers twitched. "Neal, he's just a boy. Be careful, please."

Neal's lips had begun to quiver. "I just wanna tell you, El. Don't ever even try booze. It'll kill you just like it's gonna kill me. I'm sorry for everything I've ever done that's made life hard for you. I wanted to give you everything and see you be whatever you wanted to be."

"I want to be a ballplayer like you, Daddy."

Neal shook his head and held up his free hand. The blanket slid from his shoulders. I pulled it up around him again. He smelled of the infirmary.

"Be a ballplayer, El. But don't be like me."

He turned to force his other leg under the table, rested on his elbows, and held his face in his hands. I went around and sat beside him, my knees facing away from the table. I pulled the blanket up around his shoulders again as his body jerked with sobs.

"Daddy, I forgive you," Elgin said. "I forgive you for everything."

"You always have," Neal whined. "Even when I was still makin excuses and lying about bein sorry."

Elgin looked at me and I felt the accusation.

"Give us a minute, honey," I told him, but he hesitated. I looked to the chaplain, who hurried over. I signaled him with a nod toward Elgin.

"Son, let's give your mom and dad a couple of minutes, hm?"

"I'll be right back, Daddy."

Neal remained hidden behind his knuckly hands, weeping. "I'm through lyin, Mir," he said. "I never convinced you of anything anyway, but I'm through."

Something in me needed to hear this, yet I took no joy in his pain as I once had.

"Oh, Miriam," he whimpered, "can't you forgive me? Everything you ever accused me of was true. I'm sorry for the other women, I'm sorry about the baby, I'm sorry about the old man, I'm sorry for what I've done to Elgin and to you."

I took his head in my hands and pulled him to me, cradling him like the baby he was, the pitiable, helpless, hopeless infant I had longed to rock in my arms since I lost my own at his hands.

"I need to hear you say it," he said, but I could not speak. The man would soon pay the ultimate price for his worthless past. Who was I to forgive him? How was it possible I could let go and tell him what he needed to hear? Why should he die in peace when I had to live in turmoil?

But he would not die in peace, regardless what I said. I would not lie. I could not forgive him if I didn't feel it in my heart. But even then, did I have to say it? Why was the onus on me? He could apologize for a year and cry twenty-four hours a day, and it would not bring back to me the treasures he had ripped away.

Why couldn't I let it go? His alcoholism was beyond a character weakness by now. He could not be sorry for the hold it still had on him; he could be sorry only for the choices that had brought him here. I held him and rocked him and heard his pathetic, woeful weeping.

He pulled back from me. His were the eyes of a dead man.

"If I could make it up to you, Miriam, I would work around the clock for the rest of my life. Call me a liar every time before. Say I was bein phony every time I turned over a new leaf, and you'd be right. Sometimes I thought I meant it, but I could never make it stick. This time, Mir, I got nothin to gain except your forgiveness. You won't be saying it's all right. You won't be saying you're all right or the boy's all right or that I can just forget about all the pain I've brought you.

"You won't be saying everything can be wiped away with a word. All you'll be saying is that you won't hate me forever. That's all. That's all I want. Tell me you'll think about me sometime without hatin me and everything I was. Tell me you'll think about me and remember somethin good. If you can't remember some of the fun times we had before I went crazy with the booze, at least remember that at the end I realized what I'd done and was truly, truly sorry, probably for the first time in my life."

I held him again, knowing full well that all he would take from my embrace was pity. Forgive him? Pardon him? What would that mean? I would not, would not, be phony. I would not say something I didn't mean. It would be worse than anything he had ever done to me.

"Oh, God," I said silently, "only You can forgive this man. It's not in me."

Neal stiffened in my arms. He was trying to stop crying. In his rigid shoulders I read the attitude, *If she doesn't want to forgive me, I don't want her pity either.*

I let him pull away. He wiped his eyes with his fingers. He did not appear angry. Just frustrated, as if he knew I couldn't stand a weak, blubbering man.

I remained close. I wanted to say something soothing, but I would not violate my own conscience. If forgiveness came from my lips, it had to be in my heart and mind.

"You were one good-lookin high schooler," I whispered, a smile playing at my lips.

Neal backed up and looked at me in surprise. "I was, wasn't I?" he said, a painful grin forming.

"I was the envy of every girl in that high school when I landed you."

His face contorted again and the tears came. "Yeah," he whined, "and look what I did to you. I was so proud to have you as my girl, and I spent the rest of my life ruining yours." He struggled to compose himself. "When I see what kind of a mother you've become, I only wish I'd been able to stay with you. I've got nobody but myself to blame."

He tried to bury his face in his hands again, but I took them in my own and set my face before his. "Neal Woodell, you were one scoundrel of a husband."

"I know I was."

I shushed him. "But it's all behind us now, isn't it?"

He nodded.

"Isn't it?" I repeated.

"Well, I'm sure sorry for it, I know that," he said.

"I know you are. But you snuffed out every last flicker of love I could have had for you."

"I'm not even hopin for that," he said. "I just want you to believe I'm sorry and to forgive me."

"You have been sorry so many times—"

"No, I wasn't. I was lyin then. I'm not lyin now."

His neck and shoulders felt bony. I would not forgive him simply because he was dying. I could forgive him only if I believed him. And even then, as I had prayed, it wasn't within me to forgive. God would have to do that. Who was I to be an agent of mercy and grace?

God, help me.

Neal's breath came as if he were exhausted. "Forgive me, Mir," he whispered. "Believe I'm sorry and forgive me."

I took a fluttery breath and pulled him closer. "I believe you, Neal. I believe you, and I forgive you."

43

Neal didn't stir, didn't say anything. His breathing was even and deep, as if he had fallen asleep.

I felt an airy lightness, as if I myself had been forgiven. Some dignity had been restored. For years I had been in control of this relationship. I had held the key to the lockbox of a debt of guilt. Now I had allowed the guilty to pay me. He may have had no visible response, but I felt as if I could fly.

I gently steered Neal away from me until he was sitting up straight, staring. He seemed spent. He didn't smile, didn't thank me, didn't do anything but sit. Perhaps he was stunned to silence, unable to take it in.

"We need to go soon, Neal," I said gently, wanting to run and jump and shout. Was I finally, truly free of my albatross of all these years? And had it not really been him all along, but my own reaction to him?

Oh, it had been his fault. There was no question about that. But he was in prison, and though I was divorced and humiliated, still I felt free!

"Would you like to talk to Elgin one more time?"

Neal squinted at me. "Awful tired," he said. "Yeah, I'd like to see El one more time." He touched my arm. "One more time is probably it, you know. I'm never gonna see y'all again."

I pressed my lips together and nodded.

Why didn't I say that's nonsense, that he would be fine, and that Elgin would make the trip again someday? Because I was past playing games with Neal. What was the point of polite dishonesty at this stage of a man's life?

Momma stayed with Chaplain Wallace as I went to my father again. "Are you going to be all right, Daddy?"

"Oh, I'll be all right, El. I'll be just fine now. Your mom and I got some things straight between us."

"Did she forgive you?"

"Yes, sir, she sure did."

"I didn't know if she ever would, Daddy."

"She probably shouldn't have."

"Why not? You were sorry. I knew that."

"Sometimes sorry isn't enough. And I wasn't as sorry as I am now."

I wanted to talk baseball or anything but this. But somehow asking my dad about hitting the cutoff man didn't fit now.

"El, I'll probably never see you again. I—"

"Don't say that!"

"Well, it's true."

"I'll come see you again, Daddy. I promise. And I won't wait till you're sick again."

Daddy appeared irritated. "Listen to me, boy. You ain't never goin to see me alive again. The next time, I'll be in the ground."

I began to cry.

"I know that's no way to tell a boy somethin, but I've been a bad enough father as it is by not tellin you the truth. Well, that's the truth. I'll fight this thing, but they can't fool me. It's already whipped me and I can feel it."

"Daddy, please! We can't afford to come back down here soon! If you die, I won't even be able to come back for your funeral."

Daddy actually laughed. "What do you want me to do, die today so you'll be in town for the fixins?"

"That's not funny."

"I just wanted to tell you, that's all, El. Now you can go on and blubber about it, and I guess I can't blame you. Except I was such a bad dad you shouldn't miss me too much. But it would make me feel a lot better, almost as good as your mom forgivin me, if I knew you were gonna be a better man than I ever was."

Should I tell my father that yes, I planned to be? Would that be nice? Or should I tell him that he was a good dad and that I learned a lot from him? At least the last part was true. I said nothing.

"Just tell me you'll take care of your ma, and—"

"Oh, Daddy!"

"—and that you'll be honest and not get mixed up with drinkin."

I nodded and tried to stop crying. "I love you, Daddy." I hugged his neck.

"I love you too, El, even though I was never good at—"

"I've already forgiven you, Daddy, so quit talking about it, okay?"

Daddy sighed. "Okay, El. Okay."

I pulled away and took a deep breath. "Daddy, I'm going to be the best ballplayer I can be, and I'm going to make the major leagues. I'm going to make you so proud you won't be able to stand it. When I play in my first big-league game, they'll let you out to come see me, won't they?"

"I don't know. I guess they might."

"You keep thinking about that, and I'll keep thinking about it. We'll make it happen, Daddy. I'll remember everything you taught me."

"Especially today?"

"Especially today."

Daddy rose slowly and put a hand on the table. "Do me a favor, will you, El? If I can't make it, will you tell 'em you owe a lot of your baseball success to your dad?"

"I'll tell them I owe *all* my success to my dad!"

"No, no, now, that wouldn't be honest. You know I didn't give you that skill and that brain. And your mom deserves the credit for all she done for you without a man in the house."

"I know."

"So you tell the whole story. I'll be listenin."

The next day, though Elgin's and my train was not scheduled to pull out of Birmingham until early evening, I made the difficult decision to not return and see Neal. Being closer to Hattiesburg, I made a few calls to relatives. My mother told me, "Word we get here is that Neal is dying of AIDS. Don't you dare touch him."

"That's a lie," I told her. "He's not well, but it's alcohol-related."

"Alcohol? Well, how in the world does he get booze in prison? I mean, I—"

"Momma, I gotta get off the phone, if you don't mind. My love to everyone."

I was amazed at my own reaction. I was actually defensive for Neal and insulted by the charge. Such talk was one of the reasons I had moved to Chicago, and I couldn't wait to get home.

Home. I thought of Chicago as home. I had made the final break. I didn't let my mother's comment interfere with my joy.

"I don't see why we can't see him again," Elgin said in our tiny hotel room. "We have time."

"Someday you'll understand," I said.

"You always say that."

"And I'm always right. Honey, he'd look even worse today. We wore him out. We've said all we could say, and he has done the same. Let's let it be for a while."

"But he doesn't think he's going to live much longer."

I didn't respond.

"What do you think, Momma?"

Was it time to be as honest with Elgin as I had been with Neal?

"He looks pretty sick," I said.

"You don't think I'll ever see him again, and you won't let me see him today?"

"Elgin, sit down." He sat on the bed. "I don't think any of the three of us needs the distress of another meeting just now. There's nothing more to say or do. Let's let him try to get stronger and see if he can turn this health thing around. Then when we get some more money, we can come back and see him again."

Elgin lay on his side. "You don't believe that," he said. "You know he's going to die."

"I don't know for sure."

"But you think it."

"Yes, El, I do."

"Then why can't I see him?"

"Remembering the way he was yesterday is going to be diffi-cult enough. Why would you want to risk seeing him even sicker? Anyway, he wants you to remember his last advice."

"I'll never forget it."

"Then let's leave it at that."

"Can I write to him?"

"Of course. We can give it to the chaplain when he drives us to the train."

I wrote a note, repeating what my father had said and renewing my promise to make the majors, to make Daddy proud, and to be sure to give him credit for my success.

"I still want you at my first game," I reminded him.

44

When our train finally pulled into the Illinois Central station in Chicago two days later, I heard my name.

The page was from Reverend Wallace: "Please phone me collect immediately."

I could think of only one reason. I hurried to a phone.

"Neal had an uneventful night and seemed to rally the morning after you were here," Chaplain Wallace told me. "Late the evening your train left, about midnight, he had a seizure that led to a coughing spell. The seizure and the coughing caused a blood pressure crisis and another heart attack. His kidneys failed by dawn. He was put on dialysis, but he was gone by noon. I'm sorry."

"Sir, my son gave you a note for him when—"

"I gave it to him and he read it."

"Oh, thank God."

"He had it in his hands when I left him that night."

"Would you do me a favor and tell my son that?"

When Elgin handed the phone back, he buried his head in my chest as I finished up with the chaplain.

"I want you to know, ma'am, that I believe Neal did make his peace with God sometime back. He was never terribly knowledgeable or articulate about his faith, but apparently he had

250

been a churchgoer in his youth. I feel his devotion at the end was genuine."

"Thank you for telling me that."

"And how about you, ma'am? Can I be of any assistance to you in that regard?"

I assured him Elgin and I were born-again Christians and in a good church.

"Then you know God cares personally about you. I'm sorry Neal's life ended this way, but I know he was very thankful he got to see you both again. If you're unable to get to the funeral, I'll send you whatever documents are appropriate."

I could take no more time off, and I couldn't afford airfare anyway. I thanked Chaplain Wallace and sat to collect myself.

"I have to go to the funeral," Elgin said.

"Please don't make this more difficult," I said. "We cannot and we will not be going. Don't pretend I have a choice. You saw him, you talked to him, and you both got things said that needed to be said."

It was a sad trip home from the train station. I let Elgin grieve for the only father he had ever known, for the man Neal Woodell might have been, for the ballplayer he could have been. He remembered special times when it was just him and his dad, throwing, hitting, pitching, fielding, running, talking, listening, learning.

Elgin clenched and unclenched his fists, his eyes dark and narrow, lips pressed tight. I didn't want him to grow bitter.

"You understand why we can't go to the funeral," I said as we approached the hotel.

"Uh-huh. I know."

"You gonna be okay, baby?"

"I'm not sure. This really feels weird."

"Ah! You're back! And how was the trip? Let me help you with those!"

"Thank you, Ricardo. I'm afraid we suffered a death in the family, however, so we're not much in a talking mood."

"Oh, how horrible! May I ask whom?"

"Elgin's father."

"Not an old man. Sudden?"

"Heart attack and complications." I put my finger to my lips and glanced at Elgin, who was studying the floor.

"Well," Mr. Bravura said, and I would always be grateful he left it at this: "I am so sorry."

He helped carry our suitcases from the elevator to our apartment, set them in the middle of the floor, bowed to me without a word, and slipped out. Just as I was wondering if he'd had a transfusion of sensitivity, he knocked and poked his head back in.

"Forgive me, I almost forgot. A small but heavy package came for your son from Lucky's Secondhand Shop. May I run it up?"

⓪

I had undressed and was sitting on the couch when Momma brought me the heavy shoebox wrapped in brown paper. A note inside read:

> Master Woodell, Mr. Harkness has already paid me $120 for this rebuilt motor with the clutch and gears you desired. You'll notice that it can be run with or without engaging the gears. If it works as you hope, you may settle up with him. Any problems, call me at the number below. It's been a pleasure.

I set the box aside and thought about turning on the television but decided against it. I didn't even want to talk to my mother, who seemed to be watching me carefully.

Well, I thought, *Daddy won't make it to my first big-league game. But he'll be the reason I'm there.*

45

My sympathy card to Neal's parents crossed a scathing note from my own mother about my not getting Elgin "to his own father's burial. I can understand your not wanting to go, but to keep that boy away is shameful."

My own grieving for Neal was a strange, unpredictable progression of emotions. Sometimes I was overcome with melancholy. The memories didn't seem so distant now. The man I had prayed to be rid of was now more a part of my life than when he was alive and in prison. He dominated my thoughts, reminded me of how things had been.

When I found myself weeping, sometimes sobbing, I knew it wasn't over missing him or longing for a man in my life. I wept for the sad, frustrated, miserable lonely man he had become before he died.

I found it difficult to draw out Elgin now. His face was more sober, his eyes darker. He was nearing puberty. I looked forward to how manly that would make him, but I dreaded the mysterious new interests and passions. I prayed he would keep his sweet innocence, though I knew I was dreaming.

Every time I thought of Daddy, I reminded myself of my goal. I wanted to be the best baseball player I could be. My dad had drilled into me: "Find your level, find your limit, push it until you know. Only when you've done that will you be the best you can be. Don't worry about who's better or different. Your job is to be the best you can be, because you can't do more than that."

I was the best ballplayer of my age I had ever seen. I wondered if there were any others like me anywhere. If there were, I knew what they were thinking. They didn't want to compete with kids their own age any more than I did. They would want to get on a team—of teens, college kids, adults—where they could forget who was ahead for his age and just play some ball. Competitive baseball. That's what I wanted, and that's what I missed.

I worked every day at Lucky's and worked out every night in my private batting cage. The new motor for the pitching machine was so good it was scary. Not only did I use it with the gear sometimes engaged and sometimes not, but I also figured out that I could tighten a screw halfway and cause the machine to throw hundreds of pitches with no predictability.

It was like facing the monster for the first time again. I had no idea which pitch was coming, how fast, or from which angle. The thing could fire a straight pitch at my head so fast I could barely evade it, then come back with a dancing, sweeping curve that looked like it might hit me in the rear but would break across the outside of the plate. There was no more hitting a half dozen or more solid shots for every bucket of fifty-seven balls. I tried to read the spin and location of each pitch in time to dive for cover or get a bat on it. I was light on my feet, knowing I had to keep the back foot buried for a perfect swing, yet always ready to jump out of the way of a fastball at the shins.

I used only my heavy, skinny fungo bat, but I fought through lots of hitless buckets knowing I would eventually catch on. This would make hitting a baseball like breathing.

Lucky sometimes hit balls to me, but he couldn't hit hard enough to challenge me. I compared everything with what I could do in the cellar. Nothing would compete with that until I found a whole team I could match in ability. Hector Villagrande had such a team, and my goal was to make that team the next year when I was thirteen. What drove me crazy was that I knew I was ready now.

I stood at the plate in the basement with my glove on, trying to catch as many pitches in a row as possible. Once I caught fourteen straight before a wicked curve skipped off my glove, banged off the wall, and hit me in the triceps. I jumped and howled and rubbed my arm, then flung my glove at the machine.

Eventually I learned to catch fifty pitches per bucket, sometimes standing near the machine and catching the grounders and liners after they came off the wall. I dove and lurched and reached and stretched until I sweat through my clothes, and I was getting into great shape, matching my frame with muscle and coordination.

I took Raleigh Lincoln Sr. up on his offer to pitch batting practice. I needed the competition and especially some feedback, some coaching.

By the middle of the summer I was hitting only a dozen or so balls solid from each bucket, but I hit Mr. Lincoln like I owned him. The man shook his head. "It's like facing a big leaguer," he said. "I don't want to puff you up, but you hit me like nobody ever has, and I mean nobody. I can't believe your eye. Where in the world did you develop that?"

"I guess I just have a sense of the plate," I said. "My dad said good hitters walk a lot. And my stance gets both my eyes on the pitch."

"I need to have a talk with Hector," Raleigh said. "He doesn't know what he's passing up."

"His team's doing okay."

"I should say! They've only lost two and they're going to win the state. But I never knew a team that couldn't be improved. You could start on that team, boy."

"Maybe next year."

"Maybe? You don't make that team next year, and I'm gonna

get Hector fired and take it myself. You don't make it next year, I'll get you in the City League!"

I laughed. "You have to be eighteen for that."

"You'd be one of the best hitters in that league, son, and I am not putting you on."

That was the kind of encouragement I needed. How I wanted to play in a live game! I thought about pleading with Hector Villagrande to let me work out with his team. I dreamed of being so dominating, so impressive that he would have to make room for me, not just on the bench but in the starting lineup.

I continued to read and think and dream baseball. By the dead of winter, everything seemed to fall together for me.

A bad cold kept me away from the cellar for two days. That break made me sharp somehow. Though it had taken hundreds of thousands of pitches, I seemed to succeed overnight. I was hitting consistently.

I began to focus on March and local tryouts.

I didn't know what to think anymore about Elgin's obsession. It was as if his devastation at not making the team and the loss of his father had driven him deep into himself. There was a determination, a dedication in him that frightened me. Had anyone anywhere ever been so committed to anything?

One night at dinner, as the snow outside turned to slush and the spring tryouts and his thirteenth birthday approached, he said, "Momma, I'm ready for you to come to the basement and see something."

"I thought you'd never ask," I said. "What in the world have you been doing down there?"

"You're not going to believe it."

The basement was as dark as ever. Elgin's skinny little bat looked heavy and impossible to hit with. The machine was ugly and noisy. I had not seen it with the new motor, but I had heard him talk about it enough.

But what was this? The machine looked closer to the batters' boxes. "Elgin?" I said as I approached it.

He nodded. "Yup. Closer. By more than ten feet."

"You had it as close to the back wall as possible. You said—"

"I said it was only two-thirds of major-league distance. Now it's half."

He told me to stand with my body outside the doorframe, peeking in.

"Nothing should hit you, but be ready to duck," he said.

46

Elgin cleared the room of everything but himself, his helmet, his bat, and the machine, tossing everything else past me near the stairs.

The machine whirred to life, but strangely, Elgin did not hurry to the box but merely moved left and strolled in that direction. The first pitch slammed so hard off the wall that it carried all the way to the other end and whapped against the canvas drop. I jumped, ready to get out of the way, but Elgin seemed to casually study the ball. He stood just outside the left-hander's batter's box, his bat dangling from his right hand, as the next pitch swept at him and in over the plate.

He stepped into the box and set himself. The next dozen or so pitches flew all over the place. One started high and dropped into the strike zone. One appeared to be ankle-high until the last instant when it flashed up to his knees. The only pitch he didn't swing at came in right under his chin. He moved only a fraction to elude it.

On all the other pitches, Elgin turned and erupted with a controlled but mighty swing. The sound of metal on plastic resounded from the walls as each pitch was driven to the canvas. As far as I could tell there was not even a pop-up or fly ball. All sped to the other end of the room in a line, most directly over the machine.

As I watched in awe, Elgin slipped around to the other batter's box. Now a righty, he continued his barrage, stepping, swinging, driving, recoiling, doing it again and again. His eyes looked alive, narrow, piercing in the dim light. He seemed to see nothing but the ball. At that distance each pitch came in what seemed like milliseconds. How could he react? How could he hit with such authority? I knew it could be only the hours and hours of practice. They had cost him bruises and frustration. But now they had paid off—if being able to hit the hideous machine was payment enough.

Elgin had hit fifty line drives as if he and the pitches were part of the same script. "Help me pick em up!" he exulted. "I want to show you something."

I gathered up a few balls as if in a trance and dropped them into the bucket as Elgin hurried past. I wanted to compliment him, to express wonder, to ask what the future might hold. Words would not come. Apparently, he understood. He just looked at me and grinned.

He knew, I decided. There was nothing to say, nothing to be said ever. He had made himself into a miracle. I wondered if an adult athlete could have done the same. Surely a big leaguer could do this. But would he have the patience to teach himself?

As I picked up three balls in a corner, I envisioned my son on television, on programs about people who do amazing things. Was it marketable? Could he make a living at it? Would other people copy him and get better at it? "Watch this!" Elgin shouted. "Take cover!"

He poured the balls into the machine. I skipped out of the way. He leaned past me and traded his fungo bat for his glove. He stood on the plate, eyes wild as the first pitch came.

He was not quite ready, and it swept above him, hitting the wall within inches of his head. He whooped and hollered, and I wondered if he had lost his mind. I wanted to tell him to stop, to quit showing off, to not try to do something he couldn't do. But still I was speechless. What was I watching? Who was this child? Had he come from my womb? Yesterday he was a baby, a kid, who like everyone else, loved baseball. Now he was a marvelously gifted and trained and honed and polished machine with a brain, which made him so much more and better than the metal conglomeration that had helped turn him into what he was.

The pitches bounced in, swept in, sped in, dropped, rose, spun, danced, curved, slid, broke. He caught one after the other, his face set, eyes afire. As each slammed into his glove he casually shook it loose and let it bounce away like a too-small fish. Then he set himself again, left foot slightly forward, knees bent, bare hand and glove first on his knees, but only for an instant. As the sound of the machine changed slightly, he let his hand and glove fall away from his knees and he crouched even lower. His glove flashed like a turbine-powered vacuum cleaner, picking up every pitch.

Finally I found my voice. "How do you know?" I shouted.

"Know what?"

"Where the ball will go! They all look different!"

"They *are* different! You have to be ready for anything and watch where it goes and what kind of a spin it has!"

Catch and drop, catch and drop, catch and drop. He looked like a big leaguer. What team could possibly be good enough for him?

Half an hour later, as he sat at the table in the kitchenette, eating popcorn and still sweating, I could tell he was thrilled that he had impressed me. He never asked what I thought. He just sat and watched me, his smile huge, his eyes wide. I could tell he knew.

"What are we going to do, El?" I managed finally. "You have got to do something with this."

"This is nothing," he said. "This is just for baseball. This is what I'll do every day for the rest of my life to keep me sharp for hitting live pitches. That's all."

"You don't think people would pay to see you do something that no one else anywhere would even dare try?"

"Momma! I'm not a freak."

I wasn't so sure. "But you could challenge people, make them guess whether you could do it. Show them, demonstrate it. Then get them to bet that you wouldn't dare even stand in against it, let alone be able to hit it with a skinny, heavy bat."

His face fell. "Momma, even if I could do that or wanted to—which I don't—what do you think it would pay?"

"A lot."

"Millions a year?"

"Well, no, of course not, but—"

"That's what I can make as a big leaguer."

"That's a lot of years away."

"I know. But by then I'll be able to make even more. You know what? I'm on a schedule."

"To become a big leaguer?"

"Nope. That'll come when it comes. I'm on a schedule to move the machine even closer to the batters' boxes."

"Oh, Elgin, no."

"You think I can't do it?"

Would I ever again think he couldn't do anything? I didn't want to watch. I didn't want to see that machine taking aim at my son from twenty or even twenty-five feet away. I just listened to him tell of it every day for the next several weeks.

"Just for fun," he told me, "I moved the thing to about fifteen feet away. I think I finally found out what I can't hit."

We both laughed. If he came even close to that, he might be the best hitter of all time.

"You coming to my tryout a week from Saturday?"

"If you'll let me."

"From now on, I want as many people watching as I can. Lucky's bringing his family."

My heart seemed to stop. My voice was weak. "His family?"

"He's got two younger brothers and a bunch of nieces and nephews."

"Is he married?" I tried to sound casual.

"I told you, Momma. His wife died. Cancer or something."

"Uh-huh."

Luke Harkness, his two brothers, their wives and six children, and Momma were not the only spectators at the high school all-star summer traveling team tryouts. I guessed there were a hundred in the stands.

Hector Villagrande had eight spots to fill, and he required his six returning players to try out again too. There were no guarantees, and he proved that nearly every year by cutting at least one returnee.

About twenty ballplayers, plus the six returnees, had been invited. I finished second in the wind sprints to one of the returnees, a six-foot, two-hundred-pound shortstop. I finished fourth in throwing for distance, behind the shortstop, his twin-brother second baseman, and a muscular Mexican pitcher. When we ran around the entire field, I leaped to an early lead and held off a small, skinny outfielder I guessed would not make the team.

I had a little trouble running down everything hit to me in the outfield, but that was the one area in which I had the least experience. Hector and his assistants sent fly balls to the fence on almost every shot.

It was in the infield where I shined. My throws from short were straighter and truer than they had been the year before, but I knew I could not compete against the huge twin. I felt more comfortable at second where the throw was shorter, and I quickly picked up the double-play pivot. The other twin seemed to have a lock on second as well. My only hope was to hit so well that Hector would be forced to find a place for me.

Coach Villagrande saved hitting till last. He called all the players around him and assigned them to various spots in the field. Fourteen would trade off at the infield and outfield positions with every hitter. His returning catcher would handle all of batting practice. The remaining players would get ten pitches each.

The pitching was handled by a quartet of huge hurlers from the local American Legion team. Each was a big-league prospect.

The youngest was twenty, the oldest twenty-two. Three were right-handers, two white and one black. The other was a bald lefty. He didn't even have a rim of hair, nothing showing beneath the cap line.

I was sent to second where I traded off with the veteran with each new pitcher. The black right-hander was on the mound, and apparently he and his cohorts had all been told the same thing.

No mercy.

47

Though the sun was high and bright in Chicago, I sat at the tryout shivering in a light jacket, one I was embarrassed to be wearing in front of Lucky anyway.

"Should have brought my winter coat," I said idly, but I was certain he hadn't heard. He was a mother hen with his nieces and nephews and always had an eye on them, even when talking with me.

"Uh-huh," was all he said. But as I stared at Elgin, who was apparently failing in an attempt at small talk with the big twin second baseman, Luke Harkness draped his huge, wool-lined leather jacket around my shoulders.

I smiled a thank-you at him and he looked away. "I don't want *you* to be cold now," I said.

"I've got a higher thermostat than you," he said. "I'll probably have to get rid of this sweater too, before long."

"Nobody seems to be able to hit these guys," I said.

"Yeah, well, my brother and me'll hit em," the second baseman said. "Just watch."

"I expect to hit them too," I said, but the boy didn't respond. "What's your name, anyway?" I tried.

"Dirk," the boy grunted. "My turn."

"My name's Elgin," I said as Dirk glided into position to field a weak grounder. It was the first fair ball hit off the American Legion pitchers. Five hitters had gone down, and the pitchers kept rotating; sometimes two or three would throw to the same hitter.

"We all know your name, buddy," Dirk said. "You've got a lot to prove today."

I wanted to say I had proved all I needed to the last time I tried out for this team. But a buzz of excitement cruised from my seat to my head. This couldn't be better. They knew who I was and were watching to see what I could do.

"You're not going to get any base runners this morning," Hector Villagrande hollered, "so play every grounder as if you've got a guy on first and less than two outs!"

"Lefty pitching, Dirk," I whispered. "This guy gets a bat on Baldy, it's coming to you."

Dirk straightened and turned to glare at me. "Baldy happens to be my cousin!"

I wanted to apologize. I hadn't meant anything by it. I hadn't known the lefty's name, and I should have called him Lefty. But the fair, thin kid who had been so impressive in the distance run—who had swung and missed weakly at the first three pitches, somehow got his bat on this one and it rocketed between first and second, just as I predicted.

Dirk whirled too late and couldn't get his glove down or his foot out of the way and took the liner off the top of his shoe. He spun and danced and howled as the ball skittered into right.

Coach Villagrande screamed, "Are you all right?" marching from the third-base dugout to the foul line.

"Yeah! Woodell was distractin me!"

"Well, get out of there!"

I thought Hector was talking to me. He was not.

"If you can't keep your head and your glove and your butt in

the game, let somebody in there who can! Get in there, Woodell!"

"Sorry, Dirk," I said as we traded places. Dirk was red-faced
and swearing.

Two batters and a couple of dozen pitches later, a left-handed
hitter grounded sharply toward first. The first baseman came
charging, but I hollered him off. I speared the ball to my left in
the baseline, and hopped to my right with both feet while drawing the ball back.

I fired to the right of second, knowing that Dick, Dirk's twin,
would get there in time. I was right. Dick dragged his trailing
foot across the bag as he gathered in the throw and rifled the
ball to first.

The crispness, speed, and power of the play left everybody
speechless. The pitcher jogged over to slap gloves with Dick and
me. I smiled. Dick scowled.

In the stands, Lucas leaned close to me and bumped me with
his knee.

"That boy is gonna be your security someday, you know that?
He's got big league written all over him. I don't expect he'll hit
these pitchers any better'n the rest, but he won't do any worse.
And he's so much younger."

I just smiled. I had a feeling Elgin could hit these guys, any
one of them, even the left-hander.

One batter had hit a line drive to left after swinging and missing seven pitches. The only other fair balls had been the two to
second, a couple of fly balls, a few dribblers to the mound, and
some pop-ups.

Elgin could have used one of the many aluminum bats, but it
didn't surprise me when he stepped in with his wood one. He
was a purist, obsessed with the future. There was no sense getting anywhere with an advantage he could not carry with him to
the majors.

He looked like a big leaguer already, the way he dug in on the left side, pressed his helmet down with a free hand, and studied the pitcher. He took the first pitch, which was at the waist but outside by about two inches.

"Close enough to hit!" Hector called.

The next pitch would have split the plate if Elgin had not driven it to the left center field wall on one hop. The pitcher smiled and began to work harder. Elgin took every pitch that was off the plate, and none were off by more than inches. Hector barked with every taken pitch, but the line drives to all fields kept him mostly quiet.

Elgin hit six liners, a foul homer, and two foul tips, swinging and missing once against the first right-hander. He started to leave the box when the pitcher tossed the ball to the bald lefty, but Hector told him to stay in.

"I want you to take four pitches from each of the other three pitchers," he said. "And I want you to swing at every pitch, even if it's two feet off the plate."

Elgin nodded.

"Do you understand, Woodell? Because I am serious."

Elgin nodded again, keeping his eye on the pitcher.

"Let me hear you!" Hector hollered, and I winced. Why did he have to be so mean?

I was so excited I could hardly stand it. I was facing the best pitching of my life, even better than Raleigh Lincoln Sr. These guys were big and young and strong and fast and smart. Their pitches moved. They had pride. They didn't want anyone hitting them, and they didn't expect many high schoolers would. Of course, they hadn't yet faced Dick, the shortstop, who had hit over four hundred the season before. But they surely didn't guess a twelve-year-old would make them look like batting practice pitchers.

Their assignment had been—as Hector had told everyone— to show us kids what real pitching was all about. He had told us not to expect to get a bat on the ball off any of these guys.

"Then you won't be disappointed. And when they're done with you, we'll throw you some real BP and you can show us what you've got."

I made the first right-hander look hittable.

"The other guys wore him out for you," Hector said as the pitchers traded places. But that brought laughter from the crowd. They had to wonder if anybody could get me out.

"You want any warm-up pitches?" I asked the left-hander.

"Just get in there," Baldy growled. "All I want is you."

I skipped to the other side of the plate and dug in, looking up just in time to see the first pitch sailing at my head. How dare this guy do that to me in batting practice? I ducked a couple of inches and the ball skipped lightly off my helmet and banged off one of the backstop posts, rolling all the way back to the mound. I pretended not to have seen or felt the pitch.

Baldy picked up the ball and went into his windup again. He had seen me look up in time to make that small move. I was ready for the next one, which jammed me. I stepped toward third and dragged my bat through the strike zone, drilling the ball straight back at the pitcher, right to his glove. He stared at me. I stared back. The next pitch was hellacious. It came flashing toward the outside corner with as much movement as I had ever seen, other than off the machine. I swung late and missed.

Baldy looked pumped, but the strike only got me into my rhythm. I knew he couldn't sneak another hittable pitch past me. No one could. I could feel it. I was in sync, ready to hit, eager for the lefty's best stuff.

48

Just before Baldy went into his windup, Hector Villagrande shouted, "Last pitch!"

I backed out of the box and glared at the coach. I wasn't challenging him. I was just disappointed. We had just started something, and it was going to be a show. Strength against strength. Who was the best?

"I mean with this pitcher," Hector said. "You still face the other two guys."

I stepped back in, but now Baldy was glaring at the coach.

"Okay!" Hector said. "What do *you* want?"

"I want to strike him out!"

"Try," Hector said, and I heard glee in his voice.

I cracked a high, outside pitch into right center. I sent a low pitch, which would have nipped the corner, screaming past Dirk at second base. When I did the same with an inside curve, Hector chirped at me.

"Hey, hey, hey, you're not trying to show anybody up except the pitcher. You take the inside pitch to left. You can spray the outside pitches to the right side."

I had been caught. I liked seeing Dirk bend and stretch and grunt after a ball just out of his reach. These pitches, tough as they were, looked big and slow and fat compared to the ones off my pitching machine from twenty-five feet away. I had time to think, to calculate, to see the rotation, to make my judgment. I knew experts would think I was crazy if I ever said that I hit different pitches at different points on the ball.

But it was true. Though most people believed it was impossible for hitters to really see eighty-five mile an hour and faster pitches hit their bats, I knew I could. This guy was easily throwing that hard, and I hit on top of the ball to create a spin that curled it over the infield and to the ground before the outfielders could get to it. I felt I could do that all day. When I wanted height and distance, say for a deep sacrifice fly, I hit under the ball. And with every swing, I believed I was seeing the ball and the bat meet.

Baldy was sweating on this chilly morning. He made me swing and miss once and foul off three pitches. At one point he had me down one-and-two, before I flied deep to left. Hector waved the lefty out of there and let the other two righties have a shot. From the other side of the plate, I missed a few good change-ups and popped weakly twice—unusual for me—but mostly I continued to flare solid hits to all fields. I hit several grounders just out of the reach of the infielders, and when I hit one each right at the Dick and Dirk brothers, they were so eager that one overthrew first and the other muffed the play.

No one would talk about anything else that happened there. Hector brought in a true batting practice pitcher and let everyone have his raps. Everyone except me. He asked me to go across the street and take infield practice.

A coach drove hard grounders and liners at Elgin. The boy ran, crouched, dived, speared, pivoted, threw. He wasn't perfect, but he was something. What other kid that age could catch such missiles off the bat of an adult who was pushing to see how good he was?

The tryout broke up. Coach Villagrande addressed the adults, telling them when the next session would be, that some would be getting calls during the week informing them that their sons need not show up again.

There was no way Elgin could be cut this time. He was the best hitter already. He was one of the best fielders and throwers too. He didn't have the range or the arm of the twins, but they were eighteen.

Luke's relatives waved their good-byes and left with everyone else. Elgin's workout across the street continued. Hector spoke briefly with his coaches before they headed for their cars. He knelt in front of the dugout to talk to the four Legion pitchers. When they left, only Hector and Lucas and I remained in the rickety park. He peered across the street.

"Had enough?" he bellowed.

"I can play all day," Elgin said with the clear, high-pitched voice of youth. He would be thirteen in a few weeks.

It would take all my reserves to keep from sticking up for my son, from demanding to know how he could have been passed over the year before. I stood as Hector approached with Elgin, climbing gingerly up the wood steps.

"Please," he said in a charming accent. "Sit down. I need to talk to you privately."

Luke began to leave.

"Mr. Harkness is a friend of the family," I said. "May he stay?"

"Certainly."

"And Elgin?"

"Of course. I have sent a coach to see if he can get hold of Jim Koenig, coach of the local American Legion team."

"Why?"

"It may sound strange to you, ma'am, but Elgin is ready for that level."

"You know he's had very little actual game experience. Just parts of a couple of seasons and one full one."

Hector smiled shyly. "And part of that is my fault, is it not?"

I shrugged.

"Of course it is," he said. "But if my not finding him a spot last year—on my team or any other—had anything to do with the determination that made him work as hard as he has, I deserve some credit."

I smiled and said nothing. Hector continued.

"Elgin," he said, "I need to know if you felt you could hit the ball anywhere you wanted off those four pitchers."

I nodded.

"You were hitting, in other words, at my shortstop and second basemen on purpose?"

I hesitated.

"You can tell me. I know they can be difficult. Both are excellent players."

"Yes, they are."

"You made them look bad."

"I'm sorry."

"But you did it on purpose."

I nodded. "I shouldn't have. I'm sorry. They could have looked just as good if they had fielded those balls."

"You were hitting them just out of their reach."

I nodded again.

"You showed hints of being able to do that last year when I thought you were not ready. But you were not hitting off the caliber of pitchers you hit off today. Do you have any idea of your potential?"

"No, sir. That's just it. I want to play. I need game situations. It's killing me not to be able to do it in competition."

"I wish I could help you."

"I'm not going to make this team again?"

Hector held up a hand. "Last year you had the ability and not the attitude. This year you have the attitude but you're way ahead of us. I could use you. I could win the state again with you. But I would not be doing the right thing for you."

"But I want to play for this team! Put me anywhere! I need game experience."

"I know you do. But what good will it do you to hit eight or nine hundred in a league you're too good for?"

"I wouldn't mind that."

Hector laughed. "I wouldn't either, but it wouldn't be fair. Not to our opponents. Not to your teammates. Not to you."

"But what if there's no room for me on the American Legion team? Nobody's gonna let me play in a league for eighteen-year-olds."

"Son, listen. You're going to be playing somewhere this summer."

That was a relief. It scared me to think I had to jump two or three levels just to find a place to play. What if I wasn't ready?

Jim Koenig arrived, a tall, thin man with short black hair. "So you're the one who humiliated my pitchers today, huh? I could use a switch-hitter. Hector tells me you've got skills in the field too. Frankly, we had our eyes on Dirk for second base, but we hate to break up the twins. Hector tells me Dirk is better than you in the field and has a stronger arm, but if you can hit my pitchers, you'll hit a couple of hundred points higher than he would at this level."

I could hardly sit still. I wanted to discuss baseball with this fascinating, friendly man. But I couldn't speak.

"I'll make sure my guys treat you right, and past that I won't make any promises. If this was luck, if you're a fluke, you're back to Hector's team in a New York minute. Got it?"

I didn't know what a New York minute was, but I got it.

"We have ten preseason games. I'll try you at second. Probably hit you seventh or eighth. That'll tell us where you fit. I'm willing to start you and play you every inning of every preseason game, even if you bat zero. Get comfortable, find your rhythm, and show me what you've got. We start workouts Monday night and we practice or play every day for the next three weeks."

He turned to Momma. "Can he be there, Mom?"

She smiled. "He'll be there."

"And how do you feel about all this, ma'am?"

Momma seemed to think for a second. "I may never be able

to say," she said. "Proud, for sure. I can't tell you how marvelous this is."

"Well," Jim Koenig said, "I just hope I'm not doing something bad for the boy. He deserves a chance, but I'd sure hate to ruin him for the future."

49

Three weeks, five practices, and ten games later, I had made a believer out of Jim Koenig and fourteen teammates. As the only player on the team to play every inning, I had racked up these personal stats:

At Bats	Runs	Hits	Doubles	Triples	HRs	RBI	Sacrifices	Average
33	11	26	12	3	0	14	3	.788

I had gone hitless in my first game but had driven in two runs on two sacrifices—one a fly and one a bunt. In the next nine games I had at least two hits per game, twice went four-for-four, and finished with ten hits in my last eleven at bats.

That prompted another meeting with Coach Koenig, this time at the hotel with only Momma and me.

"I don't know quite how to tell you this, ma'am," the coach began, "but your son is a phenomenon, almost a freak of nature. I've been in the game a long time, and outside of all-star big leaguers, this boy is the best hitter I've ever seen. He doesn't get fooled. He doesn't strike out. Well, you struck out once, right?"

I nodded.

"But in that at bat he hit foul his farthest ball of the year. He's not a home run hitter yet. His power takes him only about three hundred feet. But, heck, he's a child. They shifted on him, pulled in on him, threw at him, walked him intentionally. But they couldn't stop him."

"I've enjoyed watching him," Momma said. "It's been as exciting to me as to anyone. I'm a little scared, though. What am I supposed to do with a child like this?"

"Keep him doing whatever he's doing. He's a natural who also works hard. If he doesn't get tired of the game, he's going to be a superstar someday."

"He's a superstar now, isn't he?" she said.

"Well, yes, ma'am, at this level. But I'm talking about the big time. The majors. This boy has unlimited potential."

Clearly Mr. Koenig had come to tell me more than this. I just sat and smiled.

"Ma'am, American Legion is top-drawer amateur baseball. Some of the best teams in the country come from Illinois. The Arlington Heights team makes the state and national tournaments almost every year, and we've been beating them the last few seasons."

I nodded.

"Stars from Legion ball play division-one college baseball. Many of them make the pros and a few have become big-leaguers. What I'm telling you is that big-league scouts watch our games."

Was he going to tell me that they would laugh at a soon-to-be thirteen-year-old on the field? That Coach Koenig will look silly counting on a kid to carry his team?

"Ma'am, we won all ten of our preseason games. I've never seen crowds like that before, and I've never seen scouts at games that don't count. They were there with their radar guns and their stopwatches. I know they were looking at our pitchers, who, by the way, didn't allow as many hits in ten games as Elgin got off them in Hector's tryouts."

I was patient.

"Do you understand what I'm trying to tell you, ma'am?"

"No, sir."

"You need a lawyer."

"Whatever for? And how could I afford one?"

"An adviser. An agent. Someone to represent you. These guys are vultures, and you've got a lot of legal things to think about."

"Like what?"

"Like the fact that I had to jump through all kinds of hoops just to get permission for Elgin to play Legion ball. Can you imagine what it would take to allow him to play professionally?"

"Oh, Mr. Koenig, when that time comes, I'm sure Billy Ray Thatcher from Hattiesburg would be happy to—"

"Ma'am, that time has come! Three scouts want to talk to you now. Don't talk to them alone. Don't sign anything, don't agree to anything. I don't know if anyone anywhere could ever clear the way for someone who hasn't graduated high school to play professionally, but if they can they will, and Elgin will be so much fresh meat. They'll grind him up, use him, and discard him."

"You're scarin me, Coach."

"I'm trying to. Can you imagine how noisy it will be if a child starts on a big-league path? It'll be the biggest thing that's ever happened to the game. No one will believe it until they see it, and if Elgin can keep doing what he's been doing, he'll be the rage."

"What about school? What about travelin? I can't afford to go with him on big trips."

"Yes, you can. That's what you negotiate. If someone wants Elgin, you're part of the package."

"But I have a job."

"You won't need a job."

"But what if Elgin loses it? What if he is injured? Gets tired of it?"

"Momma!"

"You could, El. There are no guarantees. I know the odds against a player makin a living at baseball. What are the odds for a child who just turned thirteen?"

Jim Koenig leaned back on the couch. "Now you're asking the right questions. Now you know why you need counsel."

"Would you help us?"

He held up both hands. "No way. I don't want to be accused of making money off a talent, and you need to have someone you're paying to look out for your best interests. It has to be someone you know, someone you trust. This man from Hattiesburg you mentioned—"

"Billy Ray Thatcher."

"Does he have experience with this?"

"He's Bernie Pincham's agent."

"Well, there you go. Talk to him right away. The best I can do is keep these scouts away. I won't give them your name or address or phone number."

"We use the pay phone in the hall."

"All the better. I'll send everybody to Mr. Thatcher. Uh, could I speak with you privately for a moment, ma'am?"

I cocked my head and thought. "No, sir, I think anything you want to say to me, Elgin can hear."

Koenig shrugged. "Suit yourself. I just want to tell you that you're looking at some huge money here."

"I gathered that."

"I'm talking millions." He sneaked a peek at Elgin.

"Sir?" I said.

He turned back. "Millions."

"I'd say that's a long shot, but let's say you're right. We'll just make sure Elgin gets good counsel."

"But, Mrs. Woodell. You'll likely never have to work again."

"Oh, I expect I'll be plenty busy."

I went to bed that night unable to sleep. My mind raced with my pulse. I had always dreamed of being a big-league baseball player. How soon could it happen? How old did you have to be? I'd heard of big leaguers who began in their late teens. Joe

Nuxhall pitched for the Reds when he was fifteen, but that was when a lot of the regulars were fighting in World War II.

More than anything, I wanted competition. It was nice to be noticed, and if the day came when I tore up the big leagues, I guessed that would be all right. But something inside told me that I was simply ahead. I wasn't the best ballplayer anywhere; not yet, not already.

I started the regular season batting second and playing second base, finally thirteen but still by far the youngest kid in the league. I had a little trouble in the field, sometimes getting taken out of the double play by bigger players sliding into me. I made a few more errors than someone five years older (or more) might have made. But as usual, I hit from the start.

Three games into the season I was five-for-eight with a double. I went two-for-three the next game to send my average well over .600, then saw how quickly the numbers can change when I went one-for-four the next game and was eight-for-fifteen, or .533. That put me third on the team and eighth in the league after five games.

I had already been made famous by local newspapers and television stations. It was interesting to people that a boy of thirteen had been cleared to play in a league where the next youngest player was eighteen. My mother had had to sign all kinds of papers to absolve the league of any responsibility for my health.

It was the stretch of the next five games that really put me on the map. Our Chicago Legion team—which began the season with a record of four-and-one—won five straight. I came to the plate twenty times, walked three times (twice intentionally), and was otherwise seventeen-for-seventeen.

I went three-for-three three times and four-for-four twice with three doubles and a triple. I had eight RBIs and scored five times. The five games were played in eight days. Jim Koenig said, "The kid had a nice season last week."

In the eleventh and twelfth games of the year I was oh-for-two and one-for-three, dropping my average to .702. The second-best hitter in Legion ball in the state was hitting .505. Media swamped the games, and scouts from nearly every major-league team trailed the team. Stories in the daily papers covered behind-the-scenes maneuvering to somehow get around all the rules against a minor playing professional baseball. Everyone agreed: I deserved a chance to start moving up. The City League was considered a step down from Legion ball. And I could not play for a college team unless I attended that college. The only logical next step was the pros, and that didn't seem all that logical.

I talked with my mother of nothing except the future. And I still spent just a little over an hour every night in the cellar with the machine I had come to love. I would never stop that daily regimen, I told myself. I knew it was the secret, a secret I planned to take to my grave.

In my next eight games I went twenty-for-thirty with thirteen RBIs, three triples, eight doubles, and fourteen runs. Best of all, I had a three-hit game that included a triple and a home run. I had thought I would never hit one out of a big park. I had a couple that bounced off the wall, but it was a thrill to see one drop straight down over the right field fence, just inside the line three hundred and five feet from the plate. I would not swing for the fences. I knew better. Until I grew up, I would not be a power hitter, but with the solid contact I always made, I knew the occasional home run had to come.

Batting .687 and becoming a flawless fielder, I was the heart of a fifteen-and-five team on its way to the state championship. I wondered if there was a pitcher anywhere who could get me out consistently. The best hitters in the majors were out almost seven times out of ten. What would that feel like?

50

Twenty games into the season I sent Elgin's stats to Billy Ray:

At Bats	Runs	Hits	Doubles	Triples	HRs	RBI	Sacrifices	Average
67	24	46	14	4	1	23	6	.687

Billy Ray called me at my office. "You say this is with an American Legion team?"

"Yes, sir."

"And Elgin is thirteen now?"

"Just turned."

He whistled through his teeth. "Yes, ma'am, I think I had better visit you."

Now he sat in our transient hotel flat with his briefcase on his lap, his knees together to support it, the toes of his wing tips pointing at each other.

"What I need to know, Miriam," he said, in his slow, liquid way, "is exactly what you want. I'm retiring, but I will gladly represent you for as long as Elgin plays the game. That could be a long time, but it could just as easily be a short time. I advise you to move cautiously with his best interests in mind. There is likely money to be made in short order. I expect that you would be wiser than your late husband was."

"I'm assuming that's not a question," I said. "You know me well enough."

"I know you," he said with a smile. "You probably wouldn't want a penny of Elgin's money. Neither do I, but we're both going to be involved until he's of age. I will charge you only my hourly rate. That will not come due until he has realized some income."

"Excuse me," Elgin said, "but are you sure you don't want a percentage? It could be millions."

"Oh, it likely will be," Mr. Thatcher said. "But I don't need it and I don't want it. Enough people will come to you with their hands out, and I advise you to ignore them. Very few will have your interests at heart. I never want to be accused of being one of them."

"That's why you're here," I said. "What happens now?"

"The baseball rules say a team can't draft a kid until his high school class graduates. If he doesn't sign and goes to college, he can't be drafted until after his junior year."

"Any way around it?"

"It's never been tested in baseball. When I represented Bernie Pincham things had already changed in basketball. Years ago the hardship rule was instituted where a kid could inform the league if he was an underclassman and wanted to be entered in the draft. Now it's just standard procedure. The NBA can't keep a kid out of a draft just because he's young."

"Well, that's the issue here, isn't it?" I said.

"Everyone knows you can't draft a high schooler till he graduates, but what about a junior high kid? It's never come up."

"So, what will you do?"

"Take the gentlemanly and inexpensive route first. I will inform the commissioner's office that we want Elgin in the June draft. If that is refused for any reason, I establish the hardship situation."

I stiffened.

"Now, Miriam, I know you're a hardworking and proud woman. You're solvent and even saving money. But the fact is, your income qualifies you for food stamps."

"You know better than that."

"Of course, but don't be so proud that you stand in the way of your son living out his dream. Your humble means may help make Elgin the youngest player in the history of pro sports."

"But you won't go that route unless we have to, right?"

"Right. Meanwhile, I'll set up at the Hyatt Regency downtown. Steer every request, every offer, every approach to me. I'm sure more than one team has already been in the baseball commissioner's office trying to convince him it would be in the best interests of baseball to allow a child into the June draft. On the other side will be local social workers and the huge, independent baseball machine that has always been a law unto itself. Baseball doesn't need this, but the public may force baseball's hand."

I scowled. "It's a shame Elgin can't play at a level where everybody else can compete with him."

"Then you want me to push the commissioner."

"I want Elgin to keep his priorities. No travel till school's out, and he's goin nowhere without me."

Mr. Thatcher was taking notes. "This is good," he said. "Elgin, how is your team going to feel if it loses you halfway through the season?"

"I don't know," Elgin said, "but I don't think I'd like it."

Thatcher raised his eyebrows. "If you do get into the draft and some team signs you, you're theirs."

Elgin said, "Somebody told me the rookie leagues aren't much better than Legion ball."

"Probably true," Billy Ray said. "Are you saying you don't want to sign with a team that starts you lower than, say, A ball?"

"How about double-A?" Elgin said.

Mr. Thatcher set his briefcase on the couch. "Try this on," he said. "Let's say we get you into the draft. Then you go on record that you won't sign with anybody until the Legion season is over. That'll make you look wonderful."

"I'd go to the majors right now if I thought they'd let me, but nobody's going to do that. I owe it to my team to stick with them."

"That's going to be good for Legion ball, because the crowds will start showing up for your games. We'll stipulate that who-ever signs you gets you only after the Legion season, provided they start you no lower than double-A and that you are invited to spring training with the big club next spring."

I sucked in a huge breath. Spring training in the majors? Maybe Mr. Thatcher was getting ahead of himself.

"Let me explain it this way, Elgin," he said. "Everyone will think it's a publicity stunt. I will look like a bad guy. But if you're a first-round pick, you deserve a huge signing bonus, and I'll get it for you. A double-A first-round pick who goes to spring train-ing, publicity stunt or not, gets a certain amount.

"Do I think you're going to earn a starting spot on a big-league club before you're fourteen years old next spring? Of course not. For one thing, your mother won't let you play until school's out. But you can go to spring training during spring break, and if you perform well, your stock will rise."

Momma stood and paced. "Elgin, you'd better start getting changed. Mr. Thatcher offered to drive us to the game."

More than a thousand crowded the little ball field that night. At least a dozen scouts were there, some with video cameras. On my way to infield practice, two men in suits asked to see me.

"Son, I just need a second," one of them said, and several oth-ers gathered around.

"I'll want a minute too, Elgin."

"Me too, son."

"Ho! Hey! Wait a minute over there!" It was Coach Koenig. His face was red and he was running. "Woodell, get to your po-sition if you want to play tonight! Now!"

"We just needed a second with him, Coach," one of the men said.

"I told you, he's not talking to anybody during the season. And when he's available, he will have counsel."

"Coach?" I said.

"I told you to get on the field!"

"I will, but I just wanted you to know that I have counsel. He's here."

"You have an agent?" one of the scouts demanded.

"He didn't say that!" Koenig shouted.

"He did too! Now where is he?"

"He's not an agent," I said as Koenig dragged me away. "He's an attorney, and he's right up there with my mother."

"Oh, Elgin," Koenig whined, "you never should have told em who your mother was."

51

I had just begun to tell Billy Ray about Lucas, and I was irritated that he seemed to ignore me. I stopped and waited for his attention, but when he spoke, he was still looking elsewhere.

I followed his eyes to a group of men, all seeming to hurry up the stadium steps while pretending not to. Mr. Thatcher leaned toward me. "Don't say one word, understand? Don't even acknowledge who you are."

The men approached, notebooks and business cards in hand. Some had radar guns bulging from sport coat pockets. Most wore stopwatches around their necks.

"Are you Mrs. Woodell?" two asked.

It was all I could do to keep from nodding. What could be wrong with admitting who I was?

"Depends," Mr. Thatcher answered, rising. "Who may I say is calling?"

The men looked at him, then at me, then back at him. He began distributing his cards.

"Thatcher's the name. I represent the Woodells. You may reach me by phone, fax, snail mail, or e-mail, or you may reach me for the next few days at the Hyatt Regency downtown. For now—"

"Well, I'd like to speak with you right now, if possi—"

"For now," Mr. Thatcher repeated, "I am engaged in a private conversation and do not wish to be disturbed."

"Can you tell us when you might be available?"

"During the game when Chicago is in the field. But not in the first inning."

The scouts began to take seats near Billy Ray and me.

"Gentlemen, please," Billy Ray said, "give us some space. I will talk with each of you, I promise."

The scouts moved down a few rows. "I'm sorry, Miriam. You were saying?"

"That Lucas will be here later. He wants me to start preparing Elgin for the news about us."

"That you are to be married?"

"Oh, my, no! But the other day, we uh, held hands for the first time and—"

Billy Ray grinned. "Perhaps you need me to break that news to your son."

"Don't mock me. Lucas and I have talked for hours about how seriously we take each other, and we said long ago that we would just be friends."

"I don't need to tell you, that doesn't work for long, Miriam."

"Well, we thought it might. He told me I would know if he ever changed his mind. He said he wouldn't even hold my hand unless he was in love with me."

Mr. Thatcher looked away again, clearly embarrassed. I quit talking.

He turned back to me. "Don't misunderstand my discomfort, Miriam," he said. "I miss my wife."

"Don't tell me something's happened to Miz Thatcher!"

"No, no. I was with her just this morning. But Miriam, when you have a long, happy marriage, you miss one another whenever you're apart."

"That's beautiful."

"Maybe. Your story got to me. You see, Shirley and I felt the same way when we courted. We weren't pretending to be just friends. Anyway, she felt the same way Mr. Harkness feels. I'll be pleased to meet him."

Lucas and I had taken a walk one night while Elgin was in the cellar. We had laughed a lot, talked a lot, been quiet even more. We stood closer to each other, brushed shoulders as we sat and laughed. I had held his gaze a little longer than normal, just enough to increase my pulse and wonder if my face had flushed.

On the way back to my flat, he held my elbow as we crossed the street. That implied nothing, but when we were safely across he let his hand slide down to mine. He'd silently declared himself, unless he a bad memory.

I had so longed for his touch that my hand in his was every bit as meaningful and warm and loving and sensual as an embrace. I gripped his palm firmly, trying to convey all I wanted to say.

Though we didn't touch each other again when he was saying good-bye, we might as well have. We held each other's eyes long enough to communicate.

Elgin had forgotten to take his spikes the last time he worked at Lucky's, so I'd agreed to take them there for repair. When I walked in Luke looked up and smiled. I set the shoes on the counter then thrust out my hand as if to shake his. He looked puzzled, but shook my hand. When he did, I covered his also with my other hand.

"I'm Miriam Woodell," I said. "You must be Lucky."

"I am today," he said, also covering my hands with his. And there we stood, four hands entwined, looking deeply into each other's eyes. When another customer entered he went back to business, but I was encouraged.

I wanted to confirm that he was coming to Elgin's next game, so I waited as he tagged Elgin's shoes and waited on the next customer. The man made a small purchase and thanked Luke, who said, "Now, if you want a real deal, you can have that glass bowl over there for two dollars."

The man looked at it. "You'll never sell that monstrosity," he said.

Luke laughed heartily. "Yeah, I'll probably have to pay someone to take it off my hands. Would you believe I paid nine dollars for that and had it priced at twenty for a while?"

"No!"

Luke held up a hand. "Honest. Proved I was human, didn't I?"

"Proved you were an idiot," the man said, smiling.

"We've all got those ugly glass bowls in our lives, don't we? Sure you don't want it? I'm willing to take a seven-dollar loss on it."

They both laughed as the man left.

I approached again. Luke was still smiling. "Maybe it looked pretty in the dim light of the estate sale."

I looked at the piece and shook my head. "It's so ugly it's cute."

"You like it," he said.

"I kinda do," I admitted.

"You're not serious."

"No, but sort of. I mean I wouldn't use it for anything but a conversation starter."

"It would serve that well," he said. "I'd be willing to sell it to a beautiful woman like you for what I paid for it. Nine bucks."

"You are a rascal," I said.

"Hey, if you were a friend or something I could cut you a deal, but if I remember correctly, we just met."

"Indeed," I said.

"Buy that piece before someone else snaps it up at full price, and we can shake hands again."

"A rascal," I repeated, winking at him as I left.

52

"I don't want to bother you before the game, Champ," Jim Koenig said, "but not all of those guys were scouts."

"Agents?"

"No, they'll come later. Good thing you've got your friend representing you, because agents will descend like vultures. I'm not saying there aren't some good ones, but how would you know?"

"So who were those guys?"

"Well, one was a local guy who works for *Sports Illustrated*. He was supposed to do a 'Faces in the Crowd' thing on you. Now he says they're asking him to do some full-blown deal. You'd better have your friend, uh—"

"Mr. Thatcher."

"Yeah, you'd better have Thatcher talk to him, huh?"

"I guess."

"You just concentrate on getting some hits tonight."

In the top of the first I covered first on a bunt up the line and was run over by the Arlington Heights leadoff man. I helped the runner up.

"That was bush league," I said, smiling and patting him on the rear. "Maybe next time you'd like a mouthful of cleats."

He turned and stared at me. "Lookin for trouble, Pee-wee?"

"I'm just looking to stay on my side of the baseline. Veteran like you ought to know how to do that by now."

The kid made a move toward me and the benches cleared. No way I needed to be held back. I had plotted my escape.

"You'd better stay outa my face, little man," the runner said.

"It's tough when Pee-wee helps nail you by two steps on a Little League bunt, isn't it?" I said.

My teammates roared, and the Arlington guy struggled to break free. The umpires broke it up, and the plate ump approached the visitors' bench.

"The runner was inside the line and was out regardless. That's the end of it. Any more and somebody's walkin!"

With one out and no score in the bottom of the first, I had to skip out of the way of a pitch behind my ear. The ump came charging out from behind the plate.

"Oh, don't call that!" I said. "That easy of a pitch had to be an accident!"

The umpire pointed at the pitcher.

"Slipped," the pitcher said.

"Don't let it slip again," the ump said.

The next pitch was in the dirt, a foot in front of my feet. I danced to elude it and here came the ump again.

"That's a warning, Arlington! You're a better pitcher than that!"

I laced the next pitch about two feet above the pitcher's head. The center fielder took a step in, but the ball was still rising and flew over his head. The ball hit near the bottom of the center field fence as I rounded first. It skipped to the right and I never slowed. I'd never had an inside-the-park homer before, but I could smell this one. And with all the right people in the stands.

Concentrate, I told myself. *No mistakes. Shortest distance. All speed.* I hit second with my inside foot and pivoted, shifting my attention from the ball to my third-base coach. Then the lights went out. My breath escaped in a huge grunt and I could not inhale. I was not on solid ground, could see nothing, and felt the cool night air on my head as my helmet flew away.

Where was I? What was happening? Was I dreaming? I hit on

my heels first, somersaulting backward and winding up on my back with pain in my sternum and still no breath.

I opened my eyes and panicked. I needed to breathe! Was I going to die right here in front of my mother and Mr. Thatcher and all the scouts? Was this it? Was it over? I had hardly begun!

Jim Koenig bent over me, screaming at everyone else to back off and threatening the Arlington shortstop's life. So that was it. Their leadoff man was the shortstop. I had thought he might try something if I tried to steal second or break up a double play, but I forgot all about him with an inside-the-parker on the line.

Koenig loosened my belt, but still I thrashed, desperate for air.

"You'll breathe, buddy. Give me a second. This happens all the time."

The coach reached under my lower back and lifted my rear off the ground. I felt a stretch in my chest, a building of pressure. It seemed an eternity since I'd had air in my lungs.

Koenig worked quickly, letting me back down. "Relax!" he commanded, grabbing my ankles and pressing them toward my seat, forcing my knees to my chest. When he straightened my legs again, my lungs expanded and I sucked in cool, sweet air. My head cleared, the pain got worse, and I was mad. It all came to me. That shortstop had driven an elbow into my ribs when I rounded second on the dead run, knocking the wind from me and blowing me into left field.

My eyes darted among the Arlington players while I was still on my back in the grass.

"Don't even think about it," Koenig said. "He's already been ejected."

"Do I get third?"

"I'm arguing for home. They hadn't even touched the ball yet."

I stood and buckled my belt. Worse than the pain, worse than the shortness of breath, worse than the disappointment of not legging out the homer, I was scared. Not having been able to breathe had shaken me. But I had held my own against this kid in the top of the inning. And I had stood up to the pitcher who tried to hit me. I would have taken on the shortstop again if he'd still been on the field.

I rubbed my chest, took deep breaths, and bent, hands on my knees. The umpire awarded me the plate, which threw the Arlington coach into a tizzy.

"Protest all you want," the ump said. "This kid touches third and home on his own, he stays in the game."

"Don't feel obligated," Coach Koenig said. "You can sit the rest of this one out."

"No way. I'm all right."

I didn't want to just walk around third. I broke into a trot, which brought a long ovation, even from some of the Arlington guys. Both teams were on the field again, glaring, posturing.

"Let's go, guys!" I shouted, my breastbone smarting with every step. "Let's get back to winning this thing!"

I got a chance to sit while Arlington brought in a new second baseman and moved their original one to short.

At the end of the dugout stood a solitary figure with a large paper sack under his arm. He wore a leather jacket and sported a bushy red beard. "Anything had happened to you, El, I would've been out there swinging."

"Hey, Lucky. I'm all right. Thanks for coming."

"Are you kidding? I wouldn't miss a game if I didn't have to."

"Get out. You just came to be with Mom."

"You noticed?"

"No. I'm blind."

Luke smiled and looked away. I was startled. I had been just teasing. I liked how my mother was when Lucky was around. But now what was he trying to tell me? I looked to see how serious he was. Maybe he was putting me on.

"Woodell! You in or out?"

I stood. Time to take the field again? No. What was Koenig hollering about?

"Stay in the game, buddy!" he said. "No extra points for owies, you know."

I smiled and sneaked a peek back at Lucky. He had already headed into the stands.

53

Lucas was awkward and quiet when I introduced him to Billy Ray.

"I've heard a lot about you, Mr. Harkness," Mr. Thatcher said.

"Yes, sir, same here. Thank you."

It was the top of the second, and like we expected, the scouts began burrowing their way back up to Billy Ray.

"Is this Mr. Woodell?" one asked.

Lucas laughed. "No, sir!" he said, bolder with an audience. "Lucky Harkness of Lucky's Secondhand. Come on over and I'll make ya a deal."

They were clearly not interested in anyone not related to or representing Elgin.

"Excuse me, Luke, Miriam," Mr. Thatcher said, and he led the scouts to the end of the bleachers like a pied piper.

"Brought something for you," Luke said when we were alone.

He thrust out a brown paper sack, and I knew from the shape and weight what it was. I was about to open it when Luke said, "Grounder to Elgin."

My eyes darted to my son, who raced to his left and back-handed a three-hopper near second. He fired to first to nip the runner by a half step. The crowd cheered loudly, but I knew it had been a routine play. I couldn't count the times Elgin had told me, "Teams that win make the routine plays. The tough ones won't make you or break you if you make the rest."

I felt the cool night air on the back of my neck as I pulled the hideous glass bowl from the bag.

"I'll cherish it forever," I said, laughing.

"I knew you'd love it," Luke said. "It's not so ugly in the dark, is it?"

"Oh, I don't know," I said, turning it toward the lights. "It even feels ugly."

"Like me," he said, still smiling. "Ugly even in the dark."

"You don't believe that," I said, suddenly serious. "With your hair shorter and your beard trimmed, you look younger and very attractive."

"Younger than what?" he said, eyes dancing.

"Younger than, um, you looked when I met you."

"I didn't mean to get into this, Miriam."

I loved the way he said my name, almost as if he revered it.

"I just hope you're not embarrassed to be seen hangin around with a broken-down old veteran your kid thinks looks like a biker."

"When I first saw you, I could see what he meant. Your hair was as long as your beard."

"You let me walk you home."

"You had just saved my life. I felt safe with you."

"You are," he said.

I slipped my hand into the crook of his elbow and turned to face the field. He pressed his arm close to his side, and I loved him.

"No more talk about looks," I said. "I'm proud to be seen with you."

"But you're so pretty. Heads turn everywhere you—"

"Stop," I said. "That's always bothered me. One of the things I liked about you was that you didn't leer at me."

Luke looked away and laughed.

"What?" I said, turning to face him. "You didn't leer at me, did you?"

He laughed again. "Apparently not when you were looking."

I shook my head and slid closer. "Thanks for the bowl," I said. "It'll be hard to top that."

I sat on the bench next to the only other player on the Legion team who seemed to care as much as I did about statistics. A local college sophomore, he was a reserve outfielder who hardly ever saw action, but he knew everyone's averages.

"So, what am I hitting now, Doyle?" I said.

"Under seven hundred, but two more hits and you'll be back up there. You're forty-seven for sixty-eight. You have to have forty-nine hits by your seventieth at bat to hit seven hundred right on the head."

I cocked my head. "Not a bad goal."

Doyle snorted. "Nobody else in the state is over five hundred anymore."

I nodded. "I can't start worrying about numbers now. I just think about one pitch at a time."

"You think about the count."

"Course. The count, the score, the outs, who's on, what pitch I can expect, and where to put it."

"Wish it was that easy for the rest of us."

"You think it's easy for me?" I said.

Doyle shook his head. "If it isn't, you're a good actor. I see your wheels turning from the bench to the box. It's like you decide what you need to do with a pitch, and you just do it."

"It's kind of like that, yeah," I said.

"Want to know what it's like for us humans?"

"Sure," I said, smiling. "What's it like for you humans?"

"It's like hoping not to get killed, hoping to do anything but strike out so you can fling your bat in disgust as if you can't believe you didn't hit one out."

I laughed. "Is that why you do that, Doyle?"

"We all act like we can't believe we're not batting a thousand. Then you come along and make us look sick."

"Sorry."

"Don't be. We don't mind winning. I wouldn't mind playing more, though."

"You will. I see you starting in the outfield when Andy and Toby are gone next year."

Doyle was quiet all of a sudden and went to rearrange the bat rack.

"You're in the hole, Woodell," he said when he came back. It was clear he was upset.

"What'sa matter, Doyle?"

He sat heavily. "Let me tell you something because I like you, Woodell. That last thing you said was a little obnoxious, okay?"

"I said you'd be a starter next year."

"Well, thanks a lot, okay? I'm nineteen years old, was a superstar high school player, started on a junior college team, and hit in the high three-nineties this spring. I'll probably never play with anyone as phenomenal as you, and to top it off you're thirteen years old. I should be encouraged when an expert like you tells me what a future I have with this club, but you'll forgive me if that didn't make my day."

"You want to start this year, of course," I tried, knowing I had screwed up but not sure how.

My eyes followed the crack of the bat. With a runner at third an easy double play was muffed when the third baseman dropped the liner.

"You're on deck," Doyle said.

"I'm sorry," I said. "I don't know how to talk to people."

He shook his head. "Don't worry about it. I'm just in a mood."

"Can I make it up to you somehow?" I said, moving for my bat.

"Yeah," Doyle said. "Drive in Burke."

"How?"

Doyle shook his head. "Sac fly to right."

"Wish that was a righty on the mound," I said. "Now I have to get an outside pitch to push the other way."

"The guy'll be trying to keep away from you, anyway," Doyle said. "Should be easy."

"True," I said.

The hitter ahead of me grounded sharply to third. One out, runners at second and third. I hurried to the dugout.

"Doyle, I'd rather try to drive em both in with a hit. Okay?"

"Grief, Woodell! I was only kidding! Be sure to get one of them in anyway."

I fell behind oh-and-two and had to protect the plate, even on a pitch low and away like the next one. I golfed it into right, sending the fielder down the line into foul territory. Both runners tagged up and broke with the catch. The throw skipped past the cutoff man and both runs scored.

When I got back to the bench, Doyle just sat there shaking his head.

"Incredible," he said. "You hit your sac fly to right and still drove both runs in!"

"Guy should have let that ball drop foul," I said. "Really a stupid play."

"With you hitting, he's got to try to get the out."

"No, he lets that ball drop and I've still got an oh-two count. There's still a chance to get me out with no damage. He had to know at least one would score if he caught that ball with his back to the infield."

Doyle stared at me. "You still need a couple of hits to reach seven hundred, Coach."

54

I got the two hits I needed that night. In fact, I got three, but I was also out once. My average climbed to .704.

We drubbed Arlington Heights 13-2, and I was surrounded by photographers and reporters.

"Is it true your dad is Neal Woodell?" someone asked.

I nodded.

"Is he here?"

"No, sir. He's dead. He died in, in—Alabama. I don't want to talk about it." After a few more questions, scouts pretending to be reporters asked me where I went to school, where I lived, and about my family. I dodged them and Coach Koenig dragged me away. Mr. Thatcher, Momma, and Luke waited at the edge of the crowd. When reporters saw me with them, they tried to talk to Billy Ray.

"I'll not be answering questions tonight, ladies and gentlemen," he said. He distributed several more business cards.

When we were all in Mr. Thatcher's rented car, I asked Luke, "You see that guy knock me over?"

"Sure did, but by the time I got to the fence they were already kickin him out."

"I showed that guy," I said, sighing. "And we pushed Arlington out of the race too."

I leaned forward and put my hands on Billy Ray Thatcher's shoulders, whispering in his ear as my son and Lucas talked baseball.

"I can't wait to hear what's going on," I said.

"Let me just say your lives will never be the same," Billy Ray said. "Rafer Williams is already aware of Elgin."

The baseball commissioner? Williams was the first black and the first former player to become commissioner. He had built a reputation as a hard-nosed traditionalist. How could he have already heard about Elgin?

Billy Ray's room at the Hyatt made my mouth fall open. "Must be nice," I said.

"Get used to it," he said. "It could become an everyday thing for you."

"I'm not sure I'd ever be comfortable."

Billy Ray took dessert orders and phoned them in. He amused me by eating his strawberry shortcake with a tiny, long-stemmed spoon clearly intended for something else. It made the big man look dainty.

"You called me none too soon," he said finally. "It's darn good I was at the game. You were sitting on a bubbling cauldron and didn't even know it. These scouts have been on Elgin's trail since the preseason. Koenig has done a magnificent job keeping them from Elgin and you. They're all aware of Elgin's age, and every one started with skepticism. Once they saw the numbers he was racking up, they started studying him seriously. Was he strong enough to drive a big-league fastball? How were his mechanics? Did he work hard? Was he smart, a good base runner, have all the tools?

"They have decided he's pro material, but they've got a selling job ahead of them. They're telling each other he's a myth, not worth pursuing. But in private they're begging their bosses to come see him. The brass of almost every club has contacted the commissioner's office. They're asking what they could do about signing an underage player. I doubt any of them have admitted they're referring to a thirteen-year-old."

"What does the commissioner think?" I said.

"I heard he pieced together a half dozen requests and called in the parties to find out who they were talking about. When it came out it was a kid, he hit the roof. He told them to get serious, that he was not going to be party to any publicity stunt. That scared everybody off until more teams started checking Chicago papers for Elgin's stats. Now the commissioner has a problem."

"What's that?"

"He wants to check out Elgin for himself, but what's the guy supposed to do? He can't sneak into Chicago for a private tryout. The statistics convinced him Elgin is for real. Teams are demanding a decision about Elgin's eligibility for the June draft."

"Why wouldn't he be eligible now, if he's good enough?" I said.

"Miriam, let me give you an example. A few years ago one of our lawyers took a case from Alabama. Six batboys for a double-A team in Huntsville had to quit working every night before nine o'clock. A state statute says kids under sixteen can't work that late."

"But surely batboys have been doing that for years."

"Right, until the parent of a boy who wasn't selected as a batboy complained to the Department of Industrial Relations. Then they had to enforce the statute. The law is there to protect kids from unscrupulous employers, but if a kid wants to work and has parental permission, the authorities usually look the other way. These were kids living a dream, making a few dollars a game. Elgin, even younger than those batboys, stands to make millions and travel and work in several states."

I shook my head.

Elgin piped up. "No American League for me. They'd make me a designated hitter, and I wouldn't want to be a DH for all the money in the world."

Thatcher chuckled. "That may be how much you're offered. But if you're dead set that way, I'll communicate that."

"If I decide my son can sign and travel and be up late enough to play night games during the summer, why should anybody be able to keep him from doing that? Isn't this age discrimination?"

Thatcher squeezed my shoulder. "I've never heard it used in behalf of a young person, but you have a point. You're stipulating he will not miss school and that he would travel and work only with your supervision, so to deny him that would be wrong."

"Of course it would," I said.

"Baseball is a law unto itself," the old lawyer said, "so even though we'll have to wrangle with a lot of opponents, if Rafer Williams can be convinced, we're halfway home. I expect his office will contact me."

"You wouldn't call him?"

"The silent one is in control. The one with the commodity everyone wants need not appear eager in the least."

"So now," I said, "Elgin is a commodity?"

Billy Ray looked thoughtful. "He is exactly in the position he wants to be in. If you don't want him to be a commodity, you can take him off the trading block any time you want."

55

As the four of us got off the elevator, Billy Ray Thatcher told the rest of us to take the escalator down and wait for him at the front door. But before we reached the escalator, Luke, Elgin, and I met several men that Elgin recognized as scouts.

"You must be looking for Mr. Thatcher," he said.

"Exactly."

Elgin pointed to the front desk where Mr. Thatcher stood with a stack of phone messages. He hurried over.

"I'm sorry, gentlemen. Not tonight. Please, call me in the morning, after ten."

In the car Mr. Thatcher kept staring in the rearview mirror. At a stoplight he leaped from the car and stomped back to talk to the driver behind him. He returned before the light changed.

"Really!" he said. "It's like these guys are living in an old movie."

"A scout was following us?" I said.

"They want to know where you live. They'll try to get to Elgin through you or around you if they don't get satisfaction from me. If anyone approaches you when I'm not around, just keep insisting that everything come through me. When they find out I represented Pincham, they'll know I'm not intimidated by big numbers. Who could calculate the worth of the youngest professional athlete in history?"

Mr. Thatcher dropped off Luke at his place near the second-hand shop, then wheeled around the corner and walked us to our flat.

"Just want to make sure there aren't any scouts roaming the halls," the lawyer said.

"The man at the desk would not allow that," I said.

"The one who slept through our arrival?" Thatcher said. "He gives me confidence."

In the hallway I said, "What's next?"

"I'll have my office draw up an agreement between us, but before I get serious with the baseball people, I need to know we're all on the same page."

I looked at Elgin. His eyes were heavy. "You know what I want, Momma. I want to go as far as I can as fast as I can, and no DH."

I turned to Thatcher with my brows raised. "You heard him. What he wants is what I want."

"And do you want me to do my absolute best for him financially?"

"Mr. Thatcher, I don't even know what that means."

"If he is as good as he appears, he should be worth millions and millions."

"You'd better come in a minute. I want this boy to go to bed, and I need to talk to you."

I spent the next half hour telling Billy Ray Thatcher about the Clovis Payoff. "If Elgin gets his mind messed with all this money, it'll affect his game, but more than that, I don't want to look like a mother who's used her kid to get rich. If Elgin comes into a lot of money—even if he never gets past the first level of minor-league ball—I am not going to let it get squandered."

Billy Ray removed his suit coat and loosened his tie.

"That's really all I need to hear, Miriam," he said. "I would like to do for you what Neal would never let me do. People in our office can manage your money for you, saving it, investing it, accounting for it. I'll keep you informed all the way. Every fast-buck artist in the country will be on your doorstep."

"I'm grateful," I said.

"I'm tired," he said.

I was awakened before dawn by thumping on the door. I sat up, reaching for my robe.

"Elgin?" I whispered as loud as I dared.

He hit the floor and hurried to me. "Who's that?" he mouthed.

I held him. "If it's an agent I'm gonna beat him with a pan. Ricardo's supposed to protect us."

The pounding continued.

"It's me, Mrs. Woodell! It's just me, Ricardo! You have to see this!"

I ran a hand through my hair and began unlatching the locks.

"This had better be good."

Elgin hid behind me in his underwear as I cracked the door and squinted at the light from the hall.

"Look, look!" Ricardo said, shouldering his way in. "Excuse me. Forgive me. But I knew you'd want to see this. A light, please."

I threw on a shirt and pants and returned to where Momma stood in robe and slippers and Mr. Bravura leaned over a table in his sleeveless undershirt. He spread the *Chicago Tribune* so we could both see it. My picture was on the left side of page one, announcing a story in the sports section: "Preteen Phenom Sets Sights on Majors."

In a huge story inside—with photos from the previous night's game—my whole deal was played out. Somehow, the reporter knew everything—except about the pitching machine and the name of the "family friend" who attended the game with my mother.

Poor Lucky, I thought. He would have loved the free publicity. He had introduced himself to the scouts, but not to the reporters.

Most amazing to me were quotes from the Arlington Heights players, including the leadoff man and shortstop.

"He's a player," Brian Ewart, 20, said. "I ran him over on a bunt in the first inning and he came up scrappy. After I leveled him at second on his inside-the-park homer, I got booted and he stayed in and killed us. He's got it all."

The article made a big deal of my batting average and raised the question of whether I was too good for American Legion–level baseball.

"Of course he is," Coach Jim Koenig says. "You only want to hit over five hundred in a softball league. These few kids who run up astronomical numbers are showing they're ready for the next step."
But the next step would be college, and Elgin Woodell just turned thirteen. He won't be eligible for the professional baseball draft until he graduates from high school, five years from now.
There is the possibility of some genetic advantage from the boy's father, a short-term minor-league standout in the Pittsburgh Pirate organization.
Neal L. Woodell died last year of an alcohol-related illness at the Alabama State Penitentiary in Birmingham where he was serving a lengthy term for reckless homicide while driving without a license.

I was thrilled but Momma was in tears.
"All our business, right out there for everybody," she said.
"Somebody famous right under your own roof," Ricardo said. "They even have the address here, but not the name of the place."
"That's a relief," she said. "Otherwise your phone would be ringing off the hook, and we'd have to move."
"Oh, no, we don't want that!" Ricardo said. "Stay here and I'll protect you!"

"May I keep this?" Momma said.

"Of course! I'll get more. I'd like to post this in the lobby, let people know who they're living with! Elgin, you're like royalty."

I didn't feel so special. I had dreamed of this kind of a story, but the last thing I wanted was for it to hurt Momma.

"I have to get going," she said. "I can just imagine what kind of a day I'm gonna have at work."

"I'm sorry, Momma," I said as Ricardo left.

"I guess I knew this was coming," she said. "I just didn't expect it to wake me up and slap me in the face this morning. You'd better get some breakfast and get ready for work yourself, young man."

"Momma, you think I still have to work when we're so close to going professional?"

I could tell she didn't think that was funny.

"You are an employee, Elgin. You don't quit without notice, and you don't quit without knowing where your next check is coming from. You could be years away from making money in baseball. I know everybody believes different, and I s'pose I do too. But don't start—"

"I know, Momma. Don't start counting your chickens and all that."

"Anyway, you want to just leave Lucas high and dry? He's grown fond of you, El, and he won't be happy if you up and quit on him."

"Fond of *me*? C'mon, Mom, you think I'm blind? I think I'll be seeing a lot of Lucky whether I work for him or not. Right?"

She didn't answer.

"Right?"

She was fighting a smile.

"Right, Momma?"

"You're obnoxious sometimes, Elgin, you know that?"

"Course I do. Doyle told me that last night. I'm obnoxious and rich."

"Get some breakfast."

56

"I've got a couple of errands this morning," Luke Harkness told me. "Could you watch the place while I'm gone?"

"Could I?" I loved the idea of selling, dealing, negotiating.

Luke told me how to call for help if I needed it, what to do and not to do.

"Your mom will probably kill me when she hears I left you here alone, but I won't be gone long. I'll call you in an hour or so."

"Don't worry about me, Lucky."

I strapped on the apron Luke often wore, but I had to take it halfway around my body again before I could tie it. I waited behind the cash register, rehearsing my lines. "I can let that go for fifteen. The boss paid about ten for it, so it'd be a real deal."

But no one showed up. Not one customer. Two or three peered in the window and kept moving. One did some window-shopping, but scowled and walked away. After an hour, Lucky called.

"One more stop and I'm on my way back," he said. "Any customers?"

"Nope."

"None?"

"Nope."

"What do you make of that?"

"I think they see a kid here and they don't want to come in," I said.

"Nah. Hey, if nobody comes by, I'll try to buy somethin off ya when I get there."

About ten minutes before I expected Lucky, a middle-aged woman stopped at the window, looked at the door, looked through the window again, then knocked tentatively, her eyes on me.

"It's open!" I called.

She pushed the door slowly, ringing the bell. "You're open for business?"

"Yes, ma'am. May I help you?"

"You're open then?"

Was she deaf? "Yes, ma'am."

"Well, you might want to turn your sign around then."

"Hm?"

"Your sign. It says *Closed*."

"Oh, man!"

I hurried over and turned the sign around. I smacked myself in the head.

After looking around she thanked me and passed Lucky on her way out.

"I see you noticed the sign," Luke said.

"Not till that woman showed me. You do that?"

What was different about Luke?

"Yeah. Sorry. I figured if you noticed, okay. If you didn't, well it was just a slow day and I didn't do something stupid by leaving you here alone."

"Lucky, what'd you do to yourself?"

"You can't tell?"

"Your beard is gone!"

Lucky had had some gray in his red beard, but now with it gone, including his sideburns, he looked younger. He was red-haired and freckle-faced, just like my mom, and he was a good-looking guy. He had left only a bushy mustache.

"I like it!"

"Really?"

Luke looked self-conscious as he took the apron from me and slid a crisp, new manila envelope under the counter.

"What's that?" I said.

"Personal. Listen, don't feel bad. You know we don't get much business in the morning."

"Yeah, but I feel like you don't trust me."

"Elgin, listen. You've been great. I know you won't be here much longer, but if you ever need a job, you've always got one here."

"You mean if I go into a slump?" We both laughed. "You were gonna try to buy something off me."

"Right! Where's that glass bowl, that ugly one I couldn't get rid of?"

"You know as well as I do," I said. "You think Mom wouldn't show me that?"

"You never know."

"You guys in love?"

Luke looked at the floor. "I can't speak for her," he said finally.

"Then speak for you."

"I like her an awful lot. She's a wonderful woman."

I chuckled. "Well, you're awful pretty together; she's pretty and—"

"I know, and I'm awful. Great junior high humor there, Elgin."

"You gonna get married?"

"Slow down, cowboy," Luke said. "She doesn't even know how I feel about her yet."

"The heck she doesn't. Guy gives a woman a present like that—"

"Shut up."

I giggled. "Ugly thing."

"I know, but she loved it."

"So you gonna get married or not?"

"You're way ahead of me, pal."

"Going to our church was smart, Lucky."

"Hey! I went to that church long before you did. Don't accuse me of that. That is something I'd never do."

"I know. Mom knows too. You mean a lot to her."

Luke couldn't hide his smile. "I do?"

I nodded. "So what's the deal? You guys serious, or what?"

"We haven't even talked about it yet."

"Honest?"

"Honest."

"What'd you cut the beard off for?"

"What's that got to do with anything?"

"That's what I'm asking you."

"C'mon, Elgin. I cut my beard because I've had it more than twenty years."

"That's a reason to keep it. You cut it for Momma, didn't you?"

"Didn't she like it?" Luke said.

"She's never said, but you must think she didn't."

"No, I didn't."

"Then why'd you cut it?"

"I don't know."

"C'mon."

Lucky moved around to the front of the counter and leaned back on it. "Don't you have some sweeping or somethin to do?"

"With all that free time you gave me this morning?"

"Sorry. I owe you."

"Tell me why you cut the beard and we'll be even."

"Man, Elgin, if Billy Ray Thatcher could play ball like you can pester, you two could trade jobs."

"I'm waiting."

"Your mom said something about never having seen me without the beard, so I thought maybe she deserved a peek."

⊗

When I arrived home late that afternoon, I was disappointed to find that Elgin had nothing on the stove for dinner. "I had it all ready in the refrigerator. All you had to do was—"

"I had some of it, Momma. And you don't need any."

"Elgin, I'm famished! All day interrupted by everybody stickin that newspaper under my nose, asking me how much longer I was gonna be working there. I am so glad to be home, but what am I supposed to do for dinner?"

"You've got a date."

"Mr. Thatcher's not coming by till nine-thirty. I can't wait that long to—"

"Not that one. You've got another date."

"I do?"

"Yeah, Lucky told me to tell you he's coming by for you at about six."

"You're supposed to tell me or ask me?"

"C'mon, Momma. You know you want to go out with him."

"Well, maybe I do and maybe I don't. But that's no way to ask for a date."

"So stand him up."

"What do you know about standing anyone up? Why didn't he call me at the office?"

"He said he didn't want to embarrass you. He knows how you hate having people know your business."

"He said that?"

Elgin nodded.

"How sweet."

"So, you'll be ready at six?"

"I might. What am I supposed to wear?"

"Dress up."

"He said that?"

Elgin nodded. "Maybe he's gonna pop the question tonight, huh?"

"Elgin! Lucas and I hardly know each other! We're a long way from that serious, so don't worry."

"I'm not worried. Should I be?"

"I don't know, El. Do you like him?"

"Sure I do, Momma. Do you?"

"You know I do."

"Do you love him?"

"Well, that's none of your business."

"It is if you're gonna marry him."

"I'm not going to marry him! Now will you quit sayin that?"

"Don't marry him if you don't love him."

"Elgin!"

"At least tell me if you love the guy."

"I certainly wouldn't tell you before I tell him!"

"So you do."

"I'm not saying another word."

"Don't you think I deserve to know?"

"Not before he does."

"You kissed him yet?"

"Elgin!"

"Well, have you?"

"No! And I wouldn't tell you if I had!"

"Mom, this *is* my business."

"It most certainly is not."

"You're my business, aren't you?"

I shook my head and pressed my lips tight. Actually, I was amused. I had worried what Elgin would think if Lucas and I grew more serious. He had to be wondering what it would be like to have a male figure in the family, whether he was going to be adopted by a new father. He didn't seem apprehensive.

But I was anxious about my date.

57

I headed for the basement, not wanting my mother to feel embarrassed about answering the door to the new Luke Harkness. She might want to hug him or something, but not with me there.

She had argued that I should be there because it wouldn't look right, a man coming to our place when she was alone.

"Well, Momma, he's more particular about that than you are."

I set the machine closer to the plate than ever, hoping what was happening to my career would heighten my senses. I forgot to double-check the aim of the thing before getting into the batter's box.

There was no time to even flinch. I took the first pitch on my right wrist, an inch above my hand. I dropped to the floor and scooted to my right, settling back against the wall where I was safe. I was within four feet of where the next fifty-six pitches slammed off the wall, and I covered my ears against the noise.

The spot where the ball drilled me was hot. I held it tight with my left hand, but every time I let go to look at it, I nearly screamed with pain. It didn't feel broken, but I had no experience with such injuries. I'd been hit enough times, but now all I cared about was how long I might be out.

"Lucas! You shaved your beautiful beard!"

"You're kidding, right? I thought you hated it."

"I never said I hated it," I said as I pulled the door shut and we started down the hall. "I just said I had never seen you without it."

"Well, here I am," he said.

"I like your face," I said.

"You should. Your son says I look like you."

I let out a laugh. I noticed he was carrying a manila envelope. "Now what's tonight all about?"

"I just thought we ought to have a formal date," he said. "We never really have, you know. You didn't have to accept."

"How could I have refused?" I teased. "Sent our courier back to you?"

We boarded the el a few blocks away. I had dressed as if for church. Luke wore a tie and a corduroy jacket. He looked great, but I had complimented him enough for one evening.

He took me to a family restaurant a few miles west. I felt like a teenager. And that envelope intrigued me.

The food was plain and moderately priced. I worried about Lucas spending money on me. Because he was frugal and careful, he seemed to have discretionary income. He was not in the least extravagant, but this meal alone would have been a burden for my budget.

Cradling my wrist in my other hand, I went upstairs to the flat. I held it under the cold water tap.

I turned on the Cubs and sat on the couch with a large bowl full of ice cubes, my wrist throbbing and my head aching. The cubes turned to water as the Cubs lost big. I rummaged for some change and headed to the pay phone to call Mr. Thatcher at the Hyatt.

I was impressed when Lucas paid the waitress and asked if she minded if we sat and talked awhile. The girl noticed the generous tip and smiled as she left.

"Well," Luke said, focusing on me. "I can't put this off any longer."

"You make it sound like bad news."

"Oh, it's not. At least I hope it's not. This morning, I visited Mr. Thatcher."

I squinted, my mind racing.

"I just wanted to make a few things clear to him and ask him to help me make them clear to you. One of the things I like so much about you is how unselfish you're being with Elgin. It's great that you're worried about the money and what people will think of you because of it. And Billy Ray's, uh, Mr. Thatcher's working for just his hourly fee, well, that's incredible."

"Mr. Thatcher is wonderful," I said. "Of course, his hourly fee is about half a week's salary for me."

"But he's not going to charge you unless there's some income for Elgin."

"I know that," I said evenly.

"And he's not charging you expenses, like his car and hotel and travel and all that."

Something about Lucas's having thought all this through bothered me. I knew he had overheard much of it and I had told him the rest, so why was he reminding me?

"I'm aware of that too," I said.

Luke reached for my hand. "I'm sorry, Miriam. I don't mean to be telling you anything you already know. It's just that I've become more and more impressed with Mr. Thatcher." He pulled back, producing a folder from the manila envelope. "I asked Mr. Thatcher to draw this up today, but only if he let me pay him. It was hard to talk him into it, but I finally did get to pay for the typing and copying and notary public stuff done by a service in the hotel."

I was at a loss. *What in the world?* Lucas handed me the folder with a smile.

Two pages were filled with legal mumbo jumbo, but I recognized my name and Elgin's name and "To all parties concerned as of this date and following re: present and future earnings of one Elgin Neal Woodell, etc., etc."

The thing carried "whereases" and "wherefores" and "therefores," and a "Be it known to all—" and my heart sank. My eyes darted back and forth over the pages until the words swam. I wondered if I could speak. My impulse was to jump and run, to leave the document, to find Billy Ray. How could Lucas reduce our relationship to paper and try to benefit from it?

Mr. Thatcher's line was busy, and I didn't have much change.

"Is this an emergency?" the Hyatt operator said.

"Um, yeah. It sort of is."

"If it's an emergency I can interrupt the call he's on. If it's just sort of important, I can keep an eye on when he hangs up and ring him right away."

"That would be good."

"Let me have that number."

I hung up and slid to the floor under the pay phone. I stayed there even when smelly, old Mrs. Majda gave me a dirty look while using the phone to order her nightly smelly, old pizza. I was still sitting there when Mr. Bravura's holler came that she had a delivery. She gave me the same dirty look on her way down to get it.

I only hoped Mr. Thatcher had not tried to reach me while she was on the phone.

58

I gradually regained my composure, placed the documents back in the folder, and handed them across the table. Luke was still smiling.

"Lucas, why don't you just tell me in your own words what this thing says? I don't understand the language, and I want to hear it from you."

"Okay," he said, "just so you know I went about it the right way, got it done up legally, and that it's binding with my signature."

"You can't bind anything that has to do with Elgin or me without our signatures."

Luke's smile froze. "You don't understand," he said.

"No, I don't. That's why I want to hear it from your own lips."

He stalled, opening and closing the folder, then opening it again and perusing the document. He replaced it in the envelope.

"Well, this is not easy for me to say," he began. "I wasn't very good about romantic stuff, even when I was married."

Romantic stuff? I had not imagined I could become more uncomfortable.

Lucas continued. "That was one of Lucy's complaints—that I didn't know how to express my feelings for her. But I told you once I wouldn't even hold your hand unless, unless I, you know, really cared for you."

"And you've since held my hand."

"Right." He was smiling again.

"Your late wife was right," I said. "You don't express yourself well directly."

"I'm sorry," he said, sobering quickly. "I'm trying. Don't make it more difficult for me."

Difficult for him?

"I held your hand," he said, "because I was falling in love with you." He spoke quietly, haltingly. How I had longed to hear those words. They begged a response, one I thought I had been prepared to give.

"I thought maybe we felt the same about each other," he said. "I didn't know where our relationship might lead."

I hated to be so passive, but if he had made some huge assumption about how Elgin's future would impact his, I wasn't prepared to encourage him.

"The last thing I wanted," Lucas said, "was for you to think I was, what do they call it, an opportunist."

"That's the last thing I'd want to think," I said.

"I know, even though we really don't know each other all that well yet."

"We sure don't," I said. I so wanted him to get to the point. Would this be the end of us? If it had to be, it had to be.

"So, anyway, I got to thinkin about that stupid little gift I gave you. I wasn't trying to mock you. I just wanted you to know that I hear you when you talk. And when you said that about not ever seein me without my beard, I thought, *Hey, why not? Girl I'm in love with wants to see what she might be getting herself into.* I don't want you to have any surprises—not that I'm saying we're gonna wind up spending the rest of our lives together."

"And thus this legal thing here, related to me and Elgin."

"Right."

I took a deep breath and had to fight to keep from shaking my head. "So are you ready to tell me what it says?"

"What's up, son?" Mr. Thatcher said, and I had never heard a more welcome voice. Half an hour later I had left a note for my mother and was in Billy Ray's car.

"You did the right thing," the lawyer said. "Doesn't look like the ulna or the radius is broken, but you've at least got a deep bruise on either the tendon or the membrane."

"Nothing's gonna keep me out for long," I said. "I can't slow down."

"I hope you're right, Elgin. You want to know why?"

"Sure."

"You, my young friend, are about to meet the commissioner of baseball."

"I was hoping you'd get the drift from the paper," Luke said, "but it was hard for me to understand too. What it says is that no matter what happens between you and me, this thing still stands."

"Which is?"

"Which is that I don't now, never have, and never will make any claim on any money your son or you get from his career. I mean, if he wants to give you something, that's his business, but I want it legal and clear that I would never ask, expect, demand, or even think I was entitled to anything."

I couldn't speak.

"Mr. Thatcher figured you'd appreciate it, but he didn't think you'd think it was necessary."

How could I have doubted this sweet, generous man? Why should he have to suffer for Neal's lifetime of Clovis Payoffs?

"It's not necessary, Lucas," I said, my voice thick. "But it's so you." I reached for his hand. "You said you would hold my hand only if you loved me. Would you like to know how I feel about you?"

He looked startled. "Yes!"

"Then you know what it feels like to wonder," I said. "I would like you to tell me straight out."

"I love you, Miriam, and I've loved you since long before I held your hand."

"I love you too, Lucas."

He held my gaze. "You're the only person other than my mother who calls me Lucas."

"You want me to call you somethin else?"

"No!"

"What does your daddy call you?"

Luke laughed. "Don't ask!"

The emergency room doctor told Billy Ray and me there was no break, but "some subcutaneous hemorrhaging."

"Bleeding under the skin," Billy Ray translated. "You're gonna be all right."

"It's going to hurt for a few days," the doctor said. "Maybe a few weeks."

"How about playing ball?" I said.

The doctor stepped back and looked me in the face. "It is you, isn't it? The young baseball star, am I right?"

I nodded.

"Ah, my first Chicago celebrity. Rest the wrist three days. You can then play ball and move it as much as you want. Let pain be your guide."

"You can't make that two and a half days?"

"You have a game?"

"Yes, sir."

"If you can move it without undue pain, you may play."

Luke and I were waiting in the lobby when Billy Ray and Elgin arrived at the transient hotel.

"I've been worried sick," I said, embracing Elgin.

"You got my note then?"

I nodded and looked at his bandage. "What happened?"

"It's not that bad, Momma," he said. "I'll tell you all about it, but wait till you hear Mr. Thatcher's news."

59

Too much was happening too soon. Where had I been when my son was injured? And what would a more serious injury have meant to all of us?

On top of all that, I was hopelessly, helplessly in love. I couldn't help but compare rock-solid, self-sufficient Lucas to my late husband.

I unlocked the flat, but once inside I realized that Lucas had hung back and was waiting in the hall. I peered out at him. He had the envelope in his hand.

"I'm gonna head home," he said.

"I'll be right in," I told Elgin and Billy Ray as I stepped out. "Lucas, what's wrong?"

"I just don't want to presume I have to be in on all this. You can tell me about it. It'll give us a reason to see each other again."

"I think we have reasons," I said, searching his eyes. "Just know that you're welcome."

"I know."

"Tonight was special for me," I said.

He gently pulled me toward him and slipped his hand around my waist. He held me like a fragile doll, lowered his face to mine.

"May I?" he whispered.

"You may."

His mustache tickled as he brushed his lips against mine. We kissed ony briefly, and I couldn't help scratching my nose.

"I'm sorry, Lucas. I didn't mean to spoil the moment."

He grinned. "My fault. See you tomorrow?"

I embraced him, realized I was bending his envelope, and pulled back. "I'm really a klutz tonight," I said.

"We'll get it right," he said, and he blushed.

When I went inside, Elgin piped up, "Did you kiss him, Momma?"

"Elgin! Let me see that wrist, and then you get to bed."

The wrist had been bandaged tightly with a two-inch width of white tape over a spongy cushion.

"I don't guess I can sweep Lucky's floors, huh?"

"Bed," I said.

Billy Ray Thatcher, gentleman that he was, didn't sit until I did. I flopped onto the couch and sighed aloud.

"You know what you look like?" Billy Ray said.

"I can hardly wait."

"Like a woman in love."

"It shows?"

"I'm happy for you, Miriam. He seems like a great guy."

Thatcher told me he had been on the phone most of the day. "I could fly in a team to start taking the calls," he said, "but I finally did hear from the commissioner's office. This is an unusual case, and until he decides what he's going to do, I can't really talk to any organization. Every team in the big leagues is aware of Elgin and wants to protect its interests. Apparently, there's magic in how long he has been keeping this up. Going halfway through a regular season with a batting average two hundred points higher than anyone else convinced a lot of people. They tell me twenty games at peak performance is more than a fluke. Anybody can go on a six- or even eight-game tear, but not twenty. Combine that with Elgin's age, and you've got the situation we find ourselves in."

"Which is?"

"Well, Commissioner Williams assigned someone to privately check out Elgin for him. You'll never guess who was secretly at Elgin's last half dozen games. Ronny Dressel."

"The great pitcher from when I was a kid?"

"Hall of Fame."

"Wouldn't he be recognized, at least by the scouts?"

"He's lost his hair, his coloring has changed, and he's picked up a lot of weight. He's got a limp, wears glasses, and with a hat and the right jacket or sweater, he's invisible."

"So, what does he think?"

"If salty language is any indication, he believes Elgin is for real. He thinks he could play in any rookie league right now, and he wants Rafer to meet him. We even thought of asking Luke if the meeting could take place at his apartment."

I laughed. "Well, no one would ever suspect. Oh, my! Lucas would never forget something like that!"

"Remember we heard that *Sports Illustrated* was planning a major piece? Dressel heard they got frustrated trying to get to Elgin and decided to do the story anyway. It's coming out Monday."

"Oh, no."

"I can't see how it could be negative, unless they say he's being protected too carefully or that his mercenary mother has already acquired an agent."

"Does the magazine know about the commissioner or about Mr. Dressel?"

"No one does except the three of us. We'll have to let Luke know soon, if we want to use his place. I assume he can keep a confidence."

"He will. How does Elgin's injury figure in?"

"We'll want to stall a meeting until he's at his peak again. Too bad he's got games Monday and Tuesday, because if that story hits, we're talking national media attention. You'd hate to see him have a bad game after that and make everyone think he'll fold under the spotlight."

"Elgin loves the spotlight."

A bigger than average crowd attended Monday night's game and seemed restless when I took neither batting nor infield practice. I was placed eighth in the batting order and took my position at second in the top of the first, but was passed over by the first baseman on warm-up grounders, and I was also skipped when the fielders threw the ball around after an out. I had not had one chance in the field when I stepped in right-handed to face a righty pitcher.

What stunned opposing Park Ridge, however, was that I took the first two strikes, both over the outside corner.

I hoped the pitcher, Charles Morley, would waste a pitch, but I also knew that he might reach back for his best pitch ever, wanting to strike out the phenom. If he tried to bust one in on my fists, I was ready.

"C'mon, Chuckie," the catcher bellowed. "Right past im, Chuckie baby!"

The pitch was tight and hard. I let it go. But a pitch later, on an offering identical to the first two, I squared around and bunted the ball up the first-base line. I exploded from the box, the catcher right behind me. I carefully angled for the runner's box to the right of the baseline. It would be close. With every stride my wrist was pierced with pain.

I caught up to the ball halfway up the line and saw Morley was in position to field it. The first baseman realized he would never get to it, so he retreated to cover the bag.

As Morley reached for the ball, with the catcher also charging up the line, I shouted with as low a voice as I could muster, "My play, Chuckie! Mine! I've got it!"

I was past the ball and couldn't tell if my ruse worked. My eyes were on the first baseman's eyes, and I could tell a throw was coming from behind me. The first baseman was frantically backing up the line toward the bag, so he would have to tag me for the out.

I dove headfirst into foul territory, reaching for the bag with my left hand. I heard the catch and knew the first baseman was sweeping at me, but all he got was air. The crowd went crazy.

When we were in the field, our shortstop took all the throws to second, and once he even handled a double play himself, but I knew it was unlikely I would go a whole game without a grounder at second.

Two came in the top of the sixth. The first was near first base, and I was able to underhand the ball. The second was up the middle, and I shoveled the ball to the short stop, who threw the runner out. I only hoped I was protecting my wrist enough. It hurt bad. I finished the game with two bunt singles, a strikeout, and a walk. My average dropped a point. Worse, we lost to a team we hadn't lost to for three years.

The next night we faced our toughest opponent in the league, Mount Plaines, the only team we had lost to more than once that season. They played at a newly lighted field with a thousand seats in Waycinden Park.

Usually a hundred or so fans showed up. But with the release of my feature in *Sports Illustrated* that Monday, the ballpark was jammed Tuesday night.

60

Tuesday the stands filled twenty minutes before game time, and people kept pouring in through the fourth inning. Fans lined up six-deep behind the backstop and down both foul lines, often having to be shooed out of play by the umpires.

No home run fences had been installed in the new park, so when even more people showed up they watched from beyond the light poles in the outfield. Anything that rolled into the left field corn, however, was a ground-rule double. Anywhere but into the cornfield in left was still in play, and you could take all the bases you could get.

I thought about hitting one-handed to protect my wrist but decided against it. I would rely on my bunting and my eye again.

That worked fine—two walks and a sacrifice bunt, for no official times at bat and no impact on my average—until I came to the plate in the top of the last inning when we were down by two with two out and the bases loaded. I painfully clenched and released my fist a dozen times.

A right-handed reliever was on the mound with good speed but no movement. I knew it was crazy, but I wanted to clear the bases. Somewhere in the count, I was going to have to forget about my wrist and swing away. That was going to hurt like the devil.

The pitcher missed close on the first two pitches, then threw two strikes, but not where I wanted. When the count went to three-and-two, I stepped out and the base coaches reminded the runners to run with the pitch. I dug in again, hoping this guy would try to shoot another one past me.

But I was fooled. The pitch was a change-up that seemed to die halfway to the plate, and as my bat started through the strike zone, the pitch was still hanging out there, dropping.

I had planned to try to hit it to right. I was able to adjust enough to get the bat on the ball but was so far in front that the ball shot past the heads of the third baseman and the runner at third, bounced fair at about two hundred feet out, and skipped hard toward the cornfield. I yelled as I headed toward first, partly from the pain in my wrist, and partly because a ground-rule double would drive in only the two tying runs.

But as I rounded first, the Mount Plaines left fielder made a colossal mistake. Rather than letting the ball go into the corn-field for a double, he dived and snared it, rising to try to hit the cutoff man.

As the go-ahead runner came around third, I was waved on. I slid and the relay hit me in the helmet and bounded past every-one. As the catcher raced back to get it and the pitcher hurried to cover the plate, I rounded second and stopped halfway to third.

Koenig waved and screamed at me to come, but I stood still, like a deer caught in headlights. The pitcher yelled, "Three!" and the third baseman straddled the bag. I hesitated, started, and hesitated again. Then I dove toward third. The catcher's throw was high and got away, so I scored.

As soon as I had crossed the plate I ran back out to Coach Koenig, who was furious.

"I knew I had third no matter what, Coach. I figured if I could draw the throw we might catch a break."

"But you also ignored me," Koenig said, "and you showed me up. Tell Doyle he's playing second in the bottom half."

I ran red-faced to the dugout, wishing the crowd wouldn't cheer me after I'd gotten in trouble. I was not unhappy about being taken out with a two-run lead in the ninth. My wrist needed the rest.

Doyle ran eagerly to second for the bottom of the inning. Though he was normally an outfielder, he looked comfortable. Mount Plaines scratched out an early run and had a man at third with two outs, but a pop-up to Doyle ended the game.

I had been excited about getting to meet the commissioner of baseball soon. Now I dreaded having to face my own coach.

61

As my teammates celebrated, I sat on the bench waiting for the team lecture. When Coach Koenig quieted everyone, I raised my hand. "Coach, I want to apologize for that play."

"What're you talkin about?" someone said. "That was great!"

Koenig stopped the chatter.

"I appreciate that, Woodell. It was brave and it gave us the win, but you shouldn't have done it on your own. I wish I'd thought of it."

I spent the next three days mostly in the basement. I let the machine pitch me infield grounders and liners, and though I caught most everything, I threw nothing. For hours I crouched at the plate and caught pitch after pitch from different distances. I hoped that would keep my eye and timing sharp.

The word came from Mr. Thatcher that Rafer Williams was flying to Chicago late Sunday night. He would stay with Ronny Dressel at the Glen Ellyn Holiday Inn without registering under his own name, and Ronny would drive him into the city the next morning. Then he would send for me from Lucky's apartment.

"You'll be with me, right, Mr. Thatcher?"

"Of course he will, honey," Momma said, but Billy Ray cut her off.

"I'm afraid not. We're not exactly in the driver's seat. The commissioner has set a few conditions. He wants time with Elgin alone first."

"I don't like that," Momma said. "I don't want Elgin having to wonder what's being said."

"Oh, Rafer has already assured me through Ronny that I'm next on his agenda. He'll let me know how many hoops we have to jump through. After that, it's our decision. Then the conditions, terms, limitations, and dollar levels are ours to set. The club that wins this prize will earn it."

I found it easier and easier to flex my right hand. I felt the tendon strengthening and become more elastic. By Friday morning, I was swinging a bat carefully, and it was not nearly as painful as it had been.

I had a night game Friday and a home doubleheader Saturday. I wanted to go into that once-in-a-lifetime meeting with Rafer Williams still hitting over seven hundred, more than twenty-five games into the regular season.

I was fifty-three for seventy-five for the season, hitting .7067. I could go seven for my next ten at bats and see my average drop almost a point. One more at bat than that without a hit and my average would drop to .698.

My goal with Mr. Williams was to be honest. If he wanted to know what I wanted, it was to become not just the youngest professional baseball player ever, but the youngest big leaguer ever.

By Sunday night three more victories were in the bag and the Chicago American Legion team was almost assured of a state berth. Friday night I had gone three-for-three including a home run, my batting average a tick under .718. In the Saturday doubleheader it plummeted to .682. Though I went only one-for-three in the first game and one-for-four in the second, I hit the ball as well as I had all year. I also walked twice and hit a sacrifice fly so deep to center that two runners tagged up and scored.

"I feel like DiMaggio when his hitting streak ended," I said.

"He hit harder shots in the fifty-seventh game than he had in the five games before that, but none of them fell in."

"Yeah," Doyle said, smiling. "I'd sure hate to be hitting in the high six-hundreds. You must really be down."

"Shut up, Doyle."

Mr. Thatcher's parting words to me that night: "Talk baseball with Rafer Williams. He knows the game as well as anyone."

"I know," I said. "I remember in a play-off game when—"

Mr. Thatcher held up a hand. "Excuse me, Elgin, but I have to go. Tell him that story. He'll love it. Honest."

I wanted to tell the story, and Luke and my mother were the only available ears. "Bottom of the ninth, Reds leading by one, Mets with runners at first and second with one out. Williams catching for the Reds. Mets try a double steal. Williams sees he can't get the lead runner but that the tailing runner is dogging it. He guns down the guy at second; they hold the lead runner at third. They go on to win. Gutsy, man. Gutsy play."

Luke smiled at me. "You're a little wired."

"Am I ever."

I paced.

Momma just sat, her eyes full, her face blotchy. "This waiting is gonna drive me crazy," she said. "How am I supposed to sleep? How am I supposed to work tomorrow?"

Luke put his arm around her. "You just heard a sermon on worry," he said.

She snorted. "It was pretty good too. It just didn't take, that's all."

"You think you've got worries," Luke said, "I've got scads of cleaning to do before my company comes tomorrow. I hope that gentleman from baseball doesn't mind drinking out of an old jelly glass!"

"Lucas!"

"Oh, I'll take care of him. Sounds like all he needs is a chair and something to munch. You guys go till late morning; I'll cater a fast-food lunch."

I slept no better than my mother. I heard her sighing, tossing, and turning all night. All while I was doing the same thing.

62

I showed up too early at Lucky's Secondhand Shop the next morning. The place was locked and the street deserted. I thought about moseying over to Lucky's flat, but that was not the plan. Once Rafer Williams showed up and Luke spirited him to his apartment, Luke was to meet me at the store and send me there.

I whiled away the longest hour and a half of my life sitting on the pavement, looking in the window, lying on the pavement, and hanging over the curb to watch insects in the gutter. I rested my back against the short brick wall beneath the window of Lucky's and closed my eyes against the morning sun. I was wound tight, wishing the clock would move, wishing Luke would show up.

I scrambled to my feet when I heard Luke's boots on the sidewalk.

"There's been a screwup," he said. "Mr. Williams thought everybody understood he wanted to meet with your mother first. I called your place, but that guy Bravado or whatever his name is said you'd left two hours ago and your mother an hour ago. You'd better get goin. You know the place."

I hurried toward Luke's apartment and was almost past an old man with a cane when the man stopped and said, "Woodell!"

I spun and stopped. "Yes, sir?"

The old man reached out a huge, strong hand. "Dressel. I been scoutin ya."

"Yes, sir. Nice to meet you, sir."

"Don't let that guy bully you now, hear? Don't let him compare you with big leaguers. All we're sayin is that physically you're ready for the minors. Whether you're ready in any of the other ways, who knows?"

Without another word, Ronny Dressel waved and moved on.

I felt a tingle up my spine. Who would believe I had just met a Hall of Fame pitcher and was about to have a secret meeting with a Hall of Fame catcher who was also commissioner of baseball? Would I be able to speak, or would I just melt and have to be scooped up and poured back onto the street?

When I reached Luke's apartment I thought of my dad and how proud he would be of me. I knocked.

"It's unlocked," came the huge, bass voice.

I turned the knob and pressed my knee against the door where it always stuck. It squeaked and broke free. A few feet from the door stood a chuckling giant of a black man. He was shiny bald with a rim of long, curly hair. His feet were spread and his arms folded across his chest, making his shirt cuffs and suit coat arms ride high off his wrists. Mr. Williams was about six-four and had picked up at least forty pounds since his last playing day nearly ten years before. He had become a broadcaster, then—of all things for a National Leaguer—American League president before becoming the surprise choice for commissioner. In the meantime he had become a first-ballot Hall of Famer.

"You've been here before?" Rafer Williams said, his voice too loud for the room. I looked puzzled. "You knew just how to open the door!"

When he shook my hand, my fingers disappeared. Mr. Williams pointed to the couch, and I sat. "It's mighty nice to meet you finally," he said. He removed his brown, pin-striped coat and draped it over the back of a kitchen chair, then took off his tie and stuffed it in the pocket of his coat.

I sat with my feet flat on the floor, knees together, fists on my thighs. Williams pulled the coffee table away from my knees and settled his expanse right in the middle of it. The table bowed.

I felt more at ease as Rafer Williams made himself comfortable. There was a sparkle in his eye and excitement in every move. The man sat forward, elbows on his knees, not two feet from me, and smiled. Then he pulled up his socks, still not taking his eyes from mine. He tugged at his pant legs until they rose a few inches above the tops of his socks.

The commissioner crossed his legs and held his ankle to his knee with both hands. He had a gold ring on each hand, a gold watch on his left wrist.

"See that briefcase over there?" he said.

The satchel-style bag was stuffed, papers peeking out the top.

"That's full of you. Videotapes, charts, graphs, radar gun printouts, timings of you to first, you to second, you from first to third, you around the bases. If you can measure a ballplayer by the numbers, you've been measured, buddy."

"Uh-huh." I didn't know what else to say.

"But you and me both know you don't measure a ballplayer like that, don't we? A ballplayer is measured by his head and his heart, am I right?"

I nodded. "But you can tell a lot about a guy by his numbers."

Williams stuck out his lower lip and nodded. "True enough. Like the numbers I've got on you show that you'd be about, oh, tenth or eleventh fastest runner on a big-league club, maybe third or fourth on a rookie-league team. Your arm is remarkable. You throw the ball like an eighteen-year-old. But I s'pose you know that most eighteen-year-olds would rank last on a big-league team in throwing."

I nodded.

"I thought maybe we'd talk some baseball," the commissioner continued. "You know how rarely I get to do that? Seems all I talk about is other junk—legal stuff. Contracts, deals, negotiations. If I didn't insist on goin to a ball game at least once a week I wouldn't even see one. Let's talk baseball."

"Okay."

"Let me tell you what makes you such an unusual hitter and you tell me if I'm right. It's all bat speed, right?"

I hesitated. "I used to think bat speed was pretty much everything, sir," I said. "But when I started facing faster pitchers, guys who throw in the low eighties, I had to start getting stronger. The faster the pitch, the harder it is for the bat to change its direction."

"You're right!" he chortled. "It's not just bat speed, or all these little guys would be hitting home runs all the time! You think pitches in the low eighties make a bat hard to push through the strike zone, try to turn around one in the high nineties! That ol bat seems to recoil in your hands. Ever hit offa one of those superfast pitching machines? Same feeling. You face that kind of pitching all the time, you've got to be built for it."

I nodded.

"Are you built for it? Let me see your hands."

I held them out. Williams took one in each of his.

"Resist me," he said.

He pulled my hands toward each other. I resisted but not successfully. I was off balance, had no base. My rear end was on soft cushions. The more I fought, the more Williams was able to make me lean from side to side. I planted my feet.

"Thatta boy!" Williams said. "Set yourself and hold steady."

I squared my shoulders. I was no match against the big man, but I offered more resistance when I was braced.

"Unusually strong for your age," Williams said. "Truly phenomenal. You have the body and strength of a late teen, and the baseball knowledge—so they tell me—of an adult. Better than that. The baseball knowledge of the expert adult. Your fielding and throwing are above average for American Legion, and you hit like a double- or even triple-A player."

Afraid I would sound immature, still I had to ask.

"Do you really think a double-A player would hit near seven hundred in Legion ball?"

Williams stopped and stared at the ceiling, cupping his neck in his hand.

"Now that's a good question," he said. His mind seemed to be cataloging double-A players.

I didn't want to look cocky. I looked the commissioner in the eyes and mouthed silently, "Seven hundred?"

63

I took a call at my desk from Mr. Thatcher.

"Well, of course I want to meet with him," I said. "But not until after work. How's it going with Elgin?"

"Dressel and Luke are at the shop, and Elgin left for Luke's apartment more than an hour ago."

"Well," I said, "I don't mind tellin you, I should have taken the day off. I am worthless."

"Well now, you've got me there," Williams said, seeming to enjoy himself. "A minor leaguer who would hit seven hundred in Legion ball? Hm. I remember a kid played for the Cubs some years back. Black shortstop with a gun of an arm. Hit over three-fifty two years running in triple-A. Had trouble hitting his weight his first few years in the bigs. Wound up a pretty fair hitter. I believe he could have hit seven hundred in Legion ball. Maybe a couple of others."

"So I'm hitting like a high minor leaguer," I tried. "Someone on his way to the majors."

"Course a lot more goes into making a professional ballplayer than a good bat."

"I'll do anything."

"Would you stand in against the fastest pitcher in baseball and let him throw a hundred straight pitches past you?"

"No, sir."

"I thought you said you'd do anything."

I smiled. "Anything except let him throw them past me."

Williams howled. "You're somethin, kid! I gotta give you that. Would you work out with a trainer so you wouldn't overdo it, but build yourself up to where you can change the direction of a ninety-mile-per-hour fastball? Don't nod so quick. You know it takes eight thousand pounds of force to change the motion of a ball that weighs just over five ounces from coming at you at ninety miles an hour to going the other way at over one hundred ten?"

"I've read that," I said, "but I don't understand it. I mean, how does even somebody your size, when you were playing I mean, produce eight thousand pounds of force?"

The commissioner laughed loud. "I don't know," he said. "I always wondered that myself! I'm not a physics man, but I know it has to do with more than bat speed. It's got to be strength."

Billy Ray Thatcher was on his cell phone in the back room at Lucky's. He had returned the call of the general manager of the Houston Astros.

"It's about time, Mr. Thatcher. I'm calling about this kid who's getting all the attention. There's no hope of getting him into the June draft, I suppose."

"If that happened, would Houston be interested?"

"You never know," the GM said. "I can't imagine being interested in a child."

"I hear you," Billy Ray said. "He's just a babe."

The man chuckled. "With a capital *B*?"

Billy Ray smiled. "So you're telling me what? That you're interested or that you're not interested?"

"Just to ask about the June draft. If you can't get him into that, this is all academic."

"So, let's be academic. In fact, let's be hypothetical. Let's say you could be fairly certain this boy would be the Tiger Woods of baseball. Dominate the game like no one ever has, lead the league in just about everything, win the MVP several years in a row, lead a team to the play-offs and Series year after year."

"I've seen the videos. This is a once-in-a-lifetime opportunity for all of us. I know every other team in baseball is interested, because we have first pick and we've been contacted by all of them."

"That so?"

"Personally, I'm pessimistic that the boy will be made available until he's of age. But I wouldn't trade his rights for anything I can think of."

"Not even millions?"

"No. Even though he would never pay off until the majors. But if he keeps progressing, he could be one of the youngest big leaguers in history. He'd fill every stadium every game if he could simply compete with adults. He'd pay for a long-term deal within a half season."

Thatcher laughed. "Refresh me on which of us is on which side of the bargaining table, sir."

The GM laughed. "Just let me congratulate you on the hottest property since the first Babe. Protect him, Thatcher. For the good of the game and especially the boy."

"Count on that," Billy Ray said.

"You're not serious!" Rafer Williams thundered. "Not even to Wrigley?"

I shook my head. "Never to one big-league game."

"Well, we're gonna have to see about that," Rafer said. He looked at his watch and pulled his cell phone from a pocket.

"Rafer Williams calling for Mr. Martin—Hey, Cliff! Rafer! Good! Listen, I need four tickets to Saturday night's game. Box seats, best you've got, where you'd put me, hear? No, not a luxury box. And then for the next day, you've got a midafternoon TV game, right? That's when I want a skybox, lots of food and soft drinks, all on my office. Got it? Leave em at Will Call for Luke Harkness."

I smiled.

"Now, son, I want you to tell me about your daddy."

Billy Ray Thatcher placed a call to the general manager of the Phillies.

"Give me some good news," the GM said. "Just tell me what it's going to take. What's the floor bid?"

"Congratulations," Billy Ray said. "You get to start the bidding."

"You know what the rumors are."

"Tell me."

"That the commissioner is going to have the kid scouted independently."

"Really?"

"That's what I hear. What do you hear?"

"I just hear offers," Billy Ray said.

"You think Rafer will clear the kid for the June draft?"

"I couldn't tell you."

"But do you know?"

"Of course not. I would imagine there'd be a lot of hurdles."

"I'm not so sure," the Philadelphia man said. "There'll be do-gooders and social-worker types who'll cry bloody murder. But how can you keep a guy from doing what he wants to do and is capable of doing when he has parental consent? He can be tutored for school, can't he? I mean, he's going to make millions."

"How many millions?" Thatcher asked.

They both laughed and agreed to keep in touch.

Rafer Williams's voice was soft. "So there was no goin back for the funeral? That's rough. Uh-huh. That's a rough one. Made you a better player, though, did it? Uh-huh. Wow. How's Momma doin now?"

I smiled, embarrassed. "Momma's in love with Luke Harkness."

"You don't say!"

"By the way, Luke said to just call him and he'd bring us some burgers."

"Burgers! Let's call him!"

I skipped lunch at the office and began to feel faint by early afternoon. There was little I wanted more than to talk with the commissioner and to be able to know something one way or the other about Elgin.

64

Baseball commissioner Rafer Williams tried to press a twenty-dollar bill into Luke Harkness's hand.

"No way," Luke said. "It's on me. Drink whatever you want from the fridge."

As Luke left, the commissioner swept open the refrigerator to find it stocked with several different brands of soft drinks. "What'll you have, Elgin?"

"Diet Coke."

"Good man. Stay away from the sugar. This is Monday, so I'll do the same."

Williams howled, but I didn't get it. We sat at the tiny kitchen table in vinyl-covered chairs. He had a way of talking with his mouth full without being offensive.

"Elgin, if I compared you to Jackie Robinson, do you know what I'd be saying?"

"Sure. He was the first black ballplayer to play in the major leagues. Someday I'll be the first kid."

"The question is, do you bring to your job what he brought to his? First, he was a great, great player. That helped. But when he made an out, had an oh-for-four game, made an error, well, he was everybody's nigger."

I was stunned. Momma didn't even allow that word in our house. And here was a black man saying it.

"They told him to go back to the jungle," Mr. Williams said. "He even had a rough time with his teammates."

"Yeah, until he won Rookie of the Year."

"You know your history, don't you?"

"I read a lot."

"But Jackie Robinson was a big enough man to not fight back. He had to get angry and had to feel the injustice. If just once he had attacked somebody or treated them like they treated him, he'd have ruined it for all of us. Think I'd be commissioner today if it weren't for Jackie Robinson? Not on your life. But let me tell you this, he won over a lot of people, but not everybody. Understand?"

I nodded.

"Now tell me, son, what kind of heat you've taken. There had to be a lot of kids who lost jobs because you came along."

I told him I had suffered some but that it didn't seem like much, now that I was thinking about Jackie Robinson.

"Otherwords, you've never been spit at."

I shook my head.

"Ignored?"

"Not really."

"Shunned?"

I shook my head again. "I don't guess I'm a Jackie Robinson."

The commissioner finished off another burger and took a long pull on his Diet Coke.

"See, there's where we have our problem. I don't know how much you know about the legal side of this thing, but to get you into the June draft I would have to make an exception to an old rule. Breaking old rules is part of my heritage, so I'm not against that. I'm not even all that concerned if the worst that happens is that you're a paper tiger and you flounder in the minors and never see a major-league inning. That makes us look bad, sure, for exploiting you, ruining your childhood, all that. But even if that happens, you and your mother will likely be set up for life.

"My problem is if you're good. You're not going to have any

trouble with the fans. The difficulty will come with your team-mates and your opponents. See what I'm saying?"

"Jealousy?"

"That's part of it. But think about this. You're in American Legion ball and let's say you're hitting, oh, almost seven hundred halfway through the season. You're two hundred points ahead of everybody else and cruising toward a big-league career, way ahead of schedule. Now in your next game, you're gonna face a prodigy. This is a baby. Can barely walk. He's still in diapers, get it?"

I laughed.

"And this kid is a pitcher nobody can hit off. I mean, he's allowed four hits in five games and has an ERA of zero. Okay?"

I nodded, grinning.

"He walks your leadoff man, and now you're up. What're you thinking about?"

I had been caught off guard. I said nothing.

"Are you thinking about what pitch he might throw? Or are you thinking about bunting, where to put the ball, what's the situation? What are you thinking about?"

My smile was gone. "I'm thinking how embarrassing it would be to strike out against a baby."

Rafer Williams slammed both palms on the table, crossed his arms and sat back, glaring at me. "There you go," he said. "Let me be the older guy now. I'm a catcher for the Reds. I've got a lifetime average of over .280 and I've hit over four hundred home runs. I'm gonna be a Hall of Famer, and everybody knows it. Now I'm catching and a child comes to the plate to hit. Do I want my pitcher to give up a hit, or even a walk, to a child? What am I thinking? I'm thinking, *This kid wants to play with grown-ups, he's gonna have to face grown-up pitches. This kid's gonna be on his butt the first three times my pitcher tries to put one in his ear.* Then what?"

"Am I that kid?"

"Course. Now what?"

"I'm looking for the green light on three-and-oh."

Williams shook till he almost left the chair. He raised his head and shrieked. He clapped. "You're lookin for the green! I love it! I love you! You *are* Jackie Robinson. That's just what he woulda said!"

"I hear you, sir. Nobody's going to want me to steal a base off them, get a hit, draw a walk, throw them out, tag them out. I figure I'll have to watch for hard slides, roll blocks, beanballs. I s'pose people will bunt at me, rag on me, taunt me. It'll just make me more determined."

The commissioner had a hand over his mouth, studying me.

"Let me tell you something," he said. "I'm concerned about your power. You probably haven't hit a live pitch farther than three hundred feet, right?"

"About three-ten."

"You know what that'll get you in pro ball."

I jerked up my thumb like an umpire.

"Precisely. So, let's say you can plant liners into the outfield and maybe the occasional double in the gap. Here's what clubs will do. They'll bring that outfield into two, two-fifty or so, maybe even put one of the outfielders in the infield. Then they shift the infield to take away the ground-ball hit. With two guys in the outfield, faster than any you've ever seen in Legion ball, they'll run down those flare hits. All of a sudden you're hitting a hundred."

"Then I get sent back down."

"Then you get sent back down."

"I don't think so," I said.

"Oh, you'd get sent back down."

"If I was hitting a hundred I'd expect to be. But I don't think I could be held to a one hundred average. I know I haven't faced live, ninety-mile-an-hour pitching, but I believe I can put the ball where I want to at least half the time. And I have a good eye. I'll walk a lot."

Mr. Williams cleared away the trash and motioned to the other room where this time he sat on the couch and directed me to the coffee table.

"I like your confidence," he said. "It's naive, but it's confidence. Let me ask you this: Do you have any idea how noisy it would be if I allowed you into the draft?"

"Noisy?"

"Big. Newsworthy. I know you've been drawing crowds and getting a lot of publicity, but I don't think you realize the magnitude of this. You would be known all over the world. It wouldn't be long before you wouldn't be able to go out alone. You'd be on all the talk shows, there'd probably be apparel deals, shoe deals, you name it. But I've seen superstars come and go. I've seen kids pitch in the majors right out of high school, then never pitch in the bigs again. I saw a kid come up from A ball, fresh off a perfect game, only to be hit all over the yard in a third of an inning and never come back. That's the kind of thing I need to think about."

"I probably should tell you that I have no interest in the American League."

"What?"

"They'd make me a designated hitter, and I'd hate that."

"I hated that too. That's why I never thought they'd make me president of the AL. How strongly do you feel about it?"

"I wouldn't sign with an AL team unless they guaranteed in writing I wouldn't be a DH."

"Hm. That could make you look bad."

"Maybe just American League teams would have to know."

"Elgin, if I allow you into the June draft, you won't have any more secrets as long as you live."

"You're going to let me in?"

The commissioner's arms were spread on the back of the couch. "So, you come right out and ask me, do you?"

"Sorry."

"It's all right. I was hopin you would, because if you didn't, I wasn't supposed to discuss it. But I'll tell you, in this day of agents and lawyers and spokesmen and all that, the guy who knows the least is always the guy we're all talking about—the player in question. That's not right, especially with someone like you, the Jackie Robinson of kids. So, just so you'll know from the beginning, here's where I am on this:

"A lot of people think that once we crack this door open, we'll have all manner of high school kids dropping out and running off to play baseball like they do in basketball. Well, I say we keep some limitations. Most of all, the kid would have to agree to tutoring and would have to maintain a certain grade point average and graduate. If he fell behind, he would be on the shelf until he was back on track."

I nodded and couldn't quit smiling.

"Don't get ahead of me now, son. Just because you qualify on all those doesn't make it so easy. This gets kind of complicated, so stay with me. I couldn't make it appear I was doing this on behalf of baseball, even though you and I know that if you succeeded and made the majors at some ridiculously young age, it would be the best thing that ever happened to the game. But see, if *we* came after *you*, rather than the other way around, and I allowed you in the draft because I thought you'd be exciting to watch grow, we'd look like zookeepers.

"What has to happen is that you push your way in. You've started that with your performance and your stats. But if my hand was forced, we'd look better. Understand?"

"No."

"Can you keep a secret?"

I nodded.

"I'm going to say no. No way I can let you into the draft. Now don't look at me that way. I'm going to take a position that this would not be in your best interests, even if it might be a good thing for baseball. Then I need you to force the issue. I need your attorney to threaten a lawsuit accusing us of discrimination on the basis of age, hammering away that you and your mother both want this, that she will be with you all the way, that you will be tutored, the whole bit. Public outcry will be incredible, and at some point I'll give in. I may throw out a few conditions of my own, but I'll concede that we really don't have a case and that we don't want the expense of a lawsuit we're sure to lose."

"Then what happens?"

"Then your name goes into the June draft, the Astros take you, and you're off to the races."

I felt a lump in my throat. "You mean it's up to me? If I tell

Mr. Thatcher to make you let me in the draft, that's all there is to it?"

"Except this. I wish I could guarantee that you'll be the best thing that ever happened to baseball and that you'll make the majors in a few years. I doubt you'll make it while you're still younger than Joe Nuxhall was, but I hope you make it as a teenager. I will not be a happy man if it all falls apart for you. If you get hurt or disillusioned, or if we put you in over your head, I'll feel bad and hope the money has been worth it for you. Let me remind you that it's the baseball playing itself that has gotten you where you are now, and what you do on the field will always determine how everything else goes. You quit playing at a top level, your money dries up, your endorsements disappear; your other-than-true friends, your popularity, everything else tumbles.

"But you conduct yourself like a pro, keep practicing and perfecting your skills, you will have no limits."

The commissioner reached to shake my hand.

"I want to talk to your mother. I want to talk to Mr. Thatcher. And then I want to get back to my office. Between now and the draft, you and I are going to be busy people."

I shook his hand and wanted to thank him, but no words would come. The commissioner rose from the couch as I stood. He embraced me as I fought to keep from crying.

"You're welcome," Rafer Williams said with a smile.

65

Within a week, the baseball commissioner's office announced it had been petitioned by the representative of an underage ballplayer to be allowed into the June draft. The commissioner denied the request, but soon anyone who had not heard of Elgin Woodell before was well aware of him because of Elgin's network television appearances, rallies for him, call-in shows, letter-writing campaigns, and daily news reports of the lawsuit filed by Billy Ray Thatcher of Hattiesburg, Mississippi. Even Billy Ray took on Lincolnesque proportions.

A meeting with my American Legion coaches and teammates convinced me they would be thrilled if I was drafted and left them immediately. "Thanks a lot," I said, pretending to be insulted, but they all told me they would be proud to say they had once played with me.

"We'll win the thing without you anyway," Doyle said. Everyone laughed, but that proved true. Without me the rest of the way, they would win the state and wind up third in the nationals.

Meanwhile, the commissioner held a news conference to announce what only Momma, Luke, Mr. Thatcher, and I knew:

that Williams was, "with great fear and trepidation, making this very unusual exception in the case of one very unusual young man."

The Astros, despite their pledge to never give up Elgin's rights, traded the first pick in the draft to the Atlanta Braves. The Braves had been under tremendous public pressure, from the mayor to the people, to make the southern boy their own. They gave up two frontline players, a pitcher and a center fielder, along with three future draft picks and an undisclosed amount of cash.

The Braves offered Elgin a million dollars, guaranteed, for three years. Other clubs claimed they would have paid more. The Braves maintained that they were taking an expensive risk.

Elgin proved a bargain. His arm and range and speed left him inadequate for any position in the field except first base, and though he was a small target, he caught most everything and held his own defensively in double-A ball. He was thrown at, bunted at, run over, and taunted—sometimes even by his own teammates, but when it became clear that his bat had not suffered in the transition to professional ball, he changed a lot of minds.

Mr. Thatcher and I turned down flat the suggestion by the Braves that they give me the uniform number 1/2.

"He's gonna have enough trouble fitting in without that silliness," Billy Ray said. "If he hits like a child, then give him a child's number. He's already going to look interesting in a real uniform at his size. I mean, he's big for thirteen, but he's still no adult."

I had a slow start, probably because I was nervous and getting used to a better brand of ball—plus it took Mr. Thatcher time to arrange to have the pitching machine shipped to me and set up for me in secret locations. But then I caught fire.

Record crowds and media followed him as Elgin ran his average up close to five hundred. Atlantans began calling for his promotion to triple A and even to the big club, which was floundering in fifth place. But the Braves announced that Elgin would not be moved up even to triple A during that season. He garnered just enough at bats to win the batting title by 130 points at .485.

"He could play in the big leagues today," his manager said. "I just don't know where they'd put him."

I returned exhausted to our new address, a condominium in Buckhead. We had one floor gutted, and Elgin hid the machine there and spent hours every day smashing golf balls about the place.

Visiting us at the end of the season, Luke seemed down.

"Elgin's hitting right now," I told him. "He'll be glad to see you."

"I'll be glad to see him too, but I really need to talk to you."

I led him to the huge living room, and he reminded me that he had seen the place while it was being decorated.

"Are you happy with it?" he said.

"You know me too well," I said. "Let's just say I'm happy for Elgin, because this is going to be his place someday. When he comes of age or gets married, or whatever he's going to do, I'm going to live somewhere else."

"Doesn't he want you to live with him?"

"He thinks he does. But if I were a young wife, I wouldn't want that, no matter how charming and wonderful my mother-in-law was. And you know I'm charming and wonderful."

I worried when Luke didn't smile.

"Elgin will be gettin interested in girls here soon," he said. "But he won't be marryin anybody till he's at least twenty. You could get awful used to livin like this in the meantime."

So *that* was it.

"Lucas, I will never get used to living like this. Tell you the truth, I loved the road. I loved doing for Elgin and seeing him succeed. I missed my job. I missed some of my friends. I didn't miss the bus rides. I feel a little funny sittin around here without much to do, and I know that as Elgin does even better, I'll have even less reason to work. But this is not my idea of life, Lucas. Don't think I'm going to become a woman of leisure."

"But Miriam, look at this stuff. It's gorgeous. I feel like I couldn't even invite you two to my place again. I mean, I do all right and I'm not in debt, but compared to this—"

"Why are you comparing it to this? They don't pay shop owners hundreds of thousands of dollars. I'm keepin close tabs on Elgin so he remembers where he came from. He starts getting highfalutin on me, I can still deal with him, know what I mean?"

Luke stood to look out the window. "That's one beautiful view," he said.

I stepped behind him and slipped my arms around him. "Lucas, do you not like me anymore, now that I'm livin here?"

He didn't turn around. "Are you kiddin? Miriam, I love you more than ever. It's just that I'd be holding you back. Elgin can take care of you, and why should you be hangin with a guy like me when you can run in these circles?"

"You think I'm going to meet some teammate of Elgin's, some veteran with millions of dollars, and he's gonna sweep me off my feet?"

Luke turned around, his hands at his sides. "More likely, you'll sweep him off his feet."

"You really think that," I said flatly.

"I worry about it. There's lots of guys our age in the baseball world, especially as Elgin moves up."

I took his face in my hands. "I don't want guys," I said. "I want you."

"What have I got to offer?"

"Who else would have shaved off his beard and mustache just for me? And you've kept it off. Why?"

He shrugged. "For you."

"Then you do still care about me."

"Miriam, don't kid about this, okay?"

I backed away and sat down. He looked miserable and retreated to his chair.

"Lucas, this is not an attractive side of you, this self-pitying, poor me, I'm-not-worthy-of-you thing. It sounds like you're beggin for strokes. What do you want to hear?"

He sighed. "That you still love me as much as I love you, Miriam." His voice was thick. "I want to hear that even though you could live like this, you realize that with me you probably never will."

"Have I ever said different?"

"No, but I worry."

"I don't want you to worry, Lucas. You know who I am. You know where I came from. You know how I lived just a few months ago. This is not my place, hon. This is Elgin's. He worked for it. He deserves it. I don't want it. I won't get used to it and call it mine. We're a little out of place here, you know. People look at us funny. We still carry our own grocery bags up on the elevator."

Luke laughed. "How tacky."

"Lucas, I want to tell you this once and for all and not hear another word about it, okay? I don't want you to doubt me. I never thought I'd get a second chance at love, and for it to be so much better than the first is just a gift. No matter where I am, no matter what I'm doing, no matter who I'm with, I'm not lookin for anyone but you. I'm loving you. I don't know how else to say it."

Luke leaned forward and raised his eyebrows. "I don't suppose you'd care to back up that statement?" he said.

I'd been looking for a reason to kiss him since he came in. "Sure," I said. I rose and sat on his lap, wrapping my arms around his neck. I lightly touched his lips with mine, then pressed my mouth to his as if I wanted to drink him in.

I pulled back. "I love you, Lucas. You got it?"

He laughed. I stood quickly. "That was not intended to be funny!" I turned to move away from him, but he caught my hand.

"I'm not laughing at you," he said.

"I'm the only one here!"

"No! It's funny because when I asked you if you cared to back up your statement, that wasn't what I had in mind."

"Well, I'm sorry! What did you have in mind?"

"I was thinking more of something like this."

He pulled from his pocket a small box. Before I could even reach for it, he opened it and the diamond caught the sunlight from the window.

66

I came down a tight spiral staircase, wearing my helmet and carrying my fungo bat. Momma and Luke stood there hugging.

"Hey, guys," I said, but they ignored me. "I just hit a hundred and five line drives, every one a solid shot."

Luke and Momma looked at each other, smiling. "Who cares?" they said.

The ring had been the reason Luke could not afford to travel more with Elgin and me. We agreed we should put off our wedding until just before spring training. It would be hard on a new marriage for me to be on the road much of the baseball season, especially not knowing where Elgin might land in the organization. The only thing we knew for sure was that he would be in Florida for spring training, and that would make a nice honeymoon trip. Meanwhile, Luke expanded his business and put away profits so he could invest in a home in Georgia where the three of us would live during the off-seasons while Elgin was in the minors. Elgin would work out at his place in Buckhead and continue to furnish it for the day it would become his private home.

During the off-season, Elgin's time was taken with personal appearances, school (he was a full grade ahead already), and running through his three-hour-a-day workout. I told him often how proud I was that he was not living on past achievements.

"Are you kidding, Momma? I haven't made it yet, and even when I do, I can't let up. The only way to be the best is to work the hardest, and the only practice that makes perfect—"

"Is perfect practice," I said. "Neal Woodell lives."

Luke purchased a Colonial in a modest section of Atlanta, and we did most of the refurbishing ourselves. It was during one of those sweaty, late-fall sessions with drywall dust in our hair and paint on our hands that I grew melancholy and told Luke one of my life's secrets.

"You know what I've always wanted to do? Ever since I lost my baby girl?"

Luke was drilling. He spoke between punches on the trigger. "Tell me. Just don't tell me that beatin story again."

"Why?"

"Cause it's ugly and it makes me want to kill a guy who's already dead."

"I'd like to open a home for girls."

He slowly looked up at me. "I can't believe you never told me that."

"Oh, honey, I don't expect to still do it. My life's going to be too hectic for a lot of years, especially if Elgin becomes a big leaguer and we're married and all."

"No," he said, "listen. Ever since I was in Desert Storm I've had a soft spot in my heart for orphans. Lucy and I had decided to wait to have kids till I got back, then I came back to bury her. Now it's too late for me to be a father."

"So what are you tellin me, Lucas?"

He smiled. "Keep dreamin, that's all. You never know. You might as well have somethin to do that's so big it would never get done."

"You mean taking in girls or finishing this monstrosity?"

By spring, I was on a diet and weight program scoped out for me by the Braves trainer. It was working. I had grown another inch and bulked up. I turned down winter ball because Momma and Mr. Thatcher thought it would be better for me to be in school and live at home.

I arrived in Florida with Momma and her new husband, and the media made all of us stars. Hardly anybody believed I wasn't even fourteen yet, especially after the Little League scandal of 2001. My birthday a few days later made newscasts around the country.

I asked my minor-league manager if he thought I was ready for second base.

"Uh, no."

I shrugged and took the field. If there was a surprise at spring training, it was the sheer number of great ballplayers who showed up from various levels of the organization. I was most impressed to see the guys I had watched on television. I didn't know whether to ask for autographs or make myself scarce. Some of them treated me like a batboy. Others just scowled at me and left me alone.

Three of the big-league Braves starters were great to me. Bob Henson, the left fielder; Ken Clark, the catcher; and Luis Sanchez, the shortstop, asked my mother if they could take me to dinner one night.

"We'll baby-sit," Luis told me. Elgin had a pleading look in his eye.

I realized how thrilling this could be for Elgin. And these were all family men. "Come here a moment, Mr. Sanchez."

Luis giggled as he tried to mimic my accent in spite of his own and winked at his friends as I dragged him off to the side. "I'm inclined to allow this," I said. "But you understand I don't want him at any bars. I don't even want you guys drinkin when he's with you. No funny stuff. You're responsible, and I want him home by nine."

"Oh, man!" Luis complained. "You sound like my father-in-law before he was my father-in-law!"

"Any funny stuff, Luis, and you're in deep weeds with me. And you don't want that."

"You're right. I don't. We'll just go to dinner and bring him home. We're goin to a movie, but I just realized it's probably one you wouldn't want him to see."

"What is it?"

"Let's just say we're not takin our wives, so don't ask."

"Bring him home first."

"You got it."

I was a nervous wreck from the time Ken Clark raced out of the parking lot in his BMW until I heard him pull into our driveway just after eight-thirty. Elgin had had a wonderful time.

"Man, it's going to be great growing up on this team."

"If you make it," Luke said.

"C'mon, Lucky!" Elgin said. "You're the one who's always telling me to believe in myself."

"I just don't want you getting overconfident."

"I won't. Man, those guys gossip. It's fun."

"It's also wrong," I said. "What'd they say?"

Luke fell on the floor laughing.

"There's a guy on this club with drug problems," Elgin said. "Cocaine, I think."

"Who?"

"Gerry Snyder."

"The first baseman?" Luke said. "He's been in rehab before. He's hitting good right now."

"Yeah, but these guys think he's still in trouble with the drugs."

"They shouldn't be saying that," I said. "Especially not to you."

"Oh, Momma, it makes me feel like part of the team."

Maybe so, I thought, but that was the end of his going out with the guys.

Despite all the media attention, the Braves wisely kept Elgin on a B team in spring training, playing him sparingly against the regulars and keeping the pressure off him. When he played, he played first base, and there was no harassing him because the coaches protected him. When the team left spring training for the regular season, Elgin had hit a shade over .380 but with fewer at bats than most other players. He was assigned to triple-A Richmond where he played backup first base to an overweight twenty-four-year-old named Biff Barnett who hit towering home runs to the opposite field when he wasn't striking out. He had hit .229 the previous season and showed a decent glove for a big man. The Braves had high hopes for him as a run-producer. Until Elgin Woodell showed up.

Elgin went five-for-seven in a blowout first game of a doubleheader, and when the coaches approached Biff about letting Elgin play the second game too, just to see how many hits he could get in one day, Biff jumped the club and never came back.

By the time Elgin had his first hitless game, seven weeks later, Biff Barnett was pumping gas at the family franchise station in Burns Flat, Oklahoma. Elgin was hitting over five hundred, and the country was following him in *Sports Illustrated* and the *Sporting News* and clamoring for his graduation to the bigs.

The problem was Gerry Snyder. The Braves first baseman was leading the team in RBIs and batting .310. He was one of the best glove men in the majors, a left-hander who had the ability to almost always cut down the lead runner.

The Braves contended for the Eastern Division lead during the first three months of the season, then hit a slump and found themselves ten games out of first and slipping toward fourth. Banners appeared in the stands:

"It's Time for Elgin!"

"Bring Up Woodell, Woodja?"

Had it not been for Snyder's drug problem resurfacing, the Braves had planned to quietly bring Elgin up. They told Mr.

Thatcher that they hoped to have him in uniform in Atlanta before the media found out. It wasn't that they didn't want to capitalize on his newsworthiness; they just didn't want to appear to be doing so. They had planned to sneak him into the last three innings of a makeup game, and then start him in the annual Braves vs. Richmond game at Richmond.

But two weeks before that, Gerry Snyder turned himself in. He was back on drugs and in trouble financially. He said he'd put off asking for help again because he feared his job would not be there when he got back, "and everybody in this city knows why. I played with the kid in spring training."

67

Billy Ray Thatcher flew into Atlanta early on a Wednesday morning in July and headed for Turner Field. After an hour meeting with the brass and stopping by the clubhouse to pick up a package, he drove to Luke's house.

"Ready?" he asked Luke, shaking the smiling man's hand.

"You don't even have to ask." Luke was in a new suit with a tie and new shoes. He checked his watch and patted his back pocket for his wallet. "We gonna make it?"

"Plenty of time," Thatcher said. "Plane hits the ground at eleven."

Elgin and I had booked flights quietly, at Mr. Thatcher's instruction. "Elgin doesn't need a big welcome at the airport," Billy Ray had explained.

The secret arrival worked. The press missed us.

"How'd you do last night?" Billy Ray said on the way to the condo.

"It was only my worst game this year," Elgin said. "I think that was the first time I ever struck out twice in a game."

"And in such a long career," Thatcher said. "Any hits?"

Elgin shook his head. "Hit one pretty good to center, but I'm still only getting em out there about three hundred feet. Grounded into a double play. Made an error."

"Hmph," Thatcher said. "I don't think I'd start you tonight. Leverance is on the mound."

"Nobody told me that. He's gonna win the Cy Young this year, you know. That'll be the second year in a row the Dodgers have had a guy win it. How do they always come up with that pitching? They've been doing it for decades."

Elgin tapped his foot and drummed his knee with his thumb. "Need to spend an hour or so with the machine this afternoon," he said. "How we doin on time?"

"Relax," Billy Ray said. "Just treat this like any other game."

We all laughed and I dissolved into tears. "Right, El," I said, "just another game for a fourteen-year-old starting for the Braves."

"I have to be there for the press conference at four, remember."

"I still don't know why they're doing that to you, Elgin," I said. "You don't need that today."

"Mom, if I can't handle a press conference I sure can't handle Leverance." He shook his head. "Didn't mean to bring up his name again."

As we entered the condo, Billy Ray trailing with his wrapped bundle, Elgin said he could just as well use a nap as batting practice.

"But could you sleep?" Luke asked.

"Like a baby," Elgin said, smiling.

"You're not gonna get me with that old joke," Luke said. He put his arm around Elgin and drew him close, whispering, "I couldn't be prouder if I was your own dad."

It wasn't like Luke to say things like that. I hugged him.

"How far are we from the ballpark?" I said.

Mr. Thatcher ignored the question and asked me to sit down.

"First," he said, "you need to know that no one in this room, yourself included, is more interested than I am in getting you to Turner on time. So please, quit worrying about that. You want to work out, fine. Don't overdo it. Get yourself sharp, work off a little nervousness, whatever. No matter how much you work off, there'll be plenty left over for the game.

"Now, before you get all hot and sweaty, and before you have to dress in the coat and slacks your mother selected for the press conference, I want to give you a slightly belated birthday present."

"You already got me a birthday present, Mr. Thatcher. What's this?"

"Well, it's not really from me," Thatcher said, handing me the package. "It's from your employers."

I removed the strings and tore away the brown paper, revealing the new home and away Brave uniforms. There is nothing like the real thing. I had worn leftover, football-numbered, hand-me-down jerseys in the minors that sometimes didn't even match the pants. Here were beautiful whites and grays with shiny red numbers and letters, red piping, logos in place.

"Turn that one over, honey," Momma said. "The away jersey should have your name on it."

I turned the gray Atlanta jersey over and gasped. I bit my lip hard but lost the battle against tears. Under the crisp, perfect lettering that read WOODELL were two huge and beautiful digits: 16.

My face contorted and the tears came. "Daddy's number," I said. "How did they know?"

Mr. Thatcher put a hand on my shoulder. "I wonder," he said.

I was still dabbing my eyes when Elgin emerged wearing the away uniform. He padded around in stocking feet, looking in the mirror and tugging at the cap. I still couldn't believe it. Elgin looked like a long, lanky teenager, maybe four years older than he was, but he still looked small in that uniform. Had it

been that long ago that he begged to play on a team that had
both shirts and pants?

"Sure beats that old T-shirt, doesn't it, El?"

"I can't believe this," he said, turning to show me the back
again. "I'll always think of the name on there as Dad's, not
mine."

It was sad Neal wasn't here to see this.

Elgin tried on the uniform he would wear that night. Somehow, in the pure white, he looked even smaller. *He's a child, a
baby, playing a man's game.* If people ever wondered what they
came to the ballpark for, they'd know after they saw my son play.

He would hustle on and off the field, would run out every
grounder, encourage every teammate, know every situation. He
played ball the way it was meant to be played, and he enjoyed it
as no one ever had or ever would again.

There would be those who thought no one so young and inexperienced deserved the break Elgin was getting. But I knew
better than anyone that his life had been hard. He had seen his
daddy beat me, and he had lost a sister. He had seen his daddy
ruin his own life with drink and lies. Elgin had lived in poverty
and had gone without in a society that treated lower-middle-
class people like scum.

If anybody deserved this, Elgin did. He had taken no short-
cuts, never got discouraged, always bounced back. What other
kid on earth would have spent as much time with that crazy machine that flung those rock-like balls at him from so many different directions at blinding speed? Gifted? Sure he was, but he
had begun honing his gifts from the first day.

Mr. Thatcher and Luke and I would be in a private box with
Brave executives when Elgin was introduced to the standing-
room-only crowd for the first time. I would be good for nothing,
probably not even able to clap for him. I stuffed two packets of
tissue in my purse and dressed in a way I hoped would make
Elgin, and Lucas, proud.

I wished I could have been invisible. This was Elgin's moment.
I didn't need or want the spotlight. Let him have it. He'd know
what to do with it. I would have less and less influence on him

as the season went by and as his career continued, but I felt good about that. I would stay close enough to keep him humble, to remind him who he was and who he wasn't. But tonight he would become a baseball legend, and I wouldn't get in the way of that for anything.

I stood at the rim of the crowd of reporters and cameramen at the late-afternoon press conference. I couldn't have imagined Elgin looking smaller or younger, with the manager on one side of him, the GM on the other, and the president and owner's representative behind.

"Gentlemen," the GM intoned, "I know this is a historic day, but we'll have to move it along, because this young man has to be on the field soon. He has a job."

There were the usual photos of handshakes and holding up uniforms. Then Elgin asked for the away jersey.

"This is the one I'm proudest of," he said. "My dad's number was sixteen, and of course his name was Woodell. I've learned a lot from all the coaches I've had, but I'm here because of my dad. He's gone now, but he was the one who taught me the game and made me love it and work at it. Thank you, Daddy."

68

The Turner Field scoreboard flashed that the youngest player in the history of baseball would start at first base that night, as if it was news to anyone. When I ran out for the top of the first inning, having been announced as batting eighth, I received a huge ovation from the standing-room-only crowd.

I had always dreamed of playing before a packed stadium. But now, with at least five times the people who had ever seen me play riveted on me alone, I was embarrassed and self-conscious. I had heard of having butterflies. Mine were moths.

I had taken a ball with me to warm up the infielders. How strange, throwing grounders to someone like Luis Sanchez, the shortstop I'd idolized and had met only in spring training. I was aware of every move, and nothing seemed natural. Did I look as awkward as I felt?

That nervousness subsided when Brave starter Roger Densing threw his last warm-up toss and Ken Clark rifled the ball to second. I rolled my ball toward the dugout and watched the others throw the game ball around before delivering it back to the mound.

Clark had reminded me that I should care as much about the signal as the pitcher, "because you'll start to learn where the ball is going off the bat if you know what we're throwing the guy."

I found myself hoping for a routine grounder to second so I could receive a nice, easy throw. That was the wrong attitude. I should hope for a big-league line drive right at my feet, and I should be prepared to go on automatic pilot and prove I belonged.

Maybe it had all been a fluke. What if I made a fool of myself?

Big, bearded Roger Densing was the oldest Brave, a veteran of eleven years. He'd won a Cy Young, and though his fastball had slowed into the high eighties, he was still intimidating, even to me.

Clark called for a fastball in, and the leadoff hitter skied a high pop to third. I was relieved I had not been in on the play but wished the Braves used a throw-around routine after the out that included the first baseman. I needed something to get my mind off myself and into the game. Clark jogged to the mound and motioned me to join him.

I sprinted over, embarrassed, knowing I looked like a Little Leaguer doing that. I looked expectantly at Clark, but he was looking at Densing, who turned and glared at me. He didn't make it obvious to the crowd or the TV cameras, but when he spoke softly in a gravelly voice, I heard him well.

"Who was coverin first on that play?" he said.

I didn't know what to say. "Well, I—"

"Runner was doggin it to first base. That ball drops, we still get him if our first baseman's covering. You were five feet away and watchin the play. He drops it, you try to get back, you're a small target anyway, he throws it away, and they'd have a guy in scoring position."

Wow, he thought of all that just now?

The ump started toward us to tell us to move it along. Clark backed away, slowing him. Densing continued.

"How do you think I've lasted this long? I don't care if you're three years old and the best thing that's come along since quiche on a stick. Do the little things right. We're throwin this guy low and away four straight times if we have to. He hates to walk so he's gonna put one of those in play, and it's probably gonna come to the right side. You're gonna be in on a play, Rook, so get your butt in the game."

My face burned as I hurried back. Now I was too close to the grass. Clark was waving me back. But what if they bunted? I didn't care. I would just obey. Roger Densing had blamed me for having a runner in scoring position, and nobody had reached base! Guys were sure hard to please at this level.

First pitch, hard and down, off the outside corner. Batter swings. Ball is between first and second. I had broken to my right on the swing, aware of shrill young people in the crowd, watching their youngest hero going after the ball. From the corner of my eye I see the second baseman won't reach it.

I bend and reach, still on the dead run. The ball is in my glove. Densing is all arms and belly, angling to cover first. Just like him to do it right. I pivot, plant, and fire, leading Densing by a step. The big pitcher catches up to the throw as he draws parallel with the bag and beats the runner.

I'm smacked hard on the seat by the second baseman and suddenly become aware of the delirious standing crowd. This was a play they had seen the left-handed Gerry Snyder make in his sleep. But who knew the rookie would be up to it?

Ken Clark had followed the runner down the line, and as he took the ball from Densing they both stopped and jabbed index fingers at me as if to say, "That play was yours, buddy, and it was big-league!" I could have done a cartwheel.

With two outs the third hitter sent a grounder to short. Luis looked the ball into his glove, then came up searching not for my glove but my eyes. It was as if the shortstop were saying, "See how easy we make it for you here," and I knew the joy of taking a long, hard throw straight to the glove. This was going to be fun!

I tossed the ball to the first-base umpire, who said, "Nice inning, Rook."

The Braves didn't fare much better against Leverance, the best pitcher in baseball, so I didn't come up until I led off the bottom of the third. The self-consciousness and nervousness came back in the on-deck circle as I watched the heavy, hard strikes popping the catcher's glove. As my name was announced I heard the thunderous applause, but when I stepped in left-handed, I was on automatic again.

I ran through my mind the cadence and pace and sheer, unpredictable speed of the machine I had faced that afternoon. Leverance's first pitch was a straight fastball I should have jumped on. Strike one. Would this guy dare another, just like that one? Of course he would. He wouldn't suspect a kid could hit his best pitch.

It was on the outside corner and I sent my third-base coach diving out of the way. The crowd laughed, then cheered. Was that the wild, lucky swing of a child? They could think that only until the next one came inside and I did the same to my first-base coach.

Impressive or not, I was down oh-and-two and would not likely see another hittable fastball. I waited, patient, reaching to foul off pitches close enough to be called strikes but not fat enough to drive. Eventually I ran the count full. When Leverance lost me on a pitch at chin level, the crowd was merciless to him.

Densing pushed me to second on a hit-and-run ground out, and Leverance nearly threw the ball into center on a pickoff play that might have caught me. Leadoff man Mike Martinez followed with a double in the gap, and I ran so hard I nearly stumbled twice. How sweet to feel my spikes dig into that plate and score my first big-league run.

When I got to the dugout, no one looked at me. It was as if they hadn't realized I was back.

"Well," I said, "one to nothing, huh?"

"Yup," someone said.

"Yeah?" someone else said. "How'd we score?"

"How'd we score?" I said. "Well, I just did when Martin—" but then I realized what was going on. Only then did the guys on the bench take turns shaking my hand.

I popped out in the fifth, again to a huge ovation from people who were probably impressed that I was brave enough to even get in the box. When I came to the plate batting righty against a fireballing lefty reliever in the seventh, I was welcomed by the crowd as a new friend.

"All heat," the previous hitter told me as he trudged to the bench after a strikeout. "Just try to get wood on it."

It had been years since I had simply tried to get my bat on a ball. I wasn't going to reach out and hope for the best. I was going up there to drive the ball. The first pitch was hard and tight, just off the inside corner. Ball one.

The next should be a fastball on the outside corner. If I was wrong, I might get plunked. If I was right, I would take the pitch to the opposite field.

As I slid into second ahead of the throw from right center-field, I couldn't remember having rounded first or looking to the third-base coach. I had my first major-league hit. The crowd was up and roaring. Instead of stepping to the plate to resume the game, Roger Densing stood leaning on his bat and let me have my moment.

That one was for you, Dad, I thought, and I knew my dad would be telling me to keep my head in the game. The Braves were up by three, and it was time to try to put this thing away.

Densing called to the pitcher and asked for the ball. He gave it to the batboy, who was older than I was, and the kid ran it to the dugout.

Densing sacrificed me to third, and I scored when the second baseman erred on Martinez's grounder. The Braves knocked the reliever out of the box and I batted again in the ninth, forcing a runner at second to finish one-for-three plus a walk and two runs scored.

When I got to my locker I found the ball Roger Densing had removed from the game. The big pitcher had dated it and written: "The first of many."

I stood in the bowels of the stadium at the players' exit, waiting with Luke while Mr. Thatcher went in to be at Elgin's side for the crush of the press. I looked at my husband, my lips pressed to hold back a torrent of emotion. I was grateful that Luke seemed to know there were no words worthy of the occasion.

I was proud as a mother could be, and while I was not naive enough to believe it would be all smooth sailing, I looked forward to the ride.

My man-child had achieved his dream.

Epilogue

That night while reliving the game on the sports news, Miriam heard for the first time what Elgin said after the game.

"I said before that my dad taught me baseball. But it's my mom who raised me. She did everything she could, on her own, to let me follow my dream. I love you, Momma."

Roger Densing could have had no idea how prophetic he had been.

Within a week, Elgin had been moved to sixth in the order. By the end of the season he hit second occasionally, though his speed cost the Braves a few double plays and a few runs. In seventy-two games, Elgin led the Braves in hitting at .310 and filled every stadium in which he played. The Braves finished second, six games back of the Phillies.

The following season, without a home run to his credit, he started the all-star game, led the National League in hitting at .345, and batted second on a Braves team that won the NL East by nine games but lost to the Dodgers in the play-offs four games to one. He was named Most Valuable Player, and only his having had more than 130 at bats the previous season kept him from being named Rookie of the Year.

The Braves drew an unheard of 3.6 million–plus fans that year and would not fall below that mark throughout Elgin's career. When his three-year deal expired, after he had won the batting crown again (this time at .389, the highest NL batting average in decades), he was considered the best bargain in sports history.

Sportswriters and baseball executives, to the Braves' distraction, agreed that no price was too high for a phenomenal prodigy who was the best thing that had ever happened to baseball.

Elgin Woodell would dominate baseball as no one had ever dominated a team sport. He made more than two hundred hits in a season nineteen times, including eleven straight, and led the majors in homers nine seasons, including six straight. He had two fifty-one-game hitting streaks and batted over four hundred eight times. Had it not been for an abbreviated season, due to a broken leg at age twenty-six in the middle of his most productive years, he would surely have hit more than a thousand career home runs. From age fourteen through age thirty-three, he was named MVP sixteen out of twenty years, including streaks of four, five, and seven.

When Elgin's initial three-year pact with the Braves was about to expire, Billy Ray Thatcher negotiated a most unusual deal wherein Elgin was guaranteed to be the highest-paid player in baseball for the next five years. Every time another star's contract was renegotiated and surpassed his deal, his was to be adjusted within thirty days. One year into that deal, when he became the first player in decades to hit over four hundred, the Braves renegotiated and extended the contract to cover ten years. That was the first of three similar contracts during his career.

When he was nineteen Elgin opened the Woodell Home in Atlanta for otherwise homeless girls, run by Lucas and Miriam Harkness until their retirement.

When Elgin was twenty-three, Billy Ray Thatcher and his wife Shirley died within months of each other.

Twelve years into his career, Elgin married a young woman from the Braves' public relations department. They had three girls. And a boy.

Elgin Woodell's Career Stats

Age	Ht.	Wt.	Pos.	Team	G	AB	R	H	2b	3b	HR	RBI	Avg.	MVP	NLCS	WS	Champs
14	5-9	165	1B	Atl/NL	72	158	17	49	10	3	0	20	.310				
15	5-9	174	1B	Atl/NL	160	571	84	197	29	10	0	100	.345				
16	6-0	188	1B	Atl/NL	158	570	119	222	45	9	7	118	.389		✓		
17	6-1	190	2B	Atl/NL	156	556	120	223	44	13	24	115	.401	✓			
18	6-2	195	2B	Atl/NL	156	554	116	226	41	10	27	121	.408	✓	✓	✓	
19	6-2	205	2B	Atl/NL	155	535	118	205	39	12	33	105	.383	✓	✓		
20	6-3	208	2B	Atl/NL	153	534	112	208	38	13	32	104	.390		✓	✓	✓
21	6-3	208	SS	Atl/NL	160	552	116	205	36	9	41	118	.371		✓	✓	✓
22	6-3	208	SS	Atl/NL	159	562	114	207	39	8	44	120	.369		✓		
23	6-3	208	SS	Atl/NL	160	542	122	223	47	9	43	130	.411	✓			
24	6-3	208	SS	Atl/NL	158	550	119	219	46	12	51	162	.398	✓	✓	✓	
25	6-3	208	SS	Atl/NL	158	562	144	230	47	11	49	167	.409	✓	✓	✓	✓
26	6-3	208	SS	Atl/NL	160	586	119	215	45	10	40	146	.367		✓	✓	
27	6-3	208	SS	Atl/NL	114*	394	80	166	33	8	30	83	.421				
28	6-3	208	SS	Atl/NL	155	646	140	256	50	13	58	171	.396	✓	✓	✓	
29	6-3	208	SS	Atl/NL	161	639	161	274	55	20	67	188	.429	✓	✓	✓	
30	6-3	208	SS	Atl/NL	160	635	150	263	51	21	62	189	.414	✓	✓	✓	✓
31	6-3	210	OF	Atl/NL	157	581	141	239	40	11	49	170	.411	✓	✓	✓	
32	6-3	215	OF	Atl/NL	159	572	137	227	41	8	48	161	.397	✓	✓		
33	6-3	215	OF	Atl/NL	156	551	93	218	43	9	45	162	.396	✓	✓	✓	✓
34	6-3	215	OF	Atl/NL	157	559	94	217	40	8	40	145	.388	✓	✓	✓	
35	6-3	215	1B	Atl/NL	156	572	104	209	38	9	42	141	.365	✓	✓		
36	6-3	215	1B	Atl/NL	151	553	95	191	35	6	40	131	.345				
37	6-3	216	1B	Atl/NL	140	564	104	193	30	5	37	120	.342				
38	6-3	216	1B	Atl/NL	141	556	71	185	31	3	37	101	.333				
39	6-3	219	1B	Atl/NL	140	449	60	150	28	1	30	90	.334		✓	✓	
40	6-3	221	1B	Atl/NL	130	415	50	132	20	2	22	82	.318		✓	✓	✓
27 YEARS					4042	14518	2900	5549	1041	253	998	3460	.382	16	17	13	6

*Missed 50+ games with broken leg